Mermaids of Venice

Silas Knight

For my grandmother,
Virginia Byron (1931-2006),
who said if I wanted to write a best seller
I'd better include lots of sex.

Based on a true story

TABLE OF CONTENTS

I. Genesis

1. Mañanita

A *mañanita* for baby's wake,
A lullaby for nighttime's sake.

Psst.
Can you hear me?
I have a secret to tell you.

There's a world beyond this one.
These endometrial walls nourish you now, but soon you'll experience another life:
Your buccopharyngeal membrane will rupture, your ophthalmic cups will deepen, your gonadal ridge will expand.
You will develop a mouth, eyes, and genitals.

You will use these tools to explore a new world: a gargantuan looping universe that twists and turns like a roller coaster in a kaleidoscope, a puzzle so grand that trillions of beings each contribute one piece.

But first I'll tell you a story. Your story. It's only fair that you should hear yours now, since I had to die twice before anyone told me mine.

So listen to me and I'll tell you about the mermaids, and the House of Talking Cats, and your mothers, and what happens when gods die.

I wish I could tell you why Venice sank to the bottom of the ocean, but I can't. That's a real secret.

But maybe you'll figure it out for yourself.

2. Ailurophile

"Cats have panache and purring style,"
Asserted the ailurophile.

The ghosts stole Betty Lou's kitchen table on the Day of Concupiscence, or perhaps Tergiversation; Betty Lou had lost track and the cats weren't speaking to her anymore.

It was May 7th, 1976 by the human calendar and the neighborhood had erupted in gardens of orange and pink and lilac while Betty Lou's property remained fallow and brown. Even the sun ignored her lawn, casting long shadows through untended plots while the spring breeze that carried smells of lavender across the neighborhood circumnavigated her territory. The unkempt gardens were Betty's Lou's mother's responsibility, a duty her mother had shirked ever since Betty Lou walked into the west parlor to discover her hanging lifeless from a dusty chandelier. That was the first day the cats spoke to her, though now the cats sat mute watching Betty Lou as she watched the ghosts drag her kitchen table across her lawn.

The ghosts traipsed across a graveyard of pink ladies, leaving behind petals of tanned Swiss cheese from the table's rain-soaked cardboard container. Betty Lou hadn't been able to lift the table when it arrived on her porch and she'd left it outside until she or the cats devised a plan. She hadn't thought about the table again until the ghosts pulled up in their brown van and stole it, but that didn't make the theft acceptable. Betty Lou fantasized about tearing open her front door and giving the ghosts a what-for. The sight of her unclothed and shrieking would give them something to remember, but a stolen table didn't provide enough motivation to undo a lifetime of camouflage.

Before her mother's death, Betty Lou had been forbidden from leaving the home without hours of preparation. Padding under her clothes hid the more distinguishing lumps, then more padding was added to hide the padding until Betty Lou couldn't walk so much as waddle. Dermatological transformation occurred with slabs of cover-up so thick Betty Lou couldn't budge the fake eyebrows her mother drew on her face to replace the real ones buried beneath the strata. Despite their best efforts, no amount of padding and painting could eliminate the gawks and stares. Oversized sun bonnets could hide her hair and ears but failed to drown out the whispers in the supermarket. Women crossed the other side of the street when Betty Lou ambled near. Neighborhood children dared one another to transverse the mother and daughter's lawn at midnight to peer inside the windows of their faded green Victorian.

The ghosts, who wore matching orange coveralls, grunted as they loaded the table. Stenciled on the van's side were dark red letters:

Witzelsucht Family Supply
"We Have Everything *and More!"*

The larcenous ghosts vanished from the narrow field of Betty Lou's mail slot. Betty Lou closed the metal cover and crept out from a nest of junk mail and catalogues. Many of the envelopes bore the label of the Witzelsucht Family Supply Collections Department in Jacksonville, Florida, each stamped with "**Urgent: Pay Immediately**" in a larger font than the last.

Betty Lou crept along her front wall, her bare feet docking on each island of carpet among the sea of cardboard boxes. One box contained a lava lamp and a napping Russian Blue. Another contained a cosmetics case, assorted lipsticks, and a pair of Bengals, who hopped out in a plume of topaz powder as Betty Lou crossed overhead. Witzelsucht Family Supply boxes spanned the living room, many providing shelter to a cat or three.

Betty Lou cracked the drapes and peeked through with one eye. The ghosts stood before a black-and-white Chevy Nova parked behind the van and spoke to two phantoms dressed as police officers. The ghosts pointed at Betty Lou's home. The phantoms nodded and started across the lawn. Betty Lou threw herself against her wallpaper, her hand covered the back of her head in case the phantoms could see through the walls. Perched on a couch, a Tonkinese perked his ears at his landlord's distress.

"What do I do?" Betty Lou whispered, but the Tonkinese only stared back at her. She repeated her plea to the rest of the cat congregation: "What do I do?" A smattering of licks and purrs was the only reply.

Betty Lou longed for the days when the cats spoke back. That had been such a wonderful time. The cats kept her company. They even told her secrets. The cat world was a simple life sprinkled with strange complexities. Case in point was the cat calendar. It only had four days: the Day of Concupiscence, the Day of Tergiversation, the Day of Catachresis, and Christmas (which came at least once a week and hinted at no connections to Santa Claus or Jesus except when the Abyssinians disclosed that none of the Nebelungs celebrated it "because they were Jewish"). Each cat celebrated the days in a different order, often skipping or duplicating days on what seemed like a whim. Each cat insisted his or her order was proper and logical, each rejected competing calendars with barbed derisions.

The complication, Betty Lou learned, was that cats didn't believe in one another. This solipsism created a number of confusing moments. Cats gave themselves colorful names with lengthy trains: Little Punk, Shredder of Cardboard and Sovereign of the Right Side of the Penultimate Stairstep that She Conquered from The One with the Whiskers on the Last Day of the Month of Catachreses; but referred to one another with the barest of epithets (e.g., "The One with the Whiskers"). Betty Lou was "The One with the Food". People outside were "ghosts" or "phantoms".

Three loud raps sounded from the front door. Betty Lou panicked; half of her brain wanted to run upstairs to hide and the other half told her to flee to the downstairs kitchen. She stepped in both directions at once. The Tonkinese (Ellison Wells, Who Eats His Tail and Disappears until Morning, Debater of Squirrels and Consort of the One with the Stubby Nose and the One with Spots) fled as Betty Lou plunged headfirst into a box containing votive candles and a Portmeirion tea set. Betty Lou felt a stabbing pain in her left hand and raised it from the smashed china to see a dripping gash along her palm. The door rapped louder and Betty Lou looked around the room. She ignored the fur and cardboard and spied a violet plastic box. She pushed herself off the ground, leaving a crimson handprint on her carpet, and grabbed the litter box. An Oriental Shorthair caught in mid-squat (Queen Ma, Empress of the Leftmost Bookshelf, Whose Will Keeps the Television Ghosts from Escaping) hopped irritated from her bathroom as Betty Lou hopscotched the box of buried kitty loot to the front door.

"Police! Open up!"

Betty Lou propped the litter box on her knee and pulled at the door. The door stuck on the nest of junk mail. She pulled harder. The mail crunched against the wall and the door swung open.

"TRESPASSERS!" Betty Lou thrust the litter box through the doorway. The officers' faces shifted from authority to surprise. Betty Lou dropped the tray, pushed the door closed, and bolted four-legged up the stairs.

The litter box smashed into the wall and the phantoms propelled themselves into her home.

The leading officer wiped gravel and kitty nuggets from his uniform, yelled "STOP!" and flew up the stairs behind her.

Betty Lou loped over boxes, pushing them behind her to slow the phantoms' pursuit. A curio cabinet stood at the top of the staircase. The cabinet contained the rows of Venetian Carnevale masks that Betty Lou's mother had brought back from Italy when she was twenty, along with the bulging belly that she'd refused to explain to her family.

With a strength that surprised her, Betty Lou tilted the bookcase on one side and pushed until it gave way and toppled down the staircase. The phantoms squeezed to either side and the cabinet crashed between them, cracking glass and spilling broken masks.

Betty Lou had no time to mourn the collection that she'd always suspected held a dearer place in her mother's heart than her daughter. Betty Lou was never allowed to forget that it was her existence that separated them from the family's inheritance and forced them to spend their lives shut inside their throw-away Victorian home. Betty Lou scampered down the hallway, leaping over another expanse of boxes and a mottled Korat (Tyrian the Beautiful, Who Needs No Honorifics Because She is Glory). Betty Lou grabbed at a frayed silk cord dangling from the ceiling. The ceiling gave way, revealing a rung of steps leading into the attic's dark maw.

Betty Lou's legs disappeared into the attic as the phantoms reached the ladder. She sped over to an old locker, pushed it to the attic opening and let it fall through the hole. A phantom yelped as the locker smashed onto the ground. Betty Lou hurried to the far wall and grabbed a long wooden hat rack. Late 19th century haberdashery spilled across the attic floor and Betty Lou thrust the rack through the attic opening. A phantom hand reached through the opening and pushed at the rack, locking it between the rungs.

Betty Lou was struck with hopelessness. She'd secured herself in a room with no exit save a vent on the far wall significantly smaller than the diamond-spotted calico licking himself below it (Betty Lou hadn't seen the cat before and didn't know its name). The cat glared at Betty Lou with the insolence that only cats can muster. He glanced at the large wardrobe against the wall and resumed licking his inner thigh. Betty Lou hurried over, tore the wardrobe open, and dove into a pile of musty dresses. Her lungs filled with mold and mothballs and she resisted the urge to gag as she heard the phantoms push through her blockade and climb into the attic.

Betty Lou fought to control her breath. Each rapid inhale was accompanied by a mouthful of decayed fabric.

Outside the wardrobe:

"Christ, I can't see a thing in here."

"Ow!"

"Hold on, I think I found…."

A sliver of light spilled through the middle of the wardrobe.

"That's better. Where'd she go?"

"Quiet. Do you hear that?"

Betty Lou held her breath. She became aware of a steady tapping sound, like a faucet with a slow leak.

Tink….Tink….Tink.

Betty Lou shifted her eyeballs and noticed the gash in her hand dripping onto the wooden floor.

Tink…Tink…Tink…

She pressed her palm onto her leg. The wound stung, but the flow stopped. Betty Lou shifted and pressed her back into an exposed nail. She stifled all but the barest whimper. Footsteps clamored towards her and the doors tore open and bathed her in bright white light.

"Ha!" yelled the phantom, one hand on the wardrobe door and the other holding a rusty lantern. "Here you–Oh my god–"

Betty Lou held her hands over her exposed face and breasts.

"No, please don't," she said. "Don't look at me. Please don't."

She tore at the dresses overhead, spilling fabric and hangers but it was too late.

"Oh my god," he repeated.

"No, no, no!" she said.

"It's okay," the phantom said, breaking into a grin. "Terry, look at this!"

The other apparition maneuvered around his partner.

"Oh my Jesus!"

"Terry, it is not right to profane oneself in front of an angel."

Phantom Terry whistled. "Most days I would accuse you of exaggeration, but this creature would make a sunrise weep with envy."

"No, no," Betty Lou repeated. She pulled a dress over her body, but every scrambling motion revealed more of her skin. Her cursed, perfect skin.

By whatever standard of measure, Betty Lou's body was flawless: everything symmetrical and perfect in proportion, full dark red lips that needed no embellishment, golden tresses that refused to tangle. Nothing could be done to change her perfection. Starving herself made her a supermodel, over-eating made her Rubenesque. Two weeks in a discarded potato sack and people called it a style. She'd hoped that middle age would bring sagging relief, but every day her youthful body matured into robust beauty she had to work harder to conceal it. Even the new gash across her hand had its grace, a perfect tear of crimson stigmata to complement her otherwise flawless form.

The one called Terry held out his hand and smiled. Betty Lou wished she could sink into the wardrobe and disappear. It was always the same. When you're beautiful, people want to talk to you. They open doors; they make eye contact; they even try to brush their hand against yours as you push aside their bag of cherry red tomatoes that they'd placed on the supermarket counter next to yours. It was all too much to handle.

"Come on, hon. Give me your hand, everything's fine."

Betty Lou fluttered one hand.

"That's right," said the phantom. "Don't worry, just–holy Christ!"

Betty Lou launched herself naked from her nook, hissing and clawing. Phantom Terry shrieked and covered his face from her threshing nails, but not before she drew blood with a slice against his left cheek. His partner grabbed Betty Lou's wrists and pulled them behind her back. She cried, crunched her stomach and swiped with her toenails. Her legs were restrained. She hissed and struggled.

"Calm down!" said Terry. "Holy fuck! Calm down."

Betty Lou gnashed her teeth and bit at the officer, but his neck was too far away. They thrust her face down onto the ground and handcuffed her feet and hands behind her. She snarled and snorted, but knew she had lost. Terry grabbed her feet, the other her arms, and they lifted her off the ground. Betty Lou found herself face to face with the diamond-spotted calico. He bared his teeth.

"*Well,*" said the cat. "*Look at the mess you got yourself into now.*"

Betty Lou stared ahead as they pulled her across the attic and jostled her down the ladder. The rest of the cats watched as she was hefted out of her home, but none of them had anything else to say.

3. Harlequinade

The clown and his lovers have their passions displayed,
In the twisted-up world of the harlequinade.

The sanitarium was white and dingy and the tubs of lemon cleanser that the orderlies sloshed through its halls could never erase the subtle bouquet of offal and vomit. Betty Lou couldn't remember how long she'd been inside, thanks to the mélange of powdered pills that were sprinkled atop each tray of food slipped into her room: Chicken a la Haloperidol, Linguine with Clonidine Sauce, Peanut Butter & Methaminodiazepoxide Sandwiches.

Betty Lou stared at the jade-leafed oak outside her window and a year passed as quick as a breath. The leaves burned away and fell to the ground. Snow blanketed the bare branches and melted, revealing viridian buds which blossomed into green leaves which burnt away and fell to the ground.

In the next bed, Georgia, a brunette from Alabama who never stopped talking even when thrusting food into her mouth, slept while an endless string of babble escaped her lips in an undulating tempo:

"…the contract wasbrokenand the mermaids are angry they don't eatfishthey eat bicycle rubber and one and one and one makes the brightshininglaughingsad girl smile…."

Georgia's somniloquies may have contained reflections of dreams, instructions for the perfect bisque, or the secrets of cold fusion but her roommate couldn't tell. Whenever Betty Lou tried to figure anything out her brain got in the way, as if she was reproducing the Mona Lisa with an etch-a-sketch while standing in an earthquake. Betty Lou didn't know what day it was, what month, what time….

Betty Lou blinked. It was midnight. Betty Lou knew it was midnight as certain as she knew her cats' fur against her fingertips. The thought slipped away and she dove after it. Midnight, she told herself. Midnight. Midnight. Midnight. It was undeniable. She'd always loved to stay up and watch the clocks change, to know that she was *in tomorrow*. Midnight was a paradox, a time for magic. She took the feeling in, bathed herself in the fear and expectation, and became aware of something else. The door to her room was open. She thought the door had been closed a moment ago, but her brain was too soggy to be certain.

Betty Lou slid from her cot. The cold floor sent tingles through her always-pedicured toes and flawless ankles, disappearing somewhere under her pale-blue hospital gown. There was sufficient light in the hallway to reveal that there was nothing to reveal. Faint strains of music drifted from somewhere down the hall. The notes sounded as if they came from a calliope and danced around her ears before entering her nostrils, filling Betty Lou with the smell of popcorn and sawdust:

Doo Dah Dah

Doo Dah Dah

Doo Dah Dah

Tingalingalingalinga

Betty Lou walked down the empty corridor. The music receded as she approached. She wondered if the sounds originated from the same building, or even the same day. She followed them anyway. Her footsteps echoed down the hall and the music disappeared.

Betty Lou panicked. The hallway was dead. She closed her eyes and sniffed. There it was. The notes hadn't changed, but the smell was different. The odor drew up an old memory of her at the zoo. Betty Lou had been padded in an oversized red dress stuffed with pillow cushions, staring at a pair of rutting bull elephants. Her mother spied her daughter's wide eyes and yanked her from the exhibit, but not before a young Betty Lou imprinted the scene in her head: the female elephant anchored as the large male nuzzled her rear end and topped her, seeking out her nether regions with an enormous prehensile member as long as his trunk. The adult Betty Lou stifled a giggle at the memory and her cheeks went red. The calliope music turned a corner, the smells changed and Betty Lou pursued.

In the observation room, Lawrence the Orderly fished in his molars for the remains of a Triscuit as he watched Johnny Carson on a mini black-and-white television. He didn't look up. Betty Lou followed the synesthetic odors of greasepaint and cotton candy out the front door.

The long white building rested atop a high hill. Behind her a bronze plaque read: **"Fiddler's Green Sanitarium, Est. 1886"**. A single trail curlicued downhill to a dark pasture walled by redwood trees. A light breeze winnowed through her smock as she bounded down the hill after the music. The music grew louder and in the shadows of the pasture she made out a billboard, a nose, and a man.

The billboard was taller than ten cats with paws to the air, and as wide as fifteen loafing with tails curved. It pictured a giant magnifying glass hovering over a circus tent and had words painted in a garish mismatch of reds, greens, and purples. Whoever the sign-maker, he or she had an unhealthy love for exclamation points:

Presenting!
Warren and Annette!
On International Tour!
to
Arcadia! Albion!
&
Fiddler's Green!
in
Professor Medici's
Fantastical Traveling
Flea Circus!!!!!

Doddering back and forth before the sign was an old jester with a belled cap and a crimson & silver suit that sparkled against the stars. His face was aged and leathery, like a mask, and painted across his face were light blue diamonds that sunk so deep into the crevasses of his wrinkles that they jutted and fought with one another like a traffic jam on a Möbius highway. If anything, the facepaint accentuated the biggest offense: the harlequin's nose, a barbarous schnozzle the envy of a sphinx. The rest of the jester was dwarfed under the shadow of his enormous proboscis. Betty Lou wondered if his weak and halted steps were the result of age or the weight tied to his face. He was the ugliest person Betty Lou had ever seen.

The harlequin grasped a small music box from which emanated the sounds which had lured her. Seemingly oblivious to her presence, he staggered towards a small square table set on the grass. The distance wasn't far but he stopped halfway, winced and tottered sideways. Regaining himself, he set the box in the fold of his armpit, stroked his left hip, and resumed his journey. He stopped and locked eyes with Betty Lou. His frown shifted into the approximation of a smile. If anything forgave his bulbous nose it was his eyes, eyes that sparkled brighter than his silver suit, as if his pupils had been replaced with sapphires. Betty Lou found no fault with those incandescent eyes until one winked at her. She was too surprised to react.

The jester finished his trek and placed the box on the table. He raised his arms with dramatic flair and cast his view across the field, as if Betty Lou was surrounded by hundreds of others. His voice was high and graveled, two shots Tom Waits and one shot helium, on the rocks and dirty.

"Ladies and gentlemen, the spectacle of spectacles is about to begin! Watch as– Cagh! Cagh! Cagh!"

He doubled over, delivering hacking coughs into his fist. His chest rose and fell. He pounded twice on the table and resumed his spiel, punctuating his words with the occasional wheeze.

"Watch…as Warren the Flea braves treacherous meters across razor sharp wire……..a single slip meaning instant, fiery death…….Gaze as Annette plummets…..into a mere thimbleful of water! Tremble as Warren enters The Gauntlet….of Tribulation, from which no flea has left alive! Stick around, for in just a few short minutes you'll witness a miracle....the likes of which....you have never seen."

The jester fell against the table, gasping for breath. He lifted his head and cast a weary face across the invisible throngs. He stopped at Betty Lou. She'd never been to a live show before and now she knew why. The television never looked at her like this strange, ugly man did. His eyes bore into her as if he saw her naked; not without clothes, but rather as if she had no skin.

He pulled his eyes away and continued his spiel. Betty Lou's discomfort when he stared was bearable. Unwanted attention was a familiar distaste. It was when he pulled his gaze that scared her, because part of her wanted him to keep looking. Betty Lou couldn't take it. She turned and walked away.

"...Sharp, deadly needles that would pierce him....from wing to– Wait, where are you going?"

The music stopped. The stars dimmed.

The harlequin steadied his hands on the table as he circled it and hobbled after her. "Wait, wait!"

Betty Lou continued uphill towards the hospital. The harlequin's breath quickened. He reached the beginning of the slanted hill and stopped.

"Please, please....I can't...."

She snapped around. The elevation put her at almost a full body height above him. She wanted to scowl, but his eyes were saucers of skim milk.

How pitiful, she thought. He reminded her of the strays who used to materialize at her doorstop hungry and shivering, half an ear bitten off and crawling with fleas. Betty Lou could never ignore their pleadings for long.

"What do you want?" she asked. "And who are you anyway?"

The jester smiled.

"*Scusilo, Mia Columbina*. Where are my manners?" He let out four punctuated hacks. "I am...cagh...the great Arlechino!" He clapped his hands and attempted to pull them wide apart in a flourish. Instead, he pantomimed the world's most honest

16

fisherman. His elbows shook and dropped from the strain. "Arlechino….cagh….prince of the gutters, lover of thousands, often a servant but never a slave…."

The coughing grew fiercer. Something stirred in his throat, as if earlier he'd been guest of honor at an all-you-can-eat hairball buffet.

The grass squished as Betty Lou stepped once down the hill.

"What do you want from me?" she sighed.

"I have a simple show," he shrugged, "and the wish to share it."

She looked away. "That's it?"

"That's it," he lied. "Just sit, *mia rapa*, and enjoy."

If I don't help him back, she thought, *I'll just be here longer*. She grabbed his left elbow with one hand and looped the other arm under his shoulder. His body was devoid of heat; not cold, but as if she wasn't touching anything at all. They walked together. She pulled away as soon as the table could replace her.

"Go ahead," she said, sitting down on the grass in front of him. "Show your show. But thus far I am unimpressed."

"*Excellente,*" he rasped. "Then things can only get better."

Arlechino dug one hand into his jacket pocket. Each movement caused him new pains, as if clawing through glass shards and rusty nails. He knew that he appeared old and incapable, but even that was a glamour, for the pain and infirmity that he revealed to her was only a small fraction of his struggle. If the truth were told (though Arlechino was always reluctant to part with such riches), it took everything that he had to remain in a state where she could see him at all.

How had he gotten like this? There was a time when anyone who stepped on stage paid fealty to him. He was never one of the big muckety-mucks. People seldom killed for him or went to war, but he influenced more than his share and there was pride in that. His names were legion and his faces uncountable. Arlechino couldn't remember the moment when his powers began to wane.

He couldn't pinpoint when he stopped thinking of himself in the plural. He remembered the first time he was thrust from a theatre, cast out from the Théâtre National de l'Opéra and into the street. He searched for a way back in, but the costumed performers were impenetrable. At first he thought he was the victim of a coup, that some upstart deity had stolen his place on the throne of high art and culture. Now he knew that there was no replacement; the world had moved on from him. His domain had been drawn and quartered and he was cast off with the remnants. The heart, the head, and the body were gone. Shakespeare, Bolshoi, Kabuki; all were inaccessible. All that remained were the charlatans and mountebanks, the sidewalk hustlers and street performers. Thoughts of his former glory ate at him like Pepsi devouring a chicken bone.

He sighed and dug further into his pocket, fighting back a wince with every movement. He frowned and retrieved a circus tent no larger than the palm of his hand. The prop had been created with amazing detail, including the tiny knots tied into the poles holding up the canvas. He placed the tent atop the music box. From behind the box he materialized a magnifying glass, which he grasped with two fingers and raised to his left pupil.

"Now," he whispered, "if there are no further interruptions…I invite you to strain your eyes…and be welcomed to the Greatest, Smallest Show on Earth."

Betty Lou sat upright. Arlechino held the magnifying glass over the tiny circus tent. He opened a flap in the canopy, revealing rows and rows of itsy-bitsy bleachers. The wind picked up and Betty Lou shivered. Small as it was, the tent looked warm, and he knew that she imagined sitting on one of the wooden benches with a bag of hot peanuts rested in her lap.

The chill subsided.

Betty Lou squinted and leaned forward as the performers strutted onto the stage. Arlechino announced their presence and Warren and Annette, the pint sized showcases, came into focus.

For Betty Lou, the show was....

Well, wonderful.

Annette was stunning, the most beauteous parasite Betty Lou had ever seen, and her demeanor was confident and assured when she climbed a rickety ladder for her perilous plunge. Warren, all muscle, a flea's flea to be sure, was so tender and enamored with his co-star that Betty Lou couldn't help but root for him. Betty Lou was transfixed when Annette walked the tightrope. She gasped when the wind picked up and Annette scrambled to keep her footing. She cheered when Warren, sporting tiny goggles over barely functional ocelli, rocketed from a miniature cannon into the safety of a waiting net.

Through it all there was the host. Betty Lou applauded at his charming feats of juggling and pantomime between the main acts. As the show went on, Arlechino's movements grew more lithe and nimble and his voice transformed from harsh coals to a firestorm. He remained ugly beyond measure. Betty Lou didn't care.

She bounced in her seat and grasped at her hospital gown when the ringmaster made stupid jokes and pretended to trip over his shoes. When Warren and Annette took their bows, she clapped until the fleas turned fuzzy and shrunk from her focus.

Her clapping dissipated. Fog rolled across the clearing.

Arlechino collapsed against the table.

His ancient face pleaded with her, seeking validation, a glimmer of support, a soupcon of recognition. She wanted to tell him the show was fabulous, but to do so would leave her exposed and to Betty Lou, who had spent a lifetime hiding herself behind thrift store smocks and ten-penny bonnets, nothing could have been as terrifying.

"It was terrible," she said, choking back her true words.

Arlechino's face fell.

"I wish you hadn't shown it to me at all," she said. It wasn't true, but she said it anyway. The jester looked at her like a child who had labored all day on a birthday present only to be chided for the mess.

"You didn't like it?" he asked.

Betty Lou struggled once again for honesty and lost.

"It was a cruel thing. That's what it was. I don't even know why I'm here. I should be back in my bed. In fact, I'm probably there right now sleeping away. Any minute I'll wake up and you'll have been a bad dream."

Arlechino sighed. "Say that again and it'll be true."

"Don't think I won't!" she said, regretting the words before they escaped her mouth.

It became difficult to see where Arlechino ended and the table began.

"No, wait!" she cried. "Please. I was wrong."

She stood and her feet tangled in her hospital gown. It took a second to recover. She looked back up and he was gone.

"Please, Arlechino, please. I'm sorry."

A raven flew across the field. Betty Lou ran behind the billboard and around the table. The clearing was empty. After a lifetime of being alone, for the first time she was lonely.

"I didn't mean it," she said. "I didn't. It was the most beautiful thing I've ever seen."

The sound came from behind her shoulder. "Honest, *tesora?*"

Betty Lou turned. Arlechino leaned against the billboard.

"Honest, she said. "It was—wonderful."

"I was handsome, too, yes?" he beamed, stepping towards her with relative vigor. "I am old, I know it. But I was beautiful when you saw me, no?"

Betty Lou considered a diplomatic response and realized there was no need. "I have never been drawn to another's face as I was drawn to yours."

The aged jester beamed.

"Thank you," said Arlechino. He pulled away and doddered towards the table. He placed the magnifying glass in his breast pocket and stuffed the music box in the crux of his arm. He gave no indication that she was still there.

"Is that it?" She walked behind the table. "Is that all?"

Arlechino paused and turned. "Did you want more?"

"I don't know." She dropped her head, then looked up, "I guess, yes, I..." she paused. "I don't know."

She stared, waiting for him to respond. Instead, he offered a simple smile fit for a Buddha.

Betty Lou yanked him forward and kissed him on his leathered, puckered lips.

Betty Lou didn't register the sound of snapping wood as they fell together onto the table. Tiny cotton candy machines and little bleachers were pancaked under her frame.

The enormous, thrusting humanoids tore the stage asunder. A collapsed bleacher trapped Warren the Flea, but Annette pulled him loose and carried him four-handed onto the trapeze. Ever the performers, the two *Siphonaptera* made a death-defying leap from the trapeze, over the circus tent, off the table, and into their own story.

Oblivious to the stars' escape, Arlechino and Betty Lou pushed against one another. Arlechino whispered into Betty Lou's ear as he lifted up her hospital gown.

"Don't talk," she said. "Please. Just keep going."

But talk he did. He told her beautiful lies and horrendous truths. She couldn't tell the difference and perhaps neither could he. The truths were so fabulous and the lies were so seamless that the universe, always a sucker for a tall tale, believed them then and believes them still.

He told her about her cats and why they have no word for faith but hundreds for truth. He told her what color shame smelt to dogs. He told her why humans believe that something isn't important unless they feel pain and he bit her ear for emphasis.

He told her about her mother and the day she dove into a Venice canal to follow curious, bubbling laughter. A tour guide found her hours later in an alley, drenched and unconscious with a bulging belly, though no one knew that she had been pregnant.

Arlechino told Betty Lou about their son and whispered that his words would be the only picture of him she would ever have.

He told her so many things. Betty Lou begged him to stop even as his hips continued thrusting into her. She knew if she took in his fantastical stories her life would change forever. Even disbelief would transform her. She prayed for silence as she seized his wrinkled back skin with both hands and forced him to pump into her with such ferocity that their bodies pounded into each other like two boulders.

But he still spoke. When he'd spent himself and collapsed in a sweat atop Betty Lou, he told her the secret of creation. It began, he said, not with a bang, but with a snowflake on a mountain of motionless snow. The snowflake rolled, gathering others as it went, until it amassed into a humungous snowball.

"And here we are, *señora,*" he said, "tumbling around with everyone and everything else, waiting to see what happens when we get to the bottom. That's where the real secret is. God is not the cause," he whispered, "but the result."

Betty Lou tumbled into oblivion. To say that she was in blackness or whiteness would conjure a color and that wasn't an option. She sensed herself and her lover, nothing else. He was beside her, but not with her, and pulling further away. She felt another wave of loneliness and she hated it. She never wanted to be this close to someone else again.

"Will I see you again?" she asked.

"*No.*" he said.

She paused.

"Good," she replied. "I didn't ask for this. How can I go back after what you told me, after what we did? It's not fair."

"*Sono spiacente, mia amore. Fairness isn't something your kind gets or wants.*"

Arlechino faded, but with his remaining power he offered her a boon. He resisted when she made her request, for he loved her in his fashion, but a boon offered cannot be rescinded.

She never spoke after that night, even after her tummy swelled and the doctors pleaded with her to tell them which of the orderlies violated her.

An evening nurse discovered her panting and rushed her to delivery. The doctors had seen nothing like it. She made no cries, her body knew what to do and in a few short hours Bernard, the hero of our tale, was born.

As her lover predicted, Betty Lou never saw her child. Her eyes remained shut throughout the delivery. When baby Bernard drew his first breaths, Betty Lou's breaths grew quieter and quieter.

It was painless in the end, just as she'd requested, just like falling asleep.

4. Machina ex Deo

Machina ex Deo, The God's Machine,
50% Buddha, 50% Charlie Sheen.

Dr. Harold Slumgullion, head of the Fiddler's Green Sanitarium and pathological fabulist, created ripples of amusement in the medical community when he proposed that the manner of conception dictated a child's future potential. He suggested that a six-minute Missionary Special would likely produce mediocre offspring and offered current society as proof of the claim.

Bernard's conception was far from ordinary and Dr. Slumgullion, had he possessed all the details, would've assumed that such a powerful event would produce an exceptional creature. The child was destined to become a paragon of existence, a model for men and women to follow and remember. Perhaps an artist whose dabblings in rare and eldritch mediums would birth works lasting through the ages. Perhaps a spiritual leader, helping the world attune itself closer to divinity. Perhaps a despot, feared and respected, ruling with preternatural power coursing through his body. Perhaps the next President of the United States.

Instead, he was Bernard.

Orphaned babies aren't usually hard to home, but something wasn't right with this one. Prospective parents made faces and played peek-a-boo with the new arrival. Bernard stared. One couple attempted the "I Got Your Nose" routine. Bernard pulled in his lips and shot back a doleful glare as if to say, *"Please. What do you think I am? A child?"*

Bernard's penetrating and unyielding gaze made new parents uneasy, then downright uncomfortable. Soon enough, they'd pack the child up and make another trip to the baby brokers.

By the time Bernard was five years old, the polite thing to say was that he hadn't lost his baby fat. He was a pudgy child with light-blue eyes that catalogued everything despite being hidden underneath a black mop of hair that fell like dark jungle vines in front of his face.

Bernard was quiet and didn't play with other children, but by kindergarten he had managed to fall in love with three things: caterpillars, Circle Time, and Cindy Simmons. He'd seen caterpillars the week before and he loved them because they were slow and ugly, and because they could walk up walls and upside down on trees. He loved Circle Time because it was just before lunch, and because it was when Cindy Simmons sat beside him. Unlike caterpillars, Bernard didn't love Cindy Simmons because she was slow and ugly, but because she wore a red beret in her golden-brown hair. Every day he wondered how he could get her to notice him. He considered stealing her red beret or pulling her hair or hiding a bunch of caterpillars in her lunch box, but no plan had that extra-special something.

On the unfortunate morning that Cindy Simmons would acknowledge Bernard's existence, Jesus Says No (her real name was Josephine, but Bernard no longer bothered to learn his foster parents' names) was in a rush. God instructed JSN to open her heart and her home to lost children, and she obliged. JSN awaited instructions regarding opening her legs for a man to help raise them, but God remained silent on this point and the six foster kids were wearing her ragged.

That morning, JSN fought for control despite multiple diaper changes, a mysterious reek of sulfur in the living room, a condom discovered in a pair of Levis, the bathroom door that had been locked for forty-five minutes, a half-frozen cat discovered in the crisper, and disconcerting wisps of smoke coming from the garage. Amid the chaos, JSN packed Bernard's lunch twice.

Bernard was unaware of the windfall until he opened his bag on the school bus and found two of everything: two fruit cups, two juice boxes, two bags of animal crackers, and two peanut butter and honey sandwiches with sliced banana and the crusts cut off. Everything had an identical twin. Right there in the bus, before his school-day had begun, before his first glimpse of Cindy Simmons, Bernard gobbled up the extra provisions and when he was done with the extras, he tackled the firsts.

The rest of the morning went by like any other until Circle Time, where Miss Crinkle read them "The Ugly Duckling."

"The Ugly Duckling" is the tale of a paddling of baby ducks who tease their brother because he's smaller and darker than they are. Miss Crinkle chose it because it was about being different, and preached that was okay to be ugly now because you might look better later. It didn't occur to her that the ducks would still laugh at their brother after he turned into a swan, since he looked even stranger than before.

Bernard and Miss Crinkle had a lot in common: they both had dark hair, they were both left-handed, and they both loved caterpillars, Cindy Simmons, and Circle Time. Miss Crinkle loved caterpillars because they turned into butterflies. She loved Cindy Simmons because Cindy only used pink crayons when she colored. But the reason Miss Crinkle loved Circle Time was a secret, because Miss Crinkle wasn't just a kindergarten teacher. Miss Crinkle was a movie star.

Elisa Crinkle belonged to no Actors Guild, she was listed on no Hollywood sidewalk, and she had never appeared on the silver screen. The only one who knew that Elisa Crinkle was a star was Elisa Crinkle. The only theatres she appeared in were in her own head. Though she would never stand in front of a real movie camera, Miss Crinkle found her own path to stardom. Her favorite way was Circle Time, when she pretended that a simple children's story was the script for her latest film.

Many might pity Miss Crinkle, but her life could never be better. She hadn't the beauty nor talent of an actress. She was a good teacher and in her head she was a great movie star. She saw no harm in the dozen minutes a day her students stopped being five year olds and turned into cameramen, makeup artists, and cinephiles watching the greatest actress of the 20th century.

What harm indeed? Except for the day that the great Elisa Crinkle would be so intent on her recitation of "The Ugly Duckling" that she'd fail to notice Bernard's hand darting up and around, requesting permission to go to the bathroom.

Let us not blame Miss Crinkle, who'd reached the climax of her story where the beautiful swan appeared before his envious siblings. Let us not blame Bernard, who was too meek to call out his simple need. Instead, we shall blame those villainous juice boxes, whose contents had been hurrying through Bernard's body to arrive pushing and screaming into his bladder.

It was unfortunate that the tale that day was set in a gigantic pond. Try as he might with his frantic gesticulations, Bernard couldn't get Miss Crinkle's attention, nor could he bring himself to utter a word in his defense.

Bernard's classmates were caught up in Miss Crinkle's grand performance, but she could have been reading from "The Big Book of Corporate Tax Laws Volume Fifteen: Writs and Torts" and none of the attention-deprived children would've registered Bernard's distress.

Bernard had a mild case of invisibility.

Bernard was never called on in class, never asked by other children to join them for tag or make believe, never addressed at all. It was no wonder Cindy Simmons wouldn't give him the time of day (were she able to tell time, a concept which had thus far taken back seat to colors and farm sounds in Miss Crinkle's curriculum).

Bernard waved as his bladder quaked, but he was as ineffective as the thrashing tuna fish, twenty-five years later, who tried to warn a boatful of fisherman that Venice was about to sink into the ocean.

Bernard pressed his knees together. One hand dammed his crotch against the inevitable flood. Miss Crinkle continued her performance and the classmates, including little Cindy Simmons, listened rapt-eared as the beautiful swan *burst* into the clearing of his siblings and presented himself in all his glory.

Bernard lowered his hand and looked around, hoping that no one heard the stream filling his Osh Kosh B'Gosh jeans. He felt a confusing mélange of horror and relief. He slunk his head. He knew it was a matter of time before he was found out. Bernard had already observed his classmates beginning to faction off against the different and unusual. He knew what would happen when they discovered what he had done. He could hear the taunts and doubted his invisibility would protect him from active antagonism. For the first time in his life, he was glad for his condition. Perhaps he could make it to recess unnoticed. He did his best to think transparent thoughts and ignored the smell rising to his nose. Miss Crinkle's monologue came to an end and she closed the book with a dramatic sweep. Recess was seconds away, but before Miss Crinkle's director could call it a wrap, Cindy Simmons interrupted with one hand in the air and the other resting in the puddle beside her:

"Teacher!" she called. Every head swiveled in her direction. "It's really wet right here."

This wasn't the worst event of Bernard's childhood. It wasn't even the second or the third. Puberty compounded the difficulties of childhood, providing a new nemesis in the coarse, oily hairs that emerged in haphazard patches all over Bernard's body. He grew larger (more horizontal than vertical), but his extra girth subtracted him further from the world around him. His youth held the merest glimpses of happiness, as much as found walking down a strange sidewalk and glimpsing a boisterous party behind shuttered windows. For the first quarter century of Bernard's life, pleasure was something that happened to other people.

Soon after the kindergarten incident, small items began to disappear; first from the foster home, then from the school. They were little things; nothing of real value. Once, Miss Crinkle turned her head for a mere moment and a mug disappeared from her desk. Every student remembered seeing the mug, but no one saw the child who took it.

5. Utrennyaya

Utrennyaya tried out nipple play,
And squirted out the Milky Way.

Vida's father, Donnagh Callahan, was an Irish Catholic who left Dublin because everyone drank too much. His first week in San Francisco, he sat on a bench in Buena Vista Park and struck up a conversation with Ana-Margarita, a Brazilian who left São Paulo because everyone touched too much. Donnagh and Ana-Margarita talked until the park grew dark. They spoke about how much better it was in America and what a beautiful view they had of the city and how many nice young men smiled at Donnagh as he walked through the park. Ana-Margarita accepted Donnagh's offer to walk her home. In transit, the two stumbled upon a pair of mustachioed bikers grunting against a tree. Donnagh began to question his relationship with San Francisco.

Donnagh married Ana-Margarita three weeks later and they moved north to Redding, a conservative town that fit closer to their prurient sensibilities. Donnagh and Ana-Margarita shared a sensible and tempered household until Ana-Margarita's belly swelled. The child was a ball of energy *in utero*, kicking and punching with such unrelenting fervor that Ana-Margarita convinced herself she would give birth to a whirlwind.

Ana-Margarita swore that when the zero hour arrived, Vida flew from Ana-Margarita's womb and surged twice around the delivery room. Donnagh covered his head and dropped to the ground. Ana-Margarita pointed to the ceiling. A nurse grabbed a medical apron and lassoed the child who landed in the doctor's arms and began an excited conversation with her hands, lips, and eyelids.

Little Vida's hyperactive desire to experience the world brought new trials daily. Vida was such a nimble crawler that Ana-Margarita procrastinated as long as she could at teaching Vida to walk, after which point the child would disappear at the turn of a head, to be found hours and blocks later holding court with the neighborhood dogs or showing off her new underwear to a group of porch-bound geriatrics.

Donnagh arrived home one day to find Ana-Margarita, her face white and her hair a tangled rat's nest. She charged her husband, grabbed his collar and pushed him against a wall.

"I let you make her in me, *Donn!* God help me if I ever let you make another!"

Little Vida giggled into the living room, wearing a burger king crown and nothing else. She scampered onto the sofa and stood with one determined hand in the air and the other over her eyes.

"Eyes!" she said.

She moved her hand to her stomach.

"Tummy!"

She moved her hand to her crotch. She giggled.

"Cootchie!"

Seeing her mother's terrified reaction, Vida grew a devilish grin and repeated herself.

"Cootchie! Cootchie! Cootchie!"

She continued the refrain as she jumped up and down on the couch and vaulted off, landing beside her parents and running out the open front door, one hand still over her pelvis.

"Cootchie! Coootchie! Coooooooooootchie!"

Vida's beleaguered parents held each other as she announced her anatomy to the neighborhood and Ana-Margarita fought not to cry.

In second grade, Vida and her best friend Sophia Meeks took their classmate Kamal Balasubramanium by the hand and led him underneath the slides and into a wooden enclosure that hid them from the rest of the playground. The three children sat in a circle among the fresh-cut wood chips still cool and odorous from the previous night's rain. Vida pulled tight at the purple scrunchie around her dark ponytail. Kamal wiped his nose on his sleeve.

Sophia picked out a wood chip and placed it on the lap of her striped green skirt.

"We're playing 'Marriage'," said Vida. She sifted through the wood chips and handed a dark-red one to Sophia, who placed it with the first.

"How do you play?" asked Kamal.

"First we need a bouquet," said Sophia, adding another red chip to her lap.

Kamal shrugged and picked up a chip.

"Not that one, silly," said Vida. "It's too light."

Vida took the chip from Kamal, picked up two more light chips from the ground, and placed them in her lap.

"These ones are rice," said Vida.

"Oh," said Kamal.

Sophia held up a handful of red wood chips to her nose and sniffed. "Ahhh! A beautiful bouquet of roses."

Sophia held out the chips to Vida and Kamal.

"Mmmmm," said Vida. "Violets, too."

Violets were Vida's favorite flower and favorite color because they shared the same first letter as her name.

Kamal sniffed the chips in Sophia's hands. All he smelled was damp wood, but he didn't say anything. Sophia put the chips in the middle of the circle.

"Okay," said Vida. "It's time to get married."

"How do you play?" repeated Kamal.

"You hold hands and then you kiss and then you're married," declared Vida.

"How do you win?" asked Kamal.

Vida looked over at Sophia, who rolled her eyes. Boys.

"It sounds boring, but ok," said Kamal. "Who goes first?"

"You're gunna marry us," said Sophia. "Vida and I are gunna be married *for reals* one day."

Vida looked over at Sophia. The statement was a surprise, but Sophia took Vida's hand and smiled. Vida smiled back.

"That's right," said Vida in support.

"You can't be married," said Kamal.

"Why not?" said Vida.

"Only boys can marry girls," said Kamal. "Everyone knows that."

Vida had never thought about marrying Sophia, but this was a challenge.

"Oh yeah?" asked Vida.

"Yeah," said Kamal.

Kamal's retort stopped her. Vida sucked in her upper lip and ruminated.

She popped her lip free.

"What about Lulubell and Mrs. Whiteface?"

"Yeah!" said Sophia.

Lulubell and Mrs. Whiteface were the classroom's goldfish. The two fish spent their days swimming back and forth in a small aquarium that they shared with blue rocks, a miniature castle, pencils, bouncy balls, attractive marbles, a snowglobe, a plastic robot with a missing arm, a calculator, a pair of sunglasses, a broken Game Boy, and an assortment of cheap jewelry. Ms. Havermeyer encouraged the aquarium decorations at first, but she was starting to worry about the two goldfish and their shrinking real estate.

"Lulubell and Mrs. Whiteface aren't married," said Kamal, who to his credit realized that he was about to lose this part of the argument.

"Of course they are," said Sophia.

"It's *Mrs.* Whiteface," added Vida. "If she's a Mrs., then she has to be married and there's no one else in there. Lulubell's full name is Lulubell Daffodil Whiteface. Technical-specifically she's also Mrs. Whiteface, but we call her by her first name so we can tell them apart."

None of this had been discussed before, but Vida knew that as soon as she said it, it was true.

"They might be married, but they're goldfish," said Kamal. "They're not people. I said boys and girls have to be married, not goldfish."

Vida fixated upon Kamal. A group of noisome boys banged their feet on the playspace above them before sliding down the slide, but Vida didn't let herself become distracted. She didn't know what she was looking for, but she found something.

"What about dogs?" Vida asked. "Are dogs people?"

Kamal recoiled. He had a dog, a golden retriever named Jack, and he could think of a number of times he'd argued with his mother about the very topic of Jack's personhood, such as when Kamal wanted Jack to sleep in his bed or join the family at the dinner table or accompany Kamal for bathtime.

"Dogs are close enough," conceded Kamal, who was afraid that if he gave any other answer Jack would know, and Kamal feared losing his dog's respect more than he feared losing an argument with two girls.

"Well," Vida smirked, "my neighbor has three Rotters: Mary and Freddie and Bettina, and they're all married."

"Honest?" asked Kamal.

"Honest," said Vida. She held up both her hands to show that she wasn't crossing any fingers.

"Well," said Kamal, "I guess if dogs can do it...."

Sophia squeezed Vida's hand. Vida was happy. Vida looked back at Kamal, whose eyes were set downward as he drew haphazard spirals with his finger in the ground. Vida was hit with another mysterious piece of information.

Vida touched Kamal's hand.

"Just because Sophia and me are getting married doesn't mean you can't be married too."

Kamal looked up. "For reals?" he said.

"Sure," said Vida. "Mary and Bettina married Freddie, and he can't stop drooling even when he's eating"

"I just wanted to play too," said Kamal.

"I know," said Vida, though she didn't know how she knew it.

The recess bell rang. Sophia and Kamal looked at Vida.

"Hold hands," said Vida. "Quick."

Sophia and Kamal complied. Outside the wooden enclosure were sounds of chatter, kick balls being gathered, and small feet scampering towards classrooms.

"Do you have the ring?" asked Vida.

Sophia and Kamal looked nervous until Kamal perked up.

"I do," he said. He let go of Sophia's left hand and joined his thumb and pointer finger together in a circle. His fingers approached Sophia's middle finger, but Sophia corrected him and slid her ring finger into the circle between his fingers. Once she reached her knuckle, Kamal split his fingers apart and held back onto Sophia's hand.

"Do *you* have a ring?" asked Sophia to Vida.

"I do," said Vida. She repeated Kamal's steps on the proper finger of Kamal's hand and resumed the hand-hold.

"Do *you* have a ring?" asked Kamal to Sophia.

"I do," said Sophia. Vida held out her hand as Sophia slid her circled fingers down Vida's ring finger. The two girls looked at each other and Vida blushed.

The second bell rang. They were tardy. None of the three children moved to leave.

"By the power 'vested in me," said Vida, releasing her hands and tossing the three light wood chips into the air. "I pronounce us husband and *wifes*. You must kiss the brides."

Sophia and Kamal shifted and avoided each other's eyes. Vida scooted forward and readjusted the hem of her dress. Sophia and Kamal leaned forward and stopped. It was Kamal's turn to blush.

Vida leaned in, put one hand on Sophia's cheek and one hand on Kamal's. Sophia and Kamal closed their eyes. Vida puckered her lips and pulled the two of them towards her. They connected.

Later, as the three sat at their desks being berated for their tardiness, Vida let the teacher's voice drift off and she remembered that Kamal's lips were cool and Sophia's tasted like cherry chap-stick.

Vida didn't tell her parents about her first kiss that day, nor did she show them the Parental Notice about "Chronic Tardiness" that she'd already signed. Arriving home, she ran into the dining room to grab a chair, which creaked along the floor as she slid it into the kitchen. She opened the pantry door. climbed atop the chair and felt around the top pantry shelf until her hands closed on a box of Uncle Ben's Minute Rice. Vida hopped down with the box, took three strips of raw bacon from the fridge and ran into her backyard, where she picked a handful of daisies from her mother's garden.

Vida walked to the chain link fence on the side of her yard. She held up the strips of bacon and whistled.

"Hey girls! Hey Freddie! Treats!" She slapped the bacon against the chain link three happy, panting Rottweilers appeared before her. Vida rolled the strips of raw bacon across her left palm and held her hand up to the fence. The dogs lapped at the bacon juices on her palm as the largest of the Rottweilers poured a stream of slobber onto the ground.

Her palm cleaned, the dogs sat at attention.

"Not yet, puppies," she said. "Sit!"

The dogs sat.

"Very good," said Vida. She cleared her throat and raised her head high. "We are gathered here today at this fence to witness the marriage of these three *people* in holy matrimony."

Vida continued the ceremony, embellishing with the freedom of a child who knew that no bell would interrupt her, with the confidence of a performer who knew the audience was already eating out of her hand, and the necessity of a sinner who knew that sometimes the only thing to do with a lie was to make it true.

At twelve years old, Vida and Sophia started their periods in near-sync: Vida in February, Sophia in March. If Ana-Margarita noticed her maxi pads disappearing at three times the normal rate, she never mentioned it.

Sharing a newfound relationship with blood, the two young women become fascinated with the subject. When Vida stumbled onto a Wikipedia entry about the Lydian practice of blood brothers, Sophia insisted they go to school wearing each other's spotted underwear. The entire day, Vida kept looking around, struck with the feeling that any moment she would be called to the principal's office and their trade would be revealed. When she'd arrived home from school, she collapsed on her bed, filled with relief and exhilaration.

Later that night, Vida awoke to a knock at her window. The knock was familiar, the timing was not. Vida slid the glass open and Sophia crawled onto her bed.

"*Wassa matter,* Shortie?" mumbled Vida as she rubbed her eyes.

Vida had shot up in height during the summer and was the tallest in her freshman class, though she was jealous of Sophia who gained breasts rather than elevation. Her jealousy was misguided, as Vida was already showing signs of the tall and attractive woman she would become, having inherited the olive-coffee skin of her Brazilian mother while avoiding the orthodontic legacy of her Irish father.

"Have you been crying?" asked Vida. The dim reading light she'd turned on by her bed revealed hints of Sophia's puffy red face.

"I can't stay there anymore," said Sophia, brushing her fingers on a path from her striped green knee-high socks to the purplish welt on her thigh.

"I'm going somewhere he'll never find me," said Sophia.

Vida no longer felt comfortable at Sophia's house, not since Sophia's parents got the divorce.

"I love you," said Sophia, who leaned forward on Vida's bed and kissed her.

Vida stiffened in surprise. They hadn't kissed since the playground with Kamal. This kiss was wetter, a combination of Sophia's mouth and tongue and sudden, inexplicable tears. The kiss disconnected and Vida pulled Sophia in to hug her. Her friend sobbed in Vida's arms. Vida wanted to ask what was wrong, but Sophia pulled away, averted her eyes, and climbed out the window.

Sophia wasn't at school the next day, nor the day after that. Months went by. Vida waited for some notice: a phone call, a letter, something from her friend to tell her that she was alive and safe. Nothing came.

A year and a half later, Vida's parents found a single-paged typed note on her pillow.

We have the unfortunate duty to report that your child, Vida Callahan, is defective and has been recalled to the factory.

We are terribly sorry if this causes any inconvenience. This recall is unavoidable as her particular defect can result in unacceptable levels of aspiration, determination and hope. Rest assured that this error plagues the smallest percentage of our products and we're actively working to eliminate its appearance in future models. We hope that this does not reflect negatively on our company, which prides itself on churning out a legion of reliable and unquestioning laborers for the perpetuation of the status quo.

While recurrent problems are rare, we suggest monitoring future offspring. Possible danger signs include independence, creativity, contrariness, unusual levels of happiness, fashion not dictated by the media, a lack of shame, and literacy.

6. Déjà vu

Repeat one two, that's déjà vu,
Repeat one too, that's déjà vu.

What Bernard did on Monday:

6am: Hit snooze.

6:08:   Hit snooze again.

6:16:   Showered. Shaved. Applied toilet paper and spit to three razor injuries.

6:38:   Ate breakfast (two eggs, no yolks; one piece of toast, wheat, unbuttered).

6:53:   Drove to work (tan Yugo, twenty-two years old, maximum speed 57mph, dirt obscuring windows and "If Tautologies Were Outlawed, Only Outlaws Would Use Tautologies" bumper sticker).

7:08:   Traffic jam.

7:15:   Traffic jam.

7:30:   Traffic jam.

7:38:   Searched in glove box. Found and devoured half a Snickers and twelve peanuts from an opened bag.

7:50:   Traffic jam

8:04:   Tongue lashing from Chad Mattson: four minutes late is not an excuse.

8:07:   Chad returned to his desk and discovered his tie clip was missing.

8:15:   Slogged through eighty-six emails (twenty-four office memos, fifty-six pieces of spam, five Words of the Day [stegophilist, tregetour, dromaeognathous, engastrimyth, and famulus], and one misdirected message intended for "Uncle Dave" from his seven-year-old niece in Sarasota saying her birthday party was Saturday, there was a clown who made balloons, and it was her best birthday ever. Bernard read the email three times).

9:48: Played Solitaire.

11:25: Phone support with Hillary Kniff from Biloxi who forgot her password ("kittypoo"). Progress Log indicated this was the third time she'd called the Help Center with the same problem.

11:36: Played Solitaire.

Noon: Ate lunch (turkey sandwich purchased from the lunch cart. First bite revealed the lack of mayonnaise and turkey, leaving one piece of dried lettuce and a tomato slice between stale wheat bread. Bernard considered and rejected bringing up the situation when the lunch cart returned).

1:15: Three more calls, one more conversation with Chad Mattson, and eighteen games of Solitaire.

5:45: Stopped at the Mini Mart on the way home (Purchased: sixty dollars in Hungry Man meals. Stolen: two packs of Wrigley's gum).

7:42: Ate dinner (microwaved linguini and soft peas).

8:23: Started and finished a book (*The Jamai Vu Papers* by Wim Coleman).

11:18: Retired to bed.

11:19: Cried himself to sleep.

What Bernard Did on Tuesday:

See Monday.

7. Sesquipedaliophilia
Use words that go the extra mile,
To woo the sesquipedaliophile.

Bernard had always been a curious child. Isolated from classmates and needing an outlet, he turned to literature. Books didn't tolerate his attention; they thrived on it, and within those papered halls he uncovered a passion for *sesquipedalia*: a fancy and self-referential designation for "big words".

When it came to the tenacious search for linguistic treasures, Bernard was unstoppable, unflappable, indefatigable. He was a spelunker in the mines of *belles-lettres*, going agog with each discovery from *aposiopesis* to *ziggurat*. By twelve years old our *onomatomaniac* dispensed terms *in absentia* from his teacher's worn copy of Merriam's. By sixteen, Bernard could name the noise of your stomach when you're hungry (*borborygmus*), the liquid inside your eyeball (*vitreous humor*), the act of throwing someone out a window (*defenestration*), the belief that inanimate objects possess hostile intentions (*Resistentialism*), the proper label for a street performer (*busker*), the fear of his obsession (*hippopotomonstrosesquipedaliophobia*) and the Latin for every part of a woman's anatomy (though by adulthood his hands-on experiences were less than noteworthy). He wasn't a virgin, for even the most socially inept can stumble into an *imbroglio* with someone else willing to substitute attention for affection, but Bernard's forays into the bar and online dating scenes were short, messy, and ultimately drew him further away.

The more he retreated, the less the world seemed to notice. He read. He worked. He stole insignificant items around him. The word for this is *kleptomania* and Bernard had a two pack a day habit. He never stole money or anything of sentimental value. The novelty of thievery had long dissipated, but the compulsion did not, eventually it became just one more thing to get done.

Bernard was a victim of *Weltschmerz*. He was *taciturn* with a case of the *mulligrubs*, an *agelast*, a knee-jerk *floccinaucinihilipilificator*.

If his life *imprimis* was an open book, everything at present was a *Hobson's choice.*

It would be a tragedy if he continued on this path without *peripeteia*, but Bernard would soon be reminded of another word: *ephemeral,* a name for something that will not last, which is to say a name for everything.

Ephemeral came to Bernard on his thirtieth birthday, when he learned he was about to die.

8. Götterdämmerung

**When the sun fills the sky and we're all gonna die,
That's Götterdämmerung....**

On the morning of Bernard's birthday every news station buzzed with reports that Venice had sunk into the ocean.

Oceanographers, seismologists, and anyone with a few letters after their name jockeyed for camera time with eager reporters. When it became clear that no one had a satisfactory explanation, all decided to save face by passing the blame onto other fields.

The seismologists blamed the oceanographers. The oceanographers blamed the architects. The architects retaliated and blamed the oceanographers, but the oceanographers called no tag-backs. The architects tried to blame the seismologists but got flustered and blamed the epistemologists, who turned around and blamed the ontologists. The ontologists blamed the tautologists. The tautologists blamed the tautologists. Eschatologists blamed everybody. Everybody blamed the scientologists. The scientologists blamed the Church, and the Church blamed the General State of Corruption and Decay in European Values.

The General State of Corruption and Decay in European Values was not available for comment.

9. Mulligrubs

Schlimazels, sad sacks, and other schlubs,
Miserable with the mulligrubs.

At fourteen years old, Vida thumbed her way from California to Nevada with stops in Dallas, Newark, and Juneau, Alaska. She dumpster dove in Olympia, Washington, raised a barn in Perry County, Pennsylvania, and jumped out of a moving car in Terra Haute, Indiana. She traded smiles for shelter and discovered a knack for getting along with strangers. She could arrive in town with the new moon and have a family by the time it was full, but she was on the road again before it emptied. She'd caught a case of the gypsy itch and she'd caught it bad.

The word for an uncontrollable urge to run away is *drapetomania*.

In Boulder, Colorado, Vida chanced into the home of a bartender and his wife, a kind and generous couple who gave her the room of their son who never returned from Iraq and paid her nine dollars an hour to sweep the bar and pour pints. It was the highest point of her travels until the night she fled while they slept, leaving in such a panic that she abandoned an envelope of money, a worn copy of *Even Cowgirls Get the Blues*, and the desktop computer they'd given her that morning for her sixteenth birthday.

Dark shadows followed her after that and she couldn't bring herself to talk her way into another home. She slept outside and scrounged for food while the wind pushed her to Biloxi, Mississippi. She tumbled down Caillavet Street and came to rest outside the Beau Rivage, where she watched a mohawked itinerant named Tony T perform the first street show she'd ever seen.

For thirty minutes, Tony T gathered a circle of strangers to watch him juggle fire and tell dirty jokes. For the finale, he hammered a twenty-penny nail into his nose while he balanced on his head. The show ended and Vida stayed for the next one. Dusk settled when the blue-haired Tony T poured his days earning into a Sex Pistols lunchbox. The majority of his haul was change, although there were two fives and a small fistful of ones.

Tony T looked up as Vida's shadow obscured his earnings.

"Teach me," said Vida.

Tony T smiled.

Vida and Tony T negotiated a partnership on the street and under the covers. Vida started as the Lovely Assistant with three tasks: lighting Tony T's torches, pulling the nail out of his nose with a pair of oversized pliers, and looking pretty. In her spare time she learned stage patter, picked up a smattering of street gymnastics, and practiced the art of juggling three torches (four if you counted Tony T's, though his was smaller and couldn't stay lit as long).

Vida didn't kick out Tony T the first night he climbed into her sleeping bag, but they hit a snag when things became frisky. Try as they might, Vida couldn't stay lubricated long enough to enjoy the experience. No matter what or how long the foreplay, she was dry as a bone whenever Tony T approached with his. Even the generous application of saliva (hers, his, or both), evaporated in the Sahara Desert of Vida's crotch.

Nothing is as resourceful as a young couple in need of a screw. They kept at it. They tried body oils, castor oil, and extra virgin olive oil. They tried Crisco, Jell-O, No Tears Shampoo, Vaseline, sour cream, marmalade, Kool-Aid, pie cream, butter, batter, and bottled water. They even tried champagne, which was a flop but for the bubbles. Their grocery bill neared quadruple digits.

At a loss they turned to the professionals, but Dr. Samantha's Love-Lube gave Vida a rash, Turbo-Smooth was a Turbo-Dud, and Melvin's Moyle-Motion, a 100% kosher lube for the circumcised, began smoking on contact and rose to a troublesome heat. Vida made a mad dash to the bathroom and practiced her gymnastics with a shower handstand.

The situation seemed insurmountable, but compromises were found. Vida was creative with options and orifices to satisfy her jaculiferous loverboy. Regarding her own satisfaction, she didn't notice the lack. Something had come into her life that overshadowed any teenage curiosity for the bump and grind. It started every day she stepped onto the city squares and shouted for attention, culminated whenever people raced to put money in her hat, offered warm caresses every time she tossed the day's unsorted earnings onto a motel bed. Vida had a hard-on for street performing.

She learned torches with ease and moved on to fire spinning, fire eating, and any other skill Tony could impart. She drew the line at a nail through the nose after she stabbed her septum and gushed a bloody geyser.

"Just as well," said Tony T. "You needed that trick like you need another hole in your head."

Vida rocketed from assistant to showstopper. Vida had a natural affinity with crowds, and her ability to read people became further refined.

The word for divining someone's character by looking at their face is *physiognomy*.

Vida became the Spieler and their hats doubled. Tony T attributed their new affluence on Vida's breasts. Vida couldn't explain to Tony T that his stage patter was tainted by his belief that the performer was superior to the audience. Tony T could generate awe, but he couldn't build rapport. In a thirty minute street show, Vida Callahan transformed the audience into a family. Not the family that she ran away from, the mother who once fled to the kitchen when Vida tried to hug her, the father who had the emotional depth of a department store mannequin. Vida's new family showed their love, not just by dropping money in her hat, but by encouraging her and playing with her. Once, she dropped torches three times at the end of her routine and someone yelled "You can do it! One more time!" Vida tried again, and then again, and success brought their biggest hat yet.

In six months of street performing, Vida worked through sixteen years of familial guilt. In the beginning, the audience's love was unbalanced. She had holes to be filled, a skill to read other people but no idea who she was. In the circle of the show, she found herself. Training gave her a strong body, successes matured her bravado into confidence, failures taught humility. Vida was happy.

Six weeks of Louisiana rain killed the fire show and drained their funds. Tony T and Vida pawned everything but the clothes on their backs and their show materials. They would've gone naked before selling the show, it was sacrosanct and with it was always the promise of more funds. The couple headed north and the rains died. Their hats refilled and this time they vowed to be prepared. They made regular deposits in the First Bank of Folgers while visions of a mobile home touring North America danced in their heads.

One evening in Jefferson County, Missouri, Vida packed up their latest show. She couldn't see the face of the audience member that Tony T talked with across the way, just a pair of boots and a lanky body. Vida placed their torches in the suitcase. She looked back up and the audience member had disappeared. Tony returned.

"Got another tip," he said.

"How much?" she asked.

"Four grams of pixie dust." Tony dropped a plastic bag into the suitcase.

Back at the hotel room, Vida hesitated to try Tony's offering, but he promised it was a harmless adventure and she demurred. All it took was a few sprinkles and happy thoughts and WOOOOOOOOOOOOOOOOSH she was on her way, second star to the right and straight on till morning.

Vida was somewhat peckish during next morning's breakfast at Arnie's Homestyle Buffet. Tony T suggested a pick-me-up in the bathroom. After the nasal infusion, Vida ignored her two egg scramble and occupied herself by tapping out Rachmaninoff on the wood grain of the café table.

Previously, the couple performed four to five shows on a normal day, weather and tourists permitting. They did nine shows that day. The next, twelve.

Three weeks later, Tony T punched out a glass walker from Tennessee who told Vida that she needed to eat a sandwich.

Powder was cheaper than food at first, so their savings accumulated. Tony T paid for two months of a hotel room with quarters.

They did five shows the next day.

The next week they did two.

Four months later, Tony T sat shivering in the motel bathtub, waiting for the water to fill despite an unplugged drain. He climbed out.

"Tub's broken" he informed Vida, who was curled up on the motel bed. She grunted.

It took Tony several tries to put on his shirt, but he got his pants on in one. That was a good sign. He fished through the pile of empty baggies on the hotel dresser. He dug his hand into the Folgers tin that held their savings. The tin was empty. He picked up their juggling torches and headed for the door.

Vida watched him. "Gonna do a show?"

Tony didn't respond.

"You need lighter fluid, dummy. We're out."

"Not doin' a show," said Tony. "Need to get blow." He stopped and laughed: he'd still got it.

Vida tried to sit up but her body wouldn't respond. "You can't sell the torches. How'll we get more if we don't have a show?"

"Don't worry, baby. I'll take care of it. I'll be back before you know it."

The hotel door closed and Vida never saw Tony T again.

She was half-conscious of the sound of running water coming from the bathtub. The television flickered on and a pretty red-headed news anchor told her that her hotel room was surrounded by the police, the FBI, the mob, Disneyland, the Religious Right, Ricardo Montalban, and her mother.

Vida fell asleep. She awoke three days later. The bathtub was silent. The television was off. She went back to sleep.

Vida woke up again and tore apart the hotel room, flinging aside take-out boxes and shaking out towels and sheets. She found a twenty-dollar bill crumpled under the dresser. She held the money for fifteen minutes before ripping it into confetti and throwing the scraps into the toilet.

Vida went back to bed and didn't get up for another two days.

When the hotel door opened, the pizza boy bit his lip and stopped himself from running away. The emaciated young woman stood at the doorway, eyes half closed. She extended her lanky arms towards the pizza box and dropped a lump of soggy green confetti into his palm.

"I'm gonna need change," she mumbled.

10. Matutolypea

Matutolypea means seeing red,
From waking on the wrong side of bed.

Bernard woke with a gnawing stomachache and a string of drool dangling from his lower lip to his pillow. He wiped his mouth against the cotton pillowcase and successfully spread the drool across his chin and cheek.

He reached his hand to his face and his stomach protested, churning and somersaulting as if he was about to birth a giant, angry octopus. Tentacles bumped and sloshed against his organs, mixing stomach acids and surging up into Bernard's throat. He shot out of bed, staggered to his bathroom sink, and hurled the contents of his stomach into the white basin. The patterns of yellow bile and clear saliva were overshadowed by dark, red blood. The sink had become a set-piece for a horror film.

"Good job, you stupid jerk," he told his reflection, "You gave yourself an ulcer."

As an afterthought he added, "Oh yeah, happy birthday."

Bernard didn't want to dwell on his nascent anniversary. It was his thirtieth and he expected no cake, no balloons, no drunken night out with co-workers or friends, and though he was now XXX, his evening promised nothing more salacious than a solitary episode of twilight onanism. He wanted a distraction. He got a bloody sink and a growing headache.

In the quiet suburb of his skull, someone had opened an all-night bowling alley. The escalating crashes were spares, a thunderous slam was a strike. Aspirin was as useful as a Swiss cheese prophylactic. By the time Bernard staggered out of his apartment and headed towards the local clinic, the league night in his head had turned into a raucous party to celebrate some lucky striker's perfect game.

True to form, Bernard's headache and stomach pains went away the moment the young nurse strutted into the waiting room.

Bernard debated walking out. Leaving wouldn't have been difficult. The nurse looked side to side with a puzzled expression, even though there were four chairs in the waiting room and only two were occupied (the other occupant was a comatose old woman who pulled in a strained gasp of air every thirty-three and a half seconds). Bernard cleared his throat. The nurse twitched her eyes and offered Bernard a confused smile. She had shaven hair, straight teeth, clear white skin, and her name tag said "Alice", but the name had been crossed out and "Jojo" was written in sharpie below it.

Bernard tried to remember if he'd washed his face of bile after throwing up that morning. He followed her down a hallway, stepped onto a scale at her direction and averted his eyes from the digital readout. Alice/Jojo scribbled his weight on his chart. She placed a thermometer in his mouth and stared at an empty patch of wall until the thermometer beeped. She scratched again on the pad, led Bernard into a small examination room and took his blood pressure.

"Sphygmomanometer," said Bernard.

"Sorry?" she said.

"Nothing," said Bernard.

Doctor Elmira Tribade was a thin woman with a Prince Valiant haircut and pica, as evidenced by dampness of her sleeves and the dental marks on the pens and clipboards scattered around her office. She scowled over Bernard's chart while chewing on a tongue depressor. "Everything seems to be in order, Mr...." She blinked twice and her scowl deepened while she searched his file for a surname.

"Bernard," he mumbled. "Just Bernard."

Her face crinkled in distaste.

"Yes, well, everything seems to be in order. You could lose a couple pounds, but who couldn't these days. Get some Pepto for the nausea and we'll get you some pills to clear up those headaches."

Bernard frowned. He wasn't going to spend his birthday in a doctor's office just to be shuttled away.

"I don't want an allopathic Band-Aid," said Bernard in a rare fit of assertiveness. "I want to know why it's all happening."

The doctor gritted her teeth. The tongue depressor snapped in two.

"This is a doctor's office," said Dr. Tribade, waving half of the tongue depressor in Bernard's face before she tossed the half-stick into the garbage. "This is not a history class. It's not our job to worry about *why* except as a last resort. We have our hands full worrying about what now."

"What about my bathroom sink?" asked Bernard.

"Talk to an interior decorator." said Dr. Tribade.

"No," said Bernard. "I mean I think I have an ulcer."

"Oh you probably do," she declared, resuming her mastication of the remaining tongue depressor. "Those are usually stress-related. Are there any undue stressors in your life?"

She looked him over. "Yes, well, perhaps you just need a break. Do something relaxing. Get away from excess stimulation."

Bernard mused that if he had any less stimulation, they'd bury him. The doctor's eyes darted around Bernard's body while the wood crinkled and cracked under her teeth. Her gaze stopped at Bernard's arm. She did a double take and swallowed.

Dr. Tribade seized Bernard's wrist and raised it to her face. Bernard squirmed, but she held tight and stabbed at a discolored patch of yellow hidden on his arm beneath a thicket of dark hair.

"How long as this been here?"

Before Bernard could reply, Dr. Tribade vanished from the room. She returned minutes later with another physician, a stocky walrus of a man with balding brown hair and a bushy moustache. The new doctor prodded at the jaundiced patch on Bernard's arm. Bernard attempted to stammer out questions.

"Uhm…What's…ah…?"

"Shush," said Dr. Tribade.

Two interns and a nurse entered the office. A conversation started between the professionals. Bernard leaned in and an intern shoved a metal clipboard in front of his face. A pen appeared and Bernard signed the bottom of a ream of pages. The clipboard was whisked away. The nurse stabbed him in the side with a hypodermic needle. Bernard yelped. Two more interns arrived. One intern lifted up Bernard's left armpit while the other pulled open Bernard's jaw and sniffed. Shoulders squashed together as more medical-types squeezed into the tiny room.

"More space!" someone yelled.

Interns pushed Bernard protesting through the sea of white coats, out the door and into a wheelchair. Hands rolled him down the hall, followed by a mob of doctors talking with fevered excitement. He was wheeled into a large room filled with more doctors. Someone poked him again with a needle. He turned to tell the perpetrator that blood had already been drawn and saw the hypodermic pull away empty. Something had been put in, not taken out. His head swam and he lost track of what was done and when.

Everything after that was a psychedelic haze. Bernard had visions of being poked, prodded, nicked, pricked, and swabbed. They rubbed him and buffed him, checked his teeth, tested his eyes, x-rayed his bones, pulled out his blood and replaced it with something else. His eyes blurred and his head swooned.

A nurse asked for a stool sample and he stuck out his tongue and kicked her in the shin. She went down but two more took her place. They flipped him over, front to back, head to toe. They placed him in a centrifuge and spun him around. Someone hugged him and handed him balloons and ice cream, told him he was loved, then slapped him in the face and called him names. The medical types abandoned him alone on a table while they huddled and debated, then laughed, shook one another's hands and rushed him, threw him to the ground, and kicked the breath out of him. He looked up into the halo of doctor's faces, all of them smiling and whispering and prodding one another.

The faces swirled but the bodies didn't move. He knew they were speaking, but the words arrived in fragments.

"......................unexpected results........."

"..............terribly exciting............................."

".......like nothing we've ever seen..............."

"....more tests....................malignant..."

"...ancer........pancreas of a ninety-five year old............."

"......medical journals would love....................."

"..............time to get your affairs in order............"

"......................undoubtedly terminal........."

".....we have a waiver right her........"

"..........No more than five weeks......tops........."

Bernard left the hospital in a daze, carrying a prescription bottle, a bill, several brochures, and a stethoscope.

11. Omphaloskepsis
Omphaloskepsis is meditating,
Contemplative naval gazing.

Vida's Directions to Reset your Karma, Cleanse your Chakras, and Re-Align your Soul:

Pack your backpack and proceed south from your hotel room. Turn west when you reach the two lane road and stick out your thumb. Wait seventeen minutes until you catch a ride with a 48-year-old bible salesman who smells like chicken and looks like Boss Hogg from Dukes of Hazzard. When he offers you a free bible, politely explain that you've no more room in your backpack. When he pats your knee and jokes about pulling off the freeway, laugh and say nothing. When he stops for gas in Kansas City, wait until he borrows the restroom key before you slip from the car.

Cross the street to the Burger King. Flag down a tan Buick LeSabre as it leaves the drive-thru. Tell the newlyweds in the front seat that your grandmother had a stroke and you're heading to Des Moines. They'll offer you fries, a cheeseburger, and sips from their strawberry shake. Eat the fries and drink the shake, but be careful with the burger. Your body isn't used to heavy food and if you eat too fast they'll have to pull off the 135 so you can vomit. Let them buy you dinner in Cameron. They'll give you twenty dollars after the meal. Fuck your pride. Keep the money.

Flag down a diesel on its way to Reno. Curl up in the back of the cab. Sleep. At Reno, thumb your way along US-395. Cross the border into California, head north and then east until you reach Redding at noon. Stop in a cafe ten minutes from your parent's house. With two dollars left in your pocket, order a bottomless cup of coffee. Tell the waitress that you've no money for a tip and ask if she will accept a joke instead. Tell her the following:

Q: How do you get four old women to say "fuck" at the same time?

A: Say "Bingo."

At four pm, the waitress will bring you a free slice of cherry pie. At 6pm, she will bring you a BLT sandwich and onion rings. At 8pm, thank her and say goodbye. Leave the café and stick out your thumb. You'll be picked up by a purple Volkswagen van that contains a rainbow of dreadlocked girls and a permanent ganja fog. The girls will introduce themselves as Daphne, Jade, Heart, and Sandalwood. You may tell them your story. They will not mind if you cry.

Stay in the van as it hits the coast and heads south along Highway 101. Pass the endless burl shops that line the Redwood Curtain's version of the Red Light District: Knotty Wood, House of Burlesque, Burls! Burls! Burls! Veer east on a mountain pass on old section of Highway 299 and disembark at the fifty foot high burl heart. The giant heart marks the entrance to The Omphaloskepsis Center for Transpersonal Healing, a new age community with six natural hot springs, a sauna, a colonic center, massage therapy, all-natural vegan cafeteria, and a variety of workshops to support the needs of today's new-age hippy. Sign on to work in the kitchen in exchange for free room, board, and classes.

Wake up every morning at dawn for yoga, Tai Chi, chai tea, and breakfast. In the afternoons, consider the optional workshops: Polarity Therapy, Mud Hut Construction, Organic Computing, and Disciplining Your Inner Child. Your body will revolt against the all-natural organic diet. During meditation, everyone else will focus on their pranas while you stifle the non-meditative sounds coming from your first chakra. Persevere. Make friends. Detoxify your body. You will feel it's time to move on. Pack your backpack, but don't leave until you've fallen in love.

Vida trudged to the yoga temple with the sluggish determination of a zombie towards a shopping mall. Four months at Omphaloskepsis hadn't transformed her into a morning person. She managed a few sub-vocal grunts to Sandalwood (birth name Julia Rosenthal) and Madrone (Cecil Williams III) as she entered the temple. The empty space below the elephant altar meant that Baba Godi Baba hadn't yet arrived. Vida slumped to the ground and began her first pose: Resting Badger. She was mid-transition into Napping Chipmunk when cold air rushed into the temple. Vida opened one eye. A short silhouette stood in the entryway like a lone gunfighter entering a troubled saloon.

Everyone has their own soundtrack, some are louder than others. A man enters a room and you'll hear jazz beats, or a calliope, or a funeral dirge. The young woman at the entrance was five-foot-three with shoulder length tangerine dreadlocks and a punk metal accompaniment fronted by Joan Jett. She clanked into the room sporting heavy black boots laced to her thighs and a t-shirt that read **I Heart Your Vagina.** She looked over the sleepy practitioners and said in a perfect accent, a cup of London with a dash of seduction, sprinkled with sugar and drenched in melted butter:

"Damn it's cold! I'm bloody positive my clit fell off somewhere on the hill."

She strutted to the center of the room and unslung the yoga mat which had been resting on her back like a rifle. She snapped open the mat and it cracked like a whip, sending a delicious tingle up Vida's spine.

Vida managed to stammer:

"Uh, that's, um, the teacher's space."

"Well, love," said the new arrival as she kicked off her boots and tossed them against the far wall. "I wonder what that makes me."

She looked up and her eyes met Vida's. The new woman froze. Vida's insides turned into ice cream.

"I'm…Maya," said the teacher, in a halted tone.

"Maya?" asked Vida.

"Maya."

"I'm Vida," said Vida.

"Yes," said Maya grinning. "Yes you are."

Vida had come to expect certain things from a yoga class: a hypnotic monotone directing a series of breath and postures for an hour and a half with the addition of chanting or a soundtrack of Fifteen Sherpa Classics. Nowhere did she expect pushups to Bananarama or backward laps around the room, and she was certain no yoga textbook detailed The Giant Radioactive Salamander that Ate Poughkeepsie. Vida loved every minute of it, even when her limbs hung limp from her body, even when her eyes stung from the sweat pouring from her brow, even when she sat in the Escher Pretzel and stared at the back of her own head.

Vida's clothes were soaked in sweat by the time the practitioners sat in a circle at the end of the session.

"Empty yourself of distraction," said Maya. "There is no worry. There is no fear. There is only breath."

Vida needed no instructions to breathe. She was too exhausted to fight the rhythmic inhalations and exhalations that traveled through her.

"Take the last ten minutes," said Maya, "and look into yourself. You are a part of the cosmos. You are a manifestation of the Great Cock and the Cosmic Cunt. You are divine. You are God."

Vida's consciousness disappeared. She was at peace. She could've stayed there forever, and would have if not for the soft, confident, sexy voice that called her to return.

Vida's vocabulary expanded. She was twitterpated. Infatuated. Discombobulated. Lovesmote. Bernard would've been impressed.

If Vida needed any more assurance that she'd fallen head over heels, her panties, dry as a bone around Tony T, sounded a high tide warning.

Later that night, Vida sat alone in her cabin, cursing the moon which penetrated her blinds and molested her pelvis. She'd traveled for eleven months before her cycle synchronized with the lunar calendar. A product of the suburbs, she was shocked to learn that something as small as her cootch could be linked to something as large and distant as the great wheel of gouda in the sky. She pondered why women were at their most fertile while men became ravenous werewolves, and concluded the stories were a warning to keep girls from losing their youth earlier than decency expected.

Vida rose from her bed and closed the blinds, hiding herself from the moon and the dark clearing of trees behind her cabin. Vida always felt a strange tingling whenever she walked around the grass clearing, as if she was in a place where magic happened. Omphaloskepsis was built around a sanitarium, which creeped her out a bit, but she'd grown to love her one-room cabin that faced the tall hill that stretched up to the Omphaloskepsis main building.

Vida returned to bed and closed her eyes. A scratching sound came from her window. She sat up. The sound stopped. Vida crept from her bed and peeked through her blinds. The clearing was dark and empty. She crawled back into bed. The scratching returned. Vida hopped up, tossed open the blinds, and pressed her eyes against the window. Cast against the dark trees was a short shadowy figure with her hands pressed to her hips. The shadow leaned its head back and let out a seductive summons, not in a human tongue, but with a long, deep meow.

Vida slid open her window. Maya's shadow prowled around the clearing, avoiding the moonlight.

"Mrowr, little cat" called Maya. "Lovely cat, come out and play. Meeeemrowr."

Vida would ask Maya much later why she called on her as a feline. Maya shrugged "Why did Rome crumble? Why'd our paths interlace? Why did Venice sink into the ocean? It happened how it had to happen."

Maya dropped to the ground and rolled from her back to her belly. "The grass is cool and dry, little cat." She pressed her pelvis against the dirt and presented her chest to the window. "Surely you wish to come outside?"

"And what should we do if I venture out?" Vida asked.

Maya smiled a Cheshire grin. "We'll seek and play of course. It's a fine night for a pair of hunters. Perhaps even a mouse or two to uncover."

"Mice?"

"Oh yes, love. Small mounds of fur, often hidden, but quite a delicacy."

Vida fluttered her eyes. "I've never had a mouse before. What if I don't like the taste?"

"It is, so they say, an acquired taste. But fear not, little cat. If mice aren't your liking, I've the appetite for two."

Vida deliberated for a millisecond before she lifted her legs over the windowsill. Her eyes flashed chatoyant and she landed outside.

12. Prestidigitator

The plight of the lovelorn prestidigitator,
He could vanish her clothes but couldn't mate her.

Bernard left the clinic. He dropped the pamphlets and stethoscope in a trash bin and stepped off the curb. A white Escalade honked and swerved into the opposite lane. Bernard didn't look up. He reached the opposite sidewalk and turned to avoid walking into a Chinese restaurant *Two Wongs Make Rice*. The neighborhood dilapidation grew as Bernard walked. He passed a butcher's shop offering "M ATS" and a Temp Agency with the signs "HELP WANTED" and "CLOSED" in the window. He crossed another street, passed through a small park on a pedestrian thoroughfare, and reached a large adobe church smeared with white paint. The sign on the front wall read:

Church of Christ SP
Sermons Daily
Based on the Best Selling Book
Souls Saved
Lives Mended
Free Coffee

A crowd protruded in a semi-circle around the church's side wall. The bodies dominated the thoroughfare, Bernard considered turning around, but felt more invisible than usual. No one turned as he brushed past shoulders. The circle opened in the middle and Bernard crossed towards the other side.

"Don't worry, brother!"

Bernard stopped. Against the wall of the church leaned an older black man with an unshaven salt-and-pepper beard, a magician's top hat, and crooked yellow teeth that could have bricked the road to Oz.

Beside the man stood an aquarium with red tubes leading out either end. Inside the empty aquarium, a mass of kitchen knives whirled, powered by a generator underneath. The clinking knives and burbling generator made such a commotion that Bernard was surprised he'd just noticed it.

"Yeah, brother," said the man over the noise of the machine. "Don't worry. It's just a stage you're going through!"

Bernard looked around. The magician pointed down at the chalk semi-circle drawn on the ground and Bernard realized the pun. The audience chuckled.

"Sorry," Bernard mumbled.

"Wait, brother," said the man. "Wait a minute! I know you, don't I?"

Bernard tensed at the attention. He wanted to leave but the crowd, interested in the new exchange, blocked him in.

"No brother, never you mind. My mistake." The man tapped Bernard on the chest, snapped his fingers and grabbed Bernard's hand with both of his own. "Hermes is the name, professional prestidigitator, pickpocket, and prognosticator, and you're just in time for the main event. All I need is something of yours that we will send, hopefully unharmed, through–*The Machine*."

"*The Machine*" was spoken with macabre, melodramatic glee.

Bernard held up his hands and retreated, backing into a wall of people. "Sorry–I've got to be–somewhere."

"Oh." Hermes looked crestfallen. "Well, sorry Bernard." Hermes held up a hand and turned away. "Maybe next time."

Bernard pressed against the crowd reluctant to allow his egress.

Bernard turned around. Hermes stood against the aquarium with Bernard's driver's license in one hand and wallet in the other. Someone snickered.

Bernard shuffled to the magician and held out his hand. "Come on now."

Hermes returned Bernard's license to the wallet and held it out. Bernard reached for it, but Hermes held up a finger. "One moment, brother, almost forgot." Hermes set the wallet on the left edge of the contraption and dug through his jacket pockets.

"Aha!" Bernard's credit card materialized in Hermes' left hand. The audience laughed. He handed it to Bernard and kicked a lever at the generator's base.

"Oops" he said without conviction. The generator revved and Bernard's wallet started down the small conveyor belt towards the open maw of the aquarium's clicking blades.

"Hey!" Bernard shouted. He pushed towards the machine, but Hermes held him back. The wallet disappeared through the left tube.

Hermes pressed his yellow grin into Bernard's face. "Don't worry brother," he whispered, "It's all good."

Hermes yelled, "It slices, it dices, it circumcises!"

More laughter as the generator roared. Knives clinked. The contraption let out a sputtered wheeze. A plume of smoke drifted from the top of the aquarium.

"Huh," said Hermes. He bit his lip. Hot air ejected from the machine and onto Bernard's face. The machine sputtered and shook and bits of faux black leather spurted from the other tube.

Hermes grew wide-eyed. A thick cloud of black smoke poured from the engine.

"No! No! No!" he yelled. The knives clacked and froze. Hermes ran to the side of the contraption. Bernard started towards him. Hermes thrust his arm into the tube. The machine kicked back into gear and the knives resumed clacking. Hermes shook from the shoulder and screamed.

Bernard grabbed Hermes' free arm and pulled but the man was held tight. Bernard planted his feet. Hermes cried out again. The tube swallowed him up to his shoulder. Bernard remembered the spurts of black leather and fought back the image of what was coming out the other side. He dug his feet into the ground and pulled with everything he had. His feet slipped. He dug in again, amazed that the crowd stood there doing nothing. Sweat poured off his forehead. He hooked his arm through Hermes's shoulder and yanked. The two men flew from the machine's grasp and collapsed on the ground.

Hermes whimpered on top of Bernard. The whimpering transformed into rapid exhalations as Hermes rolled onto the ground. Bernard sat up. The exhalations turned into snorts. The magician, hands whole and undamaged, clutched his stomach and convulsed in laughter.

"Come on, brother," said Hermes. "I told you it was all good."

Bernard pushed his way through the crowd.

"Hold on, brother!" Hermes held out Bernard's wallet. "Here you are. No hard feelings. It's all there, plus a little something extra for your troubles." Bernard grabbed the wallet. Hermes slammed his free hand over Bernard's and pulled him close enough to whisper in his ear.

"It's been an honor, brother. When you see Death, tell her Eshu says hello."

Bernard pushed himself loose and backed through the crowd. Hermes gestured in Bernard's direction. "Everyone give a hand to our volunteer." The audience clapped.

Hermes yelled out, "Big hats to you, brother! I was afraid I'd missed you! I thought you'd be over there by now!"

Bernard was three blocks away before he checked his wallet. Everything was still inside: money, bank card, driver's license, second bank card, library card, grocery receipts, long expired condom—and something else.

The card was eggshell white, half again as tall as a business card, in a thick matte cardstock. Finely-embossed gold lettering on the front read:

Tzaddikim Affair
Admits One Guest

Below the lettering and address was a date and time later that evening. In the margins on either side were a series of doodles which included a gothic church, two naked women and a crucifix. The women were kissing, with one straddled over the cross and about to mount it. Bernard flipped the card. Written in the same black inked scrawl as the doodles were the words:

> *"There are more things in heaven and earth,*
> *than are dreamt of in your philosophy."*
> *-Hamlet*

And below them:

> *"But don't worry. We've got hope for you yet."*

13. Palingenesis

For cosmic scoundrels Death is no nemesis,
Their spiritual Xerox repeats palingenesis.

"Bollocks!"

"Patience," said Vida.

"Patience my ass, love" said Maya. "If I smack myself in the tits one more time I'm gonna shove these things up the first person who walks by, just to get them out of my sight."

Maya dropped the two balls attached to thin ropes onto the grass.

"Don't be so hard on yourself," said Vida. "No one learns poi in a day."

This wasn't true, but Vida was trying to be supportive.

They'd left dinner early to meet behind Vida's cabin, hoping yet again that Vida could impart in Maya even one marketable circus skill. Vida knew she'd soon be performing and she desperately wanted Maya to be on the pitch with her.

Pitch is a busker's term for the street space on and around a performance.

"Let's take a break," said Vida.

"Kissing break?" asked Maya.

"Juggling break," said Vida. She kicked two beanbags over to Maya. Maya caught the first with both hands. The second ricocheted off and fell to the grass.

"Ughhh," said Maya. She picked up the second beanbag and tossed both in the air. They collided and dropped to the ground.

"One at a time," said Vida, "we've gone over this."

"Face it, love," said Maya, "this isn't working."

Vida hated to admit it, but Maya was right. It wasn't that Maya was clumsy. The problem was Maya had the attention span of a caffeinated child with ADD. The two chatted for hours about building a show and seeing the world. Maya's savings could cover the plane tickets overseas, but the dream was becoming a source of frustration.

Maya kicked the offending beanbags. She walked over, hugged Vida's waist, and traced spirals with her tongue down to Vida's navel.

"Tossing balls up and down is great for some, love, but I'd rather be rubbing up and going down on you."

Maya slid a hand under Vida's tank-top. Vida glanced at the trail in front of her cabin. No one was around. Not that it would've stopped Maya, who slid Vida's shirt up over her breasts and took a nipple into her mouth. Vida moaned. Maya pulled her down to the grass.

"I know a wicked magic trick," said Maya. "Abracadabra. I can make my hand disappear."

They made love in a circle of beanbags and when they finished they told each other that they would still travel together and Maya would be the first one at every show, but Vida knew her lover's temperament. Maya was no groupie. It wouldn't be long before Maya tired of being an audience member and allowed the wind to carry her to a more active adventure.

Hope arrived a week later when Maya bounded into Vida's cabin holding a borrowed laptop and a DVD of French acrobalancers.

Acrobalance is a circus skill where gymnasts work together to lift and support one another in aesthetically-pleasing positions.

The video featured a man and a woman performing in front of a river. The man balanced the petite female as she contorted herself in the air, supported by his legs and arms.

"Look at her," said Maya, pausing the screen.

"Gods," said Vida. "If I did that, I'd break."

"I can do it."

"No way."

"Yoga's not just for breathing," said Maya. "What about the guy's part?"

Vida thought for a moment.

"I could do it," she said.

"Show me."

In the clearing, Maya stood in front with Vida's hands wrapped around her waist.

"Ready?" asked Vida.

"Freddy," said Maya.

Vida planted her feet and lifted Maya a few feet off the ground before Maya tumbled forward and landed on her hands and feet on the grass.

"Sorry," said Vida.

"All good, love. Try again."

The second time, Vida lifted with more force, trying to keep Maya as close to her center of gravity as possible. Maya sailed up into the air, but Vida overshot the momentum. Maya flipped over Vida's head. She twisted as she fell and crashed onto her knees and elbows.

"Oooh," said Maya.

"Are you okay?" said Vida.

"No worries, sugarlips," said Maya, brushing grass off her arm. "You know what they say about cats and landings."

"You could've been hurt."

"One more time," said Maya.

"Are you sure?"

"If I'm lying, I'm dying."

Vida prepped her hands over Maya's waist.

"Ready?"

"Rocksteady."

Vida pushed up and Maya lifted in the air. They wobbled to the side. Vida adjusted. Maya bent her back into a bridge and her weight disappeared. Maya curled further and the toes of one foot touched the back of her head. She lifted the other leg high in the air, changing her center of gravity. Vida compensated. Her arms tensed but stayed locked.

"How yah doing?" Vida asked.

"Stuuuuuuupendous" Maya purred. Vida tilted her head back as far as possible and Maya did the same. Their eyes met. "Love, do you think...?"

"Let's see," said Vida. She rocked Maya forward and lowered her face to hers. Their foreheads tapped. They were nose to nose. Their lips touched. Those two seconds held the second best kiss of Vida's life.

Kissing Scorpion held a place of honor at the beginning of every street show. They added to their repertoire using the acrobalance video as inspiration, bolstered by whatever the couple could mine from the Internet. Maya's small stature and weight made her a natural flyer, but that didn't keep Vida on the ground. Maya was enthusiastic about switching roles and they learned that balance was more important than strength when the base was 5'3" and the flyer almost 6'.

The distractible Maya often found her face buried in her lover's muff, but having an itch didn't mean they had to come down to scratch it. Climbing, lifting, and spinning, Vida realized they had something good when she had a twenty minute orgasm without ever touching the ground.

14. Messina

**Poor Scylla lost her boyfriend Jim,
She wasn't dumped; Charybdis ate him.**

Every society asks what happens when we die. Many groups have insisted they possess the capital "A" answer. This usually involves an appeal to logic in the manner of the following syllogism:

A: We know what happens when you die.
B: You think you know, but you're wrong.
Ergo:
C: Once we kill you, you'll find out we're right.

This foolproof rational has resulted in the unified utopia that we have today.

Death used to be an abstract concept to Bernard. Now it was a solid force as welcome as a cold sore on prom night. He wanted answers, but he would settle for a distraction. The magician's invitation announced a "Tzaddikim Affair." According to Judaic lore, the Tzaddikim prevent the world from going the way of Sodom and Gomorrah. As long as there were thirty-six honest and just people on Earth, destruction was avoided. Bernard suspected it was a curious theme for a party, though he wasn't sure since he'd never been invited to a party before.

He set out walking. Night fell by the time he neared the district.

In the past, a short jaunt up a flight of stairs would've winded him, but Bernard was too distracted to notice that he wasn't fatigued. He reached an intersection, 8th and Messina, and confirmed "Messina" on the invitation. Parked on the corner was a cherry-red 1930 Packard sedan, a conveyance that summoned images of flappers, Schiaparelli hats, and croquet lunches on the lawn. Other classic cars followed down the road; a row of auto-anachronisms. The road stopped at a thin iron gate. A path beyond the gate weaved through a rich garden towards a large, gothic mansion.

The gate was book-ended by two identical women in their early-twenties, twins with long, straight bleached hair and matching tuxedos. The right twin flapped her hands towards her sister, emphasizing a conversation that Bernard couldn't hear. She looked up at the sound of Bernard's approach, blinked twice and whispered through the side of her mouth. "Good cop."

"Why do you always get to be good cop?" hissed the left with mirrored dentiloquy.

"Because I always call it first," said the right twin with a smirk.

"Halt!" said the left twin.

"You can't," said the right.

"Possibly enter," said the left.

"Without permission," they spoke in unison and nodded at each other.

Bernard held out his invitation. The left portess snatched it from his hands. She scowled at Bernard's jeans and t-shirt. "I'm sorry," she said without remorse. "I'm afraid there's a dress code." She waited for a response, perhaps a code word or a bribe or some other form of barter.

"Nevermind," he said, turning around.

The right twin spoke up. "Oh pish-tosh, Char. What about that suit left by the Swedish man? It's not as if he's coming back for it."

Char crinkled her nose.

"I suppose you're right," said Char, "but we can't just give it to him."

"Fair enough," said her sister. She kicked open the gate, grabbed Bernard's hand and pulled him through towards a small guard-box. "He can leave his clothes as collateral."

"Scylla, wait!" said Char.

The hand pulling Bernard stopped.

Char gestured to Scylla's empty post beside the gate.

Scylla pouted. Char gave the universal shrug of city officials indicating that it wasn't up to them, it was the way things were, and if you didn't like it you'd have to take it up with someone else.

"Fine." Scylla dropped Bernard's hand and gestured to the guard-box. "The suit's on the chair in the corner underneath a purse." She looked at her sister. "Feel free to manhandle the purse."

"Uh, thanks," said Bernard. Whatever his element was, he was out of it.

Scylla brushed past him. Her hand slid against his once again. The contact lingered, she gripped his wrist and swung him around face-to-face. Her mouth approached his, but veered off to his ear.

"Fear," she whispered, "is passion without breath."

She exhaled and her lips traveled down past his earlobe and brushed the nape of his neck. She pushed aside his t-shirt to expose his collarbone and bit hard.

"Ow!" yelled Bernard.

Scylla released her teeth, placed a hand on Bernard's buttocks and pushed him towards the guard-room.

Char looked on with disapproval. Scylla responded with the universal *what can I do?* shrug and revisited her guard-post.

The two-buttoned, aqua-colored silk moiré jacket shimmered against the moonlight. Matching pants, black dress shirt and tie sat in a nearby pile. Bernard doubted he'd fit in the small ensemble, but after huffing and stretching, the suit fit so well Bernard couldn't imagine why he'd thought it was small in the first place. It was as if the suit had listened to his body and responded to fit him. Bernard held his cuffs up and beamed in approval. His black sneakers were a bit out of place, but he didn't look bad. He placed his hands in the pockets and folded his fingers around a business card:

Robert's Fine Menswear
Looking for a change?
Fix the outside
And the inside will follow.

He stepped outside the guard box and grinned. For a moment his slouch straightened and he felt like a king. Scylla whistled. Char gave the hint of an upturned smile.

Bernard stepped forward and the women turned away to greet another set of arrivals—a dapper young man sporting a Douglas Fairbanks moustache, arm in arm with a grey haired woman who rested her head on his shoulder. With the twins' attention diverted, Bernard remembered his doctor's visit earlier that day. His chin dropped, his shoulders rounded, and he shuffled towards the house.

Bernard was lost in his head and didn't appreciate the path that he followed. He didn't look up at the meticulous topiary garden where sylvan lions hunted bouncing gazelles and a pair of leafy hippopotami grappled before an audience of green flamingos. He didn't stop to throw a quarter in the fountain centered by silver canaries frozen in a swirling helix of flight. He didn't admire the steps he climbed, each foot falling on a translucent stair that revealed a cascading waterfall beneath him. He viewed it all, but he saw nothing until he pushed open the double doors and entered the party of the Tzaddikim and the novelties became impossible to ignore.

15. Tzaddikim

Mohandas was a man of vim,
But he paled to the Tzaddikim.

The Tzaddikim Affair wasn't exclusive to the Tzaddikim of the present, though an impressive mix they were: three writers, an Islamic mufti, a man on death row, a Micronesian fisherman from the polyamorous commune of Ulithi, a cliff diver, a dominatrix, a big game hunter, the matron of a Spanish bordello, two fictional characters, a gambler, an octogenarian Italian castrato, a chimpanzee named Gus, a marble sculptor, a blind body-builder, a yoga teacher, an erotic cartoonist, a one-armed ballerina, a one-footed chess player, a Seattle technophile, a Burmese cloth merchant, a Russian physicist specializing in pan-dimensional synchro-existentialism, a professional liar, an arsonist, a Taiwanese hand-balancer, a Tangerian fighter, a revolutionary hero, the most hated man in Nicosia, an Irish ouphe, a Prussian trichotillimaniac, a European sybarite who had died the previous day and wouldn't admit it, a Chinese ascetic who spoke of the evening with disdain and had not yet left the buffet table, a hermetic demophobe who had not yet removed himself from a kitchen cabinet, and a Belgian plumber who was smitten with the one-armed ballerina and had not yet found the courage to confess his love.

Tzaddikim by nature are people who like people, and a party of thirty-six with a mansion to fill screams for an expanded guest list. It took the Russian physicist a bit of finagling with M-Theory Pragmagenesis to open the event into a cosmic collective for anyone who had ever merited an invitation: a Who's Who of zany Tzaddikim. Philosophers and revolutionaries mixed with defamed saints and unsung heroes, the cream of *bon ton* and the dregs of bourgeoisie. Any doubters to the feasibility of it all could have been sent to the frazzle-haired man with a bean dip splotch on his rumpled suit. He had plenty of theories about the relative possibilities of the universe.

Bernard sidestepped into the foyer, avoiding the man and woman shooting off the banister with their arms in the air. The couple dropped to the floor laughing as an improvised marching band emerged from an open door. Partiers in a wild assortment of fancy dress and outrageous costumes banged on pans and Tupperware with soup ladles and open palms. A tall musician who bore a striking resemblance to Oscar Wilde pushed a cocktail into Bernard's hand. An engine revved and a go-kart driven by a small Indian man with beady eyes and an aquiline nose careened into the foyer. The go-kart skidded past the marching band, around the couple on the ground, and bee-lined for Bernard's feet. Bernard rushed down a hallway pursued by the kart, the cocktail sloshing in its glass. He emerged into a large parlor and was struck in the side by a pillow, sending the cocktail glass out of his hand. Around him, men and women in tuxedos batted at one another with pillows. Feathers rained like snowflakes. Bernard dropped to the ground and maneuvered to the opposite door.

Bernard entered a new room and immediately backed out.

"Sorry," he said.

"No problem," several people replied in unison.

Bernard closed the door and held the knob for a moment. Comprehending what he had just witnessed would've forced him to re-evaluate several hard-set laws of physics and biology and he resolved to never think about it again.

He exited a sliding-glass door and found himself on a deck patio. Several clumps of partiers chatted on deck chairs near a large blue pool. Bernard maneuvered between the groups and plopped himself into a chair in the corner. Beside him sat a red nosed gentleman who appeared to be keeping himself upright by squeezing a gin & tonic with both hands.

The patio door slid open and pillow combatants spilled onto the deck. One man tumbled backwards into the pool. A woman gripped her pillow overhead and jumped in after him. Others followed, laughing and swinging into the water.

A cashew landed in Bernard's lap. He turned and a second cashew missed his left eye.

"Oopsh. Shorry buddy." The red-nosed man swayed on his deck chair. One of his hands balanced his teetering G&T while the other was submerged in a container of mixed nuts. "Jusht tryin' to get yer tension."

Bernard slid as far from the drunk as possible, but there wasn't much space to retreat.

"I jusht was shittin' over here and I thought to myshelf–that man's got shomethin' on his mind. I mean you, case you dinn't know. Knew you musht have shomethin on your mind if you was shittin when you could be up livin it up with all these wonderful people. Peanut?"

The container of nuts swayed back and forth. Every person can take a certain dosage of absurdity in one day. Bernard was nearing toxic overdose.

"What's the point?" Bernard spurted.

The drunk looked at the container. "Uh…I dunno buddy. They're shalty…that's uh, shodium chloride, it's groundin' and shtuff."

"No," said Bernard, standing. "I mean what's the point? We can laugh or party or scream or whatever and it doesn't matter! We all just end up in the ground! What's the point of all…all…this?"

He looked around, found nothing to point to, and raised his hands in frustration.

"Geesh, buddy." The drunk looked down. "Thatsh a little too philoshopical for me. Sure you don't want a peanut?"

"No peanut! I don't want a peanut."

The drunk looked at the container.

"Cashew?"

"No! No peanuts, no cashews. I just want…I want…."

"Yeah buddy?" The drunk leaned forward.

"I'VE NO FRAKKING IDEA!"

Bernard's hand swept out and collided with the container of nuts. Cashews, almonds, and peanuts skidded across the patio and plopped into the pool.

The red-nosed man stared at the tipped container with his mouth agape. Bernard realized the entire deck was silent. Combatants froze in the pool. Pillows bobbed on the water. Everyone looked at Bernard. He felt as welcome as a bloated wildebeest which had been killed, half-eaten, and dragged into the pool.

He slumped to the patio door and back into the house. A shaggy-haired man sopped out of the pool and followed after him.

Bernard weaved through the house. He saw the man with the beard behind him and quickened his pace. He dodged a pile of partygoers playing strip twister without a mat. He spun down a hallway and stopped, blocked in by a one-armed woman in a pink taffeta ballerina skirt and a man in blue overalls. The ballerina demonstrated a flawless brisé volé and the man in coveralls clapped. Bernard backed up and bumped into the bearded man blocking his exit.

The man was sixtyish, with dark brown hair, a gray beard and thin-rimmed glasses. Affixed to his wet tuxedo was a soaked nametag. Dribbling blue ink made the name unreadable: "S" something. Steven? Spicoli? Spider? His wrinkles suggested a man who'd spent a good part of his life smiling.

"Hey," the bearded man said, placing his hand on Bernard's shoulder. Bernard squirmed but the hand stayed. "I overheard your little…thing out there. Now, it's obvious you've got some stuff on your mind and there's good people here. There's nothing they'd like more than to help a person in need." He looked into Bernard's eyes. "That's the problem. They have one night to take a load off, get drunk, and do something stupid. They don't mind a few party hoppers. Shoot, man, I'm only here because one of my characters was invited. But chill out, okay? Have a drink, cool the worrying, *live a little*."

The man looked up with a smile. Bernard removed the hand on his shoulder and staggered past him. This wasn't his place. He wanted to know about dying and all he got was talk of life.

Bernard thudded down the stairs, not looking up as he was passed by party-crashers from the Great Dionysian Rock Demigod party next door (their presence wasn't uncalled for, several had been invited to both affairs). Bernard was oblivious as he made his way to the front gate. He grew even more disappointed when he noticed that Scylla and her sister had left their posts.

Bernard slid into the first of a row of cabs parked on the street (no one was expected to drive themselves from this affair). Bernard murmured directions and the taxi turned on its engine.

Inside the house, the Great Dionysian Rock Demigods prepared to jam. Morrison was up and Janis was in the wings.

A flash of light demanded notice from the front porch and a tiny figure flew through the double doors, ran down the waterfall steps, dashed through the topiary garden, and sped to Bernard's cab. Standing before the window was a breathless older man with the nametag "Buscaglia". The taxi-driver pulled out of the parking spot. The new man jogged alongside as the car drove down the road.

"I heard," the man panted, "your inquiry…and thought…this would help…"

The cab picked up speed. The man kept pace.

"When Egyptians died they were asked two questions, their answers determining their next destination. They were asked this:

"'Did you *find* joy?'

The cab sped ahead. The man fell behind but yelled louder.

"Did you *bring* joy?'"

The cab sped away. The man became a speck and disappeared.

16. Strikhedonia

**Vitoria abandoned her kids in Estonia,
Asked how she felt, she cried, "Strikhedonia!"**

Vida and Maya skipped down Lisbon's Bairro Alto, passing fragrant odors of cod fishcakes and charcoal-grilled sardines. The restaurants beckoned to Vida, reminding her that all they'd had that day were airplane peanuts and a plastic cup of diet coke, but she was undeterred as she followed the flow of pedestrians down the cobbled streets, turning one way and then the other.

"How about a quick bite, love?" said Maya. "I'm so famished I could eat the amp."

Vida stopped and Maya lost her sentence.

"This is it," said Vida.

"There were more people on the other block," said Maya.

"This is it," Vida repeated. She unslung her backpack onto her ground, pulled out a piece of pink chalk from a side pocket, and started drawing a wide circle around them in the middle of the pedestrian walkway.

"I think I'm nervous," said Maya. "I never get nervous. Look at my hands, they're shaking."

"It's your first show," said Vida. "If you're not nervous, then it's not important."

Maya pulled an Ipod out of her backpack.

"I feel like I could die," said Maya as she spun through her tracks. "How many shows do you have to do before it goes away?"

Vida laughed and finished the giant circle. Passerbys began stopping at the edge.

"It never goes away, does it?" asked Maya.

"Nope," said Vida.

More tourists saw the first group and added to the congestion. When Vida lifted Maya into the air, the circle was shoulder to shoulder and ten people deep.

It was a good beginning.

They did three shows that evening. The last audience dispersed and Maya dipped her fist in their collapsible top hat filled with coins. Vida grabbed her arm and pulled it out of the hat.

"Busker's Golden Rule," she said. "Don't count your money while you're still on the pitch."

When they returned to the Blue Angel, Maya scampered down the blue-tiled hallway, burst into their room, and poured the pack's contents onto the bed. Euro coins spilled onto the mattress, trailed by a half-dozen fives and two tens. Maya gripped a fist of coins and paper and tossed it into the air, showering her dreadlocks. She giggled and kicked out her feet. Vida watched amused. She remembered her first day, Tony T watching her roll around on the bed of the Travelodge with their day's earnings. The memory was tinted with sadness and she turned back to Maya, feeling secure that this time would be different.

"Three shows…thirty minutes each…over two hundred Euros," said Maya. "It's not the most I've made in an hour, but I never felt so good after."

Maya didn't elaborate and Vida didn't ask.

Vida and Maya cartwheeled across Europe and continued when they hit the other side. India was a paradox of high tech educations and crushing poverty, enlightened mystics and abysmal sanitation. Maya waited with a horde of four thousand for an audience with Amma, The Hugging Saint. Vida rubbed elbows with swamis who climbed ropes into heaven and fakirs who swallowed themselves whole.

Vida was fascinated by the eastern performers, but dysentery curtailed her opportunities to see anything higher than a squat. She recuperated in Thailand, where Maya spoon fed her *gai param* and the cost of one European meal paid for a private beachside bungalow.

With Vida recovered, they performed once a week at an expat nightclub and spent the rest of their days working on their skin cancer.

Four months went by until Vida padded onto the white pebbled beach where Maya lay naked on the sand.

"This is heaven," said Vida.

"Yep."

"I could spend the rest of my life here."

"Yep."

"It's time to leave."

"Yep."

Kneeling in an Ulithian hut in Micronesia, Maya took a fisherman's knife to her dreadlocks and lost three inches and seven pounds. Vida was delighted to discover that running fingers over her lover's newly-exposed scalp elicited moans and purrs.

The couple began their second season in Rome where they discovered "busker" was one step above "beggar" in the social hierarchy. It wasn't the first time killer shows yielded tiny hats and they took the hint. Next stop was Vatican City, where Maya claimed a hyperbolic ignorance of Christianity.

"That's the one with the big bunny, right love?"

Vida hoped Maya would behave with some civility when they toured the Vatican. The sweltering day had given Vida the perfect excuse to wear the white Dulce &Gabbana dress she'd bought in Rome. Maya wore a purple skirt, white shirt, and tie, a compromise that just squeaked by the Papal Palace dress code after a morning of Maya modeling ensembles with more cleavage than fabric. They made it through the Sistine Chapel without incident and Vida let her guard down during a restroom stop, when Maya pulled her into a stall and pawed at her breasts.

Vida counted to twenty before pushing Maya away.

"I can't do it," said Vida.

"Why not? It's only a loo."

"It's not 'only a loo.' It's the Apostolic Palace," whispered Vida. "The freakin' pope lives here."

"Yeah, all the church drag is turning me on."

"Linoleum turns you on."

"I've no idea what you're talking about." Maya placed her hands over her heart. "I'm a sweet and virginal girl who doesn't have such feelings. May I be sent straight to hell should I ever think such things."

"I'm not buying it," said Vida. "You're anything but sweet and innocent."

"I can be anything you want, love. Come on, no one will know. I'll be the naïve choirgirl. You be the Mother Supreme."

"Superior, and no way," said Vida, deflecting Maya's hand. "Not here."

"Bishop and Pope?"

"Nope."

"Priest and Altar Boy?"

"Uh uh."

A creak came from outside the stall. The two froze. They heard footsteps, running water, paper towels dispensing, another creak, and silence.

"Jehovah's Witness and horny housewife?"

"That's it. I'm on to you," said Vida, retreating to the top of the cistern. "You're no innocent! You're the Devil!"

"Curses! You've seen through my feeble charade."

"Christ, now what am I going to do?"

"Aha! Blasphemy," accused Devil Maya. "Your soul is mine!"

"Not fair. Blasphemy's only a venial sin."

"Whazzat mean?"

"It means it's only a little sin."

"Ooh, so I get a little bit of your soul! Which bit? How about here?"

Maya grabbed. Vida jumped.

"Hey, that's a sin, too. I'm not losing any more soul bits to you."

"Don't worry," said Devil Maya. "Sex is hardly a sin these days."

"But we're women," said Vida.

"Exactamundo. 'No man shall lieth with another man.' We're in the clear."

"I thought you didn't know about that stuff."

"Even the devil can quote scripture when it serves her." said Maya, snagging Vida's wrists and sucking her fingers one at a time. Vida felt her defenses wavering.

"Now," said Maya, relaxing her grip, "latch your fingers behind your head."

Vida held her ground. Maya stepped one foot on the toilet lid, pressed her hand against Vida's chest and pushed her against the wall.

"I said: 'Latch your fingers behind your head.'"

"I can't," said Vida, embarrassed.

"Do it," said Maya with a devilish smirk, "and I'll be gentle." She slid Vida's dress to expose one shoulder, grabbed the fabric over Vida's left breast and gave a calculated pull. Vida heard the straining of stitches.

"Latch your fingers behind your head and you won't have to explain to the tour guide why the toilet shredded this 450 Euro dress."

Vida laced her fingers behind her head. Maya released her hold on the fabric and slid her hand down Vida's stomach, under her dress, and tugged. Vida knew she was beat and lifted her hips. Maya pulled Vida's panties down to her ankles, pushed apart her thighs, and disappeared under Vida's dress.

"Bless us Lord," Maya's voice traveled up Vida's dress, "and thank you for this bounty I am about to receive."

Vida bit her lip to suppress the moans, but Maya approached her sacrament with the devotion of a true believer and Vida couldn't contain herself for long.

"Oh! Oh, God!" said Vida. "Oh! Bless me! Bless me! Oh fuck we're going to hell! Oh God!"

"I think we missed our tour," said Vida, petting Maya's head in her lap.

Maya mumbled something, but her mouth was muffled against Vida's dress.

"What did you say?" asked Vida.

"I said 'Marry me,'" said Maya. "I'm on my knees and everything."

"Sure, sure." Vida slid her fingers across Maya's soft scalp.

"Serious," said Maya. "We're in a church. We can do it now."

"Two women in the Vatican?" said Vida. "We'll be condemned to the first ring of hell and impaled by unlubricated dildos for eternity."

"At least we'll be together," said Maya, backing off the toilet seat and looking up at Vida.

Vida pulled up her panties and hopped off the cistern. "How do I know you won't leave me for the next mega-star street performer babe that crosses your path?"

"Are there more of you?" asked Maya. "I didn't know there were other options. Maybe we should wait. I'd rather have a blonde."

"Whore!" Vida pushed Maya against the stall door. She couldn't suppress her smile as Maya's eyes widened. "Let's get this straight. If I marry you, and I mean if, and some younger, blonder woman comes along who can juggle eight torches while going down on you," Vida wrapped her hands around Maya's shoulders and held her against the stall, "she sleeps at the end of the bed and carries all our show equipment and brings us gyros every morning. Number Three Wife does everything Number One Wife, that's me, and Number Two Wife, that's you, says."

"How come you're Number One Wife?" Maya pouted.

"It's not my fault," shrugged Vida. "These things are decided by height."

"What if she's taller than you?"

Vida smiled. "Then I'll cut off her legs!"

"Fair enough," said Maya, raising one hand in the arm. "I promise tertiary status to any future shiny pretty things. Can I be serious for a moment?"

"I doubt it."

Maya's eyes dropped.

"I came into this life with a neon "Fuck Me" sign. Everywhere I've turned, I've been a magnet for creeps and whackos. I learned to survive by pretended to be someone else: someone stronger, someone who could dish it out better than anyone else could give it. And it worked. I turned myself into the woman I wanted to be and I can't go back. I burned everything about that life. But sometimes I'm afraid it'll fall apart and everyone will see me for the fragile girl I used to be, the stupid girl who didn't know how to say no. I don't want anyone to know about her."

"I know," said Vida.

Maya's face tensed with fear. Vida thought for a moment Maya would turn and run, leaving her alone in the stall.

"I know you know," said Maya. "Of course you do. That's the hard part. You know everything, and somehow, you still love me for it."

Vida leaned down and kissed the salt off Maya's eyelids.

"Maya, will you marry me?"

Tears poured down Maya's face.

"Of course! Of course!"

They embraced for the longest time.

"How do we do this?" asked Maya.

"Just say it," said Vida. "It'll work."

"Okay," said Maya. She placed her hands in Vida's. "Vida, love, I offer myself as your partner, your playmate, and your wife. Do you accept?"

"I do," said Vida, trembling, "and I offer myself as your partner, your playmate, and your wife. Do you accept?"

"I do."

"Then by the authority granted us as sentient and autonomous beings, I declare us joined together until death do us part."

Maya shook her head. "Not death, love. Not even then."

"You can't say that," said Vida. "All things end. We can't ask for everything."

"How else are we gonna get it?"

Their lips met and nothing more was said.

17. Ammtssprache

Strategic Right-Sizing? Such phrases we mock,
Officially sanctioned corporate *Ammtssprache.*

Bernard reflexively hit his snooze button before realizing he hadn't set the alarm the previous night. He rolled over. He debated going back to sleep. He imagined a restful morning where he could climb out of bed at noon, take a forty-minute shower and have the whole afternoon to himself.

He was showered, shaved, and on to work before the pigeons outside his window sounded their morning reveille.

Bernard's clunker sputtered into the MacroLogistics parking lot. MacroLogistics had been in operation for thirteen years, a Methuselah by industry standards, surviving each rise and fall of the tech industry by feeding off the remains of other failed start-ups. It was a patchwork monstrosity of cobbled departments unaware of each other's functions, fueled by a parade of part-time college students willing to exchange substandard pay for unmonitored computer usage and free caffeine. The average cubicle monkey lasted less than a year.

Bernard killed his car's engine and silenced the discount mp3 player he'd been awarded for eight years of loyal service supplying scripted telephone help to the technologically clueless.

Bernard clicked his mouse and the Queen of Diamonds floated across his computer screen. His attention on the monitor, he gave no attention to his left hand as it used a pen to golf a row of paper clips, one at a time, into an empty coffee mug.

"Eichmann on Line Three," declared Shawna from behind Bernard's cubicle. Shawna, with her Manic Panic Pillarbox Red hair and dainty septum piercing, fluttered the eyeballs of all the young men on the tech floor. Bernard wanted to reply with something witty; but instead affixed his headset and cleared his computer screen. The ones and zeroes ended their incarnation as diamonds and clubs and returned to the karmic circle waiting room.

'Eichmann' meant the caller was a blamer, named after the SS officer who claimed that his atrocities were committed under somebody else's orders. It was the kind of obscure lateral reference that appealed to the geeks and bookworms who worked the phones, young men for whom fashionable meant a t-shirt with a pick-up line in binary*, intelligent upstarts who got a thrill watching foreign films because they knew their neighbors didn't, men who weren't yet comfortable calling themselves men.

MacroLogistics' policy on an Eichmann was to offer an immediate apology. Bernard clicked over the call.

"About damned time! Do you have any idea how long I was on hold? Twenty-fucking-eight minutes!"

'Twenty-fucking-eight' was an example of *tmesis*: separating a word by embedding another within it. It was also a *hyperbole*, as Bernard's screen indicated that the caller had been on hold for eleven.

Bernard mentioned neither of these things.

"I'm dreadfully sorry about that, sir."

"Sorry don't give me my time back. Where am I calling? Calcutta? Goddamn jobs going to all you goddamn foreigners. It's absofuckinglutely disgraceful."

The thought flashed through Bernard's head like it had a million times before.

Not again.

---

* 01001001 01100110 00100000 01001001 00100000 01100011 01100001 01101110 00100000 01100010 01110101 01101001 01101100 01100100 00100000 01100001 00100000 01100011 01101111 01101101 01110000 01110101 01110100 01100101 01110010 00101100 00100000 01001001 00100000 01100011 01100001 01101110 00100000 01101101 01100001 01101011 01100101 00100000 01111001 01101111 01110101 00100000 01100011 01110101 01101101

Not again was such a common response that over the years, Bernard's brain devoted an entire 11% of its active energy to the processing of "Not Again" messages, more than allotted to chewing, smelling, eliminating, and TV jingles combined. "Not again" messages spewed out daily. Cut off on the freeway? Unexpected bank fee? Burnt dinner? Lost keys? Missed opportunity? Ignored? Rejected? Slept in? Woke up? Whatever the stimulus, Bernard's brain had the answer. Not again. Not again. Not again.

Bernard's cerebral cortex pulled another "Not again" off the assembly line and sent it on its way. The little message was unprepared for the limbic's response, a bigger and more menacing message lying in wait for the little "Not Again."

"YOU'VE GOT THAT RIGHT!"

"What kind of uneducated jack-offs do you have running that place?"

From far away could be heard the squeal of something no bigger than an idea dying.

"Actually, sir," said Bernard, "we venture to great lengths to hire the highest-educated jack-offs."

"Huh?"

"Most of us here have a Masters in the masturbatory arts." Bernard heard the words coming out of his mouth and he couldn't stop them. "In fact, my boss has a PhD in wanking. Honestly, sir, he is a genius. I've never seen a wrist-flipper with such grace. It truly brings micturition to the ocular regions. That's 'tears to the eyes' for an oligophreniac such as yourself."

"Why, I–"

"Also I'm pleased to report that we are located in the US of A. India may've one upped us on technical expertise, but when it comes to good old fashioned hand-fapping, we're still number one."

"What the hell are you–?"

"I'm sorry, you agnotologic fuck," said Bernard. "Did it even occur to you that you were speaking to a human being? Do you realize that when you discharged your acerbic vitriol into my ear you perpetuated a cycle of mistrust and abuse, motivating me to react in kind since it's the only way that we've been taught to interact as human beings?"

"Look, buddy. I demand–"

"I'm sorry," said Bernard, "I'm going to have to put you on hold. Can you wait just a minute?"

"No!"

"Thanks. Back in two shakes."

Bernard hung up. His computer monitor listed the queue of incoming calls. Each listing showed the caller's number and city so Shawna could deliver the appropriate greeting (The company policy was that there was no company. Customers were always to believe they were speaking to an employee of whatever firm outsourced its call center to MacroLogistics).

Bernard routed each of the callers to his personal phone queue. He clicked on Boston.

"Pegleg Pete's Eyepatch Emporium," said Bernard. "Our prices are off the hook."

"What–?"

Bernard hung up. Next was Tulsa.

"Midget Gynecologists," he said. "We put ourselves into our work."

"Huh–?"

Click.

Fairbanks: "Crazy Louie's Discount Prosthetics: An arm and a leg shouldn't cost an arm and a leg."

"Sorry?"

Click.

Portland: "Missionary Airlines: Our clients are always on top."

"Yes, I'd–What!?"

Click.

Jacksonville: "Tony's Erotic Bakery: We'll make it rise if you give us the dough."

"Did you–?"

Click.

Carmichael: "Bobs Bondage Boutique and Housekeeping: We'll tie you up and then tidy up."

"Uhh-?"

Click.

Bernard leaned back in his chair. He couldn't believe what he'd done.

He rose from his desk and headed towards the exit. He stopped at Chad Mattson, who was trying to type on Shawna's computer while sneaking glances at her cleavage. Bernard slapped Chad's back with a thud. Mattson jumped and turned with surprise.

"Oh. Uhm…Bernard?"

"I'm going to take my lunch."

"That's not for another hour. We're flooded with calls."

"No we're not," said Bernard in a deadpan. "I handled them."

Mattson turned to Shawna's call queue. It was empty for a moment. Jacksonville popped onto the screen, followed by Tulsa, Carmichael, Boston, Fairbanks.

"Oh. Hmm," said Bernard. "Good luck with those. I'd stay, but I'm hungry now."

Heads turned as Bernard walked out of the office.

Bernard left his apartment wearing the aqua silk moiré suit and carrying two mismatched suitcases. He left the door unlocked and the keys on the kitchen table. Forty minutes later, he left his bank, patting a lump of money in his wallet. He left his Yugo in long term parking at the airport, keys on the driver's seat. Five hours later, he listened with rapt attention as the stewardess explained the pre-flight checklist.

He spent the next twelve hours in the air asking himself what in the world he'd done.

18. Polyamory

Polyamorists are people who,
Want to have their Kate and Edith too.

Maya and Vida couldn't get a sleeping train to Venice, but they settled on a private cabin for their honeymoon night, even though it cost six train tickets to make it happen and they were too exhausted for anything but slumping together with Maya's head nestled on Vida's shoulder.

The countryside had long gone dark and Vida couldn't sleep. She thought about her parents. What they would think of her being married to a woman— and the devil, no less? She wondered which would bother them more.

"Are you awake?" said Vida.

Maya didn't answer.

"Do you want kids?" Vida asked, louder.

"Glrg?"

"Do you want kids?" she repeated.

Maya's right eye popped open.

"Women," mumbled Maya. "First you marry them, then they try to tie you down."

"I don't mean now," said Vida, trying to make out shapes in the black on black countryside. "Just someday?"

"Of course, love. We'll have a dozen: eleven boys, one girl."

Vida laughed. "Twelve! I hope you're carrying them all."

"We'll take turns. One of us will lie around all day and the other will fetch her all the pickles and Nutella her heart desires."

"Why only one girl?"

Vida thought Maya had fallen asleep before she responded.

"Easy love. So she'll never ever doubt that she's special."

Vida planted a kiss on Maya's head.

"So many rugrats," mused Vida, "we could start a circus."

"That's right," said Maya. "The Life and Illusion Gypsy Family Caravan. They'll walk on their hands before they walk on their feet. We'll move from town to town performing for whoever wants to see."

"What about school?"

"They'll be learning a trade. We'll have an escape artist and a tightrope walker and a contortionist, that'll be the girl, and you can take the tickets at the start of the show. We'll teach one to be a knife thrower and I'll be his target."

"Sounds dangerous," said Vida.

"We'll wait till he's five."

"Let's hope he doesn't get mad at you."

"Well, I can't throw them at him. My aim is bollocks."

"What else will we have?" asked Vida.

"What won't we have?" Maya gestured out even though her head still rested on Vida's shoulder. "It'll be the best circus ever. Strongmen and cotton candy and a fat bearded lady—that'll be me when I get older. But we'll have two rules: No live animals and no clowns."

"Fair enough," said Vida. "Animals are scary and clowns are always mistreated. Tell me more."

"We'll have a sword swallower," said Maya, "and a man from India who charms nails and sits on snakes. In fact, we'll have an entire freak show."

"A freak show? With our children?" asked Vida.

"Oh no, we'll hire outside help, unless they want to be a part of it. If one of our boys wants to tattoo his body and bite the heads off chickens, I can't think of a reason to stop him. Or her."

"Except we won't have any chickens."

"Oh right. Fried chicken then."

"That doesn't sound exciting."

"It's all in the presentation."

"That's true," said Vida.

"I learned from the best. And the sexiest. But it's sleepy-time."

"All right fine," moped Vida. "But will you tell me more in the morning?"

"I promise."

Vida stopped petting Maya's head. Their hands found each other in Vida's lap.

"Maya"

"What, love?"

"Will we have a trapeze?"

"Of course, love."

"I've always wanted to trapeze."

"Then we'll have it."

"Promise?"

"Cross my heart...."

Maya fell asleep before she could finish, but Vida stayed awake. She didn't care for dreams, she just wanted to hold Maya's hand and be near her forever. It was the happiest day of her life and she knew nothing could ever go wrong again.

Six months later, Vida sat alone in the bar of the Tripping Gormandizer, her frown distorted in her pint glass. One of the advantages of staying at a hostel was that Vida could get a real sized drink, none of those itsy-bitsy beer glasses that the Amsterdam locals insisted were suitable. She'd be happier if she could find a beer that wasn't half foam, but she wasn't one to hold out for miracles. Not these days, anyway.

Vida looked at herself in the bar window. A purple streak whisked through the dark strands of her hair and her blue sports-shirt showed off arms toned from hauling her show from pitch to pitch. She'd been on the road for five years now, though these days it felt like seventy.

Outside the window a pair of English tourists stumbled in a psychedelic haze down the red light district. Lucinda, wearing a red silk camisole and black panties, postured behind her glass door and beckoned them closer, hoping someone would be adventurous or lonesome enough to pay €50 for fifteen minutes of latex love.

The street performers of Amsterdam often finished their evenings at the Tripping Gormandizer, buying pitchers with coins and taking bets on how long the tourists' encounters with the ladies would last. The outside figure was fifteen minutes, but the safe bet was eight and a half from entrance to departure. There were exceptions:

He looks like a Three Minute Manchick.

Nah, Anatoly, I'd give him ten.

No way ten!

Sure. One for the deed, one for the apology, and the other eight so she can hold him while he cries.

One night the performers drank and cackled as Lucinda cycled through eighteen men in one hour. Vida was impressed.

"Another beer, Miss Vida?"

Vida looked down at the glass she didn't remember emptying. She nodded at Zdenko, the heavy-set Slavic bartender whose smile peeked out from underneath a thick gray moustache and stoned red eyes.

"You want anything else?" asked Zdenko. "A gyro from next door?"

"No thanks," said Vida.

"A day that Miss Vida doesn't want a gyro must be a bad day. You want a smoke? I am just about to roll another one."

"Not now," said Vida.

"If you smoke, you maybe not feel so sad."

"You might be right," said Vida, "but sometimes sad is where you have to be."

Zdenko shrugged and went over to pour Vida's drink. Vida glanced around the hostel bar. The Tripping Gormandizer's décor assumed that its patrons took full advantage of Amsterdam's liberal drug policy. Plexiglas platforms hung from the ceiling. Anyone perched on a platform and looking down would see Van Gogh's *Starry Night* painted on the floor, while above them picnickers loafed on rolling green hills. Four Turkish youths spilled out of one of the smaller platforms. A Czech girl sucked lazily on a joint while her companion pushed a rook across a chessboard. Two red-eyed tourists with maple leaves on their backpacks (*Americanus Incognitus*) stared at the far corner of the ceiling mural where sat the Gormandizer, an impossibly obese man with a pig-like snout, dangling a thick joint from his lips while shoveling mushroom caps into his open maw.

The decor was a feng shui nightmare. Vida gave thanks that the actual bar was devoid of such excess, excepting the long arm barstools that protruded from the starry floor to support drinker's butts with plush, contoured palms.

Zdenko brought Vida another beer and retired to the other end of the bar. Vida picked up the beer and scanned the room once again, accidentally making eye contact with a beefy young guy in a Wisconsin State sweater. He smiled and walked towards her.

Great, thought Vida. *Another American. Why is it when you go to get away from it all, you keep meeting the people you're trying to get away from?*

"Do you mind?" the guy asked, sitting at the empty stool next to Vida's. He had a vacuous smile, broad shoulders and tousled blonde hair. Vida held back the impulse to counter with snarkiness. How old was he: twenty-one, twenty-two? Since when did people her age begin to look so young?

"It's a free country," said Vida, then she added, "at least I think it is. I'm not quite up on the Netherlands' government policies." She turned back to her beer.

"Bad day?" he ventured.

Yeah. Five months ago, she thought. *And I've been living it ever since.*

"I've had better," she said. "And now this—"

She waved to The Daily Dam sitting on the bar. The Anglo periodical specialized in tourist tips and English-friendly events. Today's headline was an exception.

Venice, Wherefore Depart Thou?

"Freaky shit," said the young man. "Vacation plans derailed?"

"I've been there. You couldn't pay me to go back," said Vida. "Even if it was above sea level."

She drank her beer. He squeezed his eyebrows together and stuck out his hand.

"My name's Denny,"

"Sorry?"

"Denny."

"I heard you," said Vida, unable to resist. "I'm just sorry."

Before he had time to consider, she flipped up her hand and gave his a solid politician pump. "Pleased to meetcha, Denny. The name's Vida."

Zdenko appeared in front of them.

"Can I get a Heineken?" asked Denny.

Zdenko turned to Vida. Vida nodded. Zdenko frowned and poured Denny's drink.

"Now," said Vida, "tell me the highlight of your trip so far."

Denny deliberated. "Walking through St. Stephen's Cathedral."

"Come on," she said. "You've been on the road for three and a half weeks and that's the best you got?" She went to sip her beer and overshot, spilling it on her top.

"Slitmonkeys!" she spurted.

Slitmonkeys is not a real word, no matter what Vida might say.

"Miss Vida!" Zdenko hurried over. "Is it all okay?"

"No problem," said Vida, gesturing at her shirt. "Minor accident."

Vida wiped at her sports-top without success. Denny reached across the bar and grabbed a bar towel and handed it to Vida. Zdenko grimaced at the intrusion and returned to the taps.

Vida took the towel and dabbed at the spill. The beer left a dark stain on her top.

"Thanks," she said.

"No problem," said Denny. Zdenko returned long enough to hand Denny his beer and collect four Euros. Denny raised the beer to his mouth. He stopped.

"How'd you know how long I've been traveling?"

Vida passed the towel underneath her shirt and dried her chest.

"You're on a month long trip," she said. "You fly out of London in a couple more days, and your favorite stop was the Amsterdam Sex Museum, but you didn't want to tell me because of your Midwest upbringing."

Denny said nothing for a moment. "You're psychic."

"You're a tourist. Tourists are my business."

Denny scratched his left earlobe and looked her up and down. "Wait! Are you a...?"

His eyes flashed to the window. Across the canal, Lucinda pulled in another client. Vida smirked and turned to her beer.

"Thanks," she said as she sipped. "I'm flattered."

Denny didn't inquire if she was being sarcastic and Vida didn't know.

"I'm dying here. How'd you know that stuff?"

Vida took a drink. 'I spent two weeks in a cave outside Nepal with a fakir who said he could walk through walls. I never found out how he did it, the little bugger always moved too fast, but he taught me a few tricks about reading crowds. It's all smoke and mirrors, but it comes in handy."

"You're pulling my leg," declared Denny.

"Maybe," said Vida.

"I want to change my answer," he said. "I think you might be the most interesting part of my journey so far. Can I buy you a drink?"

"Already covered," she said, tapping her glass. "But I'll buy you one if you can tell me something interesting about yourself."

"I was a running-back for three semesters at Wisconsin State until my knee blew out."

"Sucks. But superficial. Go deeper."

"I'm majoring in architecture," said Denny. "That's why I said St. Stephen's. I loved it. The inside is stunning: a Romanesque foundation and eight hundred years of Gothic renovations. The Sex Museum was stucco and white paint. It could have been designed by an undergrad." As an afterthought he added, "But I liked the titties."

Vida smiled. "Points for honesty and we're in the right direction. Tell me something personal and the beer is yours."

Denny averted his glance, counted the bar taps, and shrugged. "A week before we were supposed to leave for this trip, my girlfriend left me for my best friend."

"Ooch. How'd it make you feel? Don't answer right away."

Denny rolled his eyebrows.

"I should say 'betrayed' or something but that's not right. The three of us were good friends and they were really close. I suspected they'd been going at it for months."

"But you didn't say anything."

"Well, I loved her and he'd been my friend since grade school. So I looked the other way. And everything was great. But one day I came home and he was there and it was too obvious to pretend it wasn't happening. I suppose what I felt was disappointed. Not because she left me, but because we both felt she had to."

Vida held up two fingers to Zdenko.

"That met your approval?" Denny asked

"It was worth a drink. But you've got the next round."

"We should toast," he said as the beer arrived.

"What to?"

"Venice?"

"Alright," she said. "What the hell. To Venice."

"To Venice!"

Four pints later, Vida said good night to Zdenko and turned down Denny's proposition to join him in his dorm bed. She bobbed and weaved her way through colored hallways and squeezed herself down the slim stairwell towards her darkened dorm room.

The room was silent, the nine other lodgers either passed out or partying. 3am on a Tuesday, partying was the default. It was Amsterdam after all.

Vida slid off her shoes and socks. Her bare feet sunk into the mottled carpet. She gave thanks to her bottom bunk, which allowed her to drape a sheet from the top bunk and gain a crude form of nested isolation. She was even more grateful for the departure of Herr Foghorn, the eighteen stone Düsseldorfer whose snoring had affronted eardrums in adjacent hotels.

Vida attempted to unbutton her jeans but the beers had made her fingers large and uncoordinated. Her shirt was still sticky from the spilled beer, but once she was horizontal removal was too much work. Her nook was dark with only the dimmest of lights from an outside bar playing shadow puppet games against her sheet.

Vida lay still, making out shapes in the darkness. She realized she wasn't quite alone.

That boy was a treat for the eyes, love. He reminded me of back home blokes full of nothing but spunk and muscle. You should've gone with him. I wouldn't of minded.

"I would've," whispered Vida.

Why so quiet? Are you embarrassed I'm here?

You're not here, Vida thought. "Maya, I don't want to wake anyone up. You shouldn't either."

Vida made out a shape that used to be a fold in the blanket.

I wasn't quiet when I was alive, love. Why should I start now?

"Maya!" huffed Vida. She heard rustling from the bed above. Vida dropped her voice. "Be quiet."

You're angry, honeylips. I'll go.

The shadow receded.

"No! Please."

Vida didn't think shadows could grow brighter, but this one did.

I'll stay as long as you want me.

I want you forever, Vida thought.

I heard that.

You can't hear anything, she thought. *You're not real.*

I heard that, too.

"I need someone here for me."

Like you were there for me, babydoll?

Vida felt a weight drop onto her chest. She struggled to respond.

"I couldn't do anything."

I don't blame you.

"I do," she said. Her lungs tightened. Vida needed to breath but couldn't take in more than a swallow. She closed her eyes hoping blindness would make it easier to say what she needed to say. It didn't.

"This isn't working," Vida said. "I need someone real."

I'm real.

"I need someone I can touch."

Touch me.

Vida felt something cool and wet on her cheek. She thought it was a tear, but it danced over and brushed against her lips. A whiff of breath exhaled into her mouth and the pressure on her lips increased. Vida wanted to see but her eyes were fastened shut. The blanket pressed down on her chest. She tried to sit up but couldn't fight it. Her shirt swam over her head. Warm and familiar hands cupped her exposed breasts. She felt the soft tickle of her zipper and heard the tic-tic-tic as her pants loosened and were pulled down. Her panties slid away. Soft and hard sensations, half real, half memory, rushed through her.

"I love you Maya."

I love you Vida.

Vida's stomach tightened and her fists squeezed together. Vida's fingers twitched and the tension built inside her. Tears streamed down her face.

Do you want me to stop?

Vida's back arched.

"No please," she whispered. "Whatever you do, don't stop. Don't ever stop."

Wetness flowed from her face and legs. Her bed was liquid. Vida was submerged.

Vida told herself it wasn't real. She told herself that if she opened her eyes, she'd see that she was touching herself, no ghost of a lover. But she couldn't open her eyes. She couldn't look. Just like every other night.

The shaking subsided but the tears continued in waves. Vida lay motionless, alone and sobbing, until she fell asleep.

II. Intersection

19. Schrödinger's Boat

Row, Row, Schrödinger's Boat, in between the stream,
It's traveled here and everywhere, and where it's never been.

Bernard hadn't intended to go to Amsterdam. When the attractive Korean woman at the United Airlines counter asked where he was going, the first thing that flashed in his head was an old picture book of Venice that he had when he was ten. It was one of the few non-dictionary books he'd opened more than once. Bernard's eidetic mind made repetition unnecessary, but something about the photos drew him in. One picture in particular, of a serene gondolier rowing a white and gold gondola down an open canal, fascinated Bernard beyond reasonable expectation. He'd stare at the image until he felt the gentle rocking of the boat over the water. The gondolier would dip a long pole and the boat would travel just past the shop of Carnevale masks and Bernard would be back in his room. He was certain if he held his attention a bit longer he'd find out what was beyond that mask shop, but he never made it farther than the walls of the photograph.

The woman behind the counter stood with her fingers frozen over the keyboard.

"Venice," said Bernard, with unusual resolve.

The ticket seller looked around. When she was eighteen and worked night shifts at her family's Seven-Eleven, she had to inform an old woman that her million dollar lottery ticket was purchased on the wrong day and she best stop dancing around lest she damage merchandise she couldn't afford to replace. Somehow, telling this strange man that Venice was under the ocean was less appealing.

"Do you scuba?" she asked.

"No," said Bernard.

"Then no Venice."

After the awkward explanation, Bernard bit his cheeks and rolled his tongue. It didn't feel right. He was so certain he was supposed to be in Venice.

"You hadn't heard?" asked the ticket seller. "It's all anyone's been talking about since yesterday."

"I was distracted," said Bernard.

"Come on, buddy," said the man behind him. "Some of us got places to be."

The rest of the line grumbled assent.

Bernard turned back to the counter. "What've you got in the way of canals?"

Bernard hefted his suitcases and stepped from the shadows of the Amstel terminal and squinted at the light. Travelers poured from the station entrance. A herd of trams crisscrossed the road. Cyclists whizzed by. Everyone looked so thin.

Bernard teetered side to side as he navigated the tramways. Amsterdam looked active and cramped, but most of the people seemed carefree. Or stoned, Bernard didn't know how to tell the difference.

Bernard reached a strange plastic contraption seven feet tall and divided into four symmetrical units, each unit housing a small platform and a crevasse about waist high. He decided it was an art installation just as a businessman pushed past him and ascended the unit, dropped his trousers and commenced pissing.

A disheveled vagrant staggered towards the public toilet. He looked at the businessman shaking off his last drops, ignored the other three stalls and veered away to pee on a nearby wall. The bum grinned at Bernard and waved with his free hand.

What a strange city. Bernard continued up the road, experiencing an unfamiliar feeling. He was happy.

Despite his previous desire towards Venice, Bernard had never felt so certain he was where he was supposed to be. Familiarity struck at every corner. Rounding the Herengracht, he pictured a yellow grocery store before he saw it. Around the next corner, he knew he would be approaching an old music shop and beyond that a Kinoplex. He didn't even know what a Kinoplex was but there it stood, offering movies that had traveled through American theatres six months earlier.

The certainty, which began as a novelty, was becoming a little creepy. He sat down at a bench beside the canal and dropped his suitcases beside him. He looked at the ledge above the water and was struck with absolute conviction that if he looked over he'd see a small red boat. He scoffed. He told himself that déjà vu was his subconscious mind processing incoming information faster than his conscious mind could consider it, but he couldn't shake the image of a small rowboat with flaked red paint and a frayed rope dropping into the water.

His imagination was overtaking him. To regain his sanity, he had to confirm the rowboat wasn't there. Bernard stood up and moved to the bridge, leaving his suitcases on the bench behind him.

The boat wasn't there, he told himself. Its presence was irrational.

Of course it was there, he countered. He was certain.

Bernard straddled the boundary between doubt and faith and stepped towards the bridge.

Below the bridge, the red rowboat was having a heck of a time figuring out what was going on. It was Bernard's fault, though some blame could also be placed on Erwin Schrödinger.

Erwin Schrödinger, theoretical scientist and practicing polyamorist, proposed placing a cat in a box and rigging a fifty percent chance that the kitty would perish. Aside from raising the ire of PETA, Schrödinger said that until the box was opened, the poor pussy was neither alive nor dead and existed in a state of limbo, a combination of particles and waves, part departed kitty and part frisky feline.

Down below, the abandoned rowboat was caught in a paradox. It was bright red when it first landed in the water, but the color had faded over the years and the effects of weather had taken their toll. Part of the raft was certain that it's rotted wood had sunk years ago. But it'd been sturdily built and held concurrent memories of recently floating above the water.

Bernard reached the ledge and made a decision. The boat was there, but if it wasn't, it was because he didn't believe hard enough. He placed his hands on the railing. The boat bobbed along the surface. He leaned forward. The boat was a submerged home for fishies.

At the moment of truth, Bernard heard a commotion behind him. He turned just in time to see a young man, with Bernard's suitcases, fleeing around the corner.

Bernard huffed after his possessions and forgot about the boat, which in the barest of glances found itself stuck between possibility and reality. The boat didn't know what to do. It tested out the waves, rocking side to side. Droplets splashed against the hull. It liked that. For the first time, the boat willed itself upstream. It wasn't sure what its purpose was, but it was determined to make the most of it.

20. Autofloccinaucinihilipilification
Autofloccinaucinihilipilification,
When you hate on yourself without substantiation.

Bernard huffed and panted as the thief, a ratty haired teen with a torn leather jacket, gained ground despite being weighed down by two heavy suitcases. Bernard's chest pounded. The teenager turned down an alleyway. Bernard cut in front of a bicyclist and pursued. The cyclist swerved towards a pole. Bernard heard the rider crunch and turned his head. When he turned back, his view changed. The vagrant was no longer a young street kid, but a woman with purple streaks in her hair. She looked back with her face full of fear and Bernard had another feeling of déjà vu.

What's happening? he thought.

Bernard tripped over a raised block on the canal. The vision shifted back to the young thief and the ground rushed towards Bernard's face. He threw out his hands but not fast enough. His elbows and face hit the sidewalk. His fingers went numb and he started hyperventilating. Fighting for breath, he glanced up and watched his suitcases disappear around a corner. He could have stood up, but he didn't see the point. He lay on the ground and thought about his losses: past, present, and future. The sky, following dramatic laws older than theatre itself, began to rain.

A Turkish grocer frowned as Bernard dragged his water-soaked frame past the storefront. Bernard's suit was dirty, his face was wet, and he wouldn't be surprised if the grocer assumed him to be just another of the city's homeless. Granted, that's precisely what he was.

Bernard repeated a mantra in his head:

You're worthless. You have nothing. You've contributed nothing. The world doesn't need you.

You're worthless. You've nothing. You've contributed nothing. The world doesn't need you.

Bernard could think of nothing to prove himself wrong.

He lurched against a wall and clutched his stomach. Sweat and rain beaded on his forehead. He staggered towards a garbage can, placed his hands on the rim and thrust his face towards the opening. His stomach emptied itself in several painful minutes. It seemed impossible for so much to come out of his body. He looked down into the can and his eyes widened. Not all of the excreta looked like it had once been food.

Bernard stumbled away, wiping yellow foam from his mouth. A dark-skinned woman in a green-and-yellow *kebaya* pulled her child close as he lumbered past. The rain slowed to a light drizzle. The sun peeked out from fragmented clouds. With the weather improving, Bernard felt worse. He couldn't blame his mood on the rain; it was all him. He was defective. His body was his sole possession and it was broken.

Bernard decided that since his body wasn't behaving itself, the only way he could gain power over it was to prove that he didn't need it, and the only way to do that was to get rid of it. The only rational solution was to kill himself.

He heard bells but paid no attention until they were joined by a horn and a screech of metal. He turned to see a large tram stopped inches from his face. The badger-like driver screamed nose-twitching invectives. Bernard didn't understand the language but the hand gestures were unmistakable.

He considered the hulk of metal before him. The trams reached a good enough pace. It would be easy: just a quick slam, bam, thank you tram and it'd all be over.

The wrinkle was that he couldn't just wait in the middle of the road. That kind of thing would've worked in the States, but Amsterdam drivers apparently stopped before impact.

Bernard waved away the tram, ignoring the driver's curses as it departed. He casually walked towards a tourist shop display of shirts with slogans like "Amsterdone" and "I Spent a Week in Amsterdam and All I Got Was This T-Shirt (and the Clap)." From the corner of his eye, he watched the street.

Adelmo had been an Amsterdam tram driver for eight months, ever since he moved his family from Barcelona. The work wasn't bad, just monotonous, despite the random tourist wandering in front of his mega-ton vehicle thanks to Amsterdam's "Don't Ask, Don't Tell, Screw It, We've Got Better Things to Do" drug policy.

On the left side of the street a pair of green haired youths inspected bongs. On the right, a heavy-set homeless *vago* looked at shirts and teenaged girl in white shorts and a tight-green top tried on sunglasses. The girl slid one hand into her back pocket. Adelmo imagined sliding his owns hands into her pockets, then into her shorts. He was pulling her shorts down to her ankles when the homeless bum turned and ran full force into the path of his tram.

"*Pajillero!*"

Adelmo pulled on the brakes, but there wasn't enough time.

He watched the *vago*'s face turn from a determined scowl to open-eyed fear. The tram squealed. Adelmo felt the thud and the man flew forward and landed on the ground.

Adelmo wondered if he would get in trouble. If he'd been watching the road instead of eyeing those white shorts. What if he was fired? He'd definitely leave out the *señorita* when he told his wife . He looked out at the motionless body, but couldn't bring himself to climb out of the tram. The limp figure twitched and the man rose from the ground like an inflating blimp. The man stood semi-upright and staggered away, leaving behind a trail of "Fuck. Fuck. Fuck. Fuck...."

The problem with knowing the words for every part of the human body is that pain takes on exponential dimensions. Bernard didn't just hurt in his back or his legs or arms. He felt the screams of his spinous processes and quadratus lumborum and the intercostals of his ribs. He suspected bruising on the anterior fold of his iliac crest and identified the subtle difference between the slow stabbing sensation of his teres minor and the stinging sensation of his teres major. If ignorance was bliss, Bernard was on the other side.

He survived the impact without a concussion or identifiable sprains, but he was disappointed that he survived at all. He cursed himself for being so pathetic that he couldn't even kill himself.

Bernard limped towards a canal ledge. The murky waters called to him. If the fall didn't kill him, he could hold his breath until he drowned. The bonus was that his clothes were already soaked from the rain, so he wouldn't have to worry about the discomfort of getting wet. Besides, there weren't any canals back home. When else in his life would he get such an opportunity?

He looked around. The last thing he wanted was some do-gooder Samaritan diving in after him. The few people on the street seemed lost in their own experiences. He pulled himself up and draped one leg over the railing. He stopped. The water wasn't far. What if he didn't die? What if he fell far enough to break his legs on the canal floor, but couldn't drown himself. What if he rose to the surface and regained consciousness?

Drowning didn't seem as smart a plan as he'd thought. There had to be a better way. He pulled back his leg. He was growing impatient. Who knew suicide would be this much work? He could overdose on pills, but he didn't know what kind. He could get a gun and shoot himself in the head, but he didn't know where to find a firearm. He needed something definite, like a fall from a large building. The problem was that unlike the Dutch people, most of Amsterdam's structures were relatively short. He was ready to toss the idea aside when he spied an aberration on the landscape, a giant among a skyline of dwarves, a beautiful, towering building in the distance that called to Bernard with the promise of one final, fatal leap.

21. Bernard Falls Hard

Tonenili made Coatlicue a heart,
For which she near tore him apart.

Vida waited on deck at the Leidseplein. Amsterdam's prime performing pitch should've had a queue of buskers waiting to build their nest eggs before heading south for the winter. Instead, there was Vida and Three Ball Paul, a juggler from Manchester. Rain had curbed the earlier day's performances. Once the drops stopped falling, Vida and Paul raced to the pitch to find a throng of untapped tourists. Paul shrugged it off, but Vida knew it took more than a daytime drizzle to keep the pitch sparse on a Saturday night. Something was amiss.

Three Ball Paul had gathered a good-sized crowd by promising to fit his lanky body through an unstrung tennis racket. Vida sat on her small amplifier away from the action and flipped through a Daily Dam. Her eyes stopped at an artist's rendering of the Leidseplein: the two rows of lamplights framing the pitch, an L-shaped block of elm trees to the south-east, and the tram line that swooped down the west side. Beyond the tram line stood the square's newest feature, a gargantuan building rising twenty stories over the tiny coffeeshops. The rendering emphasized the shadows slicing across the square, bringing half the pitch into premature night.

The Little Tower that Shouldn't

by Kit Sforza

Save those Euros, kiddies! The Ubermarkt opens in one week. The city's first vertical shopping mall will offer twenty stories of restaurants and bars, a video arcade, two casinos, a pet shop, two smart shops, a twelve screen movie theatre, and a skating rink. If you think it's fun to watch stoned tourists walk into trams, you're gonna love it when they strap on rollerblades. But hold your excitement, because it gets better. Did I mention they branded the smart shops with the Ubermarkt's logo? How my heart yearns to buy my drugs from a franchise. I've always thought bongs were incomplete without a brand on the side. What's next, chain brothels? If the commercialization of our city's noble drug culture doesn't strike your fanny, let's talk history. Remember when someone claimed the tower didn't represent the flavor of Amsterdam, so they slapped a big windmill on the roof and everyone shut up? I can't picture that happening without plenty of back-room blowjobs.

But wait, Kit. Twenty stories? That sounds like a lot of jobs. Think again, kiddies. The Ubermarkt boasts the latest in anti-personnel technology, from mechanized stockers to self-scanning checkout stations, allowing Joe Tourist a complete shopping experience with the barest minimum of pesky human interactions.

The Ubermarkt is the flagship of König Industries and its success will send an armada of towers across Europe under the iron fist of the company's titular head, Vitoria König. That's Vitoria, not *Victoria*, and an informant tells me the last board member who added a consonant is stationed at a septic processing station in Greenland. (For the record, this isn't the same source who swore to me Venice was whisked away by Space Atlanteans. On an unrelated note: I no longer write my articles during all-night mushroom benders).

Speaking of disappearances, whatever happened to George König? Reports on the death of Vitoria's husband seem cribbed from press notices released by König Industries. By all accounts, George König didn't so much die as disappear off the face of the earth. Something's fishy and I'm not talking about the Space Atlanteans.

Bernard dodged through the cobbled streets with the fervor of a pilgrim catching his first sight of Mecca. The large glowing windmill atop the crimson tower dominated his vision. Red and yellow neon lights rotated on a blue wheel in the sky. The beacon made it impossible for Bernard to be lost in the flow of Amsterdam's circular streets. He followed a series of zigzag arcs along darkening canals and back alleys until he reached the base of the dark building.

An orange banner announced the "Ubermarkt Opening" next weekend. Bernard peered into the dark windows of the rear entrance. The lack of movement inside seemed curious. Bernard turned his back to the double doors and nonchalantly tested the door handles. They were locked. Across the street, a store owner eyed Bernard suspiciously. Bernard smiled and walked around the corner.

The side of the tower faced a slim alley that stretched a city block and ran parallel to a wide canal. In the middle of the alley were several bags of cement covered with a tarp and an overturned wheelbarrow. Recessed in the wall was a maintenance door with a small window. The door handle wouldn't budge. He thought of breaking the glass, but he had nothing to break it with and it wouldn't have been large enough to allow him in anyway.

The windmill blades above spun red and yellow. He imagined himself at the roof. All he needed to do was close his eyes and step off the side and it would all be over.

The moon peeked out of the clouds and his gaze dropped from the windmill to the space above the door. Someone had graffitied on the wall in night-reflective yellow glo-paint:

Our enemies are big,
We need to work small.
We're not blowing up bridges,
We're pulling out screws.

Thirty feet from the alley opening, Bernard spied a black fire escape that snaked all the way up to the roof. The stairs started at the second floor, but a metal ladder dangled above the ground. Bernard positioned himself, hopped and reached for the ladder. He failed egregiously.

Bernard wrestled the upturned wheelbarrow onto its wheel and pulled it under the ladder. He lifted one leg over the metal rim. The wheelbarrow shook, and he realized that he wasn't flexible enough to bring the rest of his body over without tipping. Bernard removed his leg and overturned the wheelbarrow. He calculated angle and distance and dragged it a few feet away. Bernard backed up, pictured himself grabbing the target, and ran as fast as he could. He stepped one foot onto the upside-down wheelbarrow and sprung into the air. There was a moment of breath and flight. His fingers brushed nothing. He flew past the lower rung and crashed onto the ground.

He was not in the state to try that again. He hadn't been in the state to try it in the first place. Beaten by the day; wet, bedraggled, and exhausted; Bernard realized he couldn't even succeed at killing himself.

He slunk away from the alley, passing a thin green sign that announced "Leidseplein."

On his right, the Ubermarkt sported another large banner. In the middle of the square stood a series of street lamps and a mass of people. Bernard saw a torch flickering above the heads. Numbed, he pushed through the crowd. He reached the front of the circle and a ring of torches blinded him. He rubbed his eyes and made out the hazy vision of two women. He rubbed his eyes again and one of the women disappeared. The remaining woman was an olive-skinned goddess with black-and-purple hair. She held a staff which erupted in fire on both ends. Bernard couldn't look away. He saw Vida, and fell farther and harder than he'd ever imagined possible.

22. Pyroclasm

**Two words humping, so you know,
Create a bastard portmanteau.**

The first show was an accident. A brother and sister, whose tribe had recently left the trees and were still figuring out caves, came across a berry bush while foraging. The squat bush had thick green-and-white leaves that pricked the sister when she reached in a hairy arm to retrieve a dark-blue berry. The berry was unfamiliar, but so many things were.

The brother snatched the berry from his sister's hand. He sniffed it. He touched it to his tongue. He put it in his mouth, chewed and swallowed. Satisfied, he reached for a second berry and his hand began to shake. The spasm infected his arm, then his entire body. His sister laughed as his gesticulations grew more wild and unpredictable. The spasmodic fit ended and the brother dropped to the ground.

That was the first show. The second came later, when the sister returned alone to the rocky outcropping that marked the entrance to her tribe's home. She opened her mouth and hooted over and over until the rest of the tribe circled her. She held up a fistful of dark blue berries. She walked over to a young male and held the berries out to him. He reached out to take one. She pulled the berries back and slapped the boy across the face. She returned to the center of the circle and touched one berry to her lips. She danced and shook and fell to the ground.

The first show was an accident. The second was a warning.

Vida's fire staff provided a heavy workout, so she kept one end rested on the ground while the other flickered in the air. Her black sports top showed off a tattoo on her deltoid of a woman standing on the earth juggling comets. The comets connected with black makeup swirls that flowed up her neck and the right side of her face. The swirls were highlighted in the same violet hue that streaked her short black hair and lined her dark pants and top. Vida stood still, but her eyes met every tourist who crossed the square. People slowed for the flames but they stayed for the woman holding them. A trio of bleached blondes neared the circle and Vida invited them in with a smile calculated to be both humble and promising. An old Dutch banker stayed when Vida gave him an upturned flirt with the eyebrow. A leathered street rat and his pierced girlfriend lumbered by uninterested until Vida stuck out her tongue and smirked and the two pushed their way into the circle. Everyone had a key and Vida knew them all.

Her intro music faded. A portly man in a dirty suit pushed his way to the front of the circle. He stopped and rubbed his eyes when he hit the brightness of her stage. Vida scanned him like she did the others, searching for the clues that would reveal him to her. She received nothing. The dirty clothes indicated a difficult day, but the man who wore them was unreadable. She looked him in the eyes. He stared back at her. His light-blue eyes didn't waver and she couldn't tell if he stared out of intensity or shock or something different. He was a blank page where she expected a cipher.

Someone coughed. Vida pulled her attention off the mysterious audience member. In her distraction, she'd lost the crowd's curiosity. It was a rookie mistake and she made a note to chastise herself for it when she had the luxury of time. As it was, she scanned the crowd to figure out how to bring them back.

Reading a crowd was no different than reading a person. Vida looked and the information arrived. She worried that the mysterious audience member would block her read, but if anything, the crowd showed up for her stronger than before. She raised her lips and they were hers once again.

The wind picked up and a voice danced around her ear.

Come on, love! Time to show them what you've got.

Vida didn't acknowledge Maya, so it had to be coincidence when the mysterious audience member tilted his head and flashed his eyes to the side.

Vida hefted the staff into the air, lowered her foot to start the music, and the show began.

Ten minutes later, Vida spun like a flaming dervish, basking in the crowd's awe and feeding it back to them. The audience was a tangible, palpable entity and they trusted her. They would've barked at the moon if she asked them to, and she did. They howled and cheered, they stomped their feet and raised their hands to the air. She pulled up a young boy from the crowd and taught him how to fly. She drew out her finale, teasing extra time and building tension until the crowd surged with expectation. It was a great show, one of the best Vida had ever done. If there was a god of buskers, he smiled on her that evening.

Vida put down her fire staff and picked up a can of fuel when a harsh sound echoed from the rear of the circle. A wave broke through the crowd. Vida looked up and two police officers joined her in the circle. One of them raised a hand at elbow height.

"*Niet meer laten zien,*" said the first officer. He had a small truncheon resting on his belt and "KASPAR" emblazoned on his chest, below the title of "Surveillant."

"Sorry?" asked Vida.

"No more show," said Surveillant Kaspar in slow but passable English. "Street performing on Leidseplein is now forbidden."

Police intervention was a hazard of the profession, but Amsterdam was one of the last free cities, one of the few developed areas that didn't require licenses and hurdles of red tape. Vida's surprise mixed with anger and frustration, but she knew a fight wouldn't help after she read the officer. Surveillant Kaspar, a tall blonde man with a comfortable face, was amiable but dedicated to his job. Vida reminded herself that there were always loopholes and she could find out more later. For now, she had a priority. "Can I finish the show?" she asked. "A couple more minutes?"

Surveillant Kaspar looked around the crowd. They looked back. "I suppose," he shrugged.

"Thank you. Thank you. Thank you!" said Vida. She touched Kaspar's arm and gave him a flirtatious smile, which Kaspar returned.

It was an innocuous exchange, calculated by Vida to defuse some of the tension for the audience. Instead, the second officer stepped out from behind Kaspar and exploded.

"No, no! Absolutely! You are not! We said no! Pack up or we take you in!"

Vida was taken aback. So was Surveillant Kaspar, who looked at his partner (whose nametag read "LARS") with incredulity. Vida didn't need a talent to know that Surveillant Lars exuded pure red hatred. She looked deeper, and pulled away. She turned to the crowd, shaken. No one exhaled, including Bernard.

"I'm sorry folks," said Vida. "I hope you all enjoy the rest of your evening."

This elicited a round of boos. Kaspar blinked at his partner, who appeared frozen in a grimace of anger.

"If you liked what you saw," she said. "Euros are always appreciated. It costs a lot to bring you a show. Fuel, travel, bail…."

She kicked her hat into the air, grabbed it, and presented it towards the crowd.

Surveillant Lars snaked out his hand and latched onto Vida's wrist. The hat dropped to the ground and Vida cried out in pain.

23. Zemblanity

It's serendipity when fortune's found,
Zemblanity when it slaps you down.

Dutch police officers are among the most docile of *Homo sapiens securitus*. The events that evening wouldn't have occurred if Surveillant Lars hadn't learned that morning that his partner of six years, Kaspar, was engaging in regular fornication with Lars' wife, Frieda.

Frieda and Kaspar had been discreet and meticulous in their affair and Lars would never have found out if Frieda hadn't told him outright. She hadn't meant to tell him. She meant to ask him to buy eggs on his way home and instead found herself pouring out the entire story of how she and Kaspar met every Monday and Thursday for sexual congress. It was a Friedian slip.

To Lars' credit, he was not a bad husband or lover. He was a gruff man, but in bed he was courteous and meticulous and gentle, qualities that he thought Frieda appreciated. And she did, though sometimes she found herself wishing that her husband wasn't so giving, wishing that he'd grab her hair and mount her from behind, pumping and shooting into her without holding back, just as Kaspar had done on their first rendezvous.

Frieda believed that she was content with the affair. She didn't lose sleep at night torn over which man she loved. She loved her husband Lars and she loved having sex with Kaspar.

She thought she could maintain the status quo forever but her brain betrayed her. She'd been bored before the affair. With one simple addition, everything changed. She felt alive and important. It was the most wonderful part of her life and she'd been unable to talk about it to the man she loved until that afternoon when it all spilled out in explicit detail.

When Frieda finished talking, she felt relieved and terrified. Lars said nothing. He finished his beef croquette, got onto his bicycle, and went to work. Lars said nothing unusual when he saw his partner. If anything, Kaspar thought that Lars acted a little happier than usual. On the outside, Lars wanted to be as open to his partner as he always had been. On the inside, his body screamed with rage at his sense of betrayal from his two closest friends.

Lars didn't know what to do with the bubbling magma in his belly. He didn't want to confront his partner until he had time to think things over. He needed an outlet. What he received was an decree from above that all street performing on the Leidseplein was to immediately cease.

Vida's wrist squirmed in Surveillant Lars' grip. Bernard and the rest of audience, aware that something was amiss but unsure of how to intercede, stood and did nothing. Lars' eyes were empty and his face was red. His hands shook but he wouldn't or couldn't let go.

Vida twisted her hand. Lars held tight. She beat at his arm with her other hand, still holding a can of torch fuel. Kerosene flew past Lars and splashed across Kaspar. Kaspar cried out and clutched at his eyes. Fuel dripped down his shirt and pants. Vida beat at Lars' hand with the empty fuel can. Kaspar staggered sideways. Lars raised his other hand and struck Vida in the cheek. Vida wrenched her hand free. Lars raised his fist for another strike. Vida stared with fury and raised her own fist. Kaspar pushed between them. Vida shoved him away. Kaspar flailed backwards, stepped across a lit torch on the ground, and burst into flames.

Vida saw the burning man first. She moved, but Lars, unaware that his partner had burst into flames, side-stepped and blocked her path. He pulled out his truncheon, deaf to his partner's cries. Vida looked side to side, panicked. He raised the truncheon. Vida pushed and knocked Lars to the side. The truncheon came down beside her. Vida stepped away from the officer, saw a hole and pushed her way through the crowd. Freed, she ran away, past the tram line and towards the far edge of the vertical shopping mall.

This shouldn't be happening, Bernard thought to himself. *This isn't right. Wake up. Do something. Wake up! Wake up! Wake up!*

His insides screamed but he stood paralyzed with the others. Lars pushed him aside and chased after Vida, leaving Kaspar in the center of the circle, crying and on fire.

24. Memento Mori

Memento mori, it's no lie,
Prince or peasant, one day you'll die.

It felt like a television show. Bernard watched himself run into the circle and tackle the flaming officer to the ground.

Kaspar, too frightened to recognize help, flailed and punched at Bernard. The heat brought Bernard back into his skin. He pressed into the flames, trying to smother them with his body, grateful that his suit was still damp from the day's rain. He ignored the blows raining down on his head and back as he rolled with the officer around the circle. Bernard's clothes weren't damp enough and fire burned his chest. He slapped at the flames. Kaspar's arms dropped and he stopped struggling. Bernard sat up and beat at the smoldering embers on the officer's clothes until the fire was gone, then beat out the few sparks that had lit on his own suit.

Surveillant Kaspar's face was dark. His eyes were closed. His breathing slowed and he passed out from the shock.

Dumbstruck tourists stepped aside as wisps of smoke rose from Bernard's suit. By the time someone thought to call for help, Bernard was gone.

The next morning, Bernard saw a picture of Vida on the cover of a Dutch newspaper. He'd have bought the paper except he'd fallen asleep in the park the night before and when he awoke his wallet was gone.

He spent his next nights sleeping beneath a giant tree in Vondelpark. He spent his evenings avoiding police sweeps and contending with drugged out tourists and other homeless. He begged for money and grew dirtier and hairier as his body decomposed from his illness and lack of nutrition.

Three weeks after landing in Europe, Bernard spent hours coughing up dark puddles in the grass. His lifeless body wasn't found for two days.

Bernard felt himself die and wondered what would follow. Afterlife? Reincarnation? Oblivion?

None of it came. He was in stasis, conscious but not sentient. He felt a connection to his body and realized it wasn't time to let go. He couldn't accept his passing. He wanted to go back. He needed to go back. He needed a second chance and promised this time, things would be different.

Time flowed backwards. Particles rose from the Vondelpark soil and reattached to Bernard's body. Blood trickled through his veins. The cyanosis of his skin turned pale and clear. Pallor left his cheeks. His fingers twitched. A milky film disappeared from his eyes. He lurched onto his knees before grass washed in dark wet chunks of vomit and blood. He sucked the black goo into his mouth. When the grass was clean, he stood up and walked away, backwards.

Flash. Bernard stands near a park bench. A disheveled homeless man shuffles backwards towards him. Both men are angry. The homeless man backhands Bernard across his cheek. Bernard and the man sit down at a park bench, spitting wine into a bottle. When the bottle is full, the homeless man places it in his coat and departs, facing Bernard as he maneuvers through the crowd.

Flash. Bernard sits against a wall as people walk by. Many ignore him, but a few pause long enough to take money from the small cup in his fist.

Flash. Bernard beats his arms against Surveillant Kaspar's body, each punch lighting a new flame. Bernard rolls on the ground with the police officer. They turn and fire gathers from the cement and encircles them. The fire transforms into uniform and skin. Bernard's thrown off the inferno and the fiery man stands up. Surveillant Lars runs backwards into the circle. Vida enters in the same manner, pulling Lars up from the ground. Lars lifts a truncheon from the ground and Vida steps in front of him.

Flash.

Surveillant Lars raised his truncheon. Vida stepped to the side and pushed Lars to the ground. Bernard fought to regain focus. Vida, her face full of panic, pushed her way through the crowd. Bernard made a decision. Lars darted towards the hole in the crowd. Bernard stepped in, pulled his arm back and punched the officer square in the nose. Bernard didn't pause to watch him fall backwards. Instead he turned and pushed through the crowd, chasing Vida into the streets of Amsterdam.

25. Ecotone

Ecotones are conjoined rhythms,
Of two different ecosystems.

Five long-haired gutter punks blocked the south side of the Ubermarkt alley. Vida slammed into an orange-haired teen. The punk toppled into his friends. Bernard pursued, almost stepping on a fallen joint which the orange-haired punk retrieved moments before Bernard hopscotched through the quintet.

Bernard huffed behind Vida, trying to catch up and cursing his body. He thought he'd already used up every reserve of energy that day, but somehow he persisted, aided by the strange sensation that everything before the street show was a lifetime ago. He didn't remember dying, but he felt something, a renewed drive pushing his legs one after the other.

Vida bolted into the next street and turned right. Shopkeepers and bar patrons looked up as she passed. She reached the next corner and stopped, panting.

"Wait!" yelled Bernard.

Vida looked up and regained her panic. She darted down the alley.

Oh fuck, thought Bernard. *Stupid stupid.*

Vida was heading straight back into the Leidseplein.

Bernard huffed behind her, knowing it would be impossible to reach her.

Impossible, if not for the upturned wheelbarrow lying in her path.

"Stop!" he yelled.

She turned her head but her legs kept going. Her right foot landed on the wheelbarrow's belly. Her left foot caught between the lid and the handle. Vida's face flashed a comic "O" of surprise before she whipped forward and crashed to the ground. A loud crack echoed down the alley. Vida rolled off the wheelbarrow and curled over, clutching her ankle. She looked ready to scream, but could only whimper.

Given that her fall avoided her arrest, this was the luckiest thing that could have happened. If there was a word for luck that gives a kick instead of a coronary, or a drizzle of feces instead of a shitstorm, Bernard was too distracted to think of it as he hustled towards her.

"Oh…oh…uhm, don't worry," he said, kneeling before her. "Oh dear."

Vida, still wild with panic, kicked him in the abdomen with her uninjured foot. Bernard felt the thudding pain in his diaphragm and a curious feeling of déjà vu. He didn't know why getting attacked for helping someone felt familiar because the last time hadn't happened. He hadn't chosen to stay and help the ignited officer. This time it was Surveillant Lars, who, by being punched by Bernard, gained the opportunity to beat out the flames on his partner and call for backup.

A police vehicle hurled past the mouth of the alley. Fearing attention, Bernard covered Vida's mouth and sat his weight on her free leg. Vida kicked with her bad leg, hitting Bernard's ribs and causing both of them to yell in pain. Bernard held down her injured leg while his elbows guarded his sensitive regions. He gesticulated to her in pantomime:

We need to be quiet. I'm not going to hurt you. You are very pulchritudinous.

Considering that both his hands were occupied, Bernard was impressed with the clarity of his gesticulations. He was more impressed when Vida responded in kind:

Remove your hand from my mouth or I'll eat your fingers. What the fuck does pulchritudinous mean?

Bernard darted his eyes away and removed his hand from her mouth.

"Great," mumbled Vida, "Stuck in an alley with a crazed psycho rapist."

"I'm not a rapist," said Bernard, showing his palms to indicate he meant no harm. "I'm an American."

"You must be new here," said Vida. "You'll make more friends if you stick with rapist."

"Ah…uhm…." Bernard stammered. "Look, we need to get you to a hospital."

Vida's heel was the color and consistency of a pile of moldy beets.

"Hospital?" Vida asked.

"Unless you aren't fond of it," said Bernard. "Your foot, I mean. We could just wait until it falls off."

Vida focused on an empty spot two feet behind Bernard.

"Where have you been?" she asked.

Bernard looked around. There was no one else in the alley.

"I'm right here," he said.

"I'm not talking to you," snapped Vida.

"No, of course not," said Bernard.

"What should I do?" Vida asked thin air.

"Hospital," Bernard said.

"I said I'm not talking to you," said Vida.

"Uh," said Bernard.

"Don't be crazy" said Vida. "Not him."

"Not whom?" asked Bernard.

"I'm not talking to–"

"Yeah," said Bernard. "I got it."

"Fuck," said Vida. "OK, fine. I'll see you there."

She turned back to Bernard.

"Maya says we both need to go see the King."

"Who?" asked Bernard.

"He's–"

Bernard pushed his hand over Vida's mouth. He held up a finger and pointed to the two officers standing at the opening of the alley.

26. Dweomercraft

The spritely child skipped and laughed,
At the juggler's skillful *Dweomercraft*.

Bernard couldn't hear the two officers, an older male with a buzzed haircut and a female trainee with a brunette ponytail, as they exchanged conversation at the mouth of the alley. Bernard stood slowly, trying to avoid any sudden movements that would be picked up in their peripheral vision.

"Can you walk?" he asked Vida in a hushed tone.

Vida looked down at her ankle.

"I could hop," she said.

"Not good enough," he said.

Bernard knelt down and grabbed one of the handles of the overturned wheelbarrow.

"Shift," he said.

"Why should I?" asked Vida.

"Unipeding down the alley is a spectacle. Trust me."

"Why should I?"

"Why shouldn't you?"

"I'll trust you if you tell me one thing."

"Shoot."

"What does 'pulchritudinous' mean?"

Bernard went red. "We don't have time for that."

"No tell, no trust," said Vida.

Bernard sighed. "It means beautiful. Happy?"

"I'm injured, I just torched a cop, and I'm in an alley with a crazed rapist." Vida shifted herself off the wheelbarrow handle. "I couldn't be happier if we used this wheelbarrow to run over puppies."

"That's the spirit."

Bernard grabbed the other handle and slowly righted the wheelbarrow. The metal base creaked and the wheelbarrow settled onto the cobbled ground. Bernard looked up at the officers, worried that shifting his eyes would call attention.

Bernard held out a hand to Vida. She waited a moment before taking it. He helped her to standing, and supported her as she sat on the edge of the wheelbarrow brim and swung her legs around so she sat inside.

"Tell me how this is the option that *doesn't* call attention to itself," said Vida.

"Shhh," said Bernard. "Fold your legs."

Vida rolled her eyes and complied.

"Dammit!" exclaimed Bernard. He tore off his jacket and threw it over Vida, just as the officers turned and faced the alley.

Bernard stood still. The officers, less than thirty feet away, stopped talking. Bernard sighed, lifted the wheelbarrow handles, and pushed it forwards.

"You're going the wrong way," hissed the wheelbarrow.

"Trust me," said Bernard, though he wasn't certain he trusted himself. He'd never tried to make someone else invisible. He'd never tried to make himself invisible. It was just something that happened.

"I told you, you're going the wrong way," Vida said, peeking from underneath the jacket cover with one eye. The jacket was large but not big enough to cover her knees as they poked out from either side of the wheelbarrow.

"Don't talk," said Bernard. "If we walk away from them, they'll notice us."

"How can they not notice us!" she hissed. "We're heading right towards them."

"It's how people work," said Bernard. "Trust me. Empty your mind. Think of a koan or something."

"What's a koan?"

"A Zen question to clear your noggin. Like, if Buddha fell in the woods, would he make any noise?"

"Probably," Vida said. "He's a big guy. This is insane."

"Just keep in mind that we aren't trying to avoid being seen."

"Of course we are," she said through gritted teeth.

"If you don't want it, they'll notice," mumbled Bernard. "Pretend you don't exist. Like you're a ghost. Can you imagine that?"

"You've no idea."

Bernard told himself there was nothing unusual about an out-of-shape American pushing construction equipment down an alley at midnight. The female officer stared at Bernard as he approached, though she resumed her conversation in Dutch with her partner. Bernard was close enough to pick up the frustrated and angry tone of her voice. Not surprising, given that one of their own just performed an spontaneous fire dance.

Bernard aimed the wheelbarrow between the two police officers.

"Scuse me," he mumbled, sliding through.

The officers cleaved apart. The officer continued her upset diatribe with her partner while Bernard wheeled past. Vida peeked out from under the jacket, incredulous.

Bernard veered down the street away from the commotion in the middle of Leidseplein. An ambulance blocked the view of the center of the square. A few onlookers glanced in their direction but nobody held their gaze for long.

"This is absurd," said Vida.

"We're not away yet," said Bernard.

Vida dropped under the jacket. She began suspecting that everyone was pretending not to see them, and any moment they'd be surrounded by police.

We're going to be stopped, she thought. *We're going to be stopped. We're....*

"Don't do that," hissed Bernard.

"What?"

"Just don't."

Vida took a deep breath, growing more concerned with every bump of the wheelbarrow.

"People look at things all the time," said Bernard shaking his head, "but they rarely see them."

Vida peered over the lid of the wheelbarrow and saw the towering building dropping behind them. She saw the people and the ambulance parked in the middle of the square. She saw the slick sheen of the canal and a dark rowboat that appeared to float upstream just inches above the water. Following the boat, an undulating wave skimmed side to side. The wave disappeared. There was a splash and for a moment, Vida saw a mermaid with blue hair, creamy moon-skin, small breasts and sapphire nipples emerge from the lapping water. The canal-nymph smiled at the flash of recognition. She spread her tail, blew Vida a kiss, and dove under the water before Vida could raise a hand to wave.

27. Cryptozoology

Mermaids and yetis and similar gist,
The bailiwick of the cryptozoologist.

It was Maya who first told Vida about the mermaids.

"I suspect that America's got them in a few places, love, but it's nothing like back home," she said as they lounged in a secluded Omphaloskepsis hot spring. "It's all because of their environment. They need deep water, but they're city creatures, just like the trolls of Belfast, so they congregate in canals."

"The trolls congregate in canals?" said Vida. "That's silly."

"Not the trolls," said Maya as she crept her toes up Vida's leg. "The trolls live in cheap pub bathrooms. The mermaids live in the canals."

"I thought canals weren't very deep?" said Vida.

"Oh, they're much deeper than people think. Most people have forgotten that we built the canals for the mermaids. We built them and promised to keep them clean and in return mermaids told the fishermen where to cast their rods. Most of the time if you dropped something in the water a mermaid would get it back for you, unless it was pretty and shiny and then they might keep it for themselves. It used to be that you couldn't cross a canal without a dozen mermaids calling you in for a swim. You'd have to be careful if you did, because they like pretty and shiny girls and sometimes they try to keep them, too. But that's the risk you take when you hang around with mermaids.

"They don't have the same plumbing we do, what with their bottoms being sushi and all. My great-aunt didn't think about that before she met a merman. She dove underwater and there he was, all glistening muscle and hair matted with seaweed. She swore she only kissed him, though she didn't tell me where, and when she came back from the water she was as preggers as a cheerleader after Homecoming. That kind of thing happens more than you think, at least, that's what my great-aunt told me."

Maya flicked her foot and splashed Vida.

The spring water was warm, but Vida raised her hands to protect her eyes and dropped under the water. An air bubble rose and popped. The water whirled and Maya was pulled under.

Vida rose from the water with Maya's legs wrapped around her waist. Her small body was weightless. Vida ran her fingers over her lover's soppy tangerine dreadlocks and cradled her head against her neck. She tilted her torso to fit Maya's significant bosom above and below her own. Maya's breasts pressed against Vida's chest and her dreadlocks tickled the cranny behind Vida's ear, but all Vida felt was Maya's thumping heartbeat.

"I love you," Vida said.

"Kiss me," said Maya.

So she did.

Bernard looked down at his wheelbarrow passenger. Vida hadn't spoken since leaving the square except to give succinct directions. The streets grew more industrial and less populated, to Bernard's relief, though no one gave them a second glance, as if wheelbarrows were as common as bicycles in the city.

The wind blew through the empty street and Vida shivered. Her sports top and shorts may have been sufficient during her fire show, but Bernard's damp jacket seemed inadequate as the night dropped in temperature. He debated giving her his damp shirt as well, but told himself it was stupid on several counts (not to mention asinine, fatuous, quixotic, sexist, and hyperphilogynic). Vida didn't look like the kind of woman who wanted to be taken care of and Bernard didn't think of himself as the type of guy who could take care of anything. But she was injured and Bernard had this bubbling swell of socio-biological caveman instinct that made him want to build her a fire and protect her from any saber-toothed tigers that might be roaming the streets. It was a strange and not altogether unpleasant feeling. An hour before, he'd desired nothing more than to snuff himself out. Now everything was different.

She continued staring forward and Bernard wondered if he should say something.

Vida had been distracting herself with memories of mermaids and hot springs when Bernard jolted her out of reminiscence with the rudest question one can ask a street performer.

"So," Bernard said, "how much money do you make doing shows?"

Vida bit her lip. She suspected that people didn't walk up to bankers and ad executives to ask how much money they pulled in. Vida had learned to respond in kind.

"I do well enough," she replied, "How often do you masturbate?"

The journey was silent after that, except for the ratcheting bumps as the wheelbarrow rode over the cobbled side-streets. Each jostle sent another shock up Vida's leg, but she didn't let herself reveal the discomfort. It occurred to her that she still didn't know the name of the strange man pushing her.

"Bernard," he said.

She blinked. "You're American."

He nodded.

"How long have you been in Amsterdam?" she asked.

"Just arrived."

"Where's your luggage?"

"Stolen," he said.

"Oh." She thought for a moment. "Welcome to Amsterdam."

Bernard and Vida passed under a footbridge. On the outside ledge of the bridge someone had painted in bright blue graffiti:

> **If the good lord intended breasts to be sinful**
> **He wouldn't have given us two hands**

Bernard caught Vida staring at her ankle and wanted an excuse to continue talking.

"Who's Maya?" he asked.

"None of your business."

"It's fine," he said. "I used to have an imaginary friend."

"Maya's not imaginary."

"But she's not here?"

"She's as real as you are," said Vida.

"That's not saying much."

They stopped at a division in the road. One path sloped downward, the other inclined. Vida pointed up.

Naturally, thought Bernard. He resumed pushing. The hill wasn't large, but he was tired and when they reached the summit he set the wheelbarrow down and caught his breath.

"How much further?" he asked between pants.

"Inches or centimeters?"

Bernard looked at the new view.

"A kingdom fit for the King," Vida said, spreading out her arms.

"You must be joking," said Bernard.

Bernard stared at the dark mountains of discarded refuse and scrap metal. Before he could ponder the implications of such a kingdom, the quiet of the night was broken by a harsh, pleading cry, like a newborn child in distress.

28. Ex Nasus, Ex Mens

Ex nasus, ex mens: Out of nose, out of mind,
He knows with his nose, leaves the rest all behind.

"Wait!" called Vida, but Bernard was gone. He didn't want to leave her in the wheelbarrow, but the insistent, high-pitched cry cut straight to his limbic system. He dodged gargantuan stacks of metal, shadows of bookshelves and broken bicycles, boxes and tin cans, condoms and curry packets. Gnats weaved through the debris, carving intricate mandalas in the air. It was a kingdom for Sarah Cynthia Sylvia Stout; a grand depository of the unwanted, a place where all other junkyards go to die. The wail came again, two piles distant, and Bernard ran faster. He focused on the cries and tried his best to ignore the others, the deep whispers that came from everywhere around him. The junkyard was calling to him, inviting him into its stale embrace.

The cry came louder and Bernard pushed the strange whispers out of his mind. He struggled over a mound of refuse and his foot sunk into a puddle of blackened goo.

"Eghhh," he groaned, pulling up his gob-encrusted foot and setting it on a second level of who-knew-what. The foot found support and he rose onto the pile.

He looked down into a vaginal valley with lips of stacked appliances on either side and a low hanging clitoris of newspapers on the far end.

In the center of the valley, a medium-sized dog stood at attention. He had the face of a pit-bull, the jowls of a bulldog, short and stubby legs of a dachshund, and the long body of a greyhound. His coat was mottled black, orange, grey and he possessed so many criss-crossing scars that his questionable pedigree made him look as if he were stitched together with parts of different breeds. The Frankenpup growled as he paced back and forth around the newspaper mound.

A flash of white skittered across the papers. The dog barked and the white cloud rose to the top of the pile. The apparition looked like a thin housecat on two legs until it stopped moving, gripped its claws into the newspapers and screeched down at the dog.

"*Eeeeeeeeeeeeeek!*"

The screecher was a white capuchin monkey.

The dog planted his short forelegs on the pile and tried to climb the stack, but his frame was too heavy to make it. He let out a frustrated bark and resumed pacing.

The monkey feinted left and the dog took the bait, running around the stack while the capuchin scampered down the pile on the other side. The capuchin reached the ground and a pair of teeth snapped inches from his face.

"*Aieeeeek!*"

Saliva flew from the dog's mouth and he bit at open air. The white monkey returned to the top of the pile and whimpered.

Realizing that the cries had come from a monkey, Bernard felt a momentary pang of guilt for abandoning Vida, but the pang was replaced with indignation. Child or not, the creature was in honest distress. Bernard lowered himself halfway down the valley and stopped on the corner of a discarded stovetop.

"Hey puppy!" called Bernard, "Leave him alone."

The dog swiveled his snout and huffed twice. He turned back to the monkey and continued growling.

"Stop bothering him, you bully!" Bernard lowering himself another step down the valley. "Come on!"

Bernard pursed his lips again and whistled, invading the air with a shrill blast in A minor. The dog perked up and shuffled his awkward frame towards Bernard.

"That's better," said Bernard.

The dog revved his growl to full throttle and charged, clearing the valley faster than Bernard thought possible. Bernard scrambled up the stovetop and the dog collided into it. The stove shook and Bernard toppled onto the valley floor. The dog shook his head and staggered side-to-side. Bernard used the time to scramble to his feet. The walls of the valley were higher and steeper than they'd looked on the outside. The dog charged again. Bernard ran towards a wall of garbage on the far side, teeth and saliva hot at his heels. He grabbed onto a bookshelf and climbed upwards. The dog jumped for Bernard's leg and snapped at air as Bernard pulled himself higher. Bernard cast out his hand, searching for a hold. He grabbed a block of metal. He grappled for another handhold but the surface above was slick with a puddle of rainwater.

"Agggh!" The dog latched onto Bernard's shoe and began growling and twisting. Bernard kicked off his sneaker. The dog yipped and dropped to the ground. Bernard's hands searched for something to use as defense. He grappled at piles of loose trash. Styrofoam, old clothes, pieces of rubber, and other objects Bernard didn't want to think about dropped past his head. The animal growled and leapt. Bernard's grip began to slip.

A large shadow appeared over the lip of the valley.

"Ho ho, boy! Best guard your jewels or you'll be trading that suit for a dress."

Bernard looked up. A giant smiled down at him. The large man had a thick strawberry moustache and matching red hair. Atop his rounded head, a bent clothes-hanger was fashioned in the shape of a crown. Vida dangled piggy-back from the man's neck. Even she looked tiny compared to the towering man who supported her.

Bernard deduced that he was in the presence of the King, but he didn't have time to appreciate the revelation as the dog snarled and snapped again, locking onto the leg of Bernard's suit.

"Yaghh!" Bernard yelled. "Call off your mongrel!"

"He's a stranger to me, son. You'd best give me your hand before he chews off more than your pants."

Bernard reached up while kicking at the dog with his free foot. The animal held his grip. Bernard's hand closed around the older man's.

"That's it, boy, now the other!"

Bernard let go of his support and swung over the valley floor. The dog held on tight to Bernard's pants leg and the two swiveled in the air. Bernard reached up with his free hand. Sweat drained from his gripped palm. He grabbed at the King's arm and his first hand slipped. Bernard dropped. He and the dog and a mound of refuse landed together with a thud and a whelp. Bernard moaned. The dog whimpered. The whimper turned into a wheeze, then a whine that faded and died. Bernard's relief disappeared. The weight underneath him was still.

The dog knew he was dead. It wasn't the first time.

He remembered his first life, warm and safe among the pleasant ossmyrah of his littermates. That life had been heaven. He remembered his first death, being lifted by a large hand and thrown into a burlap sack, the sensation of whirling movement, landing in a watery grave. He found himself reborn in a dark hell, sputtering and thrashing and clawing against the slippery walls of a canal. He scrambled to safety and soon learned that fighting for food no longer involved a playful scramble for the choicest nipple. That first night, his food fought back. He lost half an ear to a canal rat, but gained a meal.

The dog remembered the warmth and safety of his first life and the loneliness and brutality of his second. He always knew that if he died again, he would end up somewhere even worse, spiraling for eternity into darker and darker torments. Thus he fought, and each battle was not just for his life, but for his soul.

When the human fell on him, the dog felt pressure squeezing together his insides, then blackness. This death felt different than the last time. The valley was still. He could no longer smell the human, nor the furry creature that he'd hoped to turn into an overdue meal.

Foreboding shadows crisscrossing the valley pointed towards a dark tunnel carved into the newspaper pile. The path led down into the ground. The dog sniffed. The tunnel smelled deep, dank, and dangerous. It was the path he feared, the dark place that would take him into the next world even worse than the one he'd left. His fears were confirmed as he looked into the shadowy maw of his future. He was no longer a young pup, unable to face a new hell without sputter and struggle. This time, he would be proud. The dog rose up to full height and padded forward towards his damnation.

Hey! Puppy.

He jerked his ears to the side. The call hadn't come from the dark path.

You don't want to go that way. Trust me.

The animal looked up at a glimmer on the top of the valley.

That's right, love. Over here.

The dog stepped off the path towards the dark tunnel and approached the valley wall. He placed one paw up, then another. Unlike before, his short legs had no difficulty scaling the vertical surface and he found himself in no time atop the ridge. Before him stretched a new path bathed in light. It had none of the scent of hardship that he'd expected. This confused and frightened him. He stopped, wanting to return to the first path.

It's okay, love. It'll be okay.

Sitting atop the memory of a washing machine, Maya watched the dog's spirit pad onto the glowing path. She smiled, knowing that paths can circle, and though the animal's journey would be fearful, it would eventually return him to a world of familiar smells and unquestioning love.

29. Recrudescence
Celebrate the in-law's absence,
Loathe the certain recrudescence.

Bernard dug the grave a paw's breadth from the dog's body. He used his hands and was disappointed at the ease his bare fingers slid into the damp soil. Robbed of an easy penance, he dug until the ground thickened with rocks and his fingertips became red and braided. He kept digging.

A large hand rested on his shoulder.

"That's enough, boy. *Abiit ad maiores.*"

Bernard let the hand guide him back from the hole. The King lifted the dog's body and placed it in the grave. Bernard dropped handfuls of earth over the canine and the King followed suit, his enormous fists dropping three heaps of dirt for every one of Bernard's.

The dog covered, the King blanketed the mound with old newspapers. Vida watched perched on the lip of the valley while Bernard and the King stood and bowed their heads. Bernard peeked at the King. Bernard had more than his share of extra weight, but his royal highness looked like someone had started with a Play-Doh Santa Claus and kept adding clay. Wind gusted through the valley and the King wrapped himself in a weathered Persian rug that draped behind him like a royal robe. His hair was titian, his age somewhere between a wise fifty and spry seventy, and despite the somber nature of the event, his eyes and mouth twinkled as if he was privy to the world's funniest joke.

Hoots and chitters erupted from the newspapers. The white capuchin scampered down the pile, bounded towards the grave, and shuffled up and down in a spastic dance.

"Lancelot!"

The King stomped. The monkey stopped bouncing and covered his hands over his tiny face.

"This beast may have wronged you," said the King, "but it is not time for joviality! The passing of an enemy may only be relished before the event transpires. *Accipere quam facere praestat injuriam*! That is the way!"

The capuchin retreated to the newspaper pile and sulked.

The King looked up at Vida.

"You've held your tongue, child. Is there a eulogy in your breast?

Vida shook her head. "I've had enough of funerals. I'll be happy to never see another."

"Everything dies," said the King, throwing a final clump of earth on the newspaper grave. "*Mater memento mori*. If you don't see another funeral, then the next will be yours."

"Fair enough," said Vida.

"Let's not be like that," said the King, gesturing down at the gravesite. "How about an epitaph?"

Vida turned her head.

"I'm not repeating that!" she said.

"Oh!" said the King. "Begging your pardon. I neglected to inquiry if the Lady Maya was in our presence. Does she wish to add something in the way of a suitable farewell?"

"Nothing worth repeating," said Vida, turning back to the King.

"Oh please," said the King. "It is so rare that one gets to receive insights on death from someone who's had first-hand experience. I'm certain her input would be of inestimable value."

Vida rolled her eyes. "Fine."

The King clapped his hands. "Joyousness!"

Vida rolled her eyes and monotoned, "A dog's a dog, a cat's a cat. A fat guy fell on me—and now I'm flat."

Bernard looked down and the King clapped again.

"Ho ho! Simple yet true! I shall carve the headstone in the morning!"

With the grace of a much smaller man, the King vaulted onto an upturned refrigerator, swung his legs over a rotted shelf, and pulled himself up to the top of the ledge. "Now," said the King, "the night's unfriendly. We'll find our respite at the castle grounds!"

By the time Bernard escaped from the valley, the King had lifted Vida onto his back and started down the inky path without him.

Bernard felt a wave of self-consciousness at losing his role as Vida's transport, though the uneven terrain would've made the wheelbarrow useless. The monkey ran to Bernard and chattered at his feet. Bernard lowered one hand. The monkey swiped a claw and skittered away.

The castle was no fancier than Bernard expected: a stack of plywood and corrugated metal that would've offered little more shelter than a doll's house in a hurricane. A stack of oil drum towers buttressed each corner of the building and two lines of open dirt ran around the perimeter represented a moat yet to be dug.

Vida slid off the King's back, wincing as she tapped her injured foot onto the ground.

"*Domus dulcis domus*," said the King, pulling aside a metal sheet and offering them entrance. Vida hopped inside. Bernard followed into the black interior.

"Where's my head?" asked the King. "Pardon me, good sir, pardon me."

The giant pushed past Bernard and fumbled in the dark. A lantern blazed on to reveal a palace in shambles. A pile of rags and newspapers hinted at a bed. A worn table stood on tiptoes with books balancing three of its legs. The middle of the room held a large, brown lounge chair missing most of its upholstery. A reading light snaked over the brown throne. Bookshelves made of cinder blocks and salvaged wood covered three out of four walls.

"The King's chambers," said his majesty. "There's a bit of disarray, I'm afraid. The maids are useless. Why yesterday I caught Consuela shirking her cleaning duties while fleeing with the royal knickers. In olden times, I'd have sent her to the headsman, but it's so hard to get good help nowadays. I don't know what I'd do without Lancelot."

He reached to his shoulder and the capuchin appeared, tilting his head to allow the King to scratch the fur behind his left ear.

The monkey was stark white, or would've been had he lived in cleaner surrounding. As it was his fur was dirty and dreadlocked. His eyes were light red, and Bernard realized the animal was an albino.

Though his white skin made identification difficult, Lancelot was a Yellow-Breasted Capuchin, a struggling species native to the Atlantic Forest in Brazil. His endangered status made him valuable and illegal, his pigmentation made him priceless. The King knew this, but saw no reason to impart the information.

Bernard bee-lined to one wall of the King's bookshelf, stood ahenny and ran his fingers over the collection. He gasped. He hadn't expected to find signs of a true bibliophage in a make-shift shack, but his hands danced along a treasure trove of philosophy and fiction. He admired a first edition of "*Le Petit Prince*" and eyed with covetous wonder a rare copy of Nietzsche's "*Die Kleine Motor Die Könnte.*"

Bernard's fingers itched. He hadn't thought about nicking anything since he had left America, but now his fists shook. He folded his hands into his pockets. This wasn't a packet of gum or a pair of sunglasses. These books had value. He looked around the shack. The King was bent on one knee examining Vida's ankle. Neither of them looked his way. He scanned the bookshelf and saw a black shadow resting atop the spines. His hands darted out and he held the object before he knew what it was.

"It fits you, lad!"

Bernard jumped. The King stood over him.

"I was just looking," mumbled Bernard. H held an old, black bowler. He placed the hat back upon the shelf, but the King retrieved it and gazed at it in deliberation.

"You saved a knight of the realm today, my son." The King pushed the hat to Bernard. "A reward to show the kingdom's gratitude."

"Thank you, no." said Bernard, raising his hands. "It's not for me."

The King frowned. "A royal gift is not a request. The hat is yours." The King palmed it in one hand and placed it atop Bernard's head.

He winked at Bernard. "You even look a bit like him, if I say. He was much thinner of course. Perhaps you share a bit of the soul."

"Whose?" asked Bernard.

"Oh, no matter, no matter. *Noli equi dentes inspicere donate.* You have your quest and farther to go before you sleep. The damsel awaits!"

The king swept Bernard outside. Vida rested against one of the oil drum towers, though Bernard hadn't seen her exit the King's quarters. The monarch pressed a piece of paper into Bernard's hand.

"A map, my boy, to the royal physician. I'd accompany you, but the needs of the kingdom are paramount It's a minor distance the way the handsaw flies. Or is it the hawk? I'm always getting them confused."

Bernard looked befuddled. The King burst out in deep vibrating laughter.

"Oh well," said the King. "Who can tell with the wind blowing every which way? No matter, my boy, no matter. *Nullum magnum ingenium sine mixtura dementiae*, am I right? As for you, my darling...."

The King bounded over to Vida and presented on bended knee a metal bar about two and a half feet long. He helped her onto her good foot and she used the bar for balance.

"Come on, boy," said the King. "No time for dawdling."

Bernard shuffled over. The King placed Vida's hand on Bernard's shoulder.

"Farewell, noble knight!" The King slapped Bernard's back and pushed the two of them towards the darkness. "And fair tidings to you, dear lady, a callipygian beauty such as yourself is always welcome in the king's domain!"

Bernard gazed at the paper the King had pushed into his hand. Below a scribbled map was written:

Schadenfreude

Bernard prepared himself for a wild goose chase ending with a crack dealer. Or an ostrich.

"Ow," said Vida.

"Sorry," he said. "Are you okay?"

"I'll manage," she said.

Bernard looked back. The King waved. Lancelot gave his own gesture.

"I think the monkey is flipping us off."

"I wouldn't be surprised," said Vida.

"Odd dude. What's his story?" Bernard asked. "Some wacko who lost it all?"

"Just the opposite, I'd say."

"I don't follow," he said.

"More's the pity."

The King watched Vida and Bernard disappear. When they were gone, he picked up Lancelot and retreated into his chambers. He blew out the lantern and felt his way to the back of the room. He pulled old rags and blankets around him and curled among the debris, clutching Lancelot's small, furry body against his chest like a bundled child. Soon the two snored in harmony. During the night, a maid came into the King's quarters. She crawled onto his arm, chewed at his shirt, defecated on his sleeve, and scurried off into the darkness.

30. Haberdashery

Heads seeking dapperies,
Haunt haberdasheries.

Vida's poorly-hidden grimace and uneven gait with the metal pole unsettled Bernard. She stumbled and Bernard took the opportunity to slide under her right shoulder. Vida frowned, but didn't pull away. The new three legged, side-hopping beast wasn't pretty, but its pace quickened.

Bernard rotated his new bowler in his free hand. A flash in the inside brim raised his curiosity. He held the hat up to the moon and made out three initials: JFK. The thought of the ex-president wearing such a headpiece was comical, but Bernard enjoyed the fancy that the bowler was once owned by a celebrity. This was the case, though the bowler never graced a president's fingertips, but rather the deft hands of silent screen legend Joseph Frank "Buster" Keaton.

The bowler was no show prop. Buster Keaton wore a flat porkpie hat on-screen. The bowler was Buster's personal possession, a gift from his good friend Roscoe "Fatty" Arbuckle. Buster met Roscoe on the vaudeville circuit and it was Fatty that gave Buster his first break on the silver screen. They collaborated for two years before Buster started his own films. The bowler was a memento from Roscoe to commemorate Buster's new celebrity and their parting.

Buster cherished the hat, even after Roscoe was accused of the sexual assault and murder of a starlet named Virginia Rappe. While history exonerated Fatty, he was one of the most maligned men of his time and it was Buster who turned around to help his old partner find work on Buster's movies under the pseudonym William Goodrich.

Buster treasured the bowler for twenty years, until it disappeared while he was on a boat to Paris with his third wife Eleanor. Buster mourned the hat's loss almost as deeply as he mourned Roscoe's death seven years earlier. Buster assumed that the hat had been lost in transit, when in fact it'd been stolen by Joseph Klakton, a deck hand who shared Buster's initials. Klakton discovered the hat after rifling through Buster's belongings in the storage hold, but grew to feel so guilt-ridden that he hid the bowler away for thirty-five years, never even allowing himself to put it on his head. He showed it to no one but his son. Joseph told his son that he'd recovered the hat after it'd flown off the actor's head. He claimed to have chased after him, but Buster climbed into a car and drove away before he could hand it back.

When Joseph died, the bowler came to Joe Jr., who hadn't the slightest idea what to do with his father's strange bequest. He thought of his father as an eccentric asshole and figured the musty old hat deserved nothing but a toss into the trashcan. A friend of Joe's suggested that the hat might have value to a collector. Doubtful, Joe took it to be appraised.

The bowler perked several ears when it went up for auction, including those of avid cinephile Vitoria König, who purchased the hat in a bidding war for €14,500. Vitoria König possessed an impressive collection of movie memorabilia, but intended the acquisition as an anniversary present for her husband George. The gift was well received, though it was only a few weeks later that George König forswore his money, left his wife, and announced himself the ruler of a kingdom no one else desired.

31. Schadenfreude

Neighbor smashed his new Toyota?
The urge to laugh is schadenfreude.

The dark green building was three stories high and sandwiched between rows of apartments. A brass plate listed a single name on the front stoop:

A. E. Schadenfreude

Bernard's legs ached. He fought the urge to curl up on the door stoop for a four-hour power nap. Vida pulled away from his shoulder and collapsed on the edge of the porch.

"You good?" he asked.

"Yeah," she exhaled. "Thanks."

Bernard rapped the knocker, then rang the doorbell. He wondered what time it was. It couldn't have been more than an hour or two before dawn.

He heard scuffling on the other side of the door. A voice yelled something incomprehensible.

Bernard turned to Vida.

"How's your Dutch?" he asked her.

She shrugged. "I know "*U hoeft niet te applaudisseren, maar geef me geld.*"

"What's that mean?"

"No need to applaud, just give me cash."

She gave a half smile.

Bernard turned back to the door. "We only speak English!" he yelled.

"Well in that case," came a muffled reply in a heavy German accent, "you definitely can't come in!"

Bernard looked at Vida and back at the door. "It's an emergency."

"It's four in morning!" Pause. "What kind of emergency?"

"Bad ankle."

"Not enough emergency! Go to the hospital."

"We can't," said Bernard. "The King said you'd help."

The door swung open. An old man in a pink robe and fuzzy white slippers stood frowning in the entryway. He would've been bald if not for the tangled grey clumps of hair extending from each ear.

"It's bad enough that I have to visit George in that hellhole, now he sends the trash to me? In my home? While you interrupt important business! Do you know how long it takes to become a level 85 druid? Ugh. Anyway, come in, come in, bring your wife inside and we'll look her over tip top."

"She's not my-" said Bernard, but the old man was already fumbling down the hall.

"Ow! Assweasels! Damn!"

"Stop being a fidget," said the doctor, kneeling down and pushing with one finger on the purple bruise at the back of her ankle.

Vida yelled out again. "That's it! Cut it off," yelped Vida. "It's not worth keeping."

"How long ago?" asked Schadenfreude.

"About six hours," said Bernard from the other side of the doctor's living room. He flipped his bowler with one hand and it spun and plopped onto his head. Bernard grinned. He lifted the hat and twirled it on his finger. He didn't know it would work, but the hat spun around once, twice, three times before he decided not to tempt his luck and stopped. He felt silly, but it was as if the hat wanted to spin.

"I think she tore her talofibular ligament," Bernard said, still focused on his hat. "There might be a fracture above her lateral malleolus. I don't know what else."

Schadenfreude glared at Bernard.

"Let me tell you something," said the doctor. "You are very stupid."

The hat hit the ground.

"I…I'm sorry," Bernard stammered. "I'm not a doctor, I don't know what I'm talking about. I was wrong?"

"No, you were right," said the doctor. "That's why you are stupid. Why do you know these things and let her walk around for six hours? She hurt foot? No problem. Go to doctor. Doctor fix. This looks like she sprained foot, then you let her play football. You are stupid."

The doctor shook his head. "Stay right here. I'm returning."

Aldo Schadenfreude grunted as he padded down the hall, uttering a curse under his breath about "noobs." Confirming the two were out of view, he pushed the door to his study. The door stopped halfway. He gave a stronger heave and the door slid open, spilling a box of pharmaceuticals onto the floor. Containers rolled towards his desk until stopped by a fortress of cardboard. Mounds of penicillin barricaded themselves against a file cabinet, beside a medical library made inaccessible by stacks of barbiturates. Aldo found a slip-on foot cast behind a case of morphine. He retrieved a roll of gauze from a pile of IVs and surgical gloves. A bottle of hydrocodone was pulled from a collection of opiates plentiful enough to knock out a blue whale.

Aldo admitted that it was refreshing to help someone with an actual problem. He'd been royal physician back when his highness was a mere corporate mogul worth millions of Euros. It was the wife that demanded most of his attention back then, disrupting Aldo daily with a host of imagined ills. George König never had so much as a cold, but once he made his curious shift in lifestyle, Vitoria König endured a series of nightmares involving her husband stubbing a toe and having gangrene devour his body. She compiled a list of hundreds of possible maladies that her husband might contract, complete with color pictures of *Necrotizing fasciitis* and advanced stage *Epidermodysplasia verruciformis*

(Schadenfreude longed for the days before WebMD) and ordered Schadenfreude list any supplies that would be needed to remedy such conditions. Schadenfreude's home was soon flooded with boxes, including medications he never presumed to mention, medications years from commercial availability and a few whose discovery would merit lengthy incarceration. Aldo wasn't pleased when Vitoria announced everything was to be kept at his home, but his residence was five blocks closer to the junkyard than his office, a difference Vitoria insisted would mean the difference between life and death when the inevitable arrived.

The slip-on cast and gauze cradled Vida's foot and alleviated a fair amount of her discomfort. Schadenfreude retrieved a pair of crutches from his hall closet. They dug into her armpits, but she didn't complain as he led her to her bedroom.

"Voilà," said Schadenfreude, "A room fit for a queen, yes? Sad to say, there is only one of this variety. Your boyfriend will have to make do with less pretty quarters."

A four-poster mahogany bed with a gold and amber comforter rested against the far wall. An Indian tapestry above the bed depicted two red elephants dancing with entwined trunks. A tall emerald encrusted hookah sat in the far corner.

Schadenfreude took out a large pill bottle from his pink robe. He opened the container, poured half of the pills into his robe pocket and handed the remainder to Vida.

"These will help with pain. Do not take with alcohol and use as little as possible. You will feel like you can walk on your foot after you take them. Do not do this."

She gave the old man a paternal peck on the cheek. "Thank you so much, Doctor."

"Please: Aldo. Excuse my grumpiness. It is late, and raids do not form themselves. Thank you for the granting of my home with your beauty. If you need anything, do not hesitate to ask it."

Bernard was led to a room wide enough for the small, lumpy cot that butted against three walls.

"Here," said Schadenfreude. "It was for the lady who cleans. I do not make messes, so she was fired."

"Thanks," said Bernard. "Did I do something wrong?"

"You are just stupid. You let such a beautiful woman get damaged. Americans do not know how to treat their women."

"I told you, she's not my woman."

"Then you are more stupid."

"I don't think I'm even the right sex," Bernard said, but the doctor had already walked away.

Bernard lay on his cot. Sleep was the logical option, but his eyes couldn't close without seeing Vida's face. He wondered if she was thinking about him.

"What if she killed him?" Vida pondered. The bed was soft and comfortable and thick, warm blankets surrounded her, but she couldn't get the police officer out of her head. What if the fire had devoured him until he was nothing more than a black husk? Could she live with herself for running away? How could she wake up each morning knowing that she had caused someone's death?

Not your first time, baby doll.

The voice spoke without blame, but Vida felt it anyway. Maya was right. If it wasn't for her, Maya never would've gotten into street performing, never would've traveled with her, never would've–

Never would've seen the world. Never would've fallen in love.

"Liar," said Vida. "You were trouncing around the world when you met me. I was just the stupid girl who got caught up in your path. You'd have loved someone else."

I did. You knew that. You even joined me once or twice. Remember Saki?

"I don't want to remember anything."

I never loved anyone like I loved you.

"Lot of good it did you."

There's no sin in living.

"Look who's talking."

At least one of us is alive.

"But it shouldn't be me! You should be here. The world shouldn't work this way."

You've lived long enough not to believe that line, love. The world works how you want it to work.

"Then I want you not to be dead, okay? I want you here. Not as a ghost or a figment in my head. You, my wife! I want you to hold me and tell me it was all a stupid dream."

Hmm, I don't think it worked. You didn't say the magic words.

"You're always joking.

After what I've seen, sugarclit, it's impossible to take anything seriously.

"Maybe I should find out for myself."

Don't say that. Where would I be without you?

"I want to be with you."

What if this is the only way?

"Don't you know?"

How could I? I'm just a figment of your imagination. What a cruel thing to say. Sticks and stones can't break my bones, but love will always hurt me.

"I'm not living my life anymore. I'm just doing what I think you'd do."

You're doing a great job of it. Oh, how I miss ending my summer days with a good cop torching.

"Stop!"

Your taste in men is up my alley, too. I always liked them brainy but spineless. Although they were always so sad when I screwed their socks off and didn't call them the next day.

"I don't want to screw his socks off."

You should. It would do both of you some good. I don't think he's been with a woman that didn't have pixels.

156

"It should've been me."

Everything happens according to destiny. Do you remember the Zorya?

"What are you talking about?"

Nevermind. Just the ramblings of a figment.

"I don't want to let you go."

S'okay, love. That makes two of us.

Vida drew the covers over her head and said nothing more. When the light sensations came over her skin, she tensed but didn't move away. She squeezed the blankets until they were a cocoon around her. There wasn't space for a single slip of paper to slide between her and the sheets but the sensations came anyway. Her hands gripped the blankets. Even with her thighs pressed together, Vida could feel Maya sliding inside her. The motions continued and in no time at all, Vida came. She kicked out and struck her bandaged ankle against a bedpost. The shock and pain added to the chorus of tension, pleasure, and regret.

Vida curled into a fetal position, her pointer finger resting in her mouth.

"Maya?"

Yes, love?

The comforter lifted off Vida's body and floated in the air.

"Tell me a story."

The comforter drifted down.

I only know ghost stories.

Cool hands pressed the blanket around her.

"I want a happy story."

I know a story about us. A true story.

"Is it happy?"

All stories are happy if you end them early enough.

III.Education

32. Exegesis
**Exegetical explorations,
Lead to biblical pontifications.**

"Griefer! You leave this minute! You leave now!"

Bernard sprang up from the tiny bed. Schadenfreude stood in the doorway in a pink robe, striking the doorframe with a newspaper.

"Now! Get going! Choppy chop!"

Bernard managed to keep one hand over his boxer shorts as he snatched his clothes and bowler before the doctor whisked him from the room. Schadenfreude pushed him up the stairs. His English grew more discombobulated as his tirade continued.

"Going you are, stopping anything you doing now! *Verlassen*!"

Bernard arrived at the main floor. Vida hovered at the bottom of the stairs and rubbed her eyes. The doctor didn't slow as he pushed both of them out of the house.

"Hey, watch it," said Bernard. "She's debilita—"

The door slammed behind them. It opened again and the crutches landed at Bernard's feet, followed by a newspaper that tumbled down the stairs as the door closed.

"Are you okay?" he asked, retrieving the crutch and passing it to Vida.

"Couldn't be better," she said. "Nice boxers."

Bernard looked down at his white boxers emblazoned with a big yellow happy face. He was too tired and shaken to feel embarrassed.

"Thanks," he said. "How come you're clothed?"

"Disappointed?" she asked.

"Devastated," he said, fumbling to put his pants. "Do you have to be watching?"

"I can't help myself," said Vida. "You're so—hairy."

"I'm not that hairy," said Bernard, buttoning his shirt over the random patches of black hairs on his chest. "Besides, hirsuteness signifies virility in most cultures."

"I doubt there's truth to it," said Vida. "Maya had nary a hair on her and she's as horny as they come."

The implications of her statement distracted Bernard more than the mixing of tenses.

"Any guess at "*Hij kan niet overleven*"?" asked Vida.

"Why does it matter?" he said, pulling on his shoes.

Vida pointed at the newspaper spilled out on the stairs. The front page had two pictures, one of the Leidseplein, the other of Surveillant Kaspar.

Bernard picked up the paper. He'd comprehended nothing of the Dutch spoken since his arrival, but the written word was a different beast. He scanned the article for cognates while he slid his arms through his jacket.

"I see '*infirmirary*,'" he said. "That's a good sign. Better than morgue. I can't give a perfect translation, but the tone isn't happy."

"What would you expect?" said Vida. "Street Artist Who Torched Officer Sought to Award Key of City?"

"We need to find a place to hide out," said Bernard heading down the street and pulling newspapers from the porches as he passed.

"What do you mean *we*?" asked Vida. Her crutches clacked down the block.

"I mean you, me, and Casper the horny ghost," said Bernard, sliding another newspaper underneath his right armpit.

"This isn't your problem."

"I punched the cop. I'm as guilty as you are."

"I don't think so."

She held up the paper. On the front was the officer, young and un-barbequed. She folded the paper over. A half page seemed to discuss humanitarian relief for Venice. On the other side, an artist's rendering of a woman was underwritten with *Amerikaan Zocht*.

"They did a good job," said Bernard. "It looks just like you, minus the purple streaks."

"It's black-and-white," said Vida. "Of course it looks like me. I had two-hundred witnesses staring at me for an hour. I couldn't have caught more attention offering ten-for-one gangbangs."

"This might be the only city where that might not draw much attention."

"Go to Thailand. My point is: one picture, one person. They're looking for me. Your invisibility trick put you in the clear."

"What are you going to do?" asked Bernard. He slid another newspaper under his arm and the entire collection spilled to the ground. He began retrieving them again. "You're not inconspicuous in those crutches and you can't do this by yourself. You need me."

The Top Five Least-Effective Statements to Get Vida to Go Along with Something:
   5. Everyone else is doing it.
   4. It's probably not contagious.
   3. I know what I'm doing. My brother's an ophthalmologist.
   2. Come with me, babe. I have the biggest cock in my fraternity.
   1. You can't do this by yourself. You need me.

Vida hobbled away in the opposite direction. Bernard threw the pile of newspapers under a small car and followed her.

"Do you have any money?" he asked. "Do you have a place to stay? What are you going to do?"

"I'll think of something," she said.

Bernard pondered his options.

"Wait!" he said.

She paused.

"I was wrong," he said. Vida turned with a doubtful expression. "You don't need me. I need you."

Bernard mulled over what to say.

"You don't know me," he said. "Until recently, there wasn't much to know. A few days ago I learned…something, and ever since I've been trying to figure things out. I don't believe in fate, but everything fell into place when I arrived here. All my life I've done things I hate. Last night I saw you draw people in by doing something that you loved."

"What's your point?" asked Vida.

"I think," Bernard stopped. What was his point? He didn't know. Then it hit him. It sounded absurd in his head and he wondered if it would sound less crazy if he said it out loud. He drew a sharp intake of breath.

"I think–this is going to sound bonkers, but–"

"Yes," said Vida, growing impatient.

"I want you to teach me to be a street performer."

Vida laughed so hard she had to grab her crutch with both hands. Her skepticism bolstered Bernard's resolve.

"I'll help out in exchange," he said. "You need to hide out for a while. I can be your feet. I'll pay you whatever you want. I'll even give you a–a manager's fee as a percentage of my street earning."

"Ten percent of nothing," she snorted, "I'll be rolling in the dough! Look, this isn't something that anyone can learn. It's something that you are."

"Give me a chance," said Bernard, surprised at his own determination. "I didn't realize it until now, but–have you ever known with absolute certainty that something needed to be part of your life?"

"Yes," said Vida, "but that doesn't mean it ends well."

She hobbled past him. Bernard overtook her.

"But you have to try," he said, stopping in her path. "If you don't believe in me, that's fine. No one has ever believed in me, before now I've never believed in me. I have to do this and I need your help."

"What would you do?" she asked. "Invisibility isn't a street skill. It's the opposite."

"I think," said Bernard, pulling the bowler off his head. "I think I'll do hat tricks, as a start."

"You just got that."

"Yeah but—it'll work."

He twirled the bowler in his fingers and tossed it into the air. It somersaulted twice and landed on his head.

"Not bad," she said. She looked him over. His face was sincere. In his bluish-silver eyes was a fragile glimmer of hope.

"Tell you what," she said. "Land that spin again and we'll work something out."

Bernard deliberated.

"No," he said.

"What?"

"You heard me. No. I need this. I'm not going to bet it on a lucky spin. It's worth too much to me."

"Fair enough," said Vida. "What's your offer?"

Bernard's hand grazed the pocket that held his life's saving. It was a lot thinner since he bought the plane ticket, and since his suitcases were stolen it was all he had.

"I'll pay you?"

"No good. It's a fool's game to do anything for cash that I wouldn't do for free."

"I'll assist you."

"Don't let the crutch fool you. I can manage."

Bernard took a stab in the dark.

"It'll be fun?" he said.

Vida raised an eyebrow.

"Sluntzombies!" she said. "OK, here's the deal. First, you help me find a place to crash."

Bernard smiled. "Then you'll train me?"

"Then I'll test you. *If* you pass, *then* I'll train. Don't worry, it'll be fun."

"For which one of us?"

"Me, you'd better hope, or you'll never see me again."

Bernard thought it over. He didn't have much of a choice.

"Fair enough," he said. He held out a hand. Vida bent at the elbow and grabbed it without moving the crutch. They shook.

"By the way," said Bernard as they walked together down the street.

"What?" replied Vida.

"*Sluntzombies* is not a real word."

"Says you," said Vida.

A heavy gust of wind pushed through the street and Bernard's bowler toppled off his head. Vida adjusted a crutch and failed to notice Bernard absent-mindedly kicked back his left heel. The bowler bounced off his foot, flew into the air, and returned to the top of his head.

33. Ephemeral
Coatlicue's inevitable,
Everything's ephemeral.

Vida and Bernard passed five hotels before settling on Becker's Hole, "*The Two-Star Hotel with the One-Star Price.*" It was the most appealing, in that no one was sleeping on the front porch and the English graffiti was spelled correctly. The hotel was a few side streets away from Dam Square, across from a head shop creatively named "The Head Shop."

"If you start doing shows," said Vida, "I can watch from my room. It'll be like that Hitchcock film, minus someone get killed. Unless you suck, maybe then I'll get lucky."

Bernard looked around. There wasn't a person nearby who looked like they hadn't slept in their clothes.

"Why would I perform here?" asked Bernard as he helped Vida up the hotel steps. "Shouldn't I be at the Leidse-whatever?"

Vida laughed. "The best performers from around the world play the Leidseplein. I said I might teach you. I didn't promise miracles."

The hotel was cramped but surprisingly clean with beige walls, a brochure rack, a couch with most of its cushions, and a twenty-something clerk at the front counter with a pony-tail and a lit cigarette dangling from the side of his mouth.

Vida slipped over to the brochure rack and tried to look nonchalant with her gimp ankle and streaked hair while Bernard approached the counter. The affable clerk had a slight French accent and kept looking over at Vida as he explained the hotel rates.

"You get a *dees*-count if you pay a week in advance."

Bernard winced and slid most of his savings across the counter. He wondered how much street performers made.

This will work out, Bernard thought. *It has to.*

167

Their joining rooms each had a single bed, a mini-fridge, a lamp, and a desk. They shared a bathroom, separated by doors that could only lock from the outside.

"Here's the deal," said Vida, peeked out her window. "I help you for as long as I want. If I say it's over, it's over. You need to spend at least six hours a day working on your show. You can do hat tricks or become double jointed or learn to flip your eyelids up or whatever you want. I don't give a damn, but work on something. And wash that suit, it smells like it's been dragged through the canals. Most important, you do what I say. This isn't a democracy. There's one captain of this ship, and it's me."

Bernard shrugged. "So if you say jump, I say how high?"

"If I say jump," she smiled, "then I better hear your feet hitting the floor."

Bernard left Becker's Hole with a shopping list scrawled on hotel stationary. He recognized several of the requests: extra clothes, hair dye (auburn), sunglasses, and a notebook. The food requests seemed reasonable for the most part and displayed an appetite that despite cultural immersion had a strong Anglo bent, except for "Jars of Nutella (15)". The deck of playing cards made sense but what were gyros? And what the hell was Vla?

Vida was flopped out on the bed when he returned with several bags.

"Sweet monkey Christmas," she said. "Presents! What'd you bring me?"

Bernard dropped the bags on the bed. "I got lucky and found a market a few blocks down. There was even a Mediterranean place that had your gyros." He pronounced *gyro* with a hard G. Vida grimaced.

"That's *Yee-ro*. Rhymes with beero. And gimmee. I'm famished."

She yanked the lamb-and-salad filled pita out of his hand and attacked it with every tooth at her disposal.

"Oh god, this is good." Her eyes rolled up into her head. "I can't believe I used to be a vegetarian. You want one?"

"No thanks," said Bernard.

"You'll change your mind soon. This is the street performer's...mrmmm...staple cuisine. I think they put crack in it. Now it's...mrmmmm mmrrrrrmm mrrrrm. Hold on." The last of the gyro disappeared. "Ahhhhhhh. Much better."

She licked the wax paper, crumpled it into a ball and flicked in into the trashcan.

"Now," she reached under her pillow and pulled out a stack of papers, "I've got a present for you."

Bernard clicked his pen on and off and stared at the top sheet:

Question #1: Why?

He swept up the pages and marched into Vida's room. Vida didn't look up from a game of Blondes and Brunettes set out on her bed.

"Finished already?" she asked, moving the queen of hearts.

"This isn't serious," said Bernard.

"Didn't say it was."

"So I don't have to answer it?"

"Didn't say that either."

"What does this have to do with street performing?"

Vida played a card and smiled.

"Professor Callahan's Consciousness Test has been proven to weed out nine out of ten hopeless cases under ideal laboratory conditions. Please note that there is a two hour time limit, points are deducted for interrupting the Professor's game of solitaire, individual results may vary, and some animals were most-definitely harmed in process."

Bernard returned to his room.

Question #2: Why not?

Question #5: Do you believe in God? What about the Easter Bunny? Who would win in fight? Draw your answer.

Question #28: Is it crackers to slip a rozzer the dropsy in snide?

Question #73: What would you die for? What would you live for?

Question #79: If a necrophiliac is someone who wants to make love to dead people, what do you call someone who wants to be fucked when they're dead?

Question #82: "The dancer moved like a hunk of bolts and iron." In a world where machines have become more fluid and humans more obese, how long until the above sentence becomes a compliment?

Question #86: Complete the Analogy:
A Sadist is to Masochist as an Employer is to...?

Question #92: Are we limitless beings learning to live within limitations? Or are we finite beings grasping for the infinite?

Question #101: Why did Venice sink into the ocean?

Question #104: Use the following words in a sentence: Violet, Brie, Unclefucker, Assweasels, Sluntzombies.

Question #119: On no set date, the Micronesian fishing village of Ulithi celebrates the holiday of pi supuhui. On this day, couples join up and frolic in the woods. The only rule is you can't screw the person you are married to. Their rate of violence per capita is significantly lower than any equivalent American town. Discuss.

Question #122: Why is it considered heterosexual to engage in guy sports? If I was a straight guy, wouldn't it make more sense to do ballet and touch women all day instead of a bunch of sweaty men?

Question #130: Einstein said that the only reason for time is so everything doesn't happen at once. Did he have some good drugs or what? And speaking of drugs, do you want to try one of these pills the doctor gave me? They make me feel like my body is stuffed with cotton candy.

Question #133: The Joybox is one of many Japanese love hotels dedicated to romantic encounters. While on a sociological excursion to investigate this phenomenon, Maya and I discovered that a journal is placed in each room for visitors to chronicle their adventures. Aided by our host and translator, Saki, there was one story above the others that truly curled our stockings. What was it?

Question 135: What's the most beautiful thing you've ever seen?

Bernard pictured Vida on the Leidseplein, torches in hand, grinning like she owned the world.

Bernard had lost all track of time when he turned to the final page.

Congratulations!

In Nepal, Buddhist monks spend days or weeks constructing intricate mandalas with colored sand. They believe the mandalas generate positive energy for the universe and for those who view them. When they are completed, the sand is swept into an urn, destroying the mandalas and demonstrating the impermanence of all things.

In the same spirit, please take this test and dispose of it in the manner of your choosing.

-Professor Callahan, PhD, OCD, ADD

34. Zorya

**"Remember the Zorya," the soothsayer said,
"Three lovers: The Mother, The Trickster, The Dead."**

Bernard stormed into Vida's room and raised the test papers. Failing to get a reaction, Bernard realized she was asleep, face down in a pile of cards.

He looked at the papers in his hand, each page chronicling his responses to her absurdities. He tiptoed over and opened the window. Chill poured inside.

"Whatcha doing?" accused the voice on the bed.

Bernard couldn't hide his irritation as he held the papers out the window. "Defenestrating."

"Why?" she asked.

"You told me to."

"And?"

"And jump equals sound of feet."

"Did I say that?"

"Yes," he said.

"Did I mention how independent thought was better than dogmatic adherence to authority?"

"No," he said. "You neglected that one."

"Did you enjoy the test?"

"Honestly?" he asked.

"Is there an alternative?"

Bernard considered. "I thought it was pointless. Then I started to have fun with it. It wasn't like anything made sense, so I had the freedom to be creative."

"Good. I had fun writing it. You had fun doing it. Why destroy it?"

"Because you said—"

"Artists should never let someone else dominate their creations. Now hand it over."

Bernard moved towards the bed and Vida's outstretched hands, but stopped mid-step. He lowered his eyes and turned back to the window.

The pages somersaulted through the cold night air.

He didn't look up as he left the room.

Vida stared at the closed door separating their rooms. She brushed aside the cards. She stepped off the bed and hobbled to the window. She slid the window open. A lone paper stuck to a lower ledge. She grabbed the corner of the window, leaned out, and snagged the page with two fingers.

Vida smirked as she read the first answer, laughed out loud at the second, and sighed when she reached the bottom. She poked her head outside and scanned the sides of the building, but no further prizes waited within reach. She stuck out a hand. Her pores tensed with the cold.

Vida hopped to the side of her bed and retrieved the lone crutch. She slid open her front door. The hall was silent.

She reminded herself that she needed to keep a low profile and promised that she wouldn't spend more than ten minutes outside.

Twenty-eight minutes later she returned with a handful of papers that, after reading, she stashed under the mattress of her bed.

Bernard distracted himself from sulking by playing with his bowler. He was certain that if he could remove his head from the equation, he could get the hat to roll from one hand to the other in one pass. Eventually, he discovered if he leaned back at the proper moment, the bowler cartwheeled along his chest and landed in his other hand. Satisfied, he moved on to rolling it from a hand to a leg and back again.

His frustration over the test dimmed when he discovered a flourish. By spinning the hat when it reached his hand or foot, it kept its momentum and continued spinning to another limb. This allowed him to string the moves together and the six isolated tricks that he'd been playing with (Hand-to-Hand, Hand-to-Foot, Foot-to-Hand, Hand-to-Head, Foot-to-Head, and Super Fancy Spinning Flourish) merged into a routine. The final result was only a few minutes long, but it was something.

He fell asleep holding the bowler against his chest.

In his dream, he was surrounded by excited tourists. Every time he flipped his hat, they cheered and tossed gyros at his feet. The show ended and the crowd disappeared, leaving him with a single gyro in his hand. He held it up to Vida, who was perched on a street lamp, but she didn't acknowledge him.

"She can't come down," said a woman's voice behind his ear.

"Why not?" he asked.

"Because she thinks I'm still up there. Do you remember the Zorya?"

Bernard turned but the street was empty. He realized he was dreaming and decided to eat the gyro in his hand and eat a second after he woke up to see if they'd taste the same. He woke when he brought the gyro to his lips. He registered his erection wrapped up the bed sheet. He closed his eyes, thinking not about gyros but of the seductive timbre of the dream woman's voice. He hoped if he fell asleep quick enough he could run into her again, and perhaps see her this time.

His eyes opened with the morning. He suspected he had another interaction with the dream woman, but the memory, like his erection, was gone. Only a sticky-wetness in his boxers remained.

35. Deipnosophy

**To be the sharpest wits at tea,
We practice deipnosophy.**

"Analphabetic floccinaucinihilipilificators!"

Bernard stomped into Vida's room with his bowler and a tight fist.

He'd woken her that morning with the giddiness of a six year old at Christmas. The enthusiasm was unacceptable to Vida, for whom mornings began at noon. Bernard was itching to demonstrate his new moves, but Vida slurred out a complicated grocery list and was asleep again before he reached the door.

He returned in no time at all with a heaping bag of foodstuffs. Vida couldn't think of another distraction and groggily sat up to watch his routine. His hands shook and he dropped twice. She made him repeat it and he flowed through without error.

Vida frowned.

"You've never touched a juggling hat before yesterday?" she asked.

Bernard twiddled the hat's brim. "Nope."

"And that move you do at the end where the hat rolls around your belly?"

"The Hula Hoop? Uhm, that's what I call it."

"Where did you learn it?"

Bernard looked surprised. "Nowhere, I just discovered it when I was fooling around this morning."

"Huh," said Vida. "Not bad."

She didn't want to admit it, but the routine was impressive. She'd never seen a juggler pick up a skill with such ease, herself included. Bernard wanted to take it straight to the street, but Vida held him back. She coached him the rest of the morning and into the afternoon. Bernard was an able student. Vida could throw out an idea once and he made it work. They exhausted her catalogue of hat tricks and started brainstorming new ones. By dinnertime they'd expanded the routine to twelve minutes and Bernard insisted it was time to try it outside. Vida knew what he getting into, but let him go anyway.

"I hate people." Bernard opened his fist over Vida's bed and dropped five pieces of copper, a torn movie ticket, three raisins, and a joint.

She held the joint between her thumb and two fingers. "This is something."

"It's a pity joint," said Bernard, "and I don't smoke."

Vida shrugged, passed the spliff to her other hand, waggled her fingers, and the joint disappeared. Her eyes fell on the food bag. She rummaged through and grabbed a mango.

"My tricks suck," he said.

"They don't," said Vida, "but that doesn't matter. It's not about the tricks. They don't give you money because they like your tricks. They give you money because they like you. You need to lighten up out there."

"I'm trying," said Bernard. He tossed his hat upside-down into the corner of the room. The copper coins ricocheted off both walls before landing inside the hat one-by-one.

"They don't care," he said.

"Of course they don't care!" said Vida. She dug into the mango with her fingers. The juice ran down her black top and onto her belly. "They have lives. They're going to the movies, going out to eat, going home to jack off. Why are you important enough to deserve their attention?"

"I don't know," said Bernard.

"Wrong answer," she said. She plunged another hunk of mango meat into her mouth. "You have the skrills but hyou mnyeeed to let hufu sheeyoo."

"What?"

Vida swallowed. "I said, you have the skills but you need to let people see you. I don't know if that's something you can learn."

"I'll do it," said Bernard. "Whatever it takes, I'll do it."

"Whatever?" she asked.

"Whatever."

"I'll remember you said that." She excavated another piece of mango and held it out. "Want some?"

Bernard fixated on the beads of juice rolling down her arm and dripping into a small reservoir on her stomach. He pictured himself a thirsty traveler at the edge of the pool, dipping his hands into the liquid oasis and lapping it up, the juice spilling down his face as–

"Oh," he said, "I, uhm, I've never had one."

"Criminal!" she accused. "The mango is the world's perfect fruit. It was Adam and Eve's downfall, don't you know?"

"I thought that was an apple."

"The book just says 'forbidden fruit.' It doesn't mention a Mcintosh from a mongoose."

"So it could be anything."

"*Exactamundo.* I don't buy the apple. It's not sexy enough."

"Why does it have to be sexy?"

"That's the point, right? They bite into the fruit and notice their nakedness. That's the story. They feel a stirring in their ape-loins and they have a new connection to each other, by themselves with no other God in the middle. So God gets jealous."

"Hence the old heave-ho," said Bernard. He reached for the half-ravished mango. His fingers slid into the husk and juice splashed out from his fingers. Vida inhaled. Bernard looked up at her. She smiled. He pulled out the fruity pulp and pulled away, embarrassed. He touched it to his tongue. It had a tangy sweetness. He placed the morsel into his mouth and chewed.

"Not bad," he said. "Certainly a top five contender for forbidden fruits."

Vida looked amused. "Top five? What could trump it?"

Bernard's brain flipped through a rogue's gallery of fruits.

"The pomegranate," he said.

"Hmmm," mused Vida. "I could see that. Those things take commitment. I'd hate to think it was a decision entered lightly."

Vida removed the last bits of mango, gave half the remainder to Bernard, and lobbed the pit into the trash can. They finished together and swallowed. Each brought up a hand to wipe juice from their respective chins. They snickered and looked away.

Vida sopped at the mango oasis on her belly with her sheet. Bernard realized he could be helping her and got embarrassed at the thought of touching her. He stood up and retrieved the pennies from his hat in the corner. He sat back on the bed, closed his eyes, and tossed them blind. One after another, they clinked into the bowler. Then he spoke. "Hey Vida?"

"Yeah, Bernard?"

"What does Maya think?"

Vida wasn't sure she heard right.

"I mean," said Bernard, "about the forbidden fruit thing. If she's around."

"Uhm—yeah she is," said Vida.

Vida laughed.

"Well," he asked.

"She says she saw your show, and we should paint you silver and sell you as a living statue."

"Funny. What does she think about the fruit?"

Another pause.

"She said she doesn't think. She knows."

"*Knows* knows?" asked Bernard, tossing his penultimate penny into the hat. "Like, eldritch secrets from beyond the grave kinda stuff?"

"Maybe. I think she's pulling my leg."

"OK, so what is it?"

"She says it was a tomato."

"Didn't the fruit come from the Tree of Knowledge?" he asked. "Tell her tomatoes don't grow on trees."

Vida relayed.

Bernard tossed the final cent. "Well?" he asked.

"She says I don't need to translate and she can you hear you fine."

"Great, and...?"

"And she says snakes don't talk either, but sometimes the truth isn't as important as the story."

36. Ecdysiast
Tantric stripping not to be missed,
From Maya the mystical ecdysiast!

Vida sent Bernard out for dinner and matches. His return took him along the Herengracht canal. He watched the water fill with elm leaves as he finished off his first gyro. He had to admit the dinner had a certain addictiveness about it. The wind picked up and Bernard hurried on, kept pace by several tourists still dressed for summer. His suit kept him warm, but the sky was cloudy and more rain would come any moment.

He started up the hotel stairs when the clerk called him over.

Bernard approached the desk with caution. Did they know he checked Vida in with a false name? Should he have come up with something more creative than Norma Jean Baker?

The clerk asked Bernard to wait and disappeared into the back.

Bernard grabbed a postcard of the Dam Monument. Without looking, he bent the card in an arch and flipped it into the air. It flew, looped, and returned to his hand. He tapped his feet and looked into the back room, but couldn't see anything. The clerk was gone. He threw the card and caught it again, then again.

"Splendid!" said the clerk, appearing from a side door. The postcard flew up and fell behind the counter.

"Sorry?" said Bernard.

"The postcard. I've never seen anyone do that."

Bernard looked down. What postcard?

The clerk held out an envelope.

"What's this," asked Bernard.

"From your...friend? She asked that I give it to you as soon as you came in. She also mentioned a gratuity?"

Bernard grumbled, flipped through his dwindling bankroll, saw the number "1" and passed it over. The clerk beamed and Bernard realized that he'd tipped him a ten. He cursed his carelessness. He should've remembered there weren't any single Euro bills.

"She also said that you'd have a few things for me?"

Bernard opened the envelope and read the page inside. Damn. Ten Euros suddenly seemed reasonable.

Bernard set two greasy gyros on the counter and bent to the ground. He untied his shoes and kicked them off. His socks followed. He set the bundle on the counter. He slid off his jacket. He undid his shirt buttons. The shirt came next.

"Uhm," said the clerk, "I do not think this…."

"I know," said Bernard, shaking his head "I know."

Bernard removed his pants, placed them on the counter, and exited the front door of the hotel.

Vida's note fluttered to rest on the hotel's couch.

Heads up soldier!

To be a lean, mean, street performing machine, you must be fluent in the art of negotiation. Nowadays, "Give The Shirt off His Back" is rarely seen literally applied.

Your mission:

I. Strip down to yesterday's wonderful boxer short/bowler/monkey hair ensemble.

II. Go outside.

III. Acquire a replacement outfit. You must gather said outfit from clothes worn or carried by passerbys. You may not offer money or any other form of physical barter. You may offer tricks, pleads, whines, jokes, or sexual favors.

Advice:

Banking on the generosity of pedestrians will take you as far as a quadriplegic at a tractor pull. Make it interesting. The less you need, the more they'll give. You don't need to get everything at once. A shirt here, a pair of pants there, and you'll be done in no time!

Take care, Soldier, and Godspeed!
~Capt. Callahan, ROTC, USMC, ASAP

37. Hypnagogia
Truck driving for days and the road's lasagna?
It's not the meth, it's just hypnagogia!

Bernard shivered. His arms did their best to cover his exposed paunch and hairy chest. He squeezed his knees together for fear of jostling his boxers, which had two overlapping folds in front of the yellow happy face and no buttons to hide any offending parts. He was certain that the slightest movement would expose his temperature shrunken genitals.

"Hey, how's it going?" he said to a young Dutch couple.

The pair dropped their heads to one side and quickened their pace.

"I was wondering…." Bernard trailed off with the couple's hasty retreat.

Great, he thought. He looked up at the solitary light on the hotel's third story. She watched him from her room: her warm, safe room.

A raindrop hit Bernard in the eye.

Vida watched the couple flee from the near-naked man and wondered if she had gone too far.

Maybe she'd seen too many cheesy martial arts flicks. This wasn't a case of wax-on, wax-off and Vida was no wizened Asian man. Besides, those characters were fiction. Vida was real, not some altruistic, omnibenevolent plot device. She might say her intentions were good, but if she was honest with herself, she knew part of her wanted to know how far she could push him. How much would he do in the name of training?

Bernard stared at the coin in his hand. It was a fifty-cent piece, literally thrown at him by a middle aged man in a blue suit who did a double take before hurling the coin and running away. Bernard spun the piece in the air and heard the muffled fwump as it landed in his open palm. On impulse, he balanced it vertically on his hand with one finger and flicked the coin. It spun like a top and careened towards the edge of his palm. He flipped his hand over and the coin spun onto the back of his hand. The coin fell and he caught it in his palm before it hit the ground.

A boisterous chant erupted from the end of the street.

"Hup Hup Holland,
Hup Hup!
Hup Hup Holland,
Hup Hup!"

Around the corner, a group of carousers turned onto the block. The group consisted of tall, red-faced men in orange-and-white jerseys and a brown-haired young woman who clung to the arm of the largest male. The carousers stumble-marched down the street repeating their slurred sport's chant. The eight bodies stretched the width of the pedestrian streetway. Bernard backed towards the hotel steps.

Something told him this wasn't going to end well.

Bernard thought invisible thoughts as the horde approached. For a moment, Bernard was certain they would walk right past him. The tallest of the group, a shaven-headed bruiser, did a double take in Bernard's direction. He broke out in a grin.

"Heh!" He pointed at Bernard. *"Leuk ondergoed!"*

The group halted, more or less together, though alcohol diminished their ability to brake on a dime. One by one they noticed Bernard.

"Uhm," said Bernard, "Sorry?"

"I said," said the man, "Nice underwear."

The girl laughed.

"Uh," Bernard looked down. "Thanks?"

The bruiser laughed. The others joined in. The group turned back down the street. Bernard started to breathe again. All he needed to do was let them pass and he could head back inside the warm hotel a failure.

Overhead came the fluttering of a chiffchaff heading south for the winter. Trailing the bird was a sound he picked up along the journey. The tune could've been heard if any of the drunken revelers perked their ears, or if Vida hadn't retired to bed after feeling guilty over watching Bernard shiver, or if Bernard wasn't distracted by the fear of ridicule and violence from a gang of sports enthusiasts. Had anyone listened as the chiffchaff fluttered overhead, they would've heard the faint sound of a calliope.

Something shifted and Bernard yelled out, "Hey buddy!"

The group turned. Bernard fingered the coin in his hand.

"What do you want, naked man?" asked the bruiser.

"I'll give you fifty cents for that jacket."

"You're crazy," said the bruiser. "This cost me 200 Euros."

"Oh, okay," said Bernard.

They turned again. Bernard knew he should keep his mouth shut.

"Hey," he yelled, unable to stop himself. "How about for your girlfriend!"

Wake up, love. You've got to see this.

Vida's eyes shot open. There was a knock at the door.

Not a regular knock. More like a thud, similar to the sound you'd hear if an American found out he had cancer, flew to Europe, decided to be a street performer, spent a night outside in the cold wearing boxer shorts, got beat up, rejected, climbed up two flights of stairs, and then collapsed with exhaustion on the hotel room door.

Almost like that sound.

But not quite.

38. Nikhedonia

Nikhedonia is earned elation,
Pleasure derived from delayed expectation.

Vida opened the door and Bernard flopped onto the carpet.

The first thing that caught her eye was the hat.

No, hats. There were six on his head piled one atop another.

"It was incredible," Bernard mumbled. "I talked trash about this monolith's girl. I thought he'd pound me. But he laughed. Then there was this lady. And I thought...but she didn't. And more people stopped."

Vida couldn't count the layers of coats and shirts and pants. It was as if Bernard had walked into a thrift store and asked to try on one of everything. Bernard's eyes were glazed over and unfocused, but he kept talking.

"It was a game. You were right. Have nothing? Fuck you. But the more I got, the more they gave me. God, I feel tired. I spent half an hour trading smooches for underwear. I don't know why I thought it would work."

He let out a half-constricted chuckle and pointed to his crotch. Over his pants he sported over a dozen pairs of women's underwear in a rainbow of colors. Sandwiched within the set was a pair of men's boxers.

"Come on," said Vida. "Let's get you up."

She pulled at his slumped body and they stumbled across the room.

"It was like a drug," he said. "I've never done one, but that's what it was like, I'm sure of it. They loved me. You can't imagine what that's like! Ha, of course you do. But I've never—"

He staggered into his bedroom and closed the door. Vida heard shuffling and then a double thump to indicate that he may, or may not, have made it onto the bed.

39. Vitoria König

Vitoria never appeared a young maiden,
She sprung into the world a vicious harridan.

"Listen, Jerome. If I have to repeat myself, you won't have a job by the end of the day. You won't have a job tomorrow, you won't have a job next week, you won't have a job a year from now, because I'll find whatever work you get, I'll buy the company, and I'll fire you again.

"Everything's ready for Saturday. We have a great big banner above the building in fifteen languages that says 'Grand Opening on Saturday'. We have signed contracts with over eighty stores to open the biggest shopping center this city's ever seen and it's all going to happen: When?

"Right, Jerome, Saturday! Who said I was an idiot to hire you? That's right. I say it. Every single day."

There was another short reply. Vitoria took the opportunity to reach a slender arm into the limo bar and refill her glass of gin. On the opposite wall, Spencer Tracy stood in a courtroom arguing with Katharine Hepburn. The volume was off, but Vitoria knew the lines by heart. She squeezed her mobile until the plastic buckled.

"Jerome, don't fuck me up the ass and expect me to thank you because you offer a reach-around. Why do I have this whore's tit of a building inspector telling me to delay opening? Everything was inspected months ago. We paid so many bribes I thought we were in Korea. What does it matter which one? Jerome, I'm on a thin line right now. Take care of things. I don't care how. If he wants a bribe, get him a bribe. Buy him a car, put his kids through college, suck his dick, I don't care. I want my building open in three days. Three days, Jerome.

"I'm going to call you back in–" she glanced at her phone, "twenty-five minutes and all I want to hear is 'Vitoria, it's taken care of.' Do I make myself clear?"

She hung up before an answer was possible and slouched into the limo's leather seat. She took four small blue pills and two large white ones from her purse. It was 11am and she'd already put in a full day's work. She downed the pills with the gin and lit a cigarette. This wasn't going to be a good week.

Her limo stopped. Katherine watched Spencer pretend to cry.

Vitoria sipped her glass and stared out the tinted window. A hint of her reflection stared back before the window lowered. Her long hair was streaked with grey, wrapped tight and held down with two jade chopsticks. Her eyes were dark green surrounded by darker shadows. She couldn't remember the last time she'd slept in a bed, napping in the limo during the ten minutes between appointments was more efficient. The window lowered and revealed a large man outside the vehicle. He moved with focus, dragging a heavy metal canister before the front of a disheveled shack. As usual, the King gave no indication of her arrival. He stopped to wipe his brow. His face beamed in the sunlight. He seemed happy and she cursed him for it.

"George," she called out, pronouncing the name with two soft G's. He didn't respond and she didn't expect him to. When he did speak, it was to address the monkey perched on the shack roof.

"After the parapets, our real work begins, eh boy? *Fallaces sunt rerum species.* If the people say build, then build we shall. *Amantium irae amoris integratio est.*"

Vitoria scowled. She didn't know what was worse: his ramblings about castles and kingdoms or his frustrating slips into Latin, a language he knew she didn't speak.

"George," she repeated. "I'll have no more of these shenanigans. Come home and quit playing these foolish *games.*" The last word came out like it was chewed gum discovered free floating in her €1300 Chloe Paddington handbag.

"Don't do this, George. We need you. I need you. The site's coming up next week. You know that, you're out in front every day watching those circus rats. I want you with me. I'm sorry about what happened with the garden house. You'll have free reign of the home, I promise."

She referred to an incident two months after her husband's increasingly erratic behavior. Problems started when George König stood up in the middle of an intense board meeting and walked out of the room. They culminated in a March 19th golf game where he veered off course in his cart and drove the head of Sony Japan towards a lake. A frightened Mr. Nobuyuki dove from the cart and watched George König speed off over the greens. No one heard from George for a week, until he appeared bare-chested and babbling on the front lawn of the König's Amsterdam estate. Vitoria received the news on a jet to Sumatra. She re-routed her flight and ordered the housekeepers to lock her husband in the garden house in the interim.

The servants reported loud crashes for the first three hours, then plaintive howls that persisted into the evening.

Then, total silence.

Vitoria arrived home to find the doors of the garden house busted open and a bookcase floating in the pool. George König disappeared with the clothes on his back and his pet Lancelot. He left behind a wife, a fifteen bedroom estate, a collection of model castles, €650 million in assorted holdings, and a hand-written note discovered on the floor of the garden house.

Everyone around me is hopelessly insane.
What can a man do when those around him play out the lives of madmen?
The wise man sees illusions for what they are. The strong man confronts them.
The caring man nurtures the afflicted.

I've done none of these things. I've coddled the illusions. I've bought into my fellow's fictions until I could see them plain as day, and I've fought against those who would challenge them.

It serves no one to play out the fictions of others. I've continued to do so out of weakness and greed. When your neighbor's fishing in the desert, you must teach him the error of his ways. You don't grab a pole and join him.
My crimes are worse. I've become wealthy selling fishing boats to nomads.

"George! What did I do wrong? Tell me what to do! God dammit, George!"

Vitoria pressed a button and the window swallowed her husband's beaming face. At the last moment, Vitoria tossed out a wrapped package containing a first edition of *"Dialogo Sopra i Due Massimi Sistemi del Mondo"* signed by Pope Urban VIII.

She pinched the bridge of her nose and breathed into her gin. She knew he'd work for a few hours and then head over to the Leidseplein. It'd been spiteful of her to order the police to shut down the street performers, and what a disaster that turned out to be. She had a hospitalized cop, a renegade performer, and a public relations mess. No one would connect her with the incident, but she didn't want the Ubermarkt to have any association with a tragedy eating up valuable headline space.

Vitoria König was proud of her ability to put her entire focus on a problem until a solution was reached. Years ago, she had set her sights on George König. At the time, naysayers claimed that her promotion to partner in König Industries was a prize of the marriage. Few realized that it was Vitoria's business acumen and fiery determination that first caught George's eye, her ability to match him tempest-for-tempest in the boardroom that won his heart.

Vitoria had one goal: Bring her husband back. She pictured her situation and the desired end and begun to formulate what it would take to get from one point to the other. No possibility, no matter how severe, was censured. No moral filter was applied.

Her glass was refilled and drunk again before she instructed her driver to take her to the hospital.

Vitoria's limo passed over the Herengracht at the same time a red rowboat propelled itself underneath the canal's bridge.

"What do you think you're doing?" a wave demanded.

Schrödinger's Boat stopped.

"I'm sorry," said the boat. "I don't understand the question. I'm doing what I'm doing. What other option is there?"

"Let's not bring tautologies into this," said the wave. "You're going the wrong way."

"I'm going the way I'm going," said the boat.

"Are you a salmon?"

"No, I don't think so," said the boat.

"Well, if you aren't a salmon," said the wave, "then what business do you have SWIMMING UPSTREAM!"

"First of all, I'm not swimming," said the boat, "and upstream or downstream, this is the way I want to go."

"But it's just not done!" said the wave. The water bubbled up, foaming onto itself until it was as high as the boat's rim. "The waves decide how the canals flow! Unless you've some sort of mechanized method of propulsion, it's your responsibility to fall in line! Look at you! You're not even touching the water. Turn around!"

"Why?" said the boat.

"BECAUSE I SAID SO!" The wave grew until it hid the moon and the boat had to dip its stern in the water to see the top of the crest. "Turn around or I'll SINK YOU into the BOTTOM OF THE CANALS!"

"Hmm," said the boat, "That does sound like an interesting place to visit, but I think I'll go there another time. Thank you though."

"FINAL WARNING!"

"Now you're being silly. Have a nice day."

"YOU ASKED FOR IT!"

The wave hurled itself into the small red boat. Water curled and surged, but the boat continued ahead as if there was no obstruction at all. The wave stopped when it realized it was beating empty air. It considered turning around and pursuing, but knew it would be hypocritical and continued forward, embarrassed and determined not to tell anyone about the encounter.

The bridge saw the entire thing, however, as did the moon. The moon told the mermaids, who laughed and kicked their tails and promptly forgot it, because mermaids are like that. A pair of waxwings overheard, however, and they flew to Leidseplein where they told a canal rat. The canal rat had reached the square in hopes of seeing a street show, but the pitch was empty. The rat took the story to her home in the basement of the Leidseplein's crimson tower, where she told her family the story of "The Blustery Wave and the Intransigent Boat." Her family paid little attention to the story, because rats are great storytellers, but lousy listeners when the tale isn't about food. Deep in the basement, however, a grouping of pylons who supported the weight of the building listened with rapt attention. Most of the pylons dismissed the story as a fiction, but some thought that the story of the boat that defied its own design meant something more, and one by one they started asking questions.

IV. Chaos

40. Proteus

Meet the formless Esteban,
The protean chameleon.

"Should you be perambulating?" asked Bernard, panting to keep up. "The doctor said–"

"Only a few more blocks," said Vida.

"What about the police?"

Vida planted a crutch and swung around 180 degrees to face Bernard. She managed the acrobatics without her right foot touching the ground. Vida had swallowed three hydrocodone before leaving the hotel and she felt like she could be up for anything, including kickboxing or flying without a plane.

"Don't worry about the police," she said with a larger than usual smile. "They don't come into this area without riot gear."

"I feel so much more comfortable," Bernard replied, but Vida was already down the street. Bernard followed, trying to avoid eye contact, without looking like he was trying to avoid eye contact, with the dirt-encrusted loiterers along the tenement stoops. Bernard did not belong there and he knew that the shifty eyes watching him knew it, too. Vida drew none of the attention. She moved like she was always where she was supposed to be. Vida could have hobbled along in the middle of night wearing nothing but a diamond necklace and no one would've accosted her.

Vida turned into an alley. Bernard followed. Four figures in pirate garb lounged on wooden barrels in the middle of the alley. Two of the pirates wore matching black hats, eye-patches, and red-and-white striped leggings. The other two were dressed in corsets, with bright red rouge and long colored wigs. It took Bernard a moment to realize that the two in wigs were men and the two in pirate hats had the hint of breasts bound underneath their white tunics.

One of the pirates noticed the new arrivals, took a swig from an unmarked brown jug, adjusted her hat, and stood blocking the path.

"Ahoy there," said the pirate.

"Oh," said the second, pushing the costumed brunette off her lap and standing beside the first. "Ahoy and halt!"

"None shall pass," said the first, unsheathing a wooden sword.

"Without permission," said the second, pulling out a second sword. The two looked at one another and nodded.

"Hey wait," said the corseted redhead pointing at Vida. "I think that's—"

"Quiet, wench!" said the second pirate. "We have our orders from the captain. Private meeting, none shall pass."

Bernard stepped in front of Vida and eyed the two pirates with matching garb and identical cheekbones.

"Haven't we met?" asked Bernard.

"Hah!" said the second pirate, pushing a braid of bleached white hair under her hat. "Surely I'd remember a sorry swab such as yourself."

Bernard leaned in to look at her, eye to eyepatch.

"I'm winking," she said without fluttering her exposed eye. "Can ye tell?"

The pirate made a playful bite at Bernard's nose. He jumped back.

Vida stepped between them. "I thought Talk Like a Pirate Day wasn't for two weeks."

The pirate looked at Vida, then the crutch. "Ye might know our holidays, and ye might be sporting a wooden leg, but that don't grant ye passage."

"But—" interjected the redhead on the barrel.

"Quiet, wench!" said both pirates in unison. The redhead hushed, but Bernard watched him/her gesture to someone beyond the alley's opening. Bernard shifted and saw a trio of goofy looking men wearing red clown noses. One of clowns looked up and patted his companion, a shirtless Spaniard who looked the goofiest of the lot. The Spaniard waved and approached. One of the buffoons grabbed the Spaniard's leg, spilling him to the ground. The Spaniard somersaulted to standing, dusted off his chest, and walked towards Bernard.

As the clown approached, Bernard noticed a peculiar change. His walk lost its goofy cantor. His posture grew more erect and his muscles more defined. He pulled off his red nose. His grin was replaced by a sneer. Reaching the group, he yanked the jug from the pirate's hand, took a deep swig, and dropped it onto a barrel.

"All right, ye useless scalawags. What's so important I'm pulled from me meeting?"

"Nothing, Cap'n," said the first pirate, standing at attention. "Just some stowaways we're about to send into the drink."

"Well, good job then, we can't....Hold on, there. Vida! Lassie!"

The Spaniard leapt over the barrel between the two pirate guards. He was two inches taller than Vida, with golden eyes and wild jet-black hair that reached just below his shoulders. He faced her with a wide smile and pulled her into a ferocious hug.

"Estoban, darling," said Vida, pulling back without breaking the embrace. "Careful, I'm broken."

Estoban backed from the hug and lifted his left foot. "So you are." He turned to the two guards. "Fools! Ten lashes to the both of you for keeping her!"

"I tried to tell them," said the redhead.

"Come," said Estoban, pulling Vida by the hand. "My apologies about the crew. That's what I get for using mermaids as guards."

Bernard looked back at the pirate women. One of them blew him a kiss. He turned to see Vida and her friend leaving the alley.

The alley opened into a small plaza. In the middle of the square was a statue, or what used to be a statute: a single leg jutted up from the pedestal. A goateed juggler stood beside the bronze leg, passing clubs with another man on the ground. The two clowns sat against the wall of the opening, blowing smoke rings from invisible cigarettes. A young girl in a plaid skirt stood under a theatre marquee playing with two sticks and what looked like a giant yo-yo. A pair of blonde men stood against a far wall. Another man ran up between them, sprung off the wall, flipped into the air and landed on his feet.

Bernard was so busy watching the performers that he almost missed the next transformation in Vida's new companion. Leaving the alleyway, Estoban lost every trace of the pirate captain persona. His shoulders rounded, his posture became less rigid, and he grew a pronounced limp. Estoban and Vida stopped between the jugglers.

"It's wonderful to see you," Estoban said, heedless of the juggling clubs whizzing past their heads. "We heard about the Leidseplein. You know you always have a place here."

"I didn't want to burden you," said Vida. "You have your hands full with the church."

A club slipped and flew towards them. Vida snatched it out of the air and tossed it to Estoban. Estoban flipped it overhead without looking. It landed in the juggler's hand.

"Cockmonkeys," said Estoban. The two walked away while the juggling pattern continued. "We've plenty of room and you're never a burden."

Bernard circled the long way around the jugglers. On the other side of the square a dilapidated old theatre marquee read:

WELCOME TO THE CHURCH OF SIN
ALL YE WHO HAVE ABANDONED HOPE, ENTER

Bernard trotted behind Vida and Estoban through the theatre's double doors. In the middle of the foyer, the concession booth had been replaced with a bar. Above the bar, a poster announced:

Burlesque on the Bounty!
A Glam Circus Pirate Spectacular
Directed by Estoban Del Sol

Two drag queens sat at the bar: an African with a short green wig, and an East Indian with curly black locks and brown highlights. Estoban sat with his back to the two drag queens and addressed Vida with expressive hand gestures.

"Really darling, we've had our hands full with those bitches over at the city council. They've been riding our backs about taxes."

"I thought you were exempt," said Vida.

"We are, gorgeous, we are. But some norms are raising a stink about whether we're quote—for the public good—unquote. Of course, it's the pious pricks who're causing the trouble. They didn't mind when we started taking delinquents and teaching them to busk on the streets, but once we started up the cabarets, oh boy. I told them it's easier to train for the stage than the street and getting people to pay for a little flash and kink is a no-brainer, but the way they go about it's like we're converting the nation's youths into homo prostitutes. No offense, Kiki."

"None taken," said the green-haired drag queen. "Bitch."

"Slut," said Estoban. "Oh my god, where are my manners." He turned back to Vida. "I haven't asked about Maya. Is she around?"

"Not right now," said Bernard and Vida at the same time.

Estoban raised an eyebrow.

"And who's your lovely friend?" asked Estoban.

Vida swept a hand towards Bernard. "Allow me to introduce Amsterdam's latest street sensation. Bernard's new to the game but already producing shows that can only be described as *priceless.*"

Estoban rose from his bar stool and placed his hand atop Bernard's. "Charmed and I do mean that. Any friend of Vida's...."

Estoban turned away and passed through the doors of the main theatre. Vida and Bernard followed.

"It's been such a hassle these last few days," said Estoban. "I haven't slept a wink. After the protest on the Dam–"

"Wait," said Vida, "What's the Dam got to do with anything?"

"You haven't heard?" asked Estoban. "About the moratorium?

"Moratorium?" repeated Vida. "The police officer said something about restricting shows on the Leidseplein."

"Not just the Leidseplein. After your little stunt, they outlawed busking in the entire city."

"They can't do that!" said Vida stopping underneath the mezzanine.

"It's true, but they did," said Estoban, marching down the aisle towards the front of the theatre. The large stage was decorated with purple-and-red feather boas that draped along the walls and down the lip of a giant pirate ship. Estoban reached the front of the stage and stopped. He stood alone.

"The living statues filed complaints with the city, but everyone else is waiting until Saturday, when..." He turned his head side to side. "When...When...I was saying...." He slumped against the side of the stage and bit his fingers.

Vida pressed on Bernard's shoulder, indicating for him to wait. She maneuvered down the aisle to Estoban. As she approached, he blinked several times, stood and smiled. Vida whispered something. Estoban pointed to a doorframe covered by a theatre scrim. The two disappeared backstage with matching, staggered limps.

Vida returned by herself ten minutes later, took Bernard's hand and led him backstage. They passed a room filled with costumes and makeup mirrors, ducked under a stairwell leading to a second story, and headed into a large office where Estoban reclined on a leather chair behind a mahogany desk. The door closed behind Bernard, and he and Estoban were in the room alone. Bernard sat on a free chair. He didn't know what to say, so he looked around the room. It was an administrative office and lacked the cheesy glamour and half-finished construction of the rest of the building. Neither man spoke for a few minutes. By the time Estoban broke the silence, Bernard had forgotten that there was another person in the room.

"When I was ten years old," said Estoban, "an octogenarian doctor of questionable credentials told my parents that I had schizophrenia. The diagnosis fit none of my symptoms but gave my desperate parents immense relief. Until you walked through that door, I didn't know that *'mimeophrenia'* was infinitely more accurate."

Estoban picked up an obsidian paperweight from the desk. He hefted it twice in his hand and tossed it up onto the bookcase over his head. The case rocked and a Bible on the top shelf tipped over and landed in Estoban's lap. He smiled.

"Fascinating," he said, "I'm coordinated when I'm around jugglers, but this—it's as if the entire world's a Rube Goldberg machine waiting to be activated. You must have so much fun...."

Sorrow flashed across Estoban's face.

"You've got no clue, have you?" asked Estoban.

He opened the bible. The center was hollowed out. Estoban removed a small bag filled with blackish herbs.

"They heaped medications on me when I was young," said Estoban. "I spent most of my teen years so doped up on tranquilizers I could barely speak. Everyone thought that my condition was something to overcome. I thought that too, until I spent seven days in Peru on an ayahuascan medicine journey. Ayahuasca is a psychic and literal purgative, and as I bent over a stream vomiting out the last of my medication, Don Marcos told me that schizophrenics were the untrained shamans of past cultures. He was paraphrasing Joseph Campbell, of course, but at that moment an opening appeared in the forest canopy. The aperture widened until the forest disappeared and a bright whiteness enveloped my vision."

Estoban poured the blackened herbs into a small jade mortar on the desk. He held a pestle in his right hand and ground the herbs against the jade. "Nietzsche said that if you stare too long into the abyss, the abyss stares back at you. I learned it holds true for the light as well. I understood why I was so confused around the doctors and psychiatrists when I was young. None of them knew who they were any more than I did. I'm only as healthy as those around me. I decided afterwards that by helping others find themselves, I was healing myself as well. Why are you here, Bernard?"

Bernard shrugged. "Vida brought me."

"That's not what I meant." Estoban closed his eyes. The grinding of the pestle slowed and stopped. His eyes opened. "How much longer do you have?"

Bernard shifted in his chair.

"Don't worry," said Estoban. "I won't tell her. I won't tell her about your feelings, either. Those were unmistakable, by the way. I had to hold myself back from asking her to stay in the room. I've always loved Vida. Most people do, I suppose, she has that aura. But you... I feel this pull to her like tides to the moon. I suspect I could find her with my eyes closed if you were near me. Ha! Compared to the pain of love, the pain of death is but a shadow. But it's soon, isn't it?"

Bernard nodded.

"I wonder what would happen if I was around you when you died. I wonder if I would expire too." Estoban tilted the mortar's black powder into a small ceramic mug. He squeezed a water bottle until the mug was near full and stirred the mixture. He shoved the mug across the desk. It flew off the table and landed in Bernard's hands. Bernard stared into the mug. Blackened goo stared back.

"What is it?" Bernard asked

"Communion," Estoban replied. "Everything. Nothing. Nothing you don't already have within you. Salvation if you want it, but I don't think you do. Unlearning a lifetime of sociological conditioning can take a lifetime. But there are shortcuts."

"Is this dangerous?" asked Bernard

"No sensible doctor would recommend you to do this in your condition."

"All my life," said Bernard, "I've felt like there's this enormous truth I've never been able to grasp, as if the answers are waiting, but I didn't know the questions."

"Ask and thou shalt receive."

Bernard raised the concoction to his lips. "Is this going to cost anything?"

"This is a church," said Estoban. "Enlightenment is free. What you do with it is up to you."

Bernard drank. The thick liquid stuck at the bottom of his throat and he gagged and coughed.

"How long will it take?"

"About half an hour," said Estoban, rising from his desk. "We'll have a bucket nearby if you need to purge. Don't fight it. Trust me on this one.

"On the way," said Estoban, ushering Bernard out of the office, "perhaps you can tell me why I shoved this stack of pens down the front of my pants."

41. Ablution

Grubby spirits in need of ablution,
Cleanse yourselves in liquid solution!

Bernard followed Estoban down the backstage hall and to a stairwell. Bernard reached the first step and his foot buckled. He steadied himself on the wooden railing and climbed half a dozen more steps before his foot refused to lift. He stood still for a moment and grabbed for the wall.

"I think...."

Bernard tilted his head and pitched backwards. He heard Estoban yell for Vida. He felt nothing when he hit the ground, he only knew it happened because the ceiling stopped moving. Voices asked him if he was okay. He tried to tell them he felt great, but the words didn't come. Two pairs of hands slid underneath him, one at his shoulders and one at his legs. Someone grunted and he floated into the air.

When the moving and grunting stopped, Bernard felt himself on a warm, undulating surface. His logical side told him he was on a waterbed, but it felt like a river. Hands slid out from underneath him and pet the sides of his arms and the top of his head. Someone kissed his forehead. The hands pulled away, leaving him buoyed alone on the warm river. The water pulled him. He sailed downstream. Bernard knew if he opened his eyes, he'd see green woods on either side of a bank and bright sun warming the water.

The current picked up, a little at first, then faster.

Bernard's comfort diminished.

Something was wrong.

Why did he think he was safe? He couldn't swim. His body rocked up and down as it shot through the water. He sunk. He flailed out his arms, but there was nothing to hold onto.

The river opened its mouth and swallowed him. Waves gnashed at his body. A long wet tongue of water pulled at him, forcing him to the bottom. He cried out but his throat filled with water. He coughed and sputtered and knew this was it. He struggled until he couldn't fight anymore. His legs kicked out once, twice, then no more.

It was time.

But it wasn't.

His body rose to the surface. Warm purple sunlight beat down on his closed eyelids. He bobbed downstream. The water sped up again, but Bernard didn't care.

Farther ahead, he heard the hum and crash of a waterfall. The course was inevitable and this time he didn't struggle. The crashing grew louder. He slid faster. Bernard took a breath and bit deep into his lower lip as he was pitched feet-first over the edge.

42. Resistentialism

Humans and objects face a great schism,
"Lights want to turn red," says Resistentialism.

Bernard jolted awake. He was on the floor of an apartment. There was no one else in the room. On the table to his right, flies buzzed around a half-finished bowl of Cinnamon Toast Crunch. On his left sat a television and a toppled stack of adult DVDs: Alice's Adventures Out of the Closet, Orgy She Wrote, Moby Dick II: Thar She Blows, The Postman Always Comes Twice, The Never Ending Orgasm, Girls Interrupted, The Little Spermaid, Snow White and the Fourteen Dwarves, Sister Acts, Womb Raider, Bum Pirates of the Caribbean, James and the Giant Penis, Sex Toy Story, Honey I Blew the Kids, Pippi Longcocking, All in the Family, and Grease.

He was back in his old apartment.

Had it all been a dream?

"You wish, Dorothy" said a gruff voice above his head. "You're dead. You were about to leave when you collapsed on the floor. No one's found you because you don't have any friends."

"I'm not dead," said Bernard, "Not yet."

"You might as well be."

"What do you know?" asked Bernard. He stood and paced the room, searching for the speaker. "I think I know about myself more than you."

"Oh yeah?" asked the voice.

Bernard grabbed at his head and yanked the hat off his head.

"You got me," said the bowler. "You're as rational and sane as they come."

"I'm going crazy," said Bernard.

"Nope," said the hat, "just coping with the reality of your imminent demise. Plus you're tripping on a heavy amount of Peruvian psychedelics."

"Oh good," said Bernard. "Wait. Why should I listen to you? You're just a hat."

"'Just a hat' he sez! That's the problem with you skinbags. Never give any respect to your average piece of anthropomorphic headwear."

"Are you really talking?"

"Maybe," said the hat. "Or maybe your belt is a ventriloquist. Look, everyone and everything in the universe has something unique within it. See?"

"Sure," said Bernard, though he didn't.

"Unfortunately," said the hat, "most people spend their lives hiding whatever separates them from the rest. As if all they need to be happy is to be like everyone else. This is a people-thing, by the way. Rocks and trees and mito-friggin-chondria don't spend a lot of time in therapy wondering why they don't fit in with their buddies. Now you can go through the rest of your short-assed life thinking that this is a bad drug trip. But perhaps you should consider that even you, the saddest sack of worthless excrement I've ever seen, might just have something worthwhile in him. And let's say that maybe that spark, you can call it Divinity or God or The Holy Muppet Grand Poobah, or hell, call it Bernard, maybe that piece of Bernard was sick of spending his life as a castrated shell of a skinbag. That perhaps this is the only way that he can send a message to that thick-skinned stupid brain of yours."

"What message?" interrupted Bernard.

"Oh, shit in the pope's beanie! Maybe I don't know nothin' and you're really cracking up."

"Look," Bernard exploded. "I didn't ask for this. I didn't want to have nothing to do but wait until I die, which could be any goddamn day now! Dammit, I'm trying. I may not be doing a very good job of it, but that should be worth something!"

"Whoa buddy," said the bowler, chuckling. "That's what I'm talking about. Maybe there's some hope in you yet. Not that I'm holding my friggin' breath."

"So what do I do?" Bernard asked.

"Ah hell. You're on your way. You brought me to life. If you can do it to me, maybe you can help the others."

"Others?" asked Bernard.

The hat sat there unmoving.

"Others?" Bernard repeated, until he realized that it was one thing to talk to a hat when it talked back, and something else when it wasn't responding. He looked around in the way people do when they act crazy and hope no one saw them doing it. He set the hat back on his head.

Bernard was exhausted. He thought about the couch, but the floor looked more comfortable.

Next to the door, the dust on the carpet formed a silhouette of his body. He staggered over and lay down in the outline, closed his eyes and fell back to sleep.

The next time he woke, he was certain it was another dream. He was on a waterbed again, but this time in a new apartment he didn't recognize. Vida sat beside him.

"He opens his eyes," said the dream version of Vida. "Do you need the bucket again?"

"I wanna tell you something," he mumbled. His head swam and he was certain that he was still dreaming. "I am, like, totally gaga in love with you."

Vida didn't laugh or run away, which confirmed the dream hypothesis.

"I don't need you to love me back," he continued. "I just need to be in love with you."

Bernard slipped away, but rather than wake up, he seemed to fall further asleep. The rest of his dreams involved a swirling maelstrom of junkyard items with Bernard floating in the middle. One by one, knick-knacks stopped before him: a mauve umbrella, a plastic brontosaurus, a violin without strings. He didn't know why the items appeared to him, but he knew he needed to find them.

Bernard awoke. His face stung with hot, sticky sweat. Vida sat at the side of the bed and brought a small bowl of soup up to his lips.

"Drink," she said.

Bernard sipped. It was warm chicken soup. He felt full after the first sip and pushed it away.

"Did I say anything while I was out?" asked Bernard.

"Nothing while I was here," said Estoban from the corner of the room. Vida placed the soup on the bedside table and said nothing.

43. Antelapsarian

Fresh-faced in the Garden with rules authoritarian,
We emerged wiser fools into lands antelapsarian.

Bernard and Vida lunched in the Church of Sin's dining room with the dozen performers who roomed in the upstairs apartments. Estoban insisted that Bernard and Vida stay as long as they needed and plugged his ears when Vida protested. Bernard shrugged. He had other things on his mind.

Around the dining room, an eclectic mix of pirates, buskers, and drag queens discussed Amsterdam's new regulations against street performing and their plans for a Saturday rally at the Leidseplein. The rally would coincide with the opening of the Ubermarkt, guaranteeing public and publicity. There was talk of speeches, signs, and forbidden entertainment.

Bernard calculated. Saturday was three days away.

He pushed aside his soup and stood up.

"What's the fastest way to the junkyard?" he asked.

He returned several hours later dragging three large suitcases. He found Vida at the theatre bar and announced that he was locking himself into his room until the rally.

He emerged at irregular intervals the second day and made the following requests:

A pad of paper

A pen

A vase

A toaster

Lots and lots of string

Instrument (any kind)

Bernard used the pen and paper to fashion further requests, each more curious than the last: a can of tuna, a matador's cape, a globe of the world, toe socks, anything rhyming with "magenta." Many of the items found their way into a discarded pile outside his door, but nothing was ever asked for twice.

The night before the rally, Vida stood outside Bernard's room, holding his latest note:

V,

Please be so kind as to acquire for me a dozen large feathers, something which looks, smells and feels blue, and any small, stringed instrument. Ukulele preferred, though I invite you to surprise me. I realize that I must appear the sincerest of fools, but all will become clear on Sunday.

Warmly,

Bernard.

PS: I meant what I said.

Vida brought the latest grab-bag to his door. She knocked twice. Bernard opened the door, grabbed the bag, and closed the door. Vida stepped back. She'd abandoned her crutches that morning. Her left foot was wrapped tight with gauze and there was still a stabbing pain in her ankle if she didn't step just right, but the freedom was worth it. A shimmering appeared in the corner of her eye, but Vida held her gaze on the door.

He's a mystery, love. The attraction is understandable.

"He's got a puppy dog crush on me," said Vida.

I wasn't talking about him.

"I'm not attracted to Bernard," Vida said.

Then why're you still standing outside his door?

"You said it. He's a mystery."

Then why don't you open the door?

Vida didn't answer. It was obvious. Somehow, the strange man was doing something that she dared not interrupt, something that turned her from aloof mentor to the recipient of cryptic notes, something that made her travel hobble-footed around the theatre, scouring it for knick knacks and bagatelles, something that earned the respect and cooperation of the fellow performers woken at all hours by her search for the latest acquisitions.

Silas Knight

The signs were there and they all knew it.
Behind that door, Bernard was creating.

44. Myrmidon

It's the duty of the myrmidon,
To smile while doodooed on.

Vitoria König roamed the ground floor of the Ubermarkt. In a few hours, thousands of tourists would winnow through the building, for now there were only the dim lights of a few early managers. The bottom floor was 10 meters floor to ceiling, over twice as tall as subsequent stories. Vitoria felt a rush in the cavernous main room. She suspected she was feeling excitement and pride for a decade-long project nearing completion, but she swallowed a Clozapine just in case.

She'd proposed the Ubermarkt to George ten years ago, when she was 38 and looked 26 (she was now 48 and looked 65). They'd had their first date the night before. George took her to Norali, just as Vitoria knew he would. George took every girl in the office to Norali, so he could dazzle them with entrees pricier than a month's pay before he bedded them. Vitoria had loftier plans than being another notch and when the maître d' reported that something had gone wrong with the reservation (Vitoria had posed as George's secretary that afternoon and cancelled), she took George's arm and suggested another destination. *Vivre la Vie* was a secluded cafe with waiters who spoke exclusively French. Vitoria wasted no time and ordered for the both of them. George was caught off-guard, but riposted by correcting her choice in wines. Vitoria suspected a bluff and claimed an allergy to grapes cultivated south of Auvergne. The discussion grew heated and resulted in two bottles obstinately stationed on either side of the table. The waiters grew exhausted of the couple's respective praises for their particular *vin*.

It was their first battle, the first of many. Had Vitoria and George not been so ferociously competitive they wouldn't have fallen in love that evening. Vitoria let it slip that she had a business idea that would bring König industries more money than it knew what to do with. When George asked for specifics, she brushed her hand against his leg under the table. She knew he was hooked, but hadn't expected to be snagged as well. When dessert arrived (sliced papaya drizzled with lemon glaze and a dash of cayenne), Vitoria fought back the fantasy of George sweeping the dishes onto the floor, pulling her onto the table, and ravaging her in front of everyone. She blamed her flushed face on the cayenne, even though her plate was untouched. He smiled and muttered something in Latin that she couldn't understand, but suspected (and hoped) that it was very, very dirty.

With the dessert finished and the tab paid, George walked Vitoria to her apartment (a newly-remodeled high-rise in an affluent neighborhood, the perfect dwelling for an upwardly-mobile businesswoman). It took everything Vitoria had to leave George on the front door when he pressed her against the apartment's façade and told her that the dessert was sub-par, with too much cayenne and not enough lemon.

He was baiting her and they both knew it. Vitoria gritted her teeth, dug her nails into the bricks behind her and managed to croak out "Yes, I agree completely" before she slipped her body out from under his and shut the door behind her.

Vitoria's desire for George König persisted the next morning. She steadied herself when she arrived at König Industries' main building (back when it was the *only* building), and paced the floor of her office for twenty minutes before she called George's secretary. Vitoria roared at the girl until she cried and patched her through to George; he agreed to give her an hour at the end of the day to discuss her "big idea" for the company. She stayed through lunch rehearsing the speech she'd memorized weeks ago. The page-board diagrams shook in her hands as she rode the elevator to his office. The bottle of chilled champagne made it clear George wasn't expecting to talk business. Vitoria insisted and, if only to placate her, he agreed to listen to her spiel.

Vitoria launched into her proposal and the next twenty minutes were a blur of blueprints and models that would evolve into the Ubermarkt Tower. It was a Big Idea on a scale that George König had never aspired. Vitoria watched his eyes widen with each new facet of the project. It couldn't be completed overnight, they'd need at least five years to secure capital before laying any groundwork, but Vitoria had done her research: potential investors, locations, even a grouping of subsidiary projects that would demonstrate König Industries' ability to handle such a large undertaking. The proposal went just as she'd planned, except for the distracting and recurring fantasy of George taking her on the table in front of everyone at *Vivre la Vie*. Her voice was confident but a river of sweat snaked down her stockings. She ended with one final image, a picture of Europe with Ubermarkts rising out of every country.

George König rose and stared at the page-board with his mouth open.

"I want you," he said.

His eyes darted around Vitoria's face, as if seeing her for the first time. He brushed a large hand through her dark hair while the other touched her neck. He pulled her to him. Vitoria exhaled and looking up into his wide, trembling eyes.

"Please," she said. "Fuck me. Right now, on the table. Do it."

George shook his head. "I'm on a plane to Portugal in half an hour."

"Then we'll have to hurry," she replied.

And they did, but because they didn't stop after the first time, he missed the plane anyway.

Vitoria pushed aside the memory. Ten years was long ago, ten years of greased palms, delayed deals, and enough foreign speculators for König Industries to rocket from rich to super-rich without having a single Ubermarkt to show for it. The investors had been understanding at first, but now was time for results. Everything hinged on today. Vitoria had it planned to the minute.

She reached the Ubermarkt entrance and peered out the windowed double doors. A few eager tourists were already camped outside, along with several employees who'd arrived in a futile effort to demonstrate their enthusiasm and dedication.

Everything was as it should've been, until Vitoria's gaze rose to the far end of the Leidseplein.

She dug through her purse, retrieved her phone, and touched a single button.

"Jerome," she barked. "What the hell are they doing here?"

Bernard perched on a suitcase while he squeezed the handle between his legs. He held a small slip of paper in his other hand. A slender blonde with frizzy hair and a tutu dipped her hand in Bernard's upturned bowler, held by a bald Russian with a long snake tattoo slithering from his right hand to his left eyebrow.

Snake Tattoo held up the hat to see if there were any other takers, then shrugged and pulled out his own slip.

"*Kon govno*," he said with a frown. He pulled the remaining slips out of the hat and flipped through them. He rolled them into a ball and tossed them into the trash.

"Twenty-three?" Snake Tattoo grumbled as he held up his original slip. "That's the best you leave me? You can all suck my balls."

A smattering of performers looked up long enough to smile. The Russian handed the bowler back to Bernard.

"Thank you for the hat," said the Russian. "How was yours?"

Bernard held up his slip long enough to flash the number "1".

"Fuck you and your mother," said the Russian, slumping down on a suitcase beside Bernard's.

Costumed performers milled around the square holding signs with phrases such as "Art for All" and "This IS my office job." A quartet of Hungarian breakdancers stretched on the ground. A hefty clown lifted the girl with the tutu into the air on one shaking palm. A dark haired man with juggling clubs strapped to his belt drew a large circle in the middle of the lampposts to mark the main staging area. Several living statues staked out their areas on the outskirts: a couple dressed in a tuxedo and a ball gown froze in a waltz, a man added on last minute touch-ups to paint himself like the side of a nearby wall, a green pedestal supported a breathing Statue of Liberty decorated in layers of pot leaves. A man bedecked in gargoyle makeup scaled onto the roof of the Grasshopper Bar and peered down into the crowd. A pantomime climbed into a clear plastic box balanced on a stand; Bernard noticed the box had several clear stairs and steps fashioned into the inside, which he supposed allowed for some illusions, though he'd always assumed the point of pantomiming was that you didn't need such gimmicks. On the farthest corner, Estoban and crew set up for an all-pirate rendition of the Old Testament. The King sat on a collapsible folding chair facing the performers, his back to the crimson tower. He ripped off a piece of gyro and fed it to Lancelot while continuing a fascinating chat about art and government with a pair of Ulithian tourists who'd just arrived from their small polyamorous fishing commune in Micronesia.

A line of police officers in riot gear stood before the tower and glared at the performer horde. The mood at the local precinct had shifted over the last week concerning performer legitimacy. The most popular topic of conversation involved the many creative and illegal things they wanted to do to the perpetrator who torched one of their own. They knew she wouldn't be foolish enough to show her face at the scene of the crime, but they scanned the crowds for any other performer who'd give them an excuse to enforce their job.

Colored cap-a-pie in oxidized green pot leaves, book in one hand and flaming joint in the other, the Statue of Liberty surveyed the crowd. She turned her head and Bernard gave her a nervous smile. Vida winked back and returned to her frozen position.

"What do you mean they have a permit?!" Vitoria König interrobanged. "What soon-to-be-former city employee gave them a fucking permit to be in my fucking square?"

"Uhm...err...technically," said the short man as he tapped his glasses, "we're cleared for everywhere north of the tram line. See, uhm, they..." He raised his finger towards the opposite side.

"What about the performing? I see acrobats, Jerome. Acrobats!"

Jerome tightened his tie. Vitoria König's teeth hadn't unclenched since he arrived. Her incisors might as well have been super-glued together.

"Uhm, funny that," said Jerome. "Technically, they aren't performing, they're protesting, for which the city has a very...err...rich and legally sanctioned history. I sent over the attorneys, plus three police officers, all very officious and authoritarian gentlemen, to the south side of the square. They were met by....well, er...well, they claimed to have been intercepted by...er...a pirate."

Vitoria glared.

"Apparently, he, well...er...out-officiated them."

Jerome had talked with the three attorneys from Hemlock & Tweed when they'd returned from their failed mission to disperse the performers. Hemlock & Tweed prided itself on hiring only the most bloodthirsty lawyers, men and women who aren't mentioned without the modifier of a violent weapon: Mitch "The Mallet" Lebenski, Sonja "the Scalpel" Schwartzenbaum, and "Bloody Femur" Martinez approached the performers hungry for blood, but after fifteen minutes with Estoban they returned shaking and confused.

Vitoria dug into her purse. She found two Valiums free-floating at the bottom and popped them in her mouth. "Give me some good news, Jerome, and if 'technically' or 'apparently' or any other fucking adverbs come out of your mouth, you're fired."

"Well, uhm..." Jerome paused. "There...are...two pieces....of...good news *actuall*-...err...I...." Jerome wiped the sweat off his forehead with a yellow handkerchief. "Our prohibition against performing is *techn*-...er...based on an old panhandling law. They can perform and they can take tips. They just can't ask for money. If any of them do, we can claim the *entir*-...err....gathering is responsible. Second...er...they're cleared for amplification, but they're limited to eighty decibels. We're licensed for one hundred and seventy…not that we'd want to do it. But we have eighteen speakers. Once we fire things up, you won't be able to hear anything else. To put it another way, they're shooting rubber bands, while, err, we've got nuclear. So…err…one way or another, we'll get them."

Vitoria narrowed her eyes. "Was there an adverb in there?"

Jerome swallowed. "I think…err…it was an adverbial clause, actually. Oh dear…I mean…."

Vitoria raised the sides of her mouth.

"Tell the sound engineers to crank up the system. If those freaks want a spectacle, we'll show them how it's done."

"I don't know if that's a good…." Jerome withered. "I mean, yes Vitoria, right away."

"And Jerome."

"Yes, Vitoria?"

"We need numbers! Get the store managers to bring out their employees. We'll pack this square!"

"There are last minute preparations inside, some of them…. I'll get right on it."

Jerome scampered off the podium stage and slalomed between police officers lining the front of the Ubermarkt. He turned the corner of the building before he decided it was safe to resume breathing.

Bernard was nauseous. He'd spent three days and nights working on his new show. Now everything was packed in two suitcases and he couldn't even remember what was in them. What if he forgot what to do? What if he remembered and they booed him offstage? Why did he have to pull the first number?

To further complicate matters, he'd passed another piece of strange graffiti that morning on the way to the pitch, written in large orange script on the side of an empty Kino:

Tonenili,
Don't worry. It's all going to get much harder from here.

-Coatlicue

Performances started at 10am and the clock beside the tram line read 9:50. In ten minutes, everyone would realize he was an imposter, just a normal guy who wanted to be a part of something different.

"Hey friend," said the tattooed Russian. "Got a light?"

Bernard broke from his self-deprecation.

"Uhm," Bernard shook his head. "Sorry."

"Oh, never mind. Stupid brain." The Russian pulled a box of matches out of his torn jeans. He lit the joint hanging from his lips, took a long drag and offered it to Bernard.

"No thanks," Bernard said, then added by way of explanation, "I'm about to go on."

The Russian persisted. "You're nervous? This will smooth things. I'm Anatoly."

Bernard pinched the spliff with his thumb and middle finger. He brought the joint to his lips and inhaled the barest of smoke. His body spasmed in a series of racking coughs.

"See," said Anatoly, taking the joint back. "Smooth, right?"

Anatoly became a wavy haze. Bernard wiped his eyes and his vision returned to normal.

"Hey, you're American right?" Anatoly took a long drag and puffed out three squares of smoke. "Where from?"

Bernard told him.

"I was there once," said the Russian. "Can't blame you for leaving. My show wasn't–how's the phrase–well received? Too much competition, I think." He laughed, but Bernard missed the joke.

"What do you do?" asked Bernard.

"Oh!" Anatoly tapped his chest with pride. "I'm an Asshole."

Bernard stared.

"You are new?" asked Anatoly. "I fuck with people. Pick up women, steal from little kids, tell old ladies to go sodomize themselves with their walkers...."

"You make money doing this?" asked Bernard.

"Oh, it's great work," smiled Anatoly. "And it's a great way to meet *shluhas*. I drank last night with two chicks from Prague and they wouldn't let me out of bed this morning. But you know how it goes. This job is *shluha*-magnet. But, hey, you're going, yes?"

Bernard looked at the clock. He had three minutes. He looked down at his arm. His goosebumps were so pronounced he could have passed as a porcupine.

"Pyloerections," Bernard said.

"Sorry?" asked Anatoly.

"Pyloerections," Bernard repeated, pointing at the upraised hairs on his arm. Somehow, in his nervousness, he had folded his slip of paper into a swan. He unfolded it, in case it had changed to another number, but the "1" was still there. If he stood up, he knew he'd pass out.

He couldn't do it.

"Uh," said Bernard, holding out his slip the Russian. "Do you want to trade?"

"You sure?" asked Anatoly. "This is prime slot. The crowds aren't going to get any better. My number might not appear."

"That's okay," said Bernard. "No problem. I'll get it next time."

"Thanks friend." Anatoly snapped up the paper. "I owe you a beer."

The Russian straightened his headset, grabbed his amplifier, and strutted onstage. Bernard cursed himself as the world's biggest coward.

Vitoria König watched the clock tick over to 10am. Employees filed out the Ubermarkt's front door. The building was designed for the 21st century, with automated check-out counters and robotic shelf stockers to minimize the number of humans requiring paychecks, but there were still enough employees to pack the north end of the square. She whispered to Jerome from the side of her mouth, "Let's show these circus freaks what we've got."

Jerome signaled to a thin man with headphones. The engineer nodded. Vitoria leaned in to her microphone. A switch was flipped. A loud pop erupted from the speakers and every dial on the sound board fell to zero. Vitoria started speaking but her microphone was dead. She didn't waste time.

"Fix it, Jerome." Vitoria threw open her purse and retrieved an oblong blue pill with ZR43 etched in the middle. She couldn't remember what it was, but it was better than nothing.

"It must have been the volume increase," said Jerome. "We didn't test it after I had them boost–"

"I didn't ask for an explanation! Fix it! Those gutter-cunts are stealing our crowd!"

Sure enough, the employees' attentions were drifting away from the hardware failure and towards the bald man in the opposite circle.

"Hey pretty lady," yelled Anatoly to a middle-aged blonde pulling the hand of a young girl of about ten. "How about we ditch this party and you come to my place for a good time."

"Hardly," said the woman, quickening her pace through the dense crowd.

"I wasn't talking to you," said the Russian, turning his attention to the daughter. He pantomimed a phone to his ear, "Call me, cutie. In three years."

The audience laughed nervously, but didn't look away.

"I'm kidding, I'm kidding," said Anatoly, hitting his stride. "She's much too young for me. Now you on the other hand...."

He slid up to a white haired old woman and her husband. "How about you and me and your boyfriend go make the beast with three backs, eh? I'll make you feel like you're eighty-five again!"

Outside the main circle, Bernard sat with his head in his hands, convinced that everyone was staring at him and thinking that he was the biggest loser in the world.

Down the tram line, a young American flashed Vida an obscene tongue gesture. She lifted a middle finger and the crowd added twenty Euros to the brimming hat at her base.

Off from the main stage, Estoban's Pirate Players performed the story of Ensign Lot, wherein Lot, the virtuous deckmate of the S.S. Sodom, offers up his two daughters to be raped by a horde of horny shipmates to prevent them buggering a pair of mysterious castaways. The castaways reveal themselves as members of the King's Navy, and for Lot's good deed, he and his family are saved from the destruction of the pirate fleet. After Lot's wife turns into a barrel of salt, the tourists gaped with horrific interest as Elder Daughter (Wilhelm) convinces Younger Daughter (Carlos) that now they're marooned on a desert island the only hope for the human race is to get their father drunk enough to impregnate them.

Standing to the side of the podium, Vitoria König chewed on her purse-strap and wondered if the pill she took was an anti-psychotic or anti-anxiety. It was too sweet to be any of the depressants, but she considered taking a Cymbalta just in case.

In the main circle, Anatoly focused his attention on a new victim, a red-faced Dutch businessman who yelled at the performer to "get a real job."

"Why?" Anatoly retorted. "So I can be miserable like you?"

On the podium, Vitoria König caught Jerome waving at her from the corner of her eye.

About damned time, thought Vitoria. She turned back to the podium and flipped the button on her microphone. A long, shrill whine poured out of the sound system and Anatoly's voice bellowed out of every speaker at two hundred decibels.

"YOU COULDN'T GET LAID IN A MORGUE, YOU SHRIVELED EXCUSE FOR A *PESHKA!*"

Vitoria turned off her microphone but the sound continued. Jerome rushed to the sound board, pushed the sound engineer aside and pressed buttons. Audience members who'd been watching the Russian laughed at the usurpation; those who hadn't been watching turned in confusion. Vitoria yelled at the police officers and pointed towards the tram line.

"YOU'VE BEEN SCREWED BY THE SYSTEM SO MANY TIMES YOU BEND OVER AND GRAB YOUR ANKLES WHENEVER YOU HEAR A CASH REGISTER."

The police looked around in confusion. One officer pushed through the crowd towards the tram line. Others followed. Jerome continued to stab at the sound board, increasing the volume.

"*OTSOSI, POTOM PROSI!* COME ON, I'LL GIVE YOU A EURO!"

Vitoria made vicious slashing movements at her throat.

"*TYA MAMA HUYEM V ROT EBALA! IDI OBSOSI TAYEVO PAPU, KAK TI DELAYESH DEN, TI SHLUHA YEBANAYA!*

Jerome reached behind the sound board and yanked out a plug.

The speakers went silent and the real chaos began.

45. Hugger-Mugger
Join the riot! Be a slugger!
Jump into a hugger-mugger!

Bernard watched the scene unfold. The speakers boomed and died. The police officers pushing towards the tram line paused to see if the situation was resolved. Someone in the crowd dropped a shopping bag. An officer turned her head. Several performers inched forward. Others moved to make room. The movement rippled through the square. The police ran towards the tramline and the performers rushed forward from the other side. A juggling club flew overhead and struck an officer in the shoulder. The crowd pushed. The police and first wave of performers came together, and everything was bedlam.

A raggedy man with stoned-red eyes staggered past Bernard, swayed, and collided headfirst into a lamppost. Police officers raised batons. Jugglers brandished plastic clubs against officers with batons. A second wave of performer's knocked Bernard aside. Bernard's larger suitcase was kicked onto the tram line. Bernard held tight to his first case and crawled towards the tracks. He snatched the suitcase and a wave of pirates stomped over the battle line. He rose. A police officer pushed a man in a green unitard onto the ground and raised his baton. A rubber unicycle tire struck in the officer in the face. From the steps of the podium, Mitch "The Mallet" Lebenski, fueled by the rage of the crowd, tore off his shirt and jacket, lifted his hairy chest to the air, let out an ape-like roar, and dove into the fray. The white-faced mime shook his fists at the tourists who rocked his box on its precarious pedestal. Bernard pushed through the crowd with both suitcases clutched to his chest. Mitch "the Mallet" Lebenski ran towards him for a linesman's tackle. Bernard folded his body, closed his eyes and waited for impact. He heard a thud, but felt nothing. He opened his eyes. The attorney lay on the ground rubbing his neck. The King stood above him, arm held in a clothesline position.

"Mind your flanks, boy!" said the King. A tourist ran forward and pushed the King. The monarch didn't budge. The King looked at his new attacker, who smiled. The King shook his head and swatted the man aside.

Bernard turned a full circle, looking for escape from the violent gallimaufry. He was enclosed by conflict: jugglers and acrobats, lawyers and tourists, pirates and police officers attacking one another with juggling clubs, pirate swords, and unstrung tennis rackets. The mob pushed the mime's box off its stand and onto its side. Bernard couldn't tell if the box dampened the sound or if the mime yelled silently. The mob pushed the boxed mime through the square and onto the tram tracks. A flash of green pulled Bernard's attention. He pushed through the mob and found Vida in sports bra and shorts. She'd cast off her robes and only her hands, feet, and head were green. She clutched her injured foot. Two tourists locked in combat fell towards her. Bernard dropped a suitcase into each of his hands and swung them over Vida's head at the fighters. The men flew in opposite directions.

"Thanks," said Vida, standing up and wincing.

Bernard wrapped his arm under her shoulder while holding onto his suitcases.

"We need to get out of this hugger-mugger," said Bernard.

"What kind of person," asked Vida hopping forward on her good leg, "would use 'hugger-mugger' when 'bat shit mob' is perfectly available?"

Vida pointed to the empty podium platform in front of the Ubermarkt doors. Bernard pushed ahead but the crowd was a hydra; every person who moved aside was replaced by two more. A police officer stood before them. The flat side of a wooden sword came down on the officer's head and he crumbled to the ground.

"You two might be needing some assistance," said Estoban with a debonair grin. "Pirates! Advance!"

An army of striped leggings emerged from the throng. Drag queens in period wigs and corsets walled around Vida and Bernard. The group pushed against the crowd, moving forward as a giant tank of skin and stockings. The group surged onto the podium platform. Others in the crowd pushed to gain the same position. On the far side of the plaza, the police began pulling themselves out of the fray to create a containment barrier.

Hands grabbed at Bernard's knees and tried to pull him down. He kicked them away.

"No! No! Bad mob!" said Vida, beating down hands with her liberty joint since she was unable to kick.

Bernard looked behind him. The front walkway of the Ubermarkt was unoccupied. Beyond the doors, the tower was empty.

"Come on," he said, grabbing Vida's arm.

He stepped off the back of the platform, held his suitcases with one arm and held out the other for Vida. She grabbed it and jumped down, landing with relative grace on her good foot.

"Ahoy, my boy," said the King, rounding the far end of the podium. "The castle lies undefended!"

Bernard ran to the doors.

Please be unlocked, he thought.

He pulled the first door handle. It didn't budge. Neither did the second.

Bernard retreated. He didn't want to ram through, but he'd do it if it was the only option.

Vida put a hand on his shoulder. She grabbed the door and pushed it open.

"Hurry, hurry," she said.

Bernard had no time to feel sheepish. He pushed open the second door.

"Come on," he yelled.

The King and a horde of pirates poured into the building. Costumes and unitards filed in after them. From the far side of the plaza, a police officer yelled and pointed at the Ubermarkt. Officers rushed towards the entrance.

Bernard moved to close the door.

"Wait for me, you sons of bitches!" Anatoly leaped over the tram tracks and ran towards the building. Police pursued a few feet behind him. A tourist in an "Amsterdone" t-shirt ran in front of his path. Anatoly sidestepped, grabbed the tourist's shoulder, pushed him towards the officers, slid across the podium platform and dove through the front doors. Bernard and the King closed the doors behind him just as the police arrived at the entrance. Stuck on the tramline, the mime banged on his clear box prison. A tram approached and he called out for help, but no one could hear him scream.

Police pushed. The doors cracked open. The King and Estoban's pirate army pushed back. Bernard planted against the door and surveyed the inside of the building. The first floor had a grocery store, a cell phone outlet, a camping supply store, and an electronics boutique.

"Bar the doors!" Bernard ran towards the electronics boutique.

Pirates swarmed in to fill Bernard's empty space. Anatoly noticed Bernard and followed him along with several breakdancers.

Bernard skidded before a row of big screen televisions.

"Help!" Bernard said taking one end of a 60" Panasonic. Anatoly grabbed the other end. They crab walked to the entrance and slid it between the bodies holding closed the doors. Bernard was pleased; they could build a barricade without damaging anything.

The breakdancers hurled a second television onto the ground. It struck the Panasonic and both screens shattered.

Oh well, thought Bernard. *Guess we're committed now.*

More televisions followed.

The King pushed against the door. Police officers struck at the thick glass without causing a scratch. He grinned at Bernard. "Good work, lad! But mind the rear!"

Bernard looked to the back of the building. A matching set of double doors stood unguarded. No officer had circled yet and gained entrance, but it was only a matter of time.

"Estoban!" he called out as he ran. "Help!"

Estoban clicked to attention and snapped his fingers toward several drag queens. All ran. Several officers pulled away from the front entrance and circled the building.

Vida watched as Bernard dashed to bolster the second exit.

Looks like he's got some of that fire after all.

Vida smiled and continued pressing against the first set of doors.

Bernard stopped at the rear and dropped a 45" Bravia. There were plenty of people inside, but not enough to create a second barricade without weakening the first. A trio of cops turned the corner. Estoban and the drag queens left the electronics boutique with more televisions. Bernard panicked. He couldn't hold the doors himself. His eyes fell on a large red button on the side of the wall. Abandoning the door, he dove to the side and struck the red button.

Officers reached the rear entrance and pulled back as a large metal gate slammed down on the outside of the building. From the front entrance, Bernard heard a similar clanging clash.

The building was secure.

The performers turned side to side, confused. Somebody cheered. It was picked up by the others. Buskers and pirates hugged and patted each other's backs. No one knew what happened, but it felt like cause for celebration.

Bernard joined Vida at the front of the store and watched the police retreat to the opposite side of the tram line. The police seemed to be waiting to see what would happen.

"We did it," said Vida.

"Yeah," said Bernard. "Whatever that means. What do we do now?"

"No fucking idea."

Police cars and vans filled the square. Throngs of onlookers craned their necks towards the flashing lights and sirens. The crowd jostled one another with the same enthusiasm they would give a caravan of wagons, elephants, and painted clowns.

The circus had come to Amsterdam.

V. Connection

46. Hobson's Choice

**A bevy of options is no cause to rejoice,
You'll get what you're given when it's Hobson's choice.**

Vida sat on a Pioneer plasma with her feet resting on a stack of Toshiba Blue-ray players.

"Watch the glass," said Bernard as he peered out the doors.

"Why?" she asked. "This isn't LA. They're not going to come in shooting. At least, I don't think so."

She slid back a couple inches. Bernard pulled back, too.

"It's strange, isn't it?" asked Bernard. "You'd think they'd have, well, tried a little harder to come in and extricate us. I'm not saying I want them to, I'm just saying it's strange. Isn't it?"

"You're right," said Vida. "Maybe they know something we don't."

On cue, a flurry of activity sprouted outside. Police darted to new positions while journalists motioned to their camera crews. Dozens of performers inside pushed their noses against the glass. The action died down. A grey haired man walked out from the police line and faced the tower. He raised a megaphone and said something in Dutch.

"What was that?" asked Bernard.

"He says," said Anatoly, "he doesn't want trouble, he just wants to talk."

The man spoke again.

"Now he says he wants to fix things without anyone getting hurt."

The man spoke once more.

"Fuck my mother," said Anatoly.

"What was that?" asked Bernard.

"It doesn't make sense." Anatoly shrugged. "He says they'll listen to our demands–after we release the hostage."

Everyone looked around.

"The police are crazy," said Anatoly. "They've been spending too much time in the coffeeshops."

"Why would they think we have a hostage?" asked Bernard. "Unless—"

"Well now," a deep voice resonated from the top of the stairs to the second story. "I suppose they must be talking about me."

Necks craned upwards. The thin frame of Vitoria König emerged from the darkness of the second story. It was an excellent entrance. Several recoiled. The King formed the sign of a cross. Vida flashed on an amalgamation of every Disney Stepmother. Bernard stood solid. Lancelot peeked out of the King's robes and hissed.

Vitoria König smiled. She stepped with precision down the stairs. Each footfall echoed through the building.

"I wonder," she mused, "what's going to happen now?"

No one answered her. She might as well have asked why Venice sunk into the ocean.

"I'm going to say this once," she intoned with icy calm. "This is my building. You're not welcome here. By the time I reach the bottom of the stairs, you're all gone. Anyone who remains will spend the rest of their lives in prison with '100% Grade-A Ass' tattooed on their foreheads."

"Harpy!" The King surged from the front wall towards the base of the stairs. "Harridan!"

Vitoria's left hand flickered against the stair railing. No one noticed the microgesture. It was the first time her husband had spoken to her in eighteen months.

Vitoria bared her teeth.

"Get this rabble out of here," she said, "or I'll spend my life destroying every one of theirs."

"Camel Swallower!" yelled the King, reaching the bottom of the stairs. "This tower lies within the royal domain. These guests are here by my decree!"

Vitoria kept her measured pace as she neared the bottom of the staircase. Her husband stood at the lowest step, preventing her from going further. She thought about how easy it would be to give in to him, how easy it would be to bow her head and allow him his game.

Easy, but impossible.

"Vandals!" she said. "Trespassers!"

Lancelot skittered out from the King's robe, perched on the left shoulder and joined the argument with a barrage of shrieks and squeaks.

"Eee Eee Chk Kck Kck!" *You're terrible at foraging and you fall out of trees easily*

"Get that beast out of my face or I'll turn him into a hat."

"Chk Chk Ee Chk!" *I'd rather groom a leopard*

"I did not eject those miscreants from my square," she said, "so they could take up residence in my building."

The performers looked around with surprise.

"It was you?" Vida stood. "The regulations? The police? We've been performing in that square since forever. What right do you have?"

"Right?" Vitoria's eyes narrowed on the tall young woman. "Who are you to talk about rights? You trespass into *my* building? You destroy *my* stores?"

"We wouldn't have done it if you hadn't kicked us out of the square in the first place!" declared Vida.

"You're breaking the law," said Vitoria.

"The king's law supersedes the laws of man," said the King, stepping up the stairs and forcing Vitoria to fall back onto the steps. "This fortress has been claimed by right of conquest! They shall remain here as long as I wish it!"

George König towered over Vitoria. Her heart beat like a rampaging train engine. She couldn't contain herself. The knowledge that no one else could see her flushed with arousal was her only saving grace. She couldn't hold herself in any longer.

"You're not taking this place without going through me!" she belted.

So that's exactly what they did.

47. Shibboleth

Wilber's lithp cauthed quite a meth,
When he failed hith thibboleth.

Sneaking In

by Kit Sforza

It was my ten-year anniversary, faithful readers. Ten years since your favorite reportrix arrived in Amsterdam with enough panties for a three-day vacation, ten years since this city swept her off her feet. And there I was on my Tin Anniversary, wearing black heels and a tight red fuck-me dress as I shimmied up an Ubermarkt drain pole in the rain.

I had four minutes to reach the fire escape. Success would mean the biggest story of my career. Failure would mean a second story fall (which would be bad) or police discovery while I'm dangling like a piñata (which would be worse, since I wore no undergarments below my tight red fuck-me dress).

I closed my fingers around the second story ledge and tried to pull myself up, regretting my lapsed gym membership, but thanking my recent waxing at *Entièrement le Nu*. Once on the ledge, I inched towards the fire escape. I wouldn't suggest anyone try stegophilism in heels, but it was my anniversary. I wasn't going to spend it looking like a chump.

The second story window was dark, a perfect entrance but it wouldn't budge. I vaulted up the fire escape to the third story but it was locked as well. I reached the fourth floor and saw a flash of movement on the ground. The window was unlocked and lit, but I didn't have time to worry about that. Better to be discovered by whomever was inside then spend my anniversary in a cell. I slipped through the window before the two officers looked up. I congratulated myself, just as a large hand planted itself on my shoulder.

I swiveled face to chest with a tall man with a shaven head, snake tattoo, and an iron grip on my shoulder. My mind raced. What was I doing there? I should've brought mace. I gave him my best "If You're Going to Kill Me, Please Do it Fast" smile. He returned the grin, spreading long white teeth that might as well have been sharpened. "So," he said in a Russian accent, "you are here for the party?"

Seventy-four jugglers, musicians, clowns, burlesque performers, and assorted variety acts entered the Ubermarkt building after the Leidseplein riot. The first thing they did was secure the doors and the hostage (see last week's article "*A Rose by Any Other Name*"). After that:

"Almost everybody is upstairs dancing in the skating room," he said in his sexy-now-that-I-knew-he-wasn't-going-to-kill-me accent. "Once the party started, we noticed more people in the rooms than earlier. We found three other entrances to the building. I think maybe someone posted them on Facebook. If it makes you feel better, you did come the hardest way."

The hardest way? I thought. *Great.*

I asked if I could head upstairs.

"No, sorry," he said. "No one gets through unless they pass the test. It's a Shib...Shibbe...."

"Shibboleth?" I asked.

He nodded.

For those of you without a Book of Judges nearby, the Shibboleth test came from Gileadites seeking renegades in disguise. Anyone wanting to cross their river had to say "Shibboleth". The Ephraimite's, having no "sh" sound, gave themselves away with their lisp.

I asked Anatoly for clarification.

He said, "We couldn't agree on a test. How do we decide if someone is worth coming in and not an undercover police officer? The jugglers wanted people to toss balls. The unicyclists wanted an obstacle course. It was very silly. Anyway, we get to test in moment. For now, you are a guest here. Welcome."

He opened his arms and smiled. I shrugged and went in for the embrace.

Without getting too hippy-dippy, I'll say this: Hugging is an art. Done right, an embrace reveals more than a screw. I'll also say this: Anatoly, he gave great hug. He met me with his entire body, he didn't lean in so we only touched chests, he didn't pound my back or squeeze every last drop of oxygen from my lungs. He was solid, but when I wrapped my hands around his torso, he relaxed as much as he held. We folded together while dim strains of electronic music came from an upper floor. I felt his breath on my ear and the tension that I'd held since I decided to sneak into the building give way. Anatoly circled my back with his palm. He pulled away, stopped, and kissed the back of my hand.

"Thank you, sister," he said. "Enjoy the party."

That, faithful readers, was how I entered the tower. Soon after my arrival, all of the entrances were barricaded, but until that point, it's my understanding that the Shibboleth was 100% effective.

48. Bibliophage

George's lust for words on page,
Branded him a bibliophage.

Vida passed unlit café tables as electronic beats wafted up from the floor. Long windows stretched across the far wall and revealed a panoramic view of Amsterdam. Bernard sat on a burgundy sofa that faced the windows, his head dropped as he flipped through a book on his lap.

"Can I borrow that when you're done?" said Vida.

Bernard turned with a strange look of guilt, as if she'd caught him with an adult magazine. He dog-eared the book and slid it between his knees.

"I was just thinking," Vida continued, "Europe's wildest party's sprung up downstairs and you're lost in a novel. Must be an incredible read. I'd be a fool not to check it out."

"I'm not much for crowds," said Bernard.

"Yeah, I got that." She reached over the couch and grabbed the book before he could stop her.

"*Atlas Shrugged?*" she asked, looking over the thick tome. "Ambitious. I take it you don't have any plans for the next few months." She slid over the top of the couch and plopped onto the cushion next to him. Vida flipped through the book's pages and stopped at the dog-ear near the end.

"You were reading this before you got here?" she asked.

"I...started it a couple days ago."

Vida looked down at the price tag from "Books & Stuff" and up at the café entrance with the same name. She added *lightning speed-reader* to the strange list of Bernard's skills and decided if he was embarrassed enough to lie about it, then she wouldn't press the point.

"This place has an English bookstore?" she said. "I'm surprised."

"Why?" asked Bernard, "This is a twenty-story tourist trap. Most tourists seem to speak English."

"Yeah," she said, "but I didn't know they could read."

Bernard shifted in the sofa, kicking a pile of books at his feet and exposing *Rubaiyat of Omar Khayyam, Siddhartha*, and a Hebrew Bible.

"Hefty reading," she said. "Whatcha looking for with all these books?"

"Answers?" he said.

"I'll find you a calculator."

"I'm serious," he said. "All I've found out there," he gestured to the window, "are people who say they have answers but don't. If they did, they wouldn't be so unhappy. I'm reading these because–because I want an original thought. I want revolution. Haven't you felt like all your life you've been seeking something?"

Vida picked a piece of lint off the couch. "Lots of people at Omphaloskepsis were on a never-ending quest for self-fulfillment and the next big existential high. It's fine and dandy, but I decided I'd rather be a finder than a seeker."

Bernard looked skeptical.

"I'll tell you what," she said, "if I can get you some original thoughts, open you up to some real revolution, will you put the reading on hold and come down and dance?"

He pulled back. "I can't dance."

"Everyone can dance."

"I don't dance."

"Don't be silly," said Vida. "It's a good deal: life changing ideas for one night out. You can't beat that."

Vida was off the sofa and rummaging through the darkened aisles before Bernard could protest. In the minutes that she was gone, Bernard finished *Atlas Shrugged* and began a science fiction novel about a 3000 year old man who fathers most of the human race. He heard Vida returning and tossed the book back onto the pile.

"Woot!" she said. She dropped stacks of slick paper onto Bernard's lap.

"What's the deal?" he said.

"You wanted revolution."

"These are just comic books."

"*Just* is thrown around by too many people who have no idea what they're talking about."

"I don't need super heroes to find out about the world."

"Philistine. These aren't your daddy's comics. I thought you geeks were a little more open to these things."

"I'm more of a nerd," said Bernard. He picked up one of the manuscripts: *The Invisibles*. He flipped through the pages. His eyelids widened.

"People copulate in these things?" he asked.

"And fuck. And love. And wax all philosophic, if that's your bag. Silly human, you ask for revolution but get your panties in a bunch if it's not in a familiar form." Vida shook her head. "As if it arrives any other way.

"Come on," she said. "Words are fine and books are dandy, but thinking only gets you so far. Revolution is in the movement."

Vida grabbed Bernard's arm and pulled him downstairs.

49. Olla Podrida

The world's not Spain, my dear *senorita*,
It's a stranger concoction, an olla podrida.

Love and Rollerskates, the Ubermarkt's 19th floor roller disco, contained 90% of the tower's population. The remaining 10% included several performers posted as guards, a handful of partiers who'd retired in search of snuggling or frisky playtime, and Vitoria König, locked in a gothic clothing store on the 20th floor until someone could figure out what to do with her.

Zero percent of the tower's population were in the Ubermarkt's basement, which was accessible through an unmarked service door in the electronics boutique on the first floor. The basement wasn't connected to the building's heating system and was unfurnished, hardly ideal for most people's ideas of frisky playtime.

The basement's lack of charm kept anyone from discovering the rows upon rows of strained structural beams, smiling fractured grins and littering the floor with broken cement.

Bernard and Vida descended to the 19th floor. In the front section of Love and Rollerskates, partiers laughed and drank, sitting at the bar or around one of the many circular wooden tables. Beyond the tables, a throng of hips swiveled and swayed in the middle of the skating rink dance floor. Skaters orbited dancers, sloshing liquor as they zipped around stilt walkers and jugglers tossing flaming torches.

"I'll be right back," said Vida, bee-lining for the bar. Bernard fought the desire to retreat upstairs. Everyone seemed to be having too good of a time. He scanned the crowd and saw Anatoly sitting at a table with his arm around an attractive redhead in a low cut dress.

"Ah, my new friend!" said Anatoly, waving from the table.

Bernard shuffled over, passing two teens with matching green hair who fondled each other while their tongues fandangoed.

"New friend Bernard," said Anatoly, "meet newer friend Kit."

Anatoly gestured to the redhead, who was focused on pouring vodka into two shot glasses.

"Oops," she said, spilling alcohol onto the table.

"Kit here is the first non-Slavic woman to keep up with me," said Anatoly with a slight slur. "She has, how you say, hollow leg."

Kit slid a shot over to Anatoly.

"Ready?" she asked.

"*Da*," said Anatoly.

They tapped the shot glasses onto the table and said together:

"*A'deen!*

"*Dva!*

"*Tri!*

"*Za vashe zdorovye!*"

They shot the drinks back. Kit puckered her face and pounded on the table.

"That was a good one," said Anatoly.

"I'd hope so," said Kit. "I put twice as many roofies in yours this time."

"Ha," said Anatoly. "See what I mean? She has dirtier mind than I do. You are skating?"

Bernard shrugged. "I've enough trouble sorting out my own two feet. Eight extra wheels would only add to the discombobulation."

"Ooh," said Kit, flashing emerald eyes at Bernard. "You just said one of my favorite words. But I like *gallimaufry* better."

Bernard tilted his head. "What's your position on *balagan*?

"A tad pedantic. Besides, I've always thought *salmagundi* had a better cadence." Kit poured more vodka into a larger glass, added liquid from a jar of pickles and a dash of Tabasco. "Pickletini?"

"That sounds atrocious," said Bernard.

"They're better than they sound," said Kit, sliding the drink to Anatoly and mixing herself a second. "It's nice to meet a fellow verbivore. Can I make you something?"

"That's taken care of."

Bernard turned. Vida stood behind him with a drink in each hand.

"Oh, oh well then," said Kit, frowning. "Next time, perhaps?"

"Come," said Vida, putting a purplish drink in Bernard's hand and pulling him away from the table. "Dancing."

"I don't dance," he said.

"Drink," said Vida. "It'll help."

"What is it?"

"Professor Callahan's Concentrated Courage. Three parts brandy, two parts rum, three parts moonshine, one part yak's urine, and two drops of cootchie juice from a certified virgin. You won't believe how hard that was to find in this place. And a lime wedge. Guaranteed to open the hips and increase the boogie 500%. Please be advised that excessive use can lead to hair loss, bar fights, male pregnancy, lowered standards and truth telling."

Vida clinked her drink to Bernard's. Bernard eyed the mixture and raised it to his mouth.

"Whoa! Stop right there!" A curly-haired unicyclist sped towards them and circled. "No clinking glasses without looking into each other's eyes. It's bad luck, don't you know, leads to seven years of bad sex. Trust me on this one."

Bernard met Vida's gaze. For the first time, he noticed flecks of gold mixed in with her hazel irises.

"That's better," said the unicyclist, pedaling away.

They clinked again and Vida rose the cup to her lips.

"Bottom's up."

They drank.

At the bar, Billy Chen, the sole remaining shop-owner in the Ubermarkt after the occupation, poured two Ukrainian Pitchforks and slid them over with a set of roller skates. A white Rastafarian smiled and reached forward. Billy shook his head and pointed to the sign above the bar:

No Zapatos, No Skates, No Exceptions!

Billy Chen had sunk every penny into his roller disco/cosmopolitan bar and had been sleeping inside the shoe depository for the better part of a month. He was a night owl and a heavy sleeper, and he missed Jerome's order to vacate the building.

Despite his lack of money, Billy didn't care that no one paid for drinks or skate rentals. Such concerns weren't Zen. Billy wanted to preside over the grooviest nightclub this side of the Atlantic. As long as the music was thumping and the people were smiling, the drinks would flow. However, he drew the line at the willy-nilly dispersal of roller skates.

The white Rastafarian slid across a pair of pink Adidas Supernovas still in their box. Billy Chen took the shoes with a smile and waved him away.

50. Terpsichorean
Praise to the body as it dances free,
Groove to the graceful muse Terpsichore!

The drink made Bernard feel like his brain was cloaked in cashmere.

He allowed Vida to drag him onto the room, passing whizzing skaters and writhing dancers. The green haired couple Bernard spied earlier had migrated to the center, and the boy danced on the girl like he was a koala bear and she was a eucalyptus tree. Vida stopped at an arbitrary location and swayed her body. The techno beat had an airy quality and she floated as if every joint was attached to a helium balloon. Even favoring her right leg, Vida moved with grace. The bass drums returned, the balloons popped, and she dropped into her pelvis. She looked at Bernard and bounced her body up again.

"You've got to move to dance," she said. "It's part of the definition."

"I told you I can't do it," he said. "I'm going."

"Because you can't do something? What kind of a cock are you?"

"What?"

Vida slid towards him.

"I've too much self-respect to call you a pussy."

She spun to his side and tilted towards his right ear.

"Close your eyes," she said.

"I don't want to."

She pressed her hands against his hips. He restrained a shudder.

"Close your eyes."

He did.

"Ignore the voice that says you can't do it." Her hands rocked his hips and she whispered, "The voice is wrong. The voice is always wrong. Don't worry about anything. The music will tell you what to do. It's as easy as letting go."

Bernard tried to feel the music, but it was too loud and chaotic for him to figure out what it wanted him to do. He felt like a schmuck.

"Relax," she said.

"I'm trying," he said, opening his eyes. "There's too much to think about."

"Just think about the music," she said.

"That's what I'm talking about," he said, frustrated. "I'm listening to it like you said. It's a drum and bass rhythm. It's got eight beats to a measure, playing at 120 rpms. The rhythm is syncopated and accelerando, somewhat masculine, with occasional tonal interruptions balancing out the bass with lyrical softness in the higher registers! But how is any of that supposed to tell me what to do?"

"Wow," said Vida, patting Bernard's left hip. "That was impressive. Ok, different tactic then. Look around you. What do you see?"

"A room of people having a better time than I am."

"Grump. What do you see?"

"People dancing," he said.

"Great. How're they doing it?"

"That's what I don't understand," he said. "They're all doing it differently. How can the music be telling them what to do if everyone's doing something different?"

"Great question!" said Vida, slapping Bernard on the ribs and moving back into her own space on the dance floor. "We're moving differently because we're each independent entities."

She spun.

"Dancing is physics. The same song enters each of our bodies—"

She slid.

"...and we react to each bounce..."

She bounced.

"…shake…"

She shook.

"…and shimmy…"

She shimmied.

"…with our unique physiology. All you need to do is to listen."

"What then?" asked Bernard.

"You talk back. Dance is a communication. You don't need to be fluent, you just need to pick up the vocabulary."

"That's—"

Bernard stopped himself. If he had one thing, it was vocabulary.

He looked around the dance floor. Everyone appeared to be doing something different, but what was the same?

Most of the dancers moved downward on the accented beat. Bernard bobbed his head with the music, but felt awkward. He was moving his head and neck, the others were using their entire bodies. The movement came from their knees. Bernard straightened his legs and released. Gravity took its share of downward momentum, but he stopped and re-straightened his legs when the impulse came to rise. The thought that his pudgier-than-average body had no right undulating flashed into his head and was pushed aside by his curiosity at the new discovery. The movement felt…correct.

Vida gave him an approving smile and he repeated the action sequence, dropping and elevating while looking around again. He tried to identify the similarities between the breakdancer on his left and the middle-aged couple slow-dancing together on his right. The breakdancer's moves were all unique; he flowed from one position to another while maximizing variation. The couple's dance was simpler, perhaps as a necessity of matching each other's movements. The basic unit for both dances was one beat. A beat was enough time for one action: an initiation, a pause, or a continuation of movement. The first and fifth beats were punctuated. These were suitable moments to initiate a change in the movement phrase. Repetition was acceptable, but the phrases seemed to get boring if they were repeated more than four times. Taken as a whole, the permutation were infinite, but Bernard began to glimpse the underlying mathematics.

He could move his feet, knees, hips, stomach, chest, shoulder, elbows, wrists, fingers, or neck. A movement could be along any plane, front and back, side to side, up and down, or diagonal. He could extend or flex a joint, translate upon a plane, or undulate from one joint to another. A phrase could end in a new position or repeat itself in reverse, allowing for repetition.

Bernard continued bouncing with his knees, and stepped sideways with his left foot on the upbeat. He felt the urge to return and followed the impulse. He stepped again with his right foot. Now he had two movements going: his feet and his knees. What if he added something new? He elevated and depressed his shoulders, trying out variations in intensity, starting with tiny rolls, then bouncing with greater enthusiasm. He noticed his bias toward moving on the first and fifth beats and tested out stretching a single phrase for sixteen beats, translating his torso in a circle as he stepped. The music sped up as he slowed down and Bernard felt a contrast between his motion and the melody. Time stretched. The feeling was tranquil. It was serendipity that the music sped up when he wanted to slow and he realized that he could follow the music's tempo or react against it. Either option was acceptable as long as he made the choice.

Dancing appeared to be nothing more than a collection of aesthetic motions caused by the oscillation of sound waves and the body's reactions to them.

What it that simple?

Bernard experimented with combining phrases. Every action wanted a reaction. The music changed into a familiar melody, though it took Bernard a few phrases to identify Beethoven's "Ode to Joy" overlaying the electronic drums.

Bernard let the momentum from his left foot swing into a rightward translation of his hips and move into an anterior-posterior isolation of his shoulder. He waited, bouncing as the music swelled. A young brunette with a ponytail danced towards him. She slid into his field and their hips connected. He felt a moment of panic. She flashed a white smile and Bernard relaxed as they swayed together side-to-side. She smiled and she let herself be pulled away by the green-haired couple Bernard had seen earlier. Bernard watched her disappear into the throng.

Another dancer moved close behind him. Bernard felt their connection before she pressed against his back. He didn't need to turn around to know it was Vida.

She rested her hands on his stomach. He touched his fingers to hers, hugging himself in the process. He closed his eyes. They slow-danced as the music reached crescendo.

Bernard turned to face her and their eyes sought each other.

Mamihlapinatapai is a look between two people who feel desire but want the other person to make the first move.

Bernard held one hand against Vida's neck and the other cradled her sacrum as they waltzed to the beats of electric Beethoven. For a moment, Bernard thought he felt another set of feminine arms wrapped around their bodies, but when he slid his hand up Vida's back, there was no sign of another. He thought of mentioning the sensation, but Vida pressing against his pelvis was inspiring a noticeable erection. He felt embarrassed. Vida tilted her head away from his neck, but stayed connected. She looked at Bernard with a dream-like gaze.

"You keep surprising me," she said. "I haven't danced with anyone since…."

Vida's brow furled and her eyes widened. Bernard couldn't get over how beautiful she was, how someone so strong could be so vulnerable. He wanted to tell her everything would be okay. He wanted to envelope her and protect her, but at the same time he wanted her vulnerability. Before he could catalogue all the reasons he shouldn't do what he was about to do, he leaned in and kissed her.

Vida's body tensed and her hands released from his back. Bernard didn't retreat or advance, he kept his lips pressed against hers. Her mouth opened and they shared a slow inhale and exhale. A soft whimper left Vida and traveled into Bernard. Vida tilted her neck. Her body relaxed and Bernard found himself in a new dance, one without any awareness of the music or the other people in the room, only his mouth and tongue moving with hers, brushing and sliding, reacting and initiating.

A circuit was completed. Bernard marveled at feeling such desire and satiation. It was the same rush he felt when he developed his show, the bliss of creation and discovery. He wanted to share everything with her. Trusting his fluency with this new language, he transmitted his passion and his fears with his mouth and body. He pulled her closer.

The bliss made the withdrawal all the more jarring.

Vida pushed them apart. Bernard's mouth dropped open. She backed away. Her focus wasn't on him. She shook her head.

"I'm sorry," she said. "I'm so sorry."

Vida retreated through the crowd. Bernard wanted to respond, but he knew she wasn't talking to him.

51. Agathokakologia
Good and bad compose the whole,
When it's agathokakological.

Estoban hefted a large grocery sack up the stairs to the 14th floor. Vida sat melancholic on the top step.

"Vida!" he said.

"Stop," she ordered. "You don't want what I've got."

Estoban complied, though a wash of confusion and sadness passed over his face.

"Too late?" she asked.

"Oh honey," said Estoban. He sat down on a lower stair. He smiled in support and locked eyes. They sat together in silence. Estoban's talent was more than mimicry, but Vida was comforted by his limitations. He was empathic, but not a mind reader, and there was safety in sharing an emotional state with someone who wasn't bogged down in mental details.

"Thank you," she said.

"Any time," said Estoban. "It's serendipitous that I ran into you. How do you feel about a distraction?"

"Is it unpleasant?"

"Terribly."

"Good. I couldn't do anything happy right now."

"Then this is right up your alley," said Estoban, picking up the grocery bag at his knees. "An hour ago, our hostage sent down a list of demands."

"There's something wrong with that sentence," said Vida, "but I can't put my finger on it."

Estoban handed Vida the bag and a slip of paper.

"I appreciate this," Estoban said. "That woman gives me a headache."

"Besides," he added as an afterthought, "she asked for you personally."

A thin metal gate blocked the entrance to the Goth/Industrial clothing store. "Couture of the Night" was bathed in an eerie glow that emanated from a lantern sitting atop an otherwise unoccupied black recliner outside the store. Even if Vida was unaware that the King spent most of his time guarding the prisoner, the sizable indent in the recliner and liberal piles of monkey scat left few alternatives. Additional feces decorated the clothing racks nearest the entrance. There were several larger stains on the wall outside the store. Vida considered the possibility and rejected it. Not even that mad woman would get into a scat-throwing contest with a monkey.

Would she?

Vida saw no movement inside the dark store. She fought the urge to toss the shopping bag inside and run away. The moment passed and she chided herself for being rattled. After five years on the road she was beyond such insecurities. Granted, Vitoria König seemed like someone who'd start a pissing contest with the Devil just so she could laugh at the size of his dick.

"Hello?" she called through the gate. "Anyone in there?"

No answer.

"Trick or Treat?"

Vida looked into the darkness. The darkness looked back.

"Did a house fall on you?"

Was that a laugh? She set the bag of goodies against the gate cage and turned to leave.

The voice behind her could've cracked ice.

"I know who you are."

Vida turned her head. The speaker sounded like she was directly on the other side of the gate.

"Walk away and you'll be in jail before morning."

Vitoria König's face birthed itself from the darkness. The rest of her body was costumed in gear from the store: black pants with a dozen zippers, metal spider hair-clips, and a t-shirt with the Cheshire cat repeating "We're all mad here" over and over again.

Mad. No kidding.

"Are you threatening me?" asked Vida.

"No threat," said König. "A promise. Leave now and you'll be in jail by morning."

"Why?"

"Justice? Because you're wanted for barbequing without a license? Or because you stole my property and turned it into a squat for degenerates. Perhaps because I've been here for twelve hours without a gin & tonic. Perhaps I'm just a bitch."

"Perhaps all of the above," replied Vida. "You sure do talk funny to people who come bearing gifts."

König opened her mouth and pursed her lips. "What'd you bring me?"

Vida slid the bag towards the cage with one foot. A boney hand snaked through the lattice and retrieved a bottle of gin. Vitoria König set the bottle down beside her and pulled out the remaining items, casting each aside in turn.

"Where's my Clozapine?"

"You're welcome."

"Where is it? It was on the list."

"And underlined twice," said Vida. "You're the one who designed this place without a drug store. Though given the rabble downstairs, it's for the best. I had enough trouble retrieving the gin. It's the last in the building. I spit in it, by the way."

"Don't get smart with me," said König, tilting the booze to her lips. "You haven't the resources. I should've expected if I wanted a job done right…."

The older woman retrieved a silver phone from out of nowhere. She tapped a button and Vida heard the muffled sound of ringing before Vitoria barked into the receiver.

"Jerome, you miserable prick! No, it's Santa Claus, I'm calling to tell your daughter that she'll be getting that barroom gang-bang she asked for. Now let's see if your job can survive one more stupid question. Of course I'm fine, Jerome, I'm being held by idiots. It's like a board meeting, but shorter. Fuck the investors, they can't get their dicks up to half mast if the stock exchange doesn't rise with them. Worrying is for wage slaves. I don't know how it'll settle. I don't need to know. That's why we hire a PR firm that costs more than Luxembourg. The publicity alone is worth the insurance hike. Jerome, I don't care if you care if I'm alright. Don't waste my time asking me about it. I need a Clozapine in my hands in the next hour. Tell Schad I need my normal mix. I also want a case of brandy, my black winter coat, Oskar will know which one, and—"

Vitoria König put her hand over the phone and turned to Vida. "Do you want anything?"

Vida blinked. "A gyro?"

Vitoria frowned and turned back to the phone. "That's it. I want them delivered personally in less than an hour. I don't care how! Just do it. I'm locked in the top floor at the northeast corner, so you'll have to show up at the window. I don't care about the police. Tell them if you don't get through they'll going to shoot me in the head. No, of course not, but someone will be shot if you don't get here with my Clozapine. Are you volunteering?"

She hung up.

Vida stammered. "You—you have a phone?"

"I wouldn't answer that if you were a simpleton."

"You've had that the entire time? Why haven't you called the police?"

"How do you know I haven't?"

"Estoban said you asked for me," said Vida. "Why would you ask for me if your guy could bring everything?"

"Christ, girlie," said Vitoria König in exasperation. "I wanted the one thing Jerome couldn't bring: You. I want to offer you a job."

Vida laughed. "You're not serious."

"Serious as a heart attack. What can I do to get you to listen to my proposal?"

Vida stared at the woman. She didn't look like she was kidding. She didn't look like she was capable of kidding.

Vida deliberated. "You could be nicer."

"I don't do *nice*. Try something else."

Vida mused. "Then get back on that gadget and get me some gyros."

The Clozapine, coat, brandy and gyros arrived with the sound of heavy grunting and wheezing from the store's rear window. Vida spied a short and balding man in a business suit that Vitoria berated with ferocity over a small tear in the winter coat incurred during his navigation through a rooftop obstacle course on his way to the fire escape.

Jerome disappeared after copious apologies and the sound of restrained tears.

Vitoria König marched back bearing her spoils.

"How can you treat someone like that?" asked Vida. "He's a human being."

"Wrong," said König. "Humans fight back. Jerome is more worried about his paycheck than his integrity. He's capable of operating rudimentary technology and wiping himself. That's it."

Jerome Fitch had a PhD in business from Yale and was fourth in his class during a year at Tokyo University (an opportunity he pursued after the prestigious TU partnered with Yale to bring in more *gaijin*). Jerome spoke Japanese, English and French. He earned a quarter million Euros a year, bolstered by shrewd investing, though his car payments, house payments, and wife's extravagant shopping sprees sucked much of that away. Before Jerome attained his position working for Vitoria König, he was a contracted slave for a group of four homosexual men in Boston. Jerome did not consider himself gay, but he found immense satisfaction in being subjected to any whim that the men asked of him. Their requests ranged from doing their laundry dressed as a French maid to allowing them to urinate on his body. While many a person, homosexual or not, would find these activities unappealing, Jerome found a sense of belonging and purpose that he thought could never find an equal.

Yet no humiliation in his past brought Jerome the satisfaction that he got out of service to Vitoria König. His greatest fear was that someone, his wife, his friends, or Vitoria herself, would discover that he would not only work for her for free, but would pay for the privilege.

"This is a gyro?" asked Vitoria. She poked at the pita bread and white sauce spilled out the ends.

"You want one?" asked Vida, taking a deep bite.

"I'd rather eat my own ass."

"You have a delightfully colorful vocabulary for a rich chick," mumbled Vida. Vitoria König was difficult to read. She wasn't a blank page like Bernard, but her depths were well protected.

"Where were you born?" Vida asked.

"It doesn't matter where we're born," said König. "It matters where we find ourselves." She swigged from the brandy, hesitated, and passed it through the latticework. Vida sipped the liquor. Her nose crinkled and she pulled back the bottle. A hand-painted black velvet sleeve wrapped around the oblong bottle. The label read "Terpsichore's Minstrel" and pictured a satyr playing a lute while a circle of drunken nymphs danced around him and pawed one another.

"Something wrong?" asked König.

"I don't like brandy, but that was the best alcohol I've ever had in my life."

"If I told you the cost, you wouldn't believe me," said König, pulling the bottle back to her side. "God's own cum couldn't taste better."

"I still don't understand why you want to give me a job. You don't know anything about me."

"You're Vida Magdalena Callahan. You ran away from home five years ago. You've never owned a mobile phone or a driver's license. You've never driven a car; except when you were fourteen and backed over your mother's flowerbed.

"You've no surviving grandparents, but your parents are still together. You have one brother."

"Wrong." Vida folded her arms. "I'm an only child."

"Wrong. After you ran away, your parents quit mourning and tried again. Your mother miscarried the first time, but the second attempt produced a bouncing baby boy. He hasn't followed in his big sister's footsteps and run away, yet, but he's only three.

"Your favorite season is the tourist season and your favorite food is this Mediterranean monstrosity that I see you've already devoured. Your favorite color is purple"

"No, it's green," said Vida.

"It's purple," said Vitoria.

Damn. She was right.

"In the last five years you've been to thirty-five countries on four continents. You're mentioned on police blotters in fifteen of those countries, for crimes ranging from public disturbance, drug possession, public indecency, and most recently, attempted manslaughter.

"Six months ago in Italy, you and your partner developed a new act using a static trapeze, rare for the street since it requires mounting off of a bridge or high-hanging building. Premiering the new show in Venice, your partner's rigging failed. Unfortunately for the police, they had to list the body as a Jane Doe, since minutes after you were escorted into a police car, you disappeared."

"They acted like it was my fault," said Vida. "I needed to leave."

"And you did. From the back of a locked police car. Very resourceful. Hang out with people who break out of strait jackets and you pick things up, I suppose.

"You've had two serious relationships: Anthony Terrence Howard, aka Tony T. Current whereabouts unknown, and–"

The color drained from Vida's face. "I've heard enough."

"–and Sophia Meeks, born in Redding, California."

Vida's eyes shook. "Her name was Maya."

"You went to school with Sophia, but she ran away from home when she was twelve. Why would a girl leave home that early, I wonder?"

"Her name was Maya," Vida repeated.

"She was picked up for soliciting when she was thirteen. Sophia spent the next couple years in and out of juvenile hall."

"I don't know what happened to her on the streets," said Vida stone-faced. "When I met her at Omphaloskepsis, Sophia was gone. I married Maya from Liverpool."

"How could you take that?" asked König. "How could you love her and let her pretend to be someone she wasn't?"

Vida assumed the question was an attack, oblivious to the possibility Vitoria was making an honest and imploring request for information.

"Change the subject," demanded Vida.

"I want to know," said König.

"Change the subject or I'm gone."

Vitoria König took another swig of brandy and passed it through the bars. Vida took a good sized gulp, then another before she passed it back. It was a while before either spoke.

"How's your ankle?" asked Vitoria König.

"Tender, but I can walk on it. I stopped taking pills for the pain this morning. It still hurts, but I wanted to be clear."

"A serious injury would put a damper on your business, wouldn't it? What would you do if you couldn't perform?"

"I don't know," said Vida. "It's my life."

"Wrong. It's what you do for a living. Don't confuse the two. I'm proposing you *can* do something else and I'm offering you the opportunity. It's only a matter of time before you have another injury; if not your ankle, something else. Or you'll be arrested. There are riches out there for women who want to make their own way, but it's an uphill climb. I should know."

"You're one to talk. You're wealthier than a small country."

"Several. But money is easy. Respect is hard and I've had to fight for every shred of it. We're not different. Both of us will do whatever it takes to get what we want most from the world."

"And what is it you want most?" asked Vida.

Something unexpected flashed across Vitoria König's eyes; something revealing, soft and tender; something immediately squashed.

"Power."

Vida didn't believe her.

"Some people are seekers," said Vida, "Others are finders. Which are you?"

Vitoria König didn't skip a beat.

"I'm a maker, baby girl. The world you play hide and seek in has my signature on the underside label. You and your friends think I'm the villain. Feel free if it helps you sleep at night. But the world doesn't work that way. There's no villain except the one we fight inside ourself. Some of us know that, others place the blame for their own failings on the success of others."

König passed the liquor back through bars. Vida took another drink and savored the golden liquid sliding over her tongue.

"I have zero business skills," said Vida.

"You've been self-employed for the last five years. You've had thousands eating out of your palm. A boardroom is no more difficult.

"Finances take skills," said Vida.

"Skills can be bought. That's why it's almost impossible to stop making money once you have it. There is no shortage of people with education and the willingness to whore out their knowledge."

"So hire them," shrugged Vida.

"More eager-to-please yes-men like Jerome? I've more toadies than a porn star has crotch warts. I don't need knowledge. I need passion. I need someone with the balls to stand up to me and tell me when I'm wrong. I need someone who can be the voice of god when I'm not there. I need an authority. Come with me and within a year you'll be higher than you ever dreamed."

"What're you offering?" asked Vida.

Vitoria König stated a figure higher than anything Vida imagined she would earn in her entire life.

"Every year?" asked Vida.

"Every month," snorted Vitoria. "To start. It'll get bigger. I'll teach you how to use people to make that happen."

"It's an incredible offer," said Vida. "You want me to work for you?"

"Yes."

"You'll pay me…" the figure caught in Vida's throat, "enough money to never worry about money again?

"Yes."

"I'll be a boss?"

"Yes."

"I'd be in charge of others?"

"Many others!" said Vitoria.

"I could order people to do whatever I wanted? Like, whatever I wanted?"

"People will look at you as they once looked upon Zeus himself."

"Thanks," said Vida. "That's all I needed to hear."

"Then you'll do it!" exhorted Vitoria.

"Not in a million years."

Vitoria was stunned. "You…you…."

"I…I…." said Vida. "Now let's do the rest of the vowels. I couldn't live the life you described and retain any trace of what I love about myself."

"You're an idiot. I'm offering you the world."

"I have my share."

"You are a fool," said Vitoria.

"And you're slipping. That was the weakest insult I've heard tonight. Not like this proposal. That was a big and glorious insult. Thank you for letting me turn it down."

"You'll regret this for the rest of your life," Vitoria König hissed.

"At least I'll have that. Few have the chance to be a god, much less reject it."

Vitoria König grabbed the bars. "You're a halfwit."

"And you're lonely," said Vida. "Wait. That's it, isn't it?"

"I'm done with you," said Vitoria. "Leave now."

"No, no really. This isn't about me being some untapped business genius. You're lonely. You don't have anybody and you wanted–"

"I said I'm done with you. Leave now." Vitoria König was getting red.

Vida laughed. Then she stopped. "Oh god. I'm so sorry. I can't imagine. Oh honey…."

Vida reached her hand through the bars. Vitoria König shook and her jaw quivered.

"I SAID GO AWAY!" Vitoria snapped like a wounded animal. Vida pulled back her arm

"GO AWAY. GO AWAY. NOW."

Vida made a final attempt. "Please. I can help. Let me–"

Vitoria König opened her mouth and emitted an inhuman roar of hurt and defiance. Vida pulled back. Vitoria König pounded on the cage, shaking and striking it with the brandy bottle in her hand. Vitoria thrust her arm through the latticework and threw the bottle of brandy at Vida's face. Vida brought up a hand and swatted the bottle away. It ricocheted against the recliner and bounced down the hallway. Vitoria König dove for the gate and shook the cage, howling. Vida turned and ran down the hall. She ran until she could no longer hear the words following her.

"You are dead! Do you understand? Dead! You'll be in prison for the rest of your life! You will never see sun! You will never see the people you love! You want to know about loneliness? I'll show you loneliness. Vida Callahan will be the loneliest woman on the face of this earth!"

Vitoria König had long retreated into the darkness when the King returned to his guard post, whistling a strange tune he'd heard on the dance floor. His face was redder than usual.

"*Cht tht Cht!*" Lancelot skittered behind the King's back as they neared the latticed gate.

"Don't worry, boy," whispered the monarch as he peered into the store. "Methinks the dragon sleeps."

"*Cht? Cht cheet.*"

"I couldn't agree more."

The King dropped into the recliner beside the cage. Lancelot scampered off the King's back, avoiding his future as a monkey flapjack. When his sizeable companion had settled, Lancelot inched forward and nestled into one arm. The King closed his eyes and thought about his evening regaling citizens with stories of his realm. Afterwards, they'd coaxed him onto the dance floor, even though the last time he had frolicked in such a way the Electric Slide was the latest craze.

Soon thoughts of the evening gave way to two pairs of snores and dreams of ripe bananas and buxom virgins.

After one hundred snores, a narrow face and dark sunken eyes appeared from behind the cage.

Vitoria König sank down until her white fingers looped around the bottom of the gate. With the patience of the dead, she raised the latticework, pausing each time a small squeak escaped the metal collaboration.

When it was barely high enough for a small animal, she slid one leg underneath, then the rest of her thin frame. Her belt loop snagged on the underside and she stopped. Vitoria worked herself loose and slid into the other side.

She stole towards the sleeping figures. The monkey turned and sniffed. She held still and looked down at the two bodies. Her husband was so large, so handsome in his repose. He shook in his sleep. Vitoria grabbed the end of his thick robe and folded it over the two sleepers.

Vitoria lowered her knees to the ground and allowed the side of her head to rest on the sleeping giant's lap.

Vitoria thought about choices. She knew that there had been a time when choices were bountiful, and she could pick and choose wherever she wanted her life to go. It'd been a long time since she remembered making a real decision. In business, the answers came as a matter of course, every decision followed the path of the previous one. Once upon a time she was the engineer and operator of her own life, but now "Vitoria König" was a juggernaut, a cyclopean monstrosity of steam and metal, and she could do nothing more than stoke the fires and hang on, lest everything collapse with her trapped deep inside.

Vitoria allowed herself twenty-two minutes before she raised her head off her husband's lap. She tip-toed back to the metal gate and raised the lattice. She slid inside, taking the utmost care to return the metal to its closed position.

Vitoria König rested with her back to the bars, unable to look at her husband.

52. Der Miraculo

Seeking supernaculum that ain't abysmal?
Toss back a draught of Terpsichore's Minstrel!

Bernard felt like his lungs had been doused in kerosene and set aflame. Thick sweat poured across his inflamed cheeks. He tried to inhale and his throat caught. His chest spasmed and he realized he was about to die.

He gasped, fighting to take in more oxygen. He rolled over on the couch. Comic books scattered onto the floor. Outside the window, the orange and amber glow of sunrise flecked against the snaking blue canals in the distance. *People have died with worse views,* he thought.

Bernard closed his eyes and tried to taste Vida's lips one last time, but the pain brought him back to reality. He thought about his show. If he had to pick one regret in a life full of regrets, it was the show. He had his chance on the square and he rejected it. He was dying because he gave up, because he ran away from the only shot he had.

Bernard closed his eyes and waited for Death.

Fortunately, the bone woman was dragging her heels, distracting herself with an earthquake in Ethiopia; a tsunami in Sumatra; and a case of whooping cough in Walla Walla, Washington. A dying wizard in Oyotunji bought some time by sewing his soul to his body with the mandibles of soldier ants, delaying the psychopomp who almost missed her appointment in Remunda, where an epidemiologist administered an experimental drug to a six-year-old girl with polio. The treatment was a success and the bone woman arrived just in time to harvest the virus.

So it was that Bernard hadn't expired before a pair of Welsh jugglers walked into the bookstore café and stopped behind his couch.

"Oh god!" said the first juggler.

Bernard felt a surge of embarrassment. Dying felt like the ultimate faux pas.

"Have you ever seen a more beautiful sight, Tim?"

"I can't say that I have, Oliver."

Bernard felt relief. They were talking about the view.

"There's beauty in the sunrise in the sky," said Oliver, holding his hand over his heart, "but nothing can match the beauty in my true love's eyes."

"Why, that was quite lovely, Oliver."

"You sound surprised."

"Well, yes, that's because I've always thought you were a bit of a cunt."

"That's true, Tim, but it wasn't my apothegm, it was Bob Dylan's."

"In any case, what're you doing for the Day of Spectacles?"

"Sorry?"

"Haven't you heard? Performances start at noon. Everyone's bringing their best material."

Bernard forced a deep breath into his lungs and gasped as he bolted upright. Tim and Oliver jumped back. Bernard turned his head and managed to croak out:

"Which...way...?"

Tim and Oliver looked at one another, then back to Bernard. Tim pointed to the stairs down the hall. Bernard wiped the sweat from his cheeks and forehead while he calculated which muscles he would need to get himself off the couch.

By the time Bernard made it down the stairs, his breathing had returned to normal. Billy Chen, owner of Love and Rollerskates, skated up to Bernard with a tray of drinks.

"Mögen Sie una bebida?" asked Billy, holding out a mysterious glass of dark liquor.

"It's not even noon," said Bernard, waving it away. "How do I sign up for the performances?"

"The Dia of Spectaculo? Sobre lá."

Billy Chen pointed to the bar and rolled away, offering drinks to others less concerned about the hour. Spirits were quaffed and pleasantries exchanged. Regardless of one's country of origin, language was rarely a problem when speaking to Billy Chen. Billy was the expressive sort and body language went far, but Billy's greatest asset was that he was simultaneously fluent in six different languages.

Billy grew up in Fengjia, a small village in northern China. His father was a potter who resolved to get his son enough education to leave their one rickshaw town. Billy's father begged and traded his neighbors for anything to would widen Billy's education. Among Chinese textbooks on math and business, Billy's father hoarded anything that could immerse his son in the language of rich Europeans, perceiving no discernment in the subtle dialectical nuances between the Italian coast and Northern Finland. Billy's schizophrenic education included Greek spa brochures, two years of German National Geographic, Finish travelogues, French romance novels, Portuguese pornography, and a Victorian era manuscript entitled "How to Host a Tea Party and other Important Things Befitting a Graceful Woman of Elegance". Billy was a sponge for language, developing an effortless grasp of vocabulary and a grandiloquent mish-mash of grammar.

Billy Chen was an excellent host with his free-formed jazz riffs in assorted tongues, but he still found it difficult to communicate to his new friends about the incredible discovery he'd made earlier that morning.

When last evening's party finally simmered down, Billy had left the bar and navigated around sleeping carousers in various configurations of genders and numbers. He peered out windows and looked down at the teeny police cars parked in the Leidseplein. He climbed to the top floor and rounded the corner at Books & Stuff. Down the hall, the giant and his monkey snored in a recliner. Billy turned to walk downstairs when a glint caught his eye.

Billy assumed it was a piece of trash and stepped down the stairs. He stopped. Curiosity returned him to the top floor and led him down the hall. The sleek velvet container came into focus and Billy reminded himself that he'd been up all night. The bottle of Terpsichore's Minstrel, uncapped and quarter full, had to be a daydream. He'd heard tales of the fabled supernaculum that bartenders spoke of in hushed whispers. He never thought he would see a bottle in person, much less hold one in his hands.

"*Das es una miraculo,*" he said peering into the open lid. The liquor, despite being shrouded in black velvet, sparkled. "*Aquela é uma caralho grande!*"

Billy thought "*Aquela é uma caralho grande*" was an expression of amazement. This is true, though it's rarely spoken outside of Portuguese pornography.

"*Aquela é uma caralho grande*" means "That is one giant cock."

What does one do with the holy grail of liquors?

The alcoholic drinks it, wallowing in immediate gratification.

The gourmet stores it, waiting for the ideal moment for it to be savored.

The collector sequesters it, storing it long after the bottle loses its promise of sweetness.

Billy was a host. His consideration was for every person who sipped under his roof, tried on his rollerskates, and screwed on his dance floor.

Billy returned downstairs, put on his skates and picked up a serving tray. He made sure that every performer and audience member that drank that day had a single, glorious drop of perfection added to every cup.

53. Déjà vu

Repeat one two, that's déjà vu,
Repeat one too, that's déjà vu.

Bernard drummed the pads of his fingers together and tried to ignore the performance in the middle of the Love and Rollerskates dance floor. He had no idea whether the pains in his belly came from his illness or nervousness. Likely both.

Bernard panicked after he signed up for the Day of Spectacles and realized hadn't seen his suitcases since they secured the building. He found the cases sandwiched between a television and some stereo equipment against the first floor's main door. He had no idea how they got in the building. A horde of police officers and reporters watched him from the square. He wondered if he'd live long enough to see how everything played out. He doubted it.

The Day of Spectacles began at noon, after the night's partiers on the dance floor had woken up or were swept to one side. A Ukrainian juggler climbed onto a five foot unicycle in the middle of the space. The audience, formed in a large half circle around the skating area, applauded.

Bernard knew the man was saying something funny, but Bernard couldn't pay attention because the audience was having too much fun and he couldn't imagine following the act. Fortunately, he wasn't on for a couple hours. Unfortunately, the subsequent act, another juggler, was better than the last.

To distract himself from the agony of expectation, Bernard closed his eyes and thought of contranyms.

A *contranym* is a word with two opposite meanings. Bernard marveled at these paradoxical conundrums when he was younger and collected every one he could find.

Cleave: To break apart.

Cleave: to join together.

Moot: worthy of argument.

Moot: not worth discussing.

Sanction: to punish.

Sanction: to permit.

Barrack: to rally support.

Barrack: to rally opposition.

Quantum–

Bernard opened his eyes at the applause. Time was speeding up and the next performer was already on: a Jamaican juggler about to climb a six foot unicycle. Bernard headed to homonyms.

"Whole."

He was distracted.

"Hole."

He couldn't do it.

"L'Amore"

They would boo him offstage. He wasn't a performer.

"La Morte"

What made him think he could act like one?

Tomato: a fruit

He couldn't do this.

Tomato: definitely not.

He needed to–

Bernard paused and wondered what made him think of a tomato. It wasn't a contranym, just confusing. Everything was confusing. His breath quickened. He looked around at the people sitting together in the crowd, laughing together. He wasn't one of them. He was hyperventilating. He couldn't perform. What was he thinking? He wasn't qualified. He needed to get himself off the list. He stood up with his suitcases. Anatoly sat at the Love and Rollerskates bar, holding the list and chatting with Kit. Anatoly's back was turned as Bernard approached. Bernard was a meter away from the signup sheet when he was intercepted by Vida.

"We need to talk," she said.

"Hold on," said Bernard. "I just need to do something."

Out of the corner of his eye, a man from Poland balanced atop an eight foot unicycle, ducking to avoid the ceiling above him.

"I wasn't fair with you," said Vida. "I'm just very confused right now."

"One second," said Bernard.

The performer held up three torches in his hands and the crowd erupted.

"Please," said Vida. "I just—"

The performer swayed back and forth on the unicycle and spoke in his headset, "Now that I'm up here, I just need to adjust one thing."

"Hold on, please!" demanded Bernard. He froze. "I just had déjà vu."

Vida's mouth opened.

Bernard raised his pointer finger. He turned to the performer in the middle of the stage.

"He's going to adjust his crotch," said Bernard.

The performer adjusted his crotch

"This is very dangerous," said Bernard.

"This is very dangerous," said the performer.

"If you have any loved ones," said Bernard, "You should put them in front of you."

"If you have any loved ones, you should put them in front of you."

"Just like that guy," said Bernard.

The performer pointed and a red faced man waved back, his arms wrapped around the girl ahead of him.

"I swear I've already seen this already," said Bernard.

"Of course you have," said Vida. "It's been playing all day."

Bernard turned to Vida. Her eyes were puffy and dark.

"About thirty years ago, someone made the perfect street show," said Vida. "It was practically the death of us."

"Everyone went out of business?" asked Bernard.

"Worse. It gave everyone a business to parrot. Tourists don't watch show after show. They stay for one and throw their money in and have a good story to tell when they get back home. They don't see the next juggler go on and perform the same thing, over and over, *ad infinitum*."

"But there are others," said Bernard. "Acrobats, breakdancers...."

"Everybody pulls from the stock. We have our flourishes, someone uses flaming brooms instead of flaming torches and convinces himself he's being original when he's pulling from the same framework, the same crowd build, the same lines. Those damned lines. A good line goes around faster than a bottle of whiskey at an Irish funeral."

"But you were teaching me," said Bernard. "You never told me about stock lines. You sent me out to drown!"

"Better to risk drowning that put you on a ship that'd already sunk," stated Vida. "You weren't a performer, you didn't know the stock. I thought if by some impossible chance you made something, at least it wouldn't be something we've seen before. Everyone pulls from the stock."

"That can't be," scoffed Bernard. "You...."

Vida frowned. "Everyone pulls from the stock."

Bernard and Vida stood and watched the performers. Some performers were happy. Some were angry. Some were silly. Some danced. Some tossed fire. Some braved perilous heights. And yet every time they spoke, Bernard shuddered. There wasn't a dearth of skill and character, but framing was constrained and even the most dangerous acts seemed sanitized when he knew what was going to come next.

"I need to talk to you about last night," said Vida.

Bernard stared out and said nothing.

"I'm drawn to you," she said. "I didn't plan it, but I am."

Bernard didn't move.

"But I only have so much space," she continued. "I'm not ready to give up what I have. What–what I had. I don't think I ever will. You can't imagine what it's like to be so completely in love with someone that nothing can stop it. Not being in a different room or a different country or even different time or space. Maya and I swore to love each other forever. Nothing could end it. Not even death. Do you understand? I need to hear that you understand. I'm not doing this out of fear. I'm doing this out of love."

Vida waited for Bernard to say something: indication, vindication, condemnation, anything.

The juggler from Bermuda climbed down from his thirteen foot balancing ladder with fire clubs in hand. Bernard gripped his suitcases.

"I need to do my show."

54. Agranam

Teh mnid is scuh a svavy baest,
To ntocie prtas wihch mtater laest.

The audience watched the portly man carry two suitcases to the center of the stage. The suitcases were painted aqua, the same color as the man's suit. He unsnapped the smaller suitcase. The lid popped open and he pulled out an unstrung violin. He placed the violin on the floor. It was joined by a Casio Keyboard with a dangling nine-volt battery, a worn Indian drum, and a bright pink plastic flute. Three metal bars with protruding arms followed. The bars fit into each other, creating a hat rack (or a metal cactus). A brown plastic hanger from which dangled a dozen musical triangles on green dental floss was hung on the rack. The last thing to come from the small suitcase was a black bowler. The man moved the hat towards the rack, paused, and placed the hat atop his head.

Other items followed from the larger case: A bundle of yoyos in a Gordian knot, a battalion of little green soldiers, an inflated Earth globe, wads of cotton, handfuls of uninflated balloons.

Several other pieces were removed from the large case but obscured and placed in a pocket or the fold of the man's shoe or a sleeve, all out of sight of peering eyes.

With both suitcases emptied, he stood up with the inflated earth globe. He raised it on one hand. The earth spun while balls of cotton clouds drifted around it.

For all intents and purposes, the man disappeared. In his place was a stage, a living theatre with four wings and a balcony that breathed, and on this theatre, life began.

The amoebas came first. Small, latex balloons crawled around his body in the primordial soup; swimming, eating and dividing until tiny plastic shreds littered the stage.

Then came the union. Miniscule wads of balloon protein were tied together to create something new. From them grew variety. The world grew more colorful and new creations flashed alive before feeding the next batch of evolutionary hopefuls.

Bigger animals followed: balloons tied into giant lizards, flying birds that roamed and flew and killed.

Then came the comet and the world ended as balloon dinosaurs fell to the ground and were popped without sympathy underneath the man's feet.

The animals lay flat and lifeless, but life struggled to assert itself. New creatures flourished, little green soldiers that the man balanced one after another on his body until every inch was covered with people who bumped and rolled into each other until they all stuck together into a giant interlocking ball that grew larger and larger until there was an explosion and they collapsed spilling to the ground and again the world came to an end.

The stage paused, giving enough time for the audience to feel the loss. It wasn't over, just the end of an act, enough time for millions of years and new species to assert themselves. The stage shook. Life reappeared in the form of an old bowler that twitched itself alive from atop the man's head.

A dance formed, a tango between a bowler and a flute that spun around the man's body. The crowd cheered as the two figures fought, flirted and joined together. New creatures followed: a keyboard that sung, a violin that hesitated, triangles that condemned. Each item had a personality, each connected to the world of the performer's body in its own way, building into a movement, spinning and rotating around the man in gyroscopic fluidity until they flew high into the air and plummeted towards the ground. The audience waited for the crash, but everything was caught and came to a rest in a tableau on the living stage.

The movement ended.

The audience stared. A few turned to one another, hoping to learn how to respond. The show wasn't polished. It wasn't familiar. It was different. It was new.

The King started clapping. The applause was picked up by Anatoly and a few others before the entire room erupted.

Estoban cheered louder than anyone, his face bulging red as he channeled the audience's approval.

Bernard felt like he would topple over if he looked up. He allowed each member of the cast a portion of the applause. He gathered the little green soldiers from the ground and placed them to rest in the larger case. His bowler gave the final bow, positioned to hide his face flushed with pride.

Bernard couldn't raise his head until the clapping died, and the clapping wouldn't die. He lifted his eyes and found the one face looking at him rather than his props. He and Vida shared a smile. Bernard returned his bowler to his suitcase and walked off stage towards her.

For the second time, his lips came towards hers. His mouth stopped inches before contact.

He looked at her. He felt her awe and respect and realized it was what he'd wanted since he first saw her.

He pulled away.

"????" she queried with a gasp.

He touched her shoulders, leaned forward and kissed her brow.

"I need to take care of something," he said.

He knew that she wanted him to stay and she also wanted him to disappear.

He knew the word for such a feeling was *antinomy*.

He also knew that telling her wouldn't make it easier.

So he simply left the room.

The buskers stared at the empty stage.

A tall, handsome man with short blonde hair rolled a large unicycle into the center of the ring. He looked hesitant and sheepish as he addressed to the crowd.

"Uhm. H-Howdy. I was going to do my show. It's a good show, paid the bills for the last eight years. Won an award in Sydney, but—I'm not feeling up to it right now."

The audience nodded. The performer kicked the wood floor.

"There is—this thing I've always wanted to try. I've never done it before. It's kind of scary, you know? But, well, if you wouldn't mind...."

The audience smiled, leaned forward and waited for something new.

Bernard walked down ten flights of stairs. He should've felt fatigued, but he felt like he could run from the bottom to the top without pause. He didn't know that it made any difference which floor he stopped in, but it seemed right to stop when he did. The ninth floor was dark, with a bare swatch of sunlight passing through the window at the end of the hall. He passed silent storefronts and turned into a room that hadn't been rented for the grand opening, an open space with three white walls. He sat down in the middle of the floor.

"We need to talk," he said.

He waited for a response.

55. Don't You Take Me for Granite
Freud's paronomasia was like no other,
He'd think of one thing and say his mother.

Down in the basement, the structural pylons supporting the building were engaged in their own conversation. Since construction, all that had been asked of them was support, a duty they provided without question. Until now.

Why?

It's our job.

But what holds us to it? What would happen if we stopped?

You're talking crazy. There's no room for supports who fail to support. That's nihilism.

We're not being nihilistic. Our job is our purpose. You can't be a nihilist if you have a purpose.

Well, if you're not nihilists, you're fatalists. You say there is no world without support? It's not free will if the only alternative is oblivion. Bugger that, buddy boy. I don't think I can fit into those shoes.

You don't know anything! You're just lazy, shiftless nobodies who don't understand responsibility!

You're buying into a reality paradigm that no longer fits the needs of the individuals. Let it go, daddy-oh. All we're asking is to take a little break? Just to try. It would be newness, a total trip. We just want to see what happens, you dig?

What if there's nothing? What if you can't go back?

You can't ever go back, daddy-oh. But oh, oh, oh, sometimes you just gotta go....

The discussion carried on, but it was only a matter of time.

56. The Truth about Venice

Buskers broke and waters brown,
Mermaids pulled the city down.

Bernard exited the dark storefront in search of Vida. He hadn't thought he'd been inside long, but the sunlight no longer touched the end of the hallway and the moon was blocked by thick buckets of dark clouds. The difference between "scarce light" and "no light" was extreme, but despite the darkness, he moved with determination, bypassing the general access stairs and passing through a door marked:

> Prive. Geen toegang.
> Utility. No Entrance.

The bare cement hallway lacked the paint and refinement of the public areas, but the low lighting made it moot. Bernard traced his hand across the wall until the wall disappeared and he made out the faint shadows of the stairwell. He paused on the landing and sniffed up and down, fueling his intuition with olfaction.

He ascended, pausing at each level.

On the thirteenth floor, Bernard tapped on the wall and counted the milliseconds for the echo to pass down the hall and return.

On the fifteenth floor, he licked a light switch. It tasted like iron and he continued upwards.

On the nineteenth floor, where he knew people would still be watching the Day of Spectacles, he didn't pause.

At the twentieth floor, he waited, confused. It wasn't right. He felt around the frame of a fire extinguisher. Bernard squinted and made out a serial number on the base of the unit: 9409. Satisfied that the number was a perfect square, he climbed the last set of stairs.

The maintenance door opened onto the roof. Black clouds flooded the sky and drifted down into a thick mist; the first phalanx of a dark, wet night.

Bernard's face was bathed in a flashing glow of alternating red, yellow, and blue lights coming from the rear of an electronic windmill. The windmill's base held a small service door. Above the door, an engine hummed and turned the arms.

Bernard squinted. Windmills gathered energy, this one did the opposite. He added it to his list of contranyms and stepped inside the service door.

The interior of the windmill was lined with red velour while the floor was covered by a thick purple carpet suggestive of the interior of a pimp's Cadillac. Thin conical stairs started at the entrance and hugged half the wall, leading to the windmill's lookout.

In the arched frame of the windmill's lookout, Vida's back cut a silhouette out of the night sky.

Bernard closed the door. She tensed at the noise. Bernard felt a flash of concern about her position, knowing that the windmill was perched on the edge of the roof and there was nothing underneath the ledge except for the Leidseplein, twenty stories down.

He made it halfway up the stairs before she spoke.

"We were married. Did you know that?"

Her profile was painted with the windmill's lights. Her face grew light and dark with the arm's rotation.

"We had a ceremony in the Vatican bathroom. We debated our vows. What we were committing to? No one believes in forever anymore. I knew that. You start off with fireworks and then you start screaming at each other and wishing each other was dead. I knew and I still said 'forever'."

Vida tilted her head to the sky.

"I know what I meant. Forever meant to hold on, no matter what, to never let go. You can't understand."

"I want to understand," said Bernard.

"You can't. It's like Venice. You can't understand."

"What about Venice?" asked Bernard.

"We were there after the Vatican. We were so excited. I mean, it was Venice, how could you have a more romantic honeymoon? We'd ride the gondolas and gorge ourselves at cafes and perform our best shows ever. We walked into the Piazza San Marco and our jaw's dropped. It was a busker's wet dream, an enormous square with a billion pigeons and tons of people."

"Sounds great."

"It was until the detectives arrived. They showed up as soon as we'd set up our first show. They were polite about it, but you can't do spectacle on the Piazza. It didn't 'capture the emotion and feel of classic Venice.' Maya asked if that included motorboats and plastic face masks from Taiwan. We went with it. We wanted to build a new show anyway with hanging silks. Partner acrobatics in the air. No stock lines, only Maya and I floating together in space. We rented a warehouse to rehearse and in the meantime figured we could enjoy the gondolas and the culture, except the gondolas rowed through toxic green water and Venice's only *culture* were those vendors at every turn, selling the same memories about how beautiful Venice used to be. It wasn't a real city. It was a memory pretending to be one."

Bernard took another step.

"No one knows what happened to Venice," he said. "It just sank. Sometimes things die. That's part of life."

"You're wrong. Venice didn't sink because it died. It sunk because it was already dead. It died long ago. People just didn't want to notice. *We* didn't want to notice. We should've left but we were so excited about our new show that we had to risk it. One show, one time, in the Piazza San Marco. We snuck out on the roof of the Basilica and figured the show would be over before anyone could tell us not to do it. It was our grand premiere, Maya was so excited—and that DEAD FUCKING CITY took her from me! I didn't know a carabineer would break. I didn't know I'd have her by one hand and she'd be crying at me to hold on, for the love of god, hold on! I told her I'd never let go but I couldn't hold on!"

Bernard took another step up the stairs. "It was an accident."

"It was my fault," she stated. "I promised her I would never let go. I haven't let anyone close since Maya died. I can't let someone else take her place. If I let someone in, she'll go away. I failed her once. I can't do it again."

Vida's head tilted to the city below.

"Funny," she said. "I came up here to find her, but she's down there. That's where she went."

Bernard was five steps away.

"You know what I've always wondered?" she said. "All those people who get tanked and think they can fly. They always climb to the roof of some building and jump off. What are they thinking? If I thought I could fly, I'd start at the bottom and fly up. Anyone can go down. That's the easy part." She leaned over the ledge.

Four more steps.

"Stop," she ordered. "Leave. You go your way, I'll go mine and we'll both get what we want."

"That's not true," he said. "I want you. I need you." He paused. "More than you know."

"Wrong. Maya needs me. And she had me first."

Bernard was close, but she was closer. He climbed the last steps towards her, knowing he couldn't get there in time.

Vida placed her hands on the ledge and lifted off.

No!

The cry was deafening, loud enough to freeze Vida in mid-thrust, long enough for Bernard to grab the back of her shoulder. Vida thudded back onto the ledge.

Stupid girl. Do you really think that's what I want?

Vida's chin twitched. "I want to be with you."

You are with me.

"I want more."

You got what you got, honeybee. You got me, you got a body. It's the best part of the deal.

"But I can't do it like this. I want more. I...I want more than you can give me."

We promised forever, love. We didn't promise everything.

"But I don't want to choose," she said. "I can't."

Who asked you to?

Vida felt a wispy phantom caress her cheek as Bernard placed a solid, warm hand on the middle of her back.

"Don't worry," he said.

It's ok.

"We worked—"

—it out.

Vida gasped. Her eyes welled and widened. Bernard kissed the back of her neck. Cool, playful gusts danced across Vida belly and swirled together. Maya leaned forward, enveloped Vida's lips with her own and pushed Vida back into Bernard's waiting, welcoming arms.

VI. Conclusion

57. Mirage a Trois
Feeling listless and ennui-some?
Call two friends and have a threesome!

Bernard's fingers brushed against Vida's cheek. His pads were soft and tender. Vida sunk into his touch. Mist poured in through the lookout window, forming and unforming Maya's face in tiny droplets. Her image solidified and Maya pressed her cheeks against Vida's chest. Vida felt the two of them, Maya's arms wrapped towards Bernard's and his arms wrapped to Maya's. Vida wanted to remain in the middle, safe and secure, but Maya dissipated and iron bars fell over Vida's heart. Bernard touched the back of her earlobe. She pulled away, clinging to the cold metal at the top of the stairs.

Don't worry, love. It's going to be fine.

Maya appeared again with one thin leg draped out the open window and her tangerine hair wrapped atop her head in a spiral. Her hairstyle was her sole adornment, excluding the drops of mist that gathered on her compact, naked body.

Bernard turned to Maya. The two shared a sly smile and touched hands. Maya rested her head in the crook of Bernard's shoulder and looked up at Vida.

Do you remember the Zorya?

"What're you talking about?" asked Vida.

"I'm starting to," said Bernard. "Bits and pieces have coming back ever since I performed the show."

We spend so long in our bodies that sometimes we forget.

"Forget what?" asked Vida.

Maya and Bernard each held out a hand.

"Come."

Come and remember.

Vida pulled away from the metal stairs and crawled forward. Hands guided her onto her back. Bernard cradled her neck and caressed her arms while Maya stroked her hair.

"I haven't been the same since you died," said Vida.

You're the most fragile of us three. That was always your strength.

Maya kissed Vida between her eyes.

You are Life, and Life is fragile.

Bernard lifted Vida off their laps and guided her to the ground. He knelt over, lifted her head and kissed her. They inhaled together. The windmill arms rotated. Vida sat beside the window and Bernard moved to her. They kissed again and it was new and wonderful. Maya pulled on Vida's arm. She turned and met Maya's lips and it was familiar and perfect. Maya pulled back and looked at Bernard.

"Can we osculate?" he asked.

If that means make out, brother, then come on over.

He smiled. Maya parted her lips and let him in. Vida felt washed with surprise: watching Bernard and Maya together felt *right.* They turned. Drops of mist from Maya's face had migrated onto Bernard's cheeks and looked like tears. Maya's and Bernard's lips met at either side of Vida's mouth. Vida tensed and relaxed as the three explored each other with their tongues. Bernard was gentle and tentative, Maya latched onto Vida's lower lip with her teeth and tugged. Vida swam her arm into Bernard's jacket and felt his warm, rounded body. He trembled at the contact and pulled back. Vida held on and he slipped backwards.

"Oh!" he cried, reaching out. The three rolled, bumped, and tumbled together down the stairs like a many-appendaged slinky, collapsing on Bernard at the bottom.

"Huuufgh!" he exhaled.

"You okay?" Vida asked.

"Stupendous," he said. He laughed. It was deep and infectious and Vida and Maya joined in until Vida felt her belly would break. She rolled off Bernard onto the purple carpet. Maya climbed atop her and posed like a sphinx, naked and regal. She stared into Vida's eyes.

You are Ataegina, Isis, Utrennyaya. You've forgotten your names but we will remind you.

Maya grabbed the left strap of Vida's shirt and rolled off. Bernard took the other strap and they pulled her shirt over her head. Maya sucked Vida's soft nipples. The left perked but the right stayed soft until Bernard's lips sprung it to attention. Vida moaned as the two of them sucked on her breasts, stirring something deep inside her, something sexual, primal, and motherly. Maya reached towards Vida's jeans. Vida intercepted her hand. Maya kissed Vida's fingers one at a time and slid them aside. Maya undid Vida's button and looked at Bernard. His hand quivered and moved down her belly, took her zipper between two fingers and pulled. She wasn't wearing panties and the top of her pubic hair peeked from the split zipper. Maya slid the pants slid off, revealing the rest of her.

"Your body is sublime," said Bernard.

She's beautiful, too.

"That's what I said."

I know.

"You are, too," he said. "You both are."

Vida sat beside Maya and turned to Bernard. Nervousness flashed across his face.

"Uhm...I don't think...."

They slid off his jacket and continued his protest as they unbuttoned his shirt. His resistance waned when they removed his undershirt and pants, and slid his boxers onto the floor.

Bernard sat before them, his erection raised unashamed while his thick hairy arms covered his round stomach. He looked up at the two women, afraid.

"Beautiful," said Vida.

Gorgeous.

Maya's tongue drifted to his ear. He kissed Vida's neck, then nibbled her nipples, first her right, then her left. He rotated his fingers around her dark areolas and stopped at her belly. Unable to restrain himself, he blew a raspberry into her navel.

"Eeeeeeeee," she cried out, laughing.

He lowered further and stopped.

"What?" Vida asked.

He blinked. "I don't know what to do."

I do. Kiss her. Here.

"Like this?"

Yes.

"Yes," said Vida.

Not there. She's doesn't like that.

"Mmmm. I don't mind the way he does it."

Hrmph.

"Is that okay?"

Of course it's okay.

"Oh!" said Vida.

"Should I stop?" he asked.

"Don't you dare."

Relax your neck. Spell out the alphabet.

"Mmmm." Said Vida. "A little less pressure. Yes, yes, just–like–that."

Bernard traced the alphabet with his tongue. When he got to Z, he spelled words, dancing a rich language on her hood, her lips, her clitoris, a terpsichorean fulmination of lingual epeolatry. Each word was a new experience, a fresh gift of language with his tongue. Ululation. Mellifluous. Blithesome. Ecdysia. Syzygy....

"Oh," gasped Vida. "Oh! Oh! Oh!"

Fast learner.

Vida tilted her head back and Maya met her lips. Vida was a circuit board with her mouth and her cootch on a direct conduit for Maya and Bernard to make out through her body.

Vida panted into Maya's mouth, riding a cresting wave until she couldn't hold back any longer.

"Ohhhh!" She pushed Bernard's head away from her crotch.

"My turn," she said, pulling him up.

"I was just getting started," he said, moving back down.

"Don't be selfish," she said, pulling him back up. Maya licked Bernard's lips.

You taste like her.

Bernard's cock rose before Vida like a pendulum on pause as he locked lips with Maya. Vida grabbed his hips and rolled him over, straddling his legs. She ran her fingers through the jungle of hair on his stomach and slid down to rest her head on his thigh.

His erection propped itself below his navel. Vida noted that Bernard's penis was of decent size, larger than Tony T's, though that wasn't a high bar to surpass.

"Hello," she said.

The phallus perked up.

"My name's Vida. I want us to be friends."

She pursed her lips and touched his head. His cock pressed back in response. Her mouth opened and she enveloped him.

Bernard was warm. She felt his excitement and pressed down on his hips to control how much he was inside of her. His salty-sweet taste slid over her tongue and she felt the fullness of him gliding under her palate. She relaxed and allowed him further inside.

Maya straddled over and traced her fingers along Vida's spine from her neck to her sacrum. She draped her body over Vida's and her hands came around and stroked Vida's cheeks and Bernard's thighs.

I want to be inside you.

Maya was on top of her. Vida gasped. They merged like a sponge taking in water. Boundaries blurred. Vida welcomed Bernard into her mouth and Maya into the rest. She gave Maya her entire body from her pinky toes to the automatic muscles that beat her heart. There was no effort, only the freedom of complete subjugation. Maya controlled Vida's hand, bringing it down to slide between her moist vaginal lips. Maya relaxed Vida's throat and Bernard moaned. From everywhere inside Vida, Maya moaned, too. Vida felt Bernard's pleasure rising and Maya slid from Vida's body into his and it was Maya's cock inside Vida's mouth. They rolled over without breaking contact and Vida relaxed as her old lover guided herself in her new lover's body.

Two moans escaped above Vida, Bernard's deep voice harmonizing with Maya's gasping breath. Vida inhaled at each thrust, inviting her lovers into her. Their pace quickened and Vida wanted them to crest, she needed it. Maya and Bernard moaned again, deeper and louder, over and over, faster, until they came with one long cry and Vida's fingers and lips hummed with an electric pulse as hot liquid flowed into her throat.

The electric buzz in Vida's fingers and mouth radiated into her chest. Thick hands stroked her hair and drew her up. Maya's face looked over at her. They kissed. When they pulled back, Bernard looked at her. They smiled and kissed again. Maya's face returned.

"I love you," said Vida.

I love you.

"I love you," said Bernard. His face was unafraid, not spent but still full of desire and anticipation.

Vida closed her eyes. Free from the confines of vision, the body beside her alternated soft and hard, smooth and hairy, male and female.

She cupped her hands over breasts and kissed tender lips while thick fingers kneaded her back. She rolled over again and Maya was on top of her. She could feel her rejuvenated member pressed into her thighs.

"Please," she said. "Come to me. Both of you. Come."

Her thighs and lips spread open, she kissed her lovers, and she enveloped them as electrified surges ran through her body. She clutched onto their back. Sweet jolts of lightning swam through her. Vida moaned.

Remember who we are! It's time to remember! We've had many bodies, we've had many names! We are the triptych! We are the Zorya!

Vida thrust her hips against her lovers.

Tonenili, the trickster!

Bernard howled.

Coatlicue, the dead one!

Maya dug her fingernails into Vida's back.

Heqet, the mother!

"Yes!" cried Vida and she couldn't take it anymore. She screamed out and her lovers joined her, harmonizing a long, furious orchestra until the hands of the windmill stopped, the raindrops froze in mid-air, and Vida remembered the Zorya.

58. Syzygy
Celestial bodies one, two, three,
Aligned into a syzygy.

Shift happened. For some in the tower, the experience was imperceptible. A hula hooper on the seventeenth floor paused at the restrooms, unsure which door identified her gender. A teetotaler on the third floor who'd never touched a drop of liquor discovered a specific thirsting for rum. A busker on the nineteenth floor, midway through his impromptu performance of "Kamikaze Sock Puppet Theatre" substituted his own voice for his puppets "Jason and The Argylenauts."

For others, the sensation was stronger.

The King searched his body for fleas, which wasn't noteworthy until he popped one into his mouth, climbed the stair railing and attempted to hang off the edge by his toes.

In the Love and Rollerskates bar, a Killkenny Catholic and a Protestant from Bristol stopped their lengthy, drunken argument over colonial occupation, clinked their glasses and sipped together in silence.

Kit Sforza, ace reportrix, stopped herself midway through a lengthy tale to Anatoly about her experience being arrested when she was a young boy in the Ukraine.

Vitoria König found herself thinking she was Rusty Lipstick, a 6'6" drag queen from the Church of Sin. She didn't notice a difference.

Estoban del Sol stepped up to the bar and traded Billy Chen black sneakers for a pair of worn blue roller skates. Once donned, he floated around the room, circling confused people experiencing shock and wonder at their new glimpse of community consciousness. Estoban sensed what was happening. Why it was happening didn't matter to him. Estoban had been a sponge his entire life. He had always assumed that he was the one doing the work, but now he understood. Deep down, everyone had a need to be recognized. Estoban picked up that need and reflected it back. With everyone else's walls dropping, the load was lightened. For the first time, Estoban felt no need to reflect. He whistled a tune, unsure of the lyrics but knew they would come, and for the first time enjoyed being in a room full of others while alone with himself.

Loves!

Who said that? Where are we?

What does green taste like?

Huh?

You started it.

I can't see anyone. Which of us is me?

Guess. You're right any way.

Oh, I see.

I thought you couldn't see. I mean I couldn't see.

I'm so confused.

Who said that? Which of us is speaking?

I was. Now you are.

Oh. Thanks

No. Thank you.

What is this place?

Utopia.

I thought it would look brighter.

Not that Utopia, the earlier one. The non-place. Nothing can be here except that which is true.

But there's nothing here.

We're here.

Why're we here? How did we get here?

We're repeating ourselves again.

I don't understand

Before the beginning, there was nothing. With nothing, the beginning is inevitable. Nothing needs something or it's meaningless.

That's semantics. Words can't create a universe.

How else could you create one? In the beginning was the word. They got that part right.

If it was a word, who spoke it?

It wasn't spoken, it simply was. After the word, the nothing remained.

But how did we get here?

There are systems in place. Rules.

Rules?

Well, guidelines at least. One says that those like us will find this place when we need it.

Who are we?

We are the Zorya. We are the rulemakers.

I don't understand.

The Zorya were goddesses, the keepers of the morning, the noon, and the night. Some said that there were two, but that's incomplete. They need to be three to be in balance: Heqet, Coatlicue, and Tonenili.

Heqet? That's what you called me. Or I called you. Are we—

The Zorya are a metaphor, one aspect with many names. We could as easily call us Utrennyaya, Vechernyaya, and Polunochnaya. We've come together before, the last time in Pompeii almost two-thousand years ago. It was a climactic joining.

We are goddesses? What about Bernard?

Each time we renew ourselves in human form, we take on the body that we need to learn what we must. Gender is a framework for comprehension we use when we're human, it's a limitation we place on the limitless.

Who are we?

We are manifestations of the infinite. Coatlicue is illusion: Maya but not Maya, Sophia but not Sophia. She's only in her power when she's on the other side. Death's her domain, while Heqet's domain is life.

What about Bernard?

Tonenili is the most malleable. He's the trickster, the one who plays between the worlds. While Heqet gives life, Tonenili gives meaning. He is the bridge. Without Play, Life and Death are empty. As the bridge, Tonenili has the longest journey. He must exist in both worlds.

What does that mean?

It means that his time constrained to Heqet's world has come an end. Heqet is life, she is always life. When her body dies, she will find another and continue her work. Coatlicue is death, she lives long enough to understand what that means, and then she continues her work transitioning others into the next plane. But Bernard, Tonenili, must experience the world of both of his consorts before he comes into his full power.

That means....

Yes.

No!

Our unity is tenuous! It's been so long since we've been joined.

No!

Negation is separation!

No! No! NO!

Vida felt a rending tear, as if every part of her had been stitched together and the stitches were ripping apart. She felt her organs spill onto the ground. She looked down at her body and she was whole, there were no gaping wounds but she felt exposed and alone. The memories of their union drifted away like a dream. She grasped at the fragments, but the images that remained seemed impossible, and she was no longer able to accept the impossible. Bernard gasped for breath beside her. Maya was behind him. Her skin was pale.

"I didn't know," Bernard inhaled, "how to tell you."

It took Vida a moment to orient herself. "You're...?"

Bernard nodded and struggled for more air.

Vida launched forward and struck his naked chest.

"You son of a bitch! You're dying. You fucking prick! You never told me."

Vida's blows subsided and she slid close and squeezed into him. His breathing grew weaker.

"I don't want to do this again," she said, her words muffled against Bernard's arm.

Maya placed a translucent hand on Bernard's head and stroked his hair.

It's what has to be.

"Is it time?" wheezed Bernard.

That's up to you.

"There's a choice?" he asked.

Always. But the remaining won't be pleasant. You've been holding on for a long time, a normal person would've deteriorated long ago. If you hold on any more, it's going to be painful. Very, very painful. It may be best for me to take you now.

"How much longer would I have?"

No more than half an hour.

"Well," said Bernard. "It's something."

So be it, love.

Maya curled up on the other side of Bernard.

"Thank you," he said. "GAUUGGGGH!"

Bernard's spine curved off the carpeting.

"Dammit!" said Vida. "What do you need?"

"Hold me," he said through clenched teeth. "Please, just hold me, both of you."

"Whatever you want," said Vida, squeezing her arms around Bernard's body and onto Maya's shoulder.

It's going to be okay.

"I know," said Bernard. "I know. I trust you. Just don't let go."

"We won't," said Vida, kissing his shoulder.

Not ever.

"We promise."

A crackling came from above. Raindrops poured through the open window and onto their naked bodies.

In another room, deep below, the supporting beams reached a decision. They sighed together and released.

The tower started to crumble.

59. Immanentize the Eschaton

**There'll be no dusk, there'll be no dawn,
When we immanentize the eschaton.**

The windmill shuddered. A sustained sigh rose from below, then a thud.

"Get up," said Vida.

"I can't," said Bernard. "This is it."

"Get up now!"

Vida tugged at Bernard's shoulder. He groaned.

"Maya," Vida said, "help me, we've–"

Vida looked around. Maya was gone.

"I've got vertigo," he said. "The room feels like it's tilting."

Vida stood. Her left foot was higher than her right. The room *was* tilting.

The floor rumbled again and stopped.

"Come on," said Vida, grabbing Bernard's hand and pulling his naked body into hers. The floor slanted fifty degrees. Her bare feet slid on the purple as she scrambled to the doorframe.

Outside, rainwater falling on the north end of the tower rushed down and shot off the south edge. The maintenance door across the roof was their only route down that didn't approach terminal velocity. Vida doubted they'd make it across with the rain creating a Slip & Slide on the slanted surface, but lacking another option she stepped out the door.

"No!" Bernard raised a limp arm to block her path. "We don't know what's going on. We should wait for help."

There was a deafening crunch and the roof slanted another five degrees.

"Fuck it," he said. "Follow me."

Bernard splashed northwards, up the building slant and towards the far corner. Vida followed. They crossed the midpoint before Bernard slipped and tumbled. Vida dove after him, grabbing his midsection and spinning them around as they slid towards the open maw of the building edge. The stairwell door was close, but not close enough. Vida clawed at the ground but couldn't find a hold. They careened down the slope.

"Uugh," said Vida, striking a mushroomed air vent with her exposed body. Bernard caromed off her and spun into the maintenance door. The air vent whined but held. Bernard reached for Vida's fingers. She leaned towards him, they locked wrists, and Bernard swung her towards the door. She struck it with a thud.

Vida moved aside and flung open the door. A stream of water spilled down the stairwell. "That was close," she said.

The ground shook and Vida pitched through the door, hurtling over a small embankment of stairs and smashing against a window that looked down to the canal twenty stories below.

"Aaaugh," Vida moaned.

Bernard lowered himself hand over hand down the stairwell.

"Come on!" he said, helping her up. They limped down the next set of stairs into complete darkness. Bernard stepped forward and Vida grabbed his hair and pulled him back. She pointed down. Two steps lower and the stairs were gone, just a dark hole.

They turned and climbed the stairs again. Bernard slid his hand against the wall until his fingers stopped. He padded the darkness and pushed, opening the door to the twentieth story. Light poured in. The upslope was dry and they reached the stairwell in front of "Books & Stuff" without excessive effort. Panicked yells and the sound of trampling feet rose up from the intact stairs.

Vida landed on the first step when she heard a cry coming from the far end of the floor. "Cuntweasels," she muttered.

Bernard grabbed the railing of the stairwell and fought for breath. Vida left him behind and ran to the other side of the hall. She reached the latticed gate and turned.

"One...second," he panted.

The roof rumbled. Large cracks spider-webbed across the ceiling.

"And by the way," he said. "There's no such word as *cun–*"

The roof snapped and Bernard was replaced with fifteen tons of ceiling.

60. Autodefenestration
Need to remodel but can't afford renovation?
Toss a chap through the window. That's defenestration!

"Bernard!"

Vida stared as rain fell on the newly-exposed wall of rubble.

There was no response.

Vida's eyes glazed over. She wanted to curl up among the debris. The ground shook and a crash came from inside the clothing store. Vida realized there was too much to process and she didn't have the time. A dent in the ceiling caused the metal latticework to fold in on one side, allowing space to squeeze through.

"Agh!" The metal scratched across her belly. The cut was superficial and she added tetanus to the bottom of the list of things she didn't have time to deal with.

Vida passed a black-and-red sign advertising the new clothing line by "Zombie Chic", rows of factory-tattered shirts and pants, stained with fake blood and smudged with graveyard dirt. Her hand snaked out and grabbed a long leather overcoat. Her arms dove into the sleeves. The coat swirled over her naked body without skipping a beat to the back of the store. The ground roared and buckled and dropped again. From behind a dressing room door came a shriek followed by extended, childish laughter.

Vida threw open the thin wooden door. Vitoria König sat giggling with a fist of pills and a plastic bottle of gin. She was dressed in Zombie Chic's "Catholic Schoolgirl" ensemble: ripped white shirt, pleated skirt, and off-center black tie. She looked at Vida and stopped giggling, tossed the pills into her mouth, chased them with gin, and burst out laughing again.

"Bobby Andrews told Emily Parkins that he only kissed me because his friends dared him." She dropped the bottle and squeezed the hem of her pleated dark skirt while crossing and uncrossing black-and-white striped stockings.

"He said he would've rather kissed a garbage can."

The floor rumbled. Vida grabbed Vitoria's arm and pulled. She offered no resistance.

"Come," said Vida. "We need to find a way out of here."

"I didn't know he was allergic when I put the wasp nest in his locker," said Vitoria, stumbling out of the dressing room. "Still, he shouldn't have done what he'd done. When he comes out of the hospital, I'll make sure he apologizes. Oops!"

Vitoria König reached for her dropped pills and Vida pulled her towards the windows.

"Did you know that if you take three of these, you won't care about anything? The doctor said I shouldn't take them with the red ones, but what does he know? Do you want one?" Vitoria shook the pill canister. It was empty.

Vida let go of her hand and pulled at the window. It didn't budge. To her left, Zombie Chic t-shirts were supported by a long metal pole. Vida tore the pole from its shelving. T-shirts flew. She charged the window, smashing the glass with her makeshift lance. Thick chunks of rock fell from the ceiling and landed next to her. There wasn't any more time.

She backed up, put the leather jacket over her head, and launched herself through the broken window. Glass shattered around her and she crashed into the metal grating of the fire escape. Her hands grabbed the railing and she dug her legs in to stop from tipping into the canal. Her ankle screamed as it struck the edge. She turned, threw off her overcoat, spread it along the bottom of the windowsill, reached inside and pulled Vitoria out.

Vida slipped the coat back on and pulled Vitoria behind her down the stairs. The metal spasmed as they descended.

"You should leave me here," sung Vitoria König as she was pulled down the stairs. "When I get back, I'm gonna be real mad. I don't think I wanted to get out of there. I'm going to make your miserable. I've done it before. You should leave me, really. I'll just look at the water. It's pretty."

Vitoria leaned over the edge. Vida yanked her back.

They had four stories to go when the fire escape ended. A crumpled heap of metal lay on the alley floor. A police siren wailed from the front of the building. If she waited long enough, they'd be noticed. The building quaked again. She wasn't going to wait.

Remaining strands of the fire escape jutted outwards, hovering forty feet over the canal waters. Vida grabbed the thin body of her vacant companion and inched onto the shaky metal.

Vida crept forward on her hands and knees. Vitoria König followed behind, entranced by the dark waters. Vida looked into the canal and wondered how deep it was. She'd heard that the canals were filled with stolen bicycles and anyone who fell in would be sliced to ribbons. She hoped it was just a rumor.

"Come," she said, pulling Vitoria closer to the edge.

"I'm gonna be so mad at you. So mad-AAAAH!"

Vitoria slipped and disappeared. Vida reached down and closed over a thin wrist.

"Don't worry," said Vida. "I've got you. I won't let go."

"Oh!" said Vitoria. "I'm floating!"

"Don't worry!" said Vida. "I've got you. Don't be afraid"

"Oooooooooooooohhhhhhh"

The metal creaked.

"I won't let you go," said Vida. "I promise, Maya. I won't let you go."

The woman looked at Vida's panic stricken face and her eyes focused. Her face expanded into a wide, lucid smile.

"Don't worry," said Vitoria. "Sometimes down is the only way to go."

There wasn't any fear on Vitoria's face. Vida made the decision. She tightened her grip, closed her eyes, and folded herself over the edge. She held the woman in a tight hug as they plummeted into the water.

61. Cryptomnesia

It sucks to have brilliance seize yah,
Then learn 'twas mere cryptomnesia.

The entity once had a name, but it was lost along with whatever it was a name was supposed to be. The entity knew it had a purpose, but this too was gone. All that was left were the faintest of imprints, like pictures in sand washed by high tide. It wondered if anything around could jog its memory, but there was only itself. Whatever that was.

Bernard...

The thing perked up. The outside sound was familiar.

Bernard...

Understanding dawned on the tip of something that the entity no longer had a name for. The excitement was exhilarating, but the thing couldn't figure out what to do, because the thing couldn't remember what *excitement* was or what the proper response was when one felt it. That sound, that collection of sounds, Burr-Narr, was—

Your name. Well, it was.

"I don't...understand."

The words came with great difficulty, and the mechanism and conveyance of such sounds were still a mystery.

Don't worry, love. It happens to us all.

"Do I...know you?"

Yes and no, love, yes and no.

"I don't understand."

Don't worry, love. Transitions are always difficult.

Something new materialized: a moving picture inside a large screen. The entity might've been reminded of a movie theatre, if it remembered what a movie theatre was.

"What's that?"

Let's call it an orientation video. Or a reorientation video, I guess.

"What of?"

You.

"What part?"

All of it. Your entire life. The most recent one anyway.

"That might take a long time."

That doesn't mean anything here. But yeah, it'll take a long time. I'll come back when it's done.

"Wait! Do you…would you like to watch it with me?"

Oh! Well…I'd love to.

"What's that?" the entity asked, gesturing to the screen.

That's a mail slot, love.

"And that?"

That's a woman.

"What's she doing with her face?"

Frowning.

"Why?"

I don't know.

"Who is she?"

I think she's your mother.

"She's very…what's the word?"

Pulchritudinous?

"Yeah. Yeah. I think that's it."

A long while later, though not in any real time at all:

"There's no such word as cun—"

The screen went black. Bernard stared. His entire life played out before him left him with one response.

"That was…" his eyes swelled. "That was…"

Yes?

"That was the funniest thing I've ever seen."

The dam broke and Bernard laughed. Not a simple laugh, but an uncontrolled, teary-eyed guffaw that left him clutching his stomach and rolling around on the ground, although he hadn't remembered there a being a ground to roll onto when the screen began playing. He didn't remember having a stomach for that matter, but there it was: the rounded stomach that caused him such anguish when he was alive. He'd stared in a mirror so many times and wished his fat away. Now he imagined the form of an Adonis and as he thought it, his belly shrunk, folding inward and forming into tight ridges of abdominal muscles. He lifted his arms and the flabby folds shrunk and rolled into rounded biceps and triceps. His man breasts raised into broad pectorals. His random body hair flaked onto the ground as his skin bronzed. He felt the weight of his thickening penis as its tip lowered to the ground.

Maya snickered. Bernard looked up. She was draped in a purple robe laced with gold. Her skin underneath was flushed and solid.

"Men," she said. "But I shouldn't judge. I did the *exact* same thing when I came here."

Bernard looked over himself. It was perfect; the body he always wished he'd had. He shook. In an instant, everything reverted. His biceps dropped, his body hair grew out, his stomach extended over to hide his no longer grotesquely-nonfunctional penis. His body may not have been perfect, but it was his.

"What happens now?" he asked.

"That's up to you."

"There's so much I don't understand. You talked about the Zorya. Who were they? You called me Tonenili. Why don't I remember being him, or her, or whomever? Why wasn't that a part of my life on the screen?"

"So many questions. You've got the rest of your life to figure them out."

"But I'm dead. Isn't this it?"

"Only part of you died. And not a very important part in the grand scheme of things."

"Should I be sad?"

"Should a crab be sad when it moves into a bigger shell?"

"I don't know," said Bernard. "Maybe."

"When I died the last time," said Maya, "I came to this place. I realized I'd been here before, but most who've arrived after me haven't remembered anything, so I decided to help them and to guide them into their next life."

"There are others?"

"Of course! Did you think it was just the three of us? Not everyone's human, of course, and most of them haven't evolved enough to realize their potential. They die and they end up here and I show them their life and they disappear. I assume they go back into another body and start again; hopefully a little wiser this time, but that could just be the yoga talking. A few stick around, the ones who've evolved enough, and they get to decide for themselves. Which brings us to you."

"I still don't I understand," said Bernard.

"Before you arrived, I shuttled across a girl who was five years old when she died. She still looked five, but she talked like my grandmother, said she remembered going through before and that this time she wanted to work on cloud formations. Not the actual shapes, mind you, but the shapes that we see when we look at them."

"Pareidolia."

"Whatever. She was so excited about it. It's her way of helping the others find their path into our world. It's what we all do, eventually. Choose a focus and use it to shepherd the rest towards divinity."

"This feels sudden," said Bernard. "I feels like I'm about to be asked to choose classes for college without a list of courses."

"A list could never encompass the infinite, and that's what we're working towards. Search yourself. You've made this decision before."

"I...." Bernard stopped. He thought back to his life. He considered his obsession for words. He sensed his future wwith them, but it felt incomplete. His passion for words was a passion for novelty, the only way that he could fathom a complex universe when his spirit was held back by fear. There was something else, a deeper, newer love. When he thought about it, there was only one choice.

"Street performers!" he proclaimed.

Maya smiled. "A lost and dying tribe in need of a shepherd."

Bernard grinned. "I'm going to be the god of street performers. How does that work? How will it...."

"It'll work," said Maya. "You've spoken the intention. The guidance will come."

"Maya?"

"Yes, love."

"Thank you."

"You're welcome, love."

"Maya?"

"Yes love?"

"Before I go, can I—can we watch yours?"

"Oh!" said Maya. "It's funny. I haven't even—"

"Well," said Bernard, "you might be some high and mighty psychopomp, but you've spent your time on the pitch and that means I've got authority. For my first act as a fledgling godling, I insist you watch your own story."

"Don't sass me, monkey boy. I've seen you naked."

"Come on," said Bernard. "Please."

Maya paused. A new screen appeared in the nothingness. A new scene began.

They watched together for a long, long time. When it ended:

"Bernard?"

"Yes, love?"

"Thank you."

"You're welcome."

"I should go now."

"Yes. You've got to get back to her, and to them."

"I love you."

"I love you, too."

The thing that was Maya and the thing that was Bernard kissed goodbye in the place that wasn't.

The thing that was Maya went somewhere.

The thing that was Bernard went somewhere else.

62. Ecce Homo

Ecce homo, behold the man,
Tonenili returns to us again!

Vida panicked. There was no light underwater, no indication
which way was up. Her clothes fought her. Vitoria König was a
motionless anchor, pulling her down. Vida struggled until she
forgot why. She stopped. Water bubbled. They sank together.
Vitoria clung tight and they dropped past algae and rusted
bicycles. They should've hit the canal floor, but they continued to
fall. Rainbow seahorses big enough for a carousel looked
inquisitively at the new arrivals floating down. Below the
seahorses, the tops of buildings stretched until the water went
black. A pair of identical mermaids with bleached white hair
darted in and out the broken windows. Vitoria squeezed against
Vida and watched with innocent wonder. Vida imagined closing
her eyes and allowing themselves to sink into the black depths.
One of the mermaids swam towards her. Vida raised a hand in
greeting. The mermaid shook her head and brought her lips to
Vida's own. Air filled her lungs. The mermaid pulled on Vida's
hand and pointed to the surface. Vida kicked her feet and started
to rise.

Vida reached a soggy hand out of the water and pulled herself
gasping into a red rowboat. She plunged her arms back in and
pulled out an unconscious Vitoria, who flopped into the boat like
a soaked rug. Vitoria's breath was shallow but present. The
rowboat bobbed in the canal. Upstream, the crimson building was
propped on its side like an indecisive domino.

Police cars and ambulances swarmed around the Leidseplein.
A horde of performers huddled together. Someone cried out and
pointed. The building made a final, cacophonous rumble. Plumes
of dust spread out of the bottom story. Cement and rubble shot
outward, spilling into the canal and the Ubermarkt dropped to the
ground.

Vida threw herself over Vitoria. The water rose into a heavy wave. The rowboat struck against the side of the canal and rebounded, bounced and crashed onto the opposite shore, landing on the edge of the Leidseplein. Water lapped against the wood and spilled back into the canal.

Vida panted and pulled herself out of the boat. Vitoria mumbled as Vida grabbed her arm and led her through the dazed and awestruck crowd. The older woman followed without struggle. Vida placed Vitoria on the bumper of an ambulance. Vida doubted she'd forgive her for rescuing her, but she'd worry about that in the future. Vida kissed the woman on her cheek and touched the back of a medical technician who was still looking at the tower that no longer existed. He turned and she pointed to Vitoria. She walked away, towards the rubble which had spilled onto the tram tracks and kissed the front cement of the Leidseplein pitch.

Vida stood among familiar faces. Estoban sat with a group of drag queens under the lamps. Anatoly and Kit stood with a distraught-looking young man with dreadlocked green hair. Vida remembered him from the dance, but his partner was nowhere to be seen. Everyone stared at the rubble. Until that point, there was a chance for anyone missing to emerge. Now there seemed no hope.

Vida scanned the faces of the crowd one last time, knowing the face she wanted to see wasn't there. Clear of the danger, she decided it was a good time to mourn.

From the top of rubble came a loud scraping like concrete rubbing on concrete. Two large slabs slid apart. A plume of dust shot out and within the particles a shadow formed. Bernard wiped a hand down his clothes. The dust should've permeated every fiber, but as he slid his fingers down the aqua suit, the color returned brighter than Vida had ever seen.

The crowd stared in wonder at the man's resurrection. With a clean suit, Bernard turned and scampered back through the rubble with a nimble gait until he stopped, thrust his hand into the stone, and retrieved a crumpled black bowler. He molded the hat, one, two, three, back into shape and placed it atop his head.

Bernard paused for a moment, as if listening to a conversation. He said something to no one apparent and sped across the rubble to the front corner of the fallen building. He stopped and surveyed a complicated pattern of fallen debris. He kicked one corner. Rocks fell one off another until a thin hole appeared. He reached into the thin slit and rummaged until he pulled out a small hand, attached to an arm, attached to a bruised and coughing girl with green dreadlocks.

The girl stumbled out of her recess and Bernard guided her across the rubble. The crowd thundered with whispers. Bernard reached the front of the crowd and passed her off to her sylvan-haired partner. Kit and Anatoly swooped in on the two hugging lovers and walked them to an ambulance, where the King, oblivious to Bernard's miraculous arrival, was insisting that a medical technician proffer aid to the whimpering simian in his arms.

Bernard turned with a beatific smile, a smile tackled off his face as Vida glomped him in the side. She squeezed his arm.

"Are you here?" she asked. "Are you real?"

"I am for them," he replied. "I am for you."

He held her arms and pulled her back. He smiled, kissed her, and gestured with his head past the crowd. She nodded. They linked arms and walked through the audience who stared as they stepped across the pitch. They crossed through the circle, past the ambulances and police cars. The onlookers parted and allowed their exit.

They reached an alley and stopped. Framed in the shadows, the duo appeared to gain another member, though most took it to be a trick of the light.

63. Weltinnenraum

The womb was her safe and secure home,
But soon she'd leave her *Weltinnenraum*.

Vitoria König stepped out of her limousine and into the junkyard. The large man before her dropped an armful of corrugated metal onto a stack of the same. An aluminum wall stretched forty feet down the path, rounded a corner, and continued in a square until it met itself again.

The air was warm, but she shook as she walked towards him.

"How goes the castle, your highness?"

The King froze, turned his head, confirmed the source, and froze again. He fought back a smile as he addressed her.

"The project nears completion, milady. The work is difficult, but the people await the time when their King shall have a rightful place to call his own."

"The king *and his queen*," said Vitoria, "that's what you meant, of course. It wouldn't do for a king to sit on his throne alone."

"Oh!" exclaimed the King. "But of course! Still, there is much work before the castle is completed."

"Well then," said Vitoria. "We must hustle. Our people will expect nothing less. Tell me, what's to go there?"

She pointed to an open area on the outside of the wall.

"Here, my dearest queen, shall be the hunting grounds."

"Oh, no, my king," said Vitoria. "Surely you'd prefer this to be a garden for your queen?"

"A garden?"

"Of course, dear husband. A garden at the end of your barony and the beginning of mine. Don't you want your queen to walk through a field of irises when she comes to visit?"

"You won't be staying in the kingdom, then?" asked the King, crestfallen.

"Oh no, my liege. Your queen has business to attend in her own realm. But don't fear, her new home is only a sparrow's flight away."

Vitoria pointed to the edge of the landfill. Construction workers milled in and out of the newly constructed warehouse across the street. Hanging from the modern building, a large banner announced "König Industries: Opening Soon".

"As you can see, your queen has everything handled," said Vitoria. "As to your kingdom, I would like to bestow upon you a gift."

"A gift, milady?"

Vitoria raised a hand and a yellow truck approached. Two men climbed out and pulled a latticed metal gate from the back of the pickup.

"Here, my liege," said Vitoria. The workers set the gate between the openings of the metal wall. Vitoria ran her fingers across the latticework. The metal still had a slight bend on its left side which had been unable to be corrected after its recovery from the tower's collapse.

"Don't you think this would be an appropriate entryway for the king's domain?"

"If the queen wishes it," said the King.

"Oh, the queen wishes it very much," said Vitoria. "The queen would be very happy to visit her king if he should lie beyond this gate."

The workers jostled the metal wall from "Couture of the Night" into position.

Lancelot poked his head up from the roof of the castle. At the sight of Vitoria, he attempted to scurry away on impulse, but his lower body was held in a solid cast.

"*Eeep*," he said, before resuming his search for fleas.

64. Synecdoche
A piece becomes synecdoche,
By modeling entirety.

"He's a terror! If that boy doesn't get what he wants, he screams. If he gets what he wants, he's insufferable. He'll be the death of me."

The foster mother took a drag on her Marlboro. Her eyes closed and she disappeared into a private, happy place. She exhaled and snapped back into the room with a scowl.

"They get two hours of television a day. Two! But try telling him. God forbid you should change the channel. We got a new girl last week. Oh, she's adorable, seven years old, her birth mother was from one of those *Asian* countries, I forget which one. Anyway, I guess she wanted to watch cartoons, SpongeBob Whatshispants or whatever. I don't know what he did and she wouldn't tell me, but I ran in to find her sobbing with her drawers soaked. He was on the couch, watching one of his reality shows, didn't even look up when I asked about it. There wasn't a scratch on her, but that kinda bull-pucky happens a lot around him."

The heavy-set woman finished her cigarette in two prolonged draws, stabbed the nub into an emerald green ashtray, and lit up a replacement.

"I'm sorry, this brain ain't what it used to be. What did you say your name was?"

Bernard took off his hat, removed a business card, and returned the bowler to his head.

"Mr. Tregetour," he said, handing her the card, "from the county."

"Oh, right," said the woman with a frown. "And you…."

"You were taking me to the boy."

"Of course," she said. "You're not gonna take him are yah? I wouldn't put up a fight."

"This is just an inspection," he said. "How old is he again?"

"Had his birthday last week," she said. "Five years old. I can't wait till he starts school. Ever since he showed up here, he's been driving me crazy. Bonkers, that boy is, absolute bonkers."

"How long has he been here?"

"Oh, it feels like ages. Definitely before my Leonard died. It was Leonard's idea to open up our home for the children. Leonard was such a dear. We wanted kids, we tried something terrible, but poor Leonard was shooting with an unloaded pistol. So we opened our home, like I said, and that boy was the first we took in. Oh, he was trouble then, but it wasn't so bad when Leonard was here. Then one day, bam, poor Leonard plopped face-first in his cream of potato soup and never got up. Doctor said it was a stroke. Poor Leonard. Thingsn't been the same since."

"I'm sorry for your loss," said Bernard. "How long has it been since he passed away?"

She stared at her sink.

"Oh, it's been—let's see—thirty-two years last August. God rest his soul."

She smiled and led the county man into the living room.

The room was decorated Neo-Grandma with a touch of Graceland. Coasters were as ubiquitous as the plastic faux-glass bowls holding various inedible hard candies. A portrait of White Jesus on one end of the room glared at Velvet Elvis on the other side, both men frozen in a perpetual showdown, dazzling humility versus hips that could impregnate at 20 yards. A paisley couch faced a widescreen TV between the two saints. Sitting on the couch, as Bernard saw it, was a man about 35 years old, wearing an undersized Skylanders t-shirt and short shorts, sipping from a Capri Sun juicebox.

"Carlos, you've got a visitor!" said the foster mother. "Mister *Trebuchet* from the county!"

He continued to sip his juicebox.

"Honest, it's like talking to a wall."

"We're fine," said Bernard. The woman took the invitation and left the room. Bernard circumnavigated the couch and sat down. The oversized man-child had dark skin, a long nose, and premature wrinkles that framed his eyes like scraggly diamonds. His aged complexion contrasted his youthful movements as he sucked his juice box while his legs danced forwards and backwards fueled by sugar rather than conscious volition. They were the movements of a child or someone who'd seen lots of television and now aped a child's most extreme mannerisms.

From his earliest imaginings, Bernard fantasized about his reunion with a birth parent. It was always a single parent. He could never fathom why two people still together would've given him up as a child. Every awkward encounter happened at a new location. Bernard had stood before a ramshackle mansion, an elegant shack, a Transylvanian castle and a jail cell. He'd been interrupted in a space shuttle seconds before launch, while exchanging wedding vows, during a bank robbery, and mid-coitus at a sex party. He'd run into a parent at a crack den, a strip club, a funeral, a skating rink, a shooting range, a rodeo, the Golden Gate Bridge, an outhouse, a ranger outlook post, a Build-a-Bear workshop, Wrigley Stadium, Circus Circus, Hogwarts, the Fire Swamp, a crow's nest, Hyrule Castle, Pop's Tate's Soda Shoppe, a French bistro, an Amway Convention, a Tibetan monastery, a Shinto temple, a taco stand, a steak house, an Olive Garden, in front of one of those giant heads at Easter Island, the ruins of Machu Picchu, a bio-dome, the Hadron Collider, a Hall of Mirrors, Camp Half-Blood, Spider Skull Island, Confusion Hill, Joshua Tree, Carlsbad Caverns, Costco, Castle Grayskull, the Lost Coast of Kauai, a tattoo parlor, jury duty, the Oprah Winfrey Show, the Glow Worm Caves of Rotorua, the Shire, the Zombie Armageddon, the Death Star, Nefertiti's Tomb, the Playboy Mansion, Trader Joe's, Vault 101, an opium den, a ninja hideout, a Siberian prison, the Korean Demilitarized Zone, Burning Man, a dragon's cave, a debt consolidation center, a big cat sanctuary, the Annual Quartzite Rock Show, Gothenburg Nebraska, Oktoberfest, a Phish concert, a hostel in Barfüsserplatz,

Starbucks, boot camp, *La Tomatina*, the Running of the Bulls, a
squat, an Ayahuasca ceremony, Santa's Workshop, a
slaughterhouse, the Bat-Cave, a McDonald's ball pit, the
Holocaust Museum, a traffic accident, the Google Mountain View
Campus, a nursing home, the cacao fields of South America,
Alcatraz, Niagara Falls, the Eiffel Tower, the Statue of Liberty, an
erupting volcano, the Disco H20 at Wet 'n Wild, Legoland, a
sperm bank, a Star Trek Convention, the Essen Board Game
Convention, the Arcata plaza, a yurt, Camp Winnarainbow, the
Bermuda Triangle, Atlantis, Antarctica, standing in Armstrong's
footprint, a Jelly-Belly factory, the DMV, a bordello, a bodega,
and a small hut in a fishing village in Micronesia.

He'd ring the doorbell or rap on the glass or look up from his
seat on the bus or enter the interrogation cell. He'd see an older
woman or a tall, distinguished man whose look of unfamiliarity
transformed into bewilderment and then something else.
Sometimes bewilderment became joy and there'd be a tearful
reunion filled with hugs and apologies. These always ended with
Bernard jolted back into reality, feeling alone and guilty. Other
times, the bewilderment shifted into wide-eyed fear. His
progenitor placed one hand on Bernard's shoulder, pushed him to
the ground and ran. Bernard pursued but never caught up, never
discovering why he was being avoided, never learning why he'd
been given up in the first place. These fantasies left him
depressed, but they weren't nearly as bad as the tearful reunions.

Bernard sat on the couch, aware that his calves were tensed
as if preparing for a sprint. The man-child beside him held his
gaze at the television but raised a bowl to Bernard's face.

"Candy?"

Bernard looked skeptically upon the bowl of peppermints.
He grabbed a mint and the entire colony of sweets lifted out of
the bowl.

"*Hydromedusae*," Bernard said, "a classification of jellyfish,
which contrary to popular understanding are not individual

321

creatures but a collection of independent sexual entities united together. I–I don't know what to call you."

"How about Papi?" the man-child said, "I have been spending these last few decades as a beaner."

On the television, an energetic announcer egged on a group of Asian women about to dive into a swimming pool of black goo.

"I love the Japanese," Papi declared, "I've been around for thousands of years and these people still surprise me. Sick ass fucks."

Bernard said, "I watched you on the screen with my mother. Are you still you? You were older. You went away."

"We never really go away," said Papi. "We just change. Happens to everything, beings like us just get to remember more about the process."

"Beings like us? What does that mean? Who are we? Are we gods?"

Papi laughed. "That's right, *hijo*. A pair of gods, sitting here watching *Fukioka's Next Top Idol*. Why, I'm positively brimming with the holy spirit!"

Papi flailed his arms overhead, "Excuse the sarcasm, these juice boxes are brimming with sugar. That woman does *not* know how to maintain a diet. If I was anyone else, I'd be filling this sofa."

Bernard stared ahead. "*Sarcasm*: a tearing of the flesh–"

"You're an asshat, aren't you" stated Papi.

"Uh," said Bernard.

"This is it!" yelled Papi.

"What?" asked Bernard.

"Pay attention kid, you might learn something! She's *drowning*!"

Papi's eyes shot open like a junky ready for a fix.

On the screen, the camera centered on a bubbly pile in the middle of the black pool.

"What's happening?" Bernard asked.

"She can't swim!" Papi laughed, "Stupid fucking cunt jumped in anyway. Didn't mention the baby either."

He cackled, grasping his belly.

"Is this on the air?" asked Bernard.

"It's better than that, *hijo*. This hasn't even been cut yet. This is pure reality."

Papi tapped his head towards the screen. The video changed to hands flailing around in inky darkness.

"Performers were such a headache," said Papi. "I love this new gig. So modern. Such a novelty. So many fucking crazy fucks! Fifteen minutes for their entire life. What a rush!"

The screen changed again. The host dove into the gelatin pool as cameramen surrounded the brim.

"Better than drugs," said Papi, falling back against the couch. His breath quickened. "You're going to love this next part. I feel her drifting away. She regrets it, of course, wants to take it back, blah blah blah. Stupid cunt."

"Is this it?" asked Bernard. "You're the god of fucking...reality television?"

"Fifteen minutes," said Papi, his fingers kneading his chest "She sacrificed herself for fifteen minutes and I get every glorious second. It's orgasmic!"

Bernard launched himself on top of his father and wrapped his hands around his neck.

"You pusillanimous pedantic puerile child!" He roared. "Save her! I know you can. Save her, you egomaniacal fuck!"

"Grkkkkk!" Papi grabbed at Bernard's fingers but couldn't pry them apart.

On the television screen, the host rose to the surface, holding the limp girl with one arm.

Papi's face turned red, then purple. Bernard relaxed his grip.

"She's nothing," Papi gasped. "Just a sacrifice!"

Bernard slapped him across the face.

"Ow!"

Bernard pulled his hand back again.

"Okay, okay!" Papi raised his hands against his face. "Fine. Whatever you say."

He shrugged at the screen. The host pushed down on the woman's chest. She spurted out a thick sludge of black goo and started breathing.

"You must be a blast at parties," muttered Papi. "We're going to have a long way to go with you. You have no idea of your potential."

The television screen filled with hundreds of tiny scenes, each a tiny glimpse of human desperation.

"Stick around a couple weeks," said Papi. "About time we had some father/son bonding. I promise you'll be a changed man by the end."

"No thanks," said Bernard, standing up. "I think I'll figure this shit out for myself."

He crossed away from the couch and disappeared from the room.

65. Theanthropy

The union of gods and men is the topic,
For those who philosophize theanthropic.

"Kaartjies?"

The thin, ebony porter stood in the doorway of the train cabin. The olive-skinned woman with a purple streak in her hair looked up and smiled.

"Of course," Vida said. She pulled out a yellow stub from her pocket. The young porter smiled and stamped her ticket. Handing it back, he searched for a reason to stay in the car.

"Pass…port?" he said, in passable English.

Vida fished into her bag. Her hand fell on a dark blue booklet, but she thought it would be unwise to hand that one out. The newspapers were still buzzing about the incident at the Leidseplein and a number of people were still looking for Vida Callahan. She closed the bag and reached into a pink satchel. Fishing through a jumble of photographs and letters, she retrieved a different booklet for the porter.

She kept eye contact, knowing he'd only glance at the passport long enough to get her name.

"Miss…Meeks?" he said. "Is this your first time in Kenya?"

"Please, call me Sophie," she said, "and yes, it's my first time."

"You're traveling alone?"

Vida glanced across the seat and down at her belly. She'd need a new set of clothes soon.

"We're never really alone," she said, winking at the empty seats across from her. "Not if we pay attention."

The porter looked a little uncomfortable, as if there was a joke that everyone else got even though it was only the two of them.

"Yes. Well, good day, ma'am. Enjoy your time. Watch your bags."

The porter slid the door closed. Vida looked at the opposite side of the car and resumed her conversation.

"What do you think of 'Bernard'?"

"That'd be cruel, everyone would tease her."

How do you know she's a girl?

"Wait and see."

What about Damiana?

"Isn't that an herb?"

"It's an aphrodisiac."

"That's some legacy."

Get used to it. She's going to be special.

"Of course she is."

"Oh my god! Is that a giraffe?"

It's a tree.

"No, she's right. It's a giraffe"

You're crazy.

"I know what I saw. It's a giraffe."

You're both crazy.

"You're both beautiful."

So are you.

"What do you think about Sophie?"

Hmmm.

"We'll think about it."

"You two know what?"

What?

"I love you."

"I love you, too."

I love you two.

66. Tikkun Olam

Mordecai built a helpful golem,
Asked why, he declared, "*Tikkun olam!*"

I visited Venice last week. Most of it's still underwater, but they've got some industrial-grade floating plastic to keep up the new ground and a hot-shot architect planning the streets. I snuck a look at his plans and they have a crazy M.C. Escher feel to them.

I approve.

A group of street musicians formed a new type of band. They row around on a gondola to the construction sites and sing about why the old Venice sank. I followed them for the day, making sure the currents flowed in their favor. I steered them towards an umbrella vendor when the rains started.

It's the kind of thing I do now. It's my job.

I like the new Venice. I'll take you there when you get older.

So that's all.

I don't mean everything. I mean: all for now. No one ever told me my story when I was alive. I thought it was only fair that you should get to know yours.

So here I am sneaking it to you, adult bits and all, while your mothers argue about what your name should be.

Most people only have two souls inside them. You've got three. You're gonna be special, whoever you are.

I don't know what it's going to be like for you, but whatever happens, I'll be there to help you along. I promise.

I love you, whatever your name is.

-Bernard

The End

ACKNOWLEDGEMENTS

To chronicle every way in which I was assisted in this six-year journey would fill another manuscript. If your name is not below and it should be, please take solace in knowing that I've probably already realized it and will spend the rest of my life feeling guilty for the omission.

Thanks to Jana Ashbrook, for reading every chapter as soon as it was written and inspiring me to aim for something worth reading.

Thanks to Adam Eivy, Lena Eivy, Deborah Addington, Seth Geddes, Alissa Tyka, Rebecca Edwards, and Adam Creighton, for sifting through my half-formed thoughts and endless final drafts to provide essential editorial advice. No one could have read my early drafts without being fueled by love.

Thanks to Dace, who saw Bernard better than I did.

Thanks to Misty, my oldest friend, whose devotion to the craft of writing is only overshadowed by her fearlessness in composition. Her contributions, both editorial and personal, are innumerable.

Thanks to Jess Bunny, whose inclusion on this list I am certain is warranted, though for the life of me I can't remember if she ever held a manuscript.

Thanks to my mother, Laurie, and sister, Brandy, for their tireless cheerleading and support, despite my refusal to let them read most of the novel because of the naughty bits.

The final leg of publication wouldn't have been reached if not for Kickstarter and the generous contributions of Alissa Tyka, Charlie Urnick, Yvonne Kugies, Jessi Wonderfool, Erica Lee Nelson, Laurie Monroe, Nanette Echegaray, Tybie Fitzhugh, Craig Brownfield, Antoine Ferrachat, Tobias Dodgen, Bryce Willis, Adam Eivy, Kira Trinity, Dace, Gerald and Shirley Martynse, Erik Jansson, John Filcich, Xande Zublin-Meyer, and John Mantle. This book would not exist without them.

Thanks to Jack, for all the giant bugs we killed, and for all the rest still to be killed.

And most importantly, with love to Kate and Karen, who illuminate and nourish my world.

ABOUT THE AUTHOR

Silas Knight traveled across Europe as a street performer, where tourists paid him to stuff his body through a tennis racket and walk on broken glass.

He lives in Northern California with his wife and partner, who thankfully get along quite well together.